Don't Close Your Eyes

Don't Close Your Eyes

P S Cunliffe

First published in Great Britain in 2023 by

Bonnier Books UK Limited
4th Floor, Victoria House, Bloomsbury Square, London, WC1B 4DA
Owned by Bonnier Books
Sveavägen 56, Stockholm, Sweden

A CIP catalogue record for this book is available from the British Library.

ISBN: 978-1-47141-531-9

This book is typeset using Atomik ePublisher

Embla Books is an imprint of Bonnier Books UK
www.bonnierbooks.co.uk

For Bailey

Lawless London: CCTV shows heart-stopping moment jogger pushes pedestrian in front of a bus

25 September, 2018

Shocking CCTV footage has been released by the Met police that shows a woman pushed into the path of a double-decker bus.

The woman was walking across London Bridge when the jogger attacked, sending her sprawling at the exact moment a bus was approaching.

A Scotland Yard spokesman said: 'At around 7.40 a.m. on Friday, 3 August, the victim was walking to work on the east side of London Bridge, heading towards Monument Station, when the male jogger knocked her into the road and into the path of an oncoming bus. Due to the quick reactions of the driver, the victim's injuries were limited to those sustained during the fall.'

Speaking about the attack, hero bus driver, Oliver Cerioni, said that the jogger had singled out the woman. 'He looked like he was doing it on purpose. It was lucky I swerved in time, or the consequences could have been terrible, for her and for me.'

It is believed the victim suffered a broken arm and head injuries during the incident. Police have not ruled out the possibility the victim was known to the attacker.

The jogger is described as white, aged early to mid-forties, with short brown hair. He was wearing a light-grey T-shirt and dark-blue shorts. Officers are appealing for witnesses and for anyone who recognises the jogger to get in touch.

Do you know the jogger? Contact newsdesk@pressonline.uk

1

Day One: 21 November, 2022

Catherine

The sound of crying snatches me out of a dream. A flutter of panic, then I remember it's Simon's turn to see to Charlie. I reach over to his side of the bed and my hand thumps down onto cool linen. He's gone. Up already, thank goodness.

I've a full day planned, starting with the rarest of treats: a lie-in, then brunch with Lydia at London Bridge at eleven, followed by a Cézanne exhibition at Tate Modern in the afternoon. At least that's what it says in my diary. To be honest, I'm looking forward to the inevitable ditching of the exhibition in favour of day-drinking our way right through to the evening. *Quick one in the Members' Bar before we go in?* I'll say, knowing one will turn into two, and two will turn into a whole afternoon of gossip with my best friend. The thought of it is an extra blanket warming me, pulling me back towards sleep.

Then I hear the pad of tiny footsteps out on the landing.

'Mummy?' Charlie's voice is tearful, lost-sounding.

Come on, Simon. It's your turn.

A soft tap-tapping at the bedroom door.

'Go and find Daddy, darling,' I say, regretting it immediately, because the next sound I hear is the creak of the door and, when

I open my eyes, Charlie is standing at the foot of the bed in his *Hey Duggee* pyjamas.

'I'm *really* hungry, Mummy,' he says, clutching his tummy, as if he hasn't eaten in days. I check the clock on the bedside table. It's nearly eight. He should be up and dressed by now, eating his Weetabix downstairs.

'Has Daddy not made you breakfast?'

He shakes his head.

Great. The first time in forever I get a lie-in and Simon's still expecting me to attend to Charlie's every need. I throw on Simon's dressing gown, grab my phone, pick up Charlie and head out onto the landing.

'He's going to be late,' I shout, but the house is heavy with morning quiet, the only sound from downstairs the ticking of the big clock in the living room.

Unbelievable. Simon must have gone for his morning run, even after he promised not to. I thought we were on the same page, thought he understood that today was his turn to take care of Charlie and my turn to be the irresponsible one. Now Charlie's going to be late for nursery, just like the last time Simon took him in. And yes, Simon's right, we *are* the ones paying them – very handsomely as it happens – but that's hardly the point, is it?

'Come on, trouble,' I say to Charlie. 'Let's get you ready.'

I dress him in elasticated trousers, a T-shirt and his favourite dinosaur jumper then carry him downstairs. 'Walk, don't run.' I smile as I set him down in the hall. He races off to the kitchen, socked feet drumming over the floorboards. When I straighten, I see Simon's running shoes lying askew next to the front door. He must have got back without me hearing.

I march into the kitchen. 'I thought we agreed you wouldn't run this morning. The one day that I—' But I'm arguing with thin air. Charlie looks back at me, unsure of what he's done to make Mummy use her angry voice.

'Not you, darling,' I tell him. 'I was talking to Daddy.'

'Daddy's not here,' he says, giving me one of his 'silly mummy' looks.

'No. No, he isn't.'

So where the hell is he?

I move through the ground floor. Living room, dining room, Simon's office. No sign of him, and his briefcase isn't in its usual overnight spot on his desk.

I fish my phone out of the dressing gown pocket. There's a missed call from him, but it's from one forty-five this morning. Ah, I know exactly what this is. He had work drinks last night. He must have downed too many Malbecs and crashed on someone's sofa. I picture him, leaving some swanky City bar in the small hours, swaying on the pavement as he calls to let me know he's staying over at Max's, or in someone else's spare room. He's probably on his way back right now, nursing a hangover as his cab makes its way through morning traffic. Which is no good to me. Even if he gets here on time, he'll be reeking of booze. Can't have Daddy turning up at the nursery gates half-cut.

'Mummy! I'm *really* hungry!' Charlie shouts from the kitchen.

So much for my lie-in.

I make Charlie his breakfast, set him up in front of his iPad and put *Paw Patrol* on, then race upstairs, shower and dress as quickly as I can. I'm not one of those mums who turn up for the nursery drop-off looking Instagram-ready – it doesn't do to look like you're trying too hard – but I don't want to look like a slummy mummy either. I take my make-up bag downstairs and peer into the hall mirror. There's the beginnings of a spot on my chin, but apart from that I don't look awful. I dab on some concealer, then blusher and a touch of mascara. Finally, a spritz from the bottle of Chloé that Simon bought me on his last work trip to Paris.

I call out instructions to Charlie, 'Can you find your shoes, darling? Have you got your backpack ready?' No response – he's glued to his tablet. In the end I go into the kitchen and take it off him, hurry him into his coat, shoes, scarf and mittens, then give his hair a quick brush.

Charlie looks as cute as ever in his red duffel coat. Quick snap for Facebook before we leave? I reach for my phone, then reconsider. If Simon sees I've been posting pictures, he'll think I'm having a nice time and that I'm not furious with him.

I take my Burberry mac down from the stand in the hall, then change my mind. Simon prefers me in the mac, says it makes me look smart and professional. I switch it for my favourite cosy, quilted jacket.

'Ready to go?'

'Want to say goodbye to Daddy,' Charlie says, peering behind him, as if Simon has been moving around the house unseen while we've been getting ready.

'You'll see Daddy after nursery,' I say, though it wouldn't surprise me if Simon is outside when I open the front door, looking the worse for wear as he gets out of a cab. He'll give me one of his shrugs. *Sorry, love. What am I like?* It's hardly the end of the world, but I'll have to make him feel bad – that's the way these things work. Plus, he'll owe me big time now. My mind begins to run through the possibilities: who might be free when, what sort of night out I might plan. I'll mention it to Lydia over brunch, see what we can come up with.

But when I open the door, it isn't Simon on the doorstep, but two strangers. A smartly dressed young woman in a black blazer and grey pencil skirt with her hair pulled back into a glossy ponytail, and behind her a tall police officer in uniform. Charlie looks up at the uniformed officer with a mixture of fear and awe. He reaches for my hand and I enfold his tiny fingers in mine.

'Oh dear,' I say. 'Not another burglary? Who is it this time?'

Living in the most picturesque square in Borough, which also happens to be less than a ten-minute walk from London Bridge, does come with its drawbacks. Cavendish Square has seen more than its fair share of break-ins this year. So many that we – by which I mean the residents' association – successfully petitioned the council for CCTV cameras to be installed at each corner.

'Not a burglary,' the woman says.

Thank goodness. We splashed out on a fancy alarm the day after we found out Mr Michaels' house two doors down had been ransacked while he was sound asleep on the top floor, but it still makes me feel sick to think that criminals are stalking around the square at night.

'In that case, can it wait? We're running late.' I move to close the door behind us.

The woman takes out a badge and flashes it at me.

'I'm Detective Inspector Carter of the Metropolitan Police, and this is Detective Constable Chaudhari. Are you Mrs Wells? Wife of Simon Wells?'

Every muscle in my body tightens.

'What's happened? Is something wrong?'

Images flash through my mind, a flickering slideshow of catastrophe. Simon's car on its roof by the side of the road. A bloody, lifeless hand palm up on a bed of broken glass. Simon, surrounded by a gang of youths. A knife drawn from the pocket of a hoodie. Simon, unconscious in a hospital bed, life draining out of him.

Detective Inspector Carter shares a look with her colleague, then looks down at Charlie. It only lasts for a split second, this moment of silent communication between them, but it makes something plummet inside me, from sternum to gut.

'I think it would be best if we come inside,' she says, and that's when I know something truly terrible has happened.

In the sitting room, Detective Chaudhari gets down on his haunches in front of Charlie, flashes him a toothy grin.

'Do you want to show me your cars?' he says.

There are a handful of toy cars in front of Charlie's toy box that must have caught the detective's eye. Metal ones with sharp little points and edges. Charlie looks up to me for reassurance.

'It's OK.' I force a smile. 'Show the nice policeman your cars.'

Charlie releases my hand, runs over to his toy box and drops to his knees. He picks up one of his cars and shows it to DC Chaudhari.

'This my favourite,' he says. It's a tiny police car.

Detective Inspector Carter pats me on the arm and ushers me through to the kitchen. She pulls a chair out from under the table and looks down at the remains of Charlie's breakfast smeared over the seat. She hesitates, not wanting to contaminate her skirt with globs of soggy Weetabix.

'Sorry,' I say. I hurry over to the sink, wet a cloth and return to wipe the seat clean. 'Everything's been a bit rushed this morning.'

She holds up a hand. 'It's fine, Mrs Wells. Please, sit down.'

This is what they do when they have bad news. They tell you to sit down, so you don't hurt yourself when your legs give way. The slideshow of images plays through my mind again. The car, the hand, the knife, the hospital bed.

I take my seat. 'Sorry,' I say. I feel like she is frustrated with me. I don't want her to be. It feels like the news might be worse if she's frustrated with me.

'That's OK,' she says. 'Now, I need you to listen.'

'I am listening,' I tell her, though I wonder if I'll hear anything over the rush of blood in my ears and the thud of my racing heart.

'This morning we found your husband's car, parked in an isolated area of Epping Forest. It was very heavily damaged, burnt out in fact, and, I'm sorry to tell you, it looks like someone was inside the car at the time of the fire.'

And this is how my world ends.

2

Catherine

I spit a mouthful of vomit out into the sink, spattering Charlie's *Peppa Pig* bowl and matching spoon. Run the cold tap to wash it away. Christ. There's not enough air in the room. Where has all the air gone? I reach over, unlatch and push open the kitchen window as Detective Inspector Carter comes up behind me, puts a hand on my shoulder. I pull away. I don't want her to touch me.

'It's a mistake,' I tell her. 'Some sort of mistake, that's all.'

She bites her lip and her eyes go wide.

'Mrs Wells . . .' She speaks in the soft, slow way we reserve for the very old, or very young. 'I understand this must be a terrible shock—'

I don't give her the chance to finish. I take my phone from my pocket and dial Simon's number. It rings twice, then goes through to answerphone.

I leave him a message. 'Simon, for goodness' sake. Can you call, please? The police are here. They're saying something has happened to you. Someone has taken the car. Set it on fire.' I want to scream down the phone, tell him he's a selfish idiot, because his stupid behaviour has brought the police to our door. Instead I add, 'Just call me. Straight away.' And I hang up.

'Listen,' I tell Detective Carter. 'It's a misunderstanding. It has to be.'

'Black Mercedes GLE?' she says. She takes out a notepad, reads out the registration. 'Does Simon always drive to and from work, Mrs Wells?'

'Most days. He can't bear the tube at rush hour. But he wouldn't have driven home last night.' The words pour out of me in a breathless stream. 'If he's going to have a drink, he leaves the car parked at work and gets a cab home. Last night he had work drinks, so someone must have taken the car. Stolen it, I mean, and they must have had some sort of terrible accident. There'll be CCTV, in the garage at his office. You should get it checked. Plus, I had a missed call from him.'

Detective Carter's expression changes. Soft concern turns to curiosity. 'What time was this?'

I swipe my phone then hold it up, show her the screen with the details of the missed call from Simon. She takes the phone off me, scrolls through the notifications and presses a few buttons.

'You didn't speak to him?'

'I was asleep.'

'He didn't leave a message? Call back on the landline?'

Nobody calls the landline anymore. I pick the handset up off the kitchen counter and dial 1471. A voice reads out the last number stored, weeks ago. It's a number I don't recognise, certainly not Simon's.

I shake my head. 'He probably thought it best not to wake me if I didn't answer first time.' I curse myself. Why didn't the phone wake me? If it had, I could have spoken to him and I would know exactly where he is.

Carter hands the phone back. 'Right now, we're just trying to get to the bottom of things. Can you tell me when you last saw your husband?'

'Yesterday morning, before he went to work.' I place my mobile face up on the table. 'He'll probably call any minute.'

'But he didn't come home last night?'

'That's right, yes . . .'

She nods, as if to say, *Do you see? If he didn't come home, then . . .*

I snort an almost-laugh. 'He's not missing. I mean, he's not *missing* missing. He'll have stayed over at a colleague's. He's probably on his way back right now with a hangover and a dead phone battery.'

Doesn't twenty-four hours have to pass before the police consider someone missing? A grown man not being home for one night is hardly cause to assume he's dead, especially when he tried calling me at a quarter to two, barely seven hours ago.

'Is it normal? For him not to come home?' she says. She tips her head and her ponytail bounces cheerfully behind her.

There's something about her tone I don't like, that suggests she thinks Simon and I are something we are not. That he is a philanderer and I am the dumb don't-ask-don't-tell housewife, sat at home each night, turning a blind eye while he's out doing god knows what with god knows whom.

'It's not normal for him *not* to come home,' I say, 'but it happens. He has a very demanding job. Lots of travel – he's due to fly out to New York next week. He does business all over the world, so has to be available at all sorts of times to deal with important clients.'

Like the other month, when they had a contingent over from the Tokyo office who wanted to see the sights – and by sights, they meant go to strip clubs and drink themselves silly. Simon was the one forced to escort them around town, make sure they didn't get lost, or mugged, or worse. He said the whole thing was incredibly tedious, embarrassing even – it certainly sounded it to me – but that he hadn't much choice in the matter. Sometimes you had to go that extra mile, because the extra mile would be what paid off during the next round of bonuses. True, on that occasion he warned me in advance he wouldn't be home at anything like a decent hour, but it's not out of the question something similar happened last night. Clients dropping by, Simon having to act as tour guide and babysitter combined.

I pick up my phone again. There have been no notifications or alerts, but there's always a chance a message might have sneaked through. That can happen sometimes; you get a message from one person and see that you somehow missed one from somebody else hours ago. No such luck. There's nothing from Simon since his last text two days ago: *On way home, need me to pick anything up? X*

'We'll look into everything, I promise,' says Detective Carter. 'In the meantime – and I know this is difficult – we'd like you to come down to the station to look at some things, some items recovered from the scene of the incident.'

My stomach clenches like a fist. 'This is all rather premature, isn't it?' I say. Simon *promised* he would be here this morning, and he isn't. But that still doesn't mean he's missing.

I look at my phone, will it to spring into life.

Call me, you bloody idiot. Call me.

Carter says, 'Is there someone who might be able to come and look after your son? Someone he'll feel comfortable with?'

I think about Lydia, who I at least know will be free this morning, seeing as we were supposed to be sipping bottomless Prosecco over avocado on toast soon. She's good in a crisis, would be here like a shot if I asked, but she's never looked after Charlie on her own before.

'I could call my mum?' My voice is high and trembling. 'She usually does t'ai chi on Thursday mornings, but she should be finishing about now. She could probably be here in half an hour. She moved down after Dad died. Simon helped her find a lovely place in Holborn, sorted everything.'

Why am I over-explaining everything?

Maybe it's the ghost of guilt that begins to hover when talking to the police, or perhaps I just want her to know that Simon is the sort of person who is nice to his mother-in-law. A good person, a family man.

Carter nods. 'Why don't you give her a call. I can do it for you, if you'd like?'

I picture Mum receiving a call from my number and answering it to find a police detective on the other end of the line. She'd have a heart attack. Best if I do it.

She picks up right away. The second I hear her voice, tears start to come, which doesn't make sense at all because Simon is perfectly fine, but I can't stop myself.

'Oh, love. What is it?'

I don't want to put it into words.

'Can you just come, please? The police are here. They think something might have happened to Simon – which it hasn't – but can you come and take Charlie to nursery while I get things sorted?'

She says she'll call a cab, be here as soon as she can. I hang up and tell Detective Carter.

'OK,' she says. 'And if you'd like someone to go with you to the station, that might be a good idea, too.'

First, they tell you to sit, then they ask you if there's anyone who can be with you, a friend or a relative. Someone who'll be there when they leave, someone to stop you losing it completely, jumping out of the window or reaching for the knife drawer.

Lydia. I dial her number. 'Some sort of mistake, I'm sure of it,' I tell her. I ask her to meet me at the police station in Southwark.

'Christ. Of course, Cat,' she says. 'I'm putting my coat on, right now.' She still sounds half asleep.

I hang up. 'She's going to meet us there.'

Carter nods, smiles a tight-lipped little smile.

I know what she's thinking. Denial is the first stage of grief, isn't it? I read an article about it in the *Guardian* only last week, so I know exactly what she's thinking.

But that's not what this is.

I would know if Simon had died. I would have *felt* something when it happened. That invisible bond between us, I would have felt it break. So, whatever has happened, it isn't what it looks like.

It can't be.

I look at DI Carter and wonder how she could possibly understand. Has she got a partner at home? Or is she like one of those detectives we see in TV dramas, who has put her career before everything else in her life and goes home to a cold, sparsely furnished flat to mull over case files, pin photos to the walls and join them up with bits of string? Perhaps she does have a partner, but is it someone she has that invisible bond with, someone she has been with nearly half her life?

'It's a mistake,' I say. 'You don't know the first thing about him.'

'Yes, of course,' she says, and I fight the urge to grab her by her perfect ponytail and drag her out of the house.

3

Sara

Five hours earlier

There's someone in Sara's flat. It's three in the morning and someone has broken in and they are inside the flat, in the bathroom, right this second.

Sara snatches her phone from the bedside table, dials the first two digits of 999 then pauses. She can't tell if she's truly as awake and hyper-alert as she feels, or if her mind is still foggy with sleep. What if she calls the police, but is wrong? Did she double-lock the door before going to bed? Fuck. She can't remember. She listens hard, hears the sound of rushing water and a series of soft thumps. Someone moving around in the bath. Someone's definitely in there. But what sort of an intruder breaks into a stranger's flat to take a shower?

She calls out. 'Adam, is that you?'

Adam is the only other person with a set of keys, but that's only for emergencies, or in case she loses hers. He's never let himself into the flat before. Please, God, let this be the first time.

No answer. She tries again, thumb hovering over the final digit.

'Adam?' She shouts louder this time, then wishes she'd kept her mouth shut. If it is an intruder, they'll know she's home alone now.

More thuds, then the sound of the bathroom door being unlocked and opened.

'Only me,' a voice calls.

The bedroom door creaks open and Adam stands in the doorway, a towel wrapped around his waist. The streetlights outside and the thin curtains mean the bedroom is never entirely dark and his toned torso, gym-fit and still wet from the shower, is picked out in shades of orange.

'You idiot,' she says. 'You scared the shit out of me. I was about to call the police.' She puts her phone down, grabs a pillow from his side of the bed and hurls it at him. It spins in the air, thumps against his hip and lands at his feet.

'Give me a second, I'm all wet,' he says. He disappears and she hears the sounds of him fussing around in the rest of the flat. A drawer being opened in the kitchen, the rustle of a plastic bag, the sound of the kettle boiling. For a moment she feels a draught, as if he has opened a window or door.

'What the hell are you doing?' she shouts.

'There in a minute,' he calls back.

It is a ridiculous time of the morning and she has an early start, but now that the panic is subsiding, she is pleased to see him. Even if he did scare the hell out of her.

'Why didn't you text me?'

He reappears, this time without his towel. He is clutching a cup of tea and he comes over to the bed and offers it to her.

'Surprise,' he says, unconvincingly.

'Tea? Really? Have you seen the time?'

'I just thought . . .' He shrugs and sets the tea down on the bedside table, as if it's the most normal thing in the world to turn up unannounced at three in the morning and make her a cup of tea.

'Adam, what's going on?'

He climbs under the sheets, then leans over to kiss her. His hair is still damp, skin clammy. He's brushed his teeth and still smells faintly of aftershave. Sara wonders if he's drunk, if he's showered to hide something. She breathes him in, tries to smell beyond the shower gel and aftershave.

'I had a shower to save time,' he says. 'I wanted to see you before . . .' He trails off and she knows she's not going to like what he says next.

He's let her down before, when he has to work late and can't meet up as planned, or when he gets a call during dinner and has to rush off to attend an urgent meeting. When that happens, he gets this look about him, the same one he has now: blue eyes wide and guileless, mouth set in a regretful smile.

'About this week,' he says. 'I know it was important to you, and it was to me too—'

Was? He's already talking about their plans as if they aren't going to happen.

'Something's come up,' he says. 'A four-day conference, in Paris. Sorry, I won't bore you with all the details.'

'Oh, Adam,' she says, thinking that for once she would like to hear the details. If she knew more she might not feel so abandoned.

They've had their holiday planned for two months. Nothing fancy, just an isolated cottage near a pretty village on the edge of Surrey. The plan was for her to pick him up after work in her little Fiat, so he didn't have to worry about the drive. Stop somewhere on the way down to stock up on food and booze, then they could properly relax when they got there. She's had fantasies of them walking hand in hand along blustery canal paths, hunkering down in some old man's pub, with a real log fire burning in the hearth, before tipsily heading back to the cottage to spend hours in bed.

'Can't they send someone else?'

'They were supposed to,' he says. 'The guy's had some sort of accident, a car crash, or something. I'm the only one who can take his place. I can't *not* be there. I drop the ball on this and . . .' He sucks in air through his teeth and shakes his head.

While Adam often asks Sara about her work, she avoids talking about his if she can. His work is the thing that takes him away from her, makes him arrive late and leave early. Best not to mention it, in case he recalls an email he forgot to send or a call he should've made. So, while she knows he works for a trendy start-up in Soho – what's it called again? Bitsave? Bitsaver? Something like that – the details are sketchy. She knows he is high up in the company, with a big-cheese job title – Director of Something or Other – and a big-cheese salary to go with it, and that he's at the level where he's never allowed to switch off, not even on weekends.

'Fine,' she says, letting him know from her tone that nothing is fine.

'Don't be annoyed.'

'First, you don't message me to tell me you're coming, then you scare the shit out of me, and now you tell me we're not going away *and* I'm not going to see you for four days? I'm not annoyed, Adam. I'm delighted. Can't you tell?'

'Sorry.' He trails kisses over her shoulder and down her arm. 'Would you rather I hadn't come?' He reaches behind her and slides his hand under her T-shirt, rubs her back, finds the base of her spine and slips a finger under the band of her underwear.

'It's not that,' she says, but in that moment, it is precisely that. She would rather him not have come, rather him not have turned up out of the blue to ruin their holiday. And she would rather him not be tugging at her knickers, as if that's going to make her feel any better about things. A 3 a.m. booty call is definitely not the apology she deserves.

At her unresponsiveness, he removes his hands from beneath her clothes and rests his forehead against hers.

'Hey,' he says and she feels his breath on her lips. 'Babe, look at me.' She lifts her eyes to meet his. 'I'm just as annoyed as you are. But there'll be other holidays. I've called the place already and they said there's no harm done. They'll hold the deposit and we can go another time. I'll sort it out as soon as I'm back, I promise.'

She exhales, long and slow. At least he feels bad, and felt guilty enough to come and tell her in person rather than over the phone.

She nestles into his shoulder. 'I suppose it isn't the worst thing in the world, you being here.' There's no point in spiting herself by keeping him at a distance, when tomorrow he'll be gone and she won't see him for the rest of the week.

He whispers in her ear. 'I was thinking, when I get back we should start looking for a place together.'

She pulls away. 'Really?'

'Really,' he says. 'Where I am now was only ever meant to be temporary, and the commute is killing me. This place is too small for two of us. It makes perfect sense. Plus, I *want* to live with you.' Sara's heart swells. 'Why don't you start thinking of where you'd like to move to? Somewhere that'll work for both of us. Call some estate agents if you like, set up some viewings for when I'm back.'

It might be three in the morning but Sara's mind is suddenly buzzing with the possibilities. 'But how will it work?' she says. 'I can hardly afford this place on my own.'

Moving in together should mean she ends up paying less than she does now, but Adam is long past the days of slumming it like a student. What if he wants to live somewhere super-posh – and super-expensive? A house, rather than a flat? Somewhere with a balcony, or a roof terrace, or on one of those big fancy squares with a residents-only garden out front?

He kisses her quiet. 'Shh. Don't worry about it,' he says.

'Yes, but . . .'

Another kiss, then: 'I said, don't worry. We don't earn the same, so it wouldn't be fair if we paid the same rent, would it? We'll work it out. Rent for a bit, then look at buying somewhere together, outside London. That's what you want, isn't it?'

It is. They have talked about their future, in a jokey, no-pressure sort of way. She saying how it would be nice to live outside of London, somewhere with clean air and room for their kids to run around. He saying, 'Kids?' with a look of mock shock on his face, and she saying she'd like to have a boy and a girl, a few years apart, so they could look out for one another. He'd smiled and agreed that did sound nice, and his response, his calm acceptance of the idea, had opened up a pool of contentment in her belly.

'How much?' she asks. 'Just so I have an idea. They'll ask, at the estate agents.'

'Tell them we're interested in places for – oh, I don't know – seven hundred a week? Somewhere nice. North London. Definitely North. Islington, Highgate. I've always quite liked Muswell Hill. Maybe we can get a place with two bedrooms? You could use one of them as your office, if you like. Or we could use it for . . . whatever.'

Is he hinting at kids? In no world had she planned on having children in the next year, or two, but if it did happen . . . would it be such a bad thing?

Adam runs his hand down her side again. His fingers hook under her T-shirt and his skin is warm against hers, his hand on the small of her back pulling her against him. She feels his excitement and it stirs something inside her. Never mind that their week away together is ruined. They are going to move in with each other. Soon they'll spend every day together.

She holds him back long enough to take off her T-shirt and knickers then climbs on top of him. When they are finished, they fall apart and lie on their backs, breathing heavily, hot and cold at the same time.

'Do you have to go?' she whispers. She resists the temptation to ask him to take her with him. Adam hates it when she is needy.

'I have to,' he says, 'but I'm sorry. Really I am.' He lies there, eyes open, staring up at the ceiling.

There's something different about him tonight. It's in the way he is lying there, rather than wrapping his arms around her. And while they were having sex, it was in the touch of his hands and the feel of his skin. A new kind of urgency that, while not unpleasant, makes her feel a little used. He's probably just worked up about the sudden trip, maybe even anxious. She realises she has never known him to be anxious before – he is usually so confident and sure of everything. She is a little thrilled by the idea.

Nobody is one person all of the time. It can't always be about excitement: drinks and shows, nights out and sex. After seeing each other for nine months, it's time to take things to the next level. Now that they're moving in together, she will get to see all sorts of different sides to him. She'll see him when he is happy and excited, and also when he is sad or stressed or upset. That's what grown-up relationships are all about. Being with someone fully, not just for the good bits.

'Is everything OK?' She reaches out to touch his arm.

He flinches, looks at her as if she has caught him doing something he shouldn't.

'Pre-flight nerves,' he says. 'Everything's fine. Go to sleep.' He leans in and kisses her and the moment their lips part he turns away.

She closes her eyes and imagines what it will be like when they are living together, how their lives will intertwine in new ways. They'll wake up and eat breakfast together. Cook for each other, spend lazy Sundays and evenings curled up on the sofa watching television. She'll no longer get that niggling feeling in her stomach when she sees him, that sense of time as water in her hands. When they live together, they'll have all the time in the world. Her head fills with images of beautiful flats and houses, of balconies and gardens and roof terraces.

When she next opens her eyes, five hours have passed and Adam has gone.

4

Catherine

Detective Carter makes three cups of tea while we wait for Mum to arrive so we can go to the police station. She puts one on the table in front of me – as if I want a cup of tea at a time like this – and heads towards the sitting room. I hear whispers in the hall and when the door next opens it's Detective Chaudhari who comes into the kitchen. He walks over to the table and sits down. Why have they switched places?

'OK, Mrs Wells,' he says. 'Let's just try and get to the bottom of this, shall we?'

Whereas Detective Carter was a little uptight, less easy-going, Chaudhari is softly spoken and a little portly, with a round, open face.

He takes out a small notepad and pen while I pick up my phone and activate it. Still nothing. I check the switch that turns it to silent, click it back and forth – *click-click-click*. Was it on silent before I did that? Has it been on silent all morning? Is that why I missed Simon's call? I swipe the screen to make sure the ringer is at full volume, then check the battery. It's at eighty-five per cent. Good.

'Tell me about last night,' Chaudhari says. 'Where did Simon say he was going to be?'

'He said he was going out for work drinks and that he'd see me later on.'

That *is* what he said, isn't it?

I think back to the whirlwind rush of yesterday morning: feeling tired after Charlie woke in the early hours; making breakfast for the three of us; getting a very sleepy little boy ready for nursery. Did Simon actually say those words? Or am I remembering them from another morning? Am I imagining he said it because that's what I think he would have said? No. I distinctly remember him standing in the hall, smoothing down his hair and doing up his tie in the mirror, talking to me as I fastened Charlie's laces.

Work drinks tonight. Not sure how long it'll go on for . . .

That was how the argument started. *Don't forget, it's your turn to do the nursery drop-off tomorrow. Don't be late, and don't be hungover.*

I won't. I'm going for a run first thing. I won't want to feel ropy.

Oh, Simon. Do you have to?

I'll only be fifteen minutes.

But you won't, will you? Because you'll need to get showered and dressed when you get back, so it'll be more like thirty minutes, or thirty-five—

Charlie wasn't late last time.

He was. By almost half an hour.

And so on, until he begrudgingly agreed to move his run to the evening.

'Did he say who he was going to be with, or where he was going?' Chaudhari asks.

Even if he had, I wouldn't necessarily know who those people were, or where those places were. Clients I'll never meet, swanky bars I'll never visit. After a while you just sort of . . . tune it out.

'The usual places, the usual people, I suppose,' I say. 'Work friends. Clients, maybe?'

'And where is it he works?'

'Jefferson Trading. He's in stocks, works in the City, near St Paul's.'

Detective Chaudhari writes in his notepad, then says, 'Did you notice anything different about him yesterday morning? Did he seem worried or upset?'

I know what he's getting at here, and he is well off the mark. My husband is just . . . well, not the type of person who would do that. And even if he did decide to take his own life, I doubt he'd choose to do it in the most painful way imaginable.

'Nothing. He was . . . normal.'

'And did you hear from him during the day at all?'

I shake my head again. 'He checks in sometimes, to see how Charlie is, or to ask if I want him to pick anything up on his way home, but not every day, and not yesterday. I had that missed call from him, in the early hours, that's all.'

I show him the notification. He takes the phone and checks it, just like DI Carter did, then hands it back.

'How about you, Mrs Wells? Do you work at the moment?'

'I'm a GP,' I say. 'I mean, I was. I put things on hold to have Charlie, but I'm planning on going back to work once he's at school full-time. Simon would rather me be a stay-at-home mum, have a little brother or a sister for Charlie – he's a bit old-fashioned like that – but I get restless, being home all the time.'

I am talking too much again.

'So you were at home yesterday?'

'Most of the day. I picked Charlie up from nursery, got home around four and haven't left the house since. I did the same thing I do most nights when Simon isn't here. Gave Charlie his bath, put him to bed around six thirty and read him a story. Then I watched some television and sat in the kitchen, had a few glasses of wine. Tried to unwind. Went to bed around elevenish.'

Chaudhari mutters as he writes in his notebook. 'In around four. Watched television. Few glasses of wine. Bed at eleven.'

'Elevenish.'

'Elevenish. Got it.'

The kitchen door opens and Charlie comes running into the room, clearly not as taken with DI Carter as he was with her colleague. He clambers up onto his chair and starts *Paw Patrol* playing on his iPad. DI Carter rejoins Chaudhari and more questions follow, soundtracked by the adventures of a team of cartoon search-and-rescue dogs. As if my morning wasn't surreal enough.

They want contact details for Simon's friends and they want to know about his last few places of work, presumably because his drinks might have involved old colleagues. They ask who Simon's dentist is – and I really don't like to think why they want to know this. They want to check through any electrical devices of Simon's, and I hand over his laptop and iPad. They want to know who we bank with, what credit cards we have, what our financial situation looks like, whether we are in debt – of course we are, isn't everyone? – and they want some recent photographs of Simon. I scroll through my phone and select a handful. Simon in front of the Duomo in Florence holding Charlie, the two of them grinning from ear to ear. Simon on the beach wearing shorts and a T-shirt from our last holiday in Tuscany, sunburn pinking his arms. A selfie I took of us at his colleague Andrew's wedding last year. Simon, handsome in his best suit, looking up at me with a huge smile on his face and in his eyes. I remember that day, how we argued terribly when we got lost on the drive down, but ended up having drunken sex that night. Like strangers who had just met in a bar.

'You can email them to me.' Chaudhari uses his finger to slide his card across the kitchen table.

'How about this,' says DI Carter, pointing to Charlie's iPad.

'Simon's old one,' I say. 'He doesn't use it anymore, hasn't in years. Charlie uses it for watching cartoons.' I don't want her thinking we dump Charlie in front of it all the time, though I'm not sure why I care. 'Only for short periods. Simon is very strict when it comes to screen time.'

'We'd better take it, just in case.' She goes over to Charlie, crouches down next to him. 'Would you mind if I borrowed your tablet, just for a little while?' she says. 'I'll make sure you get it back.'

She picks it up and closes the case. The noise of the cartoon shuts off and Charlie frowns and looks over to me, as if I should be doing something to prevent this injustice. But it's not me he should be complaining to.

I check my phone again.

Calls, texts, voicemails. WhatsApp, Facebook.

Nothing.

I go to the settings, check the data is turned on and the Wi-Fi connected. What if Simon is trying to get through but can't because my phone isn't working?

There's a knock at the door. I spring up off my seat and race down the hall.

Please be Simon. Please, God, be Simon.

Whatever the explanation, I just want him back from wherever the hell he has been, with some silly story we will go on to tell at dinner parties for years to come.

Remember that day? The police came round and everything. They thought he had burnt to death in his bloody car! Can you imagine? And all the time he was sleeping off his hangover on Graham from Accounts' sofa.

I pull open the door and Mum is standing there, dressed in a tracksuit, gym bag slung over her shoulder. Such an odd sight. I can't remember ever seeing her in a tracksuit before.

'I was just on my way back from t'ai chi,' she says. 'What on earth has happened?'

'Simon,' I say.

All I wanted this morning was a lie-in and a chance to let my hair down, to feel like a real person, for once. And now, because of my idiot husband, who only cares about himself, the whole day is ruined. Selfish bastard.

5

Catherine

DC Chaudhari pulls the car up right outside the main entrance to the police station. Surely there should be some sort of rear entrance for people like me, who are just here to help with enquiries? But Chaudhari turns off the engine and looks over his shoulder.

'OK, Mrs Wells? If you'd like to follow us inside,' he says.

DI Carter has already got out of the passenger side. She opens the car door for me, and I step out onto the pavement, legs shaking. Passers-by eye me with curiosity. They must think I'm some sort of criminal.

I want to explain, *This isn't what it looks like.*

'If you could come this way.' Chaudhari gives me an oh-so-gentle touch on the elbow.

Lydia is waiting for me in reception. She gets to her feet the moment she sees me, rushes over and throws her arms around me, enveloping me in a comforting cloud of perfume. Jasmine, roses, vanilla. The usual Lydia smells.

'What's happened?' she says into my ear.

'They think something's happened to Simon. That he might be . . . he might be . . .' I daren't say it. 'It's a mistake.' That word again. I cling to it like a lifebuoy at sea, because if I let go of it, and start to think that it *isn't* a mistake, I'll be swept away. Drowned by the unthinkable.

'Of course it is.' Lydia rummages in her bag and pulls out a handkerchief, blots it against each of my cheeks in turn. 'It's going to be OK,' she says. 'Do you hear me? It's going to be all right.'

'Mrs Wells?' DI Carter is standing by an open door, one arm outstretched. 'If you'd like to come this way.'

Lydia holds my hand and we walk into the police station proper, but when we arrive at the interview room, they ask her to wait outside, directing her to a row of grey plastic chairs.

'What's the point in her being here if she's not allowed in the room?' I say.

Chaudhari shrugs. 'Best if we speak to you on your own for the time being,' he says. 'But she'll be outside if you need her. And we can stop for a break anytime.'

'I'll be right here,' says Lydia.

This can't be happening.

I am shown into a windowless interview room that smells faintly of lemon cleaner and given a seat on another one of those hard grey plastic chairs at a table that holds only a box of tissues. Detectives Carter and Chaudhari give me their best sad smiles before leaving the room.

'Back in a moment,' says Carter.

The door closes behind them and I am alone. How can they tell me my husband has burnt to death in our car, then leave me sitting here on my own?

I take out my phone and lay it flat on the table. I stare at it, pick it up and check again for texts, missed calls, messages, voicemails. In the last half-hour I have called Simon twelve times and left twelve messages. I've texted him, messaged him on Facebook and WhatsApp, emailed his personal and work email. Left a message with his PA, Ruth, that he must call me as soon as he gets to the office. I have left three messages on his work phone. All of this, and he has still not called back.

Something must have happened. Not what the police say has happened. But something.

The door clatters open and the detectives come in muttering their apologies. Carter places a glass of water on the table. They pull out chairs in noisy unison and take a seat across from me.

Chaudhari has an iPad with him and he says, 'Right, Mrs Wells. I'd like you to take a look at some pictures and tell me if you recognise any of the items shown. OK?'

I quickly activate my phone again, just in case. Nothing. I set it aside, put my shaking hands on my lap.

'This was found next to the car,' he says. He taps the tablet a few times then lays it flat on the table, turns it towards me and swipes to show me the first image. It's a picture of a fire-damaged rucksack. Half charred black, but with some of the original red and yellow colouring still visible. A hint of marker pen graffiti, pin badges on the arm straps. It looks like the sort of thing a teenager might own. He swipes again, shows me the same rucksack from the back, swipes again and shows it from the side.

Are they serious? The rucksack isn't Simon's. Obviously. The idea of him turning up to client meetings carrying that thing is laughable. He uses a briefcase for work, with enough room for his laptop and all the notebooks and files he might need for the day. He does own a rucksack, but it's a proper one for hiking that we bought from Cotswold Outdoor. Last time I saw it, it was on top of the wardrobe in the spare room.

'No rush,' says Detective Carter.

'Make sure you get a really good look,' says DC Chaudhari.

I don't want them to think I'm not being thorough, so I lean in and say nothing for a full ten seconds before saying, 'Sorry, I've never seen it before.'

'You're quite sure?' says Carter.

'I'm sure.'

That sense of being at sea recedes, then Chaudhari says, 'How about this? It was inside the bag,' and swipes the screen. My whole body tenses – then lets go. It's a photo of a baseball cap with a logo embroidered on the front. Black, I think, though that could just be from the fire. I can't help but smile. Simon has never owned a baseball cap, at least for as long as I have known him. It's just not his style. He spends half his life in suits. He'd look silly walking around in a smart three-piece carrying a briefcase while wearing a baseball cap. The only hat he owns is a straw, panama sort of thing we bought to keep the sun off last time we were in Italy, and I'd had to twist his arm into buying that. I said to him, he might feel silly in the hat, but he'll feel a damn sight more silly walking around with a bright red face.

I shake my head. 'It's not Simon's.'

'Take your time,' Carter says.

Chaudhari shows me another photograph of the baseball cap from a different angle, as if it will make any difference, as if I only ever see my husband's head from the left-hand side.

'No, sorry,' I say, though I'm not sorry in the slightest.

The bag and the baseball cap must belong to someone else, some other poor soul who met their end in that burning car. For the last hour I have felt so close to sinking down into the dark. Now I am swimming back towards the shore. Beneath the table I plant both feet on the floor.

Everything's going to be OK.

'Just a few more,' Chaudhari says.

Next comes a picture of part of a flyer for a music gig. The bottom half has been burnt away and most of what is left is taken up by the face of a young man looking moody and mysterious. The band in question is called The Push, and presumably he is their lead singer. The flyer has the faded look of an image that has been collaged together from photographs. Probably put through the office photocopier by someone on their lunch break. Chaudhari points to the corner of the flyer, to the venue name and address, a place called The Pit, on Bethnal Green Road.

'Did Simon ever mention this place?'

The Pit. I can just imagine it. A run-down dive with sticky floors and too-loud music, packed to the rafters with sweaty twenty-somethings swigging alcopops. Even when we were in our twenties it isn't the sort of place we would have gone to, and it certainly isn't the sort of place Simon would go to for work drinks. I don't imagine a place called The Pit has much of a wine list, and I don't imagine Simon would have much joy trying to discuss the finer points of the stock market with a rock band playing in the background.

'He's never mentioned it,' I say. 'To be honest, it's just not his sort of place. He couldn't take clients somewhere like that, it's a bit scruffy, I imagine. Plus, he's not really into live music. I mean, we go to concerts sometimes. We went to the Proms last year . . .'

'How about this?' Chaudhari swipes the screen and now there is no breath in my lungs.

It's a picture of Simon's watch.

He was wearing it the night I met him. I noticed it, not because it looked expensive and a little old-fashioned – though both those things were true – but because he kept it on in bed and the glass face was ice-cold against my skin. At some point over the following weeks he explained that it had belonged to his father, who died in a tragic accident, and that it is all he has to remember him by.

He never takes off his father's watch, except for when he showers.

In the picture, the brown leather strap is blackened and twisted and the glass face is shattered. But the resemblance to Simon's watch is undeniable. Watches are watches though, aren't they? There are millions of them and so many look alike. So many are the same size and shape as Simon's, with a leather strap and silver trim. So, maybe it isn't Simon's. Maybe it is just a watch that looks like Simon's.

'There's an inscription on the back. Some initials,' says Detective Chaudhari.

He swipes at the screen again and a new image appears of the watch's reverse and there they are, three letters engraved into the watch's steel back.

Simon's father's initials.

'No, no, no,' I hear myself say, because this can't be real.

I'm on my feet. The plastic chair tips back behind me and clatters to the floor.

'Mrs Wells . . .'

I spill out into the corridor and into Lydia's arms.

'Oh, Cat. What is it?' she says, over and over and oh, God, please tell me this isn't happening, *somebody please tell me this isn't happening and I have forgotten how to breathe somebody help me I have forgotten how to breathe.*

6

Sara

A burst of heavy metal spills out onto Essex Road as Sara kicks open the door with a scuffed Dr. Martens and emerges from the warm glow of the pub interior with a pint of lager in each hand and a packet of cheese and onion crisps clamped between her teeth. She sets the drinks down and lets the crisps drop from her mouth onto the rickety wooden table.

'Thanks.' Helen is in the middle of rolling a cigarette. She stops long enough to take a sip from her pint before resuming, pinching the line of tobacco between the tips of her fingers, rolling the paper back and forth then licking the cigarette closed. She shivers against the cold as she lights her roll-up. Sara takes her phone from her pocket and finds the first of several properties she bookmarked during her lunch hour.

'Look at this one.' She turns the screen towards Helen, swipes through the pictures.

Of all the flats she has seen for rent so far, this is her favourite. A maisonette on two floors of a Victorian house on a leafy road in North London. Inside, bright rooms with high ceilings, a white-tiled bathroom with a clawfoot bath. Country-style kitchen. Two bedrooms. 'It's in Highgate,' she says. 'Loads of celebs live round there. And it's got a garden. I mean, it's not exactly huge, but still. A *garden*. In London.'

'Nice,' says Helen, but by the twist of her mouth Sara can tell she is unimpressed. Sara takes another look at the listing. Maybe it is a bit old-fashioned. A little *too* grown up. You could never throw a party in a place like that. You'd be forever worried about spilling wine on the sofa, or getting a cigarette burn on the carpet.

She selects the next tab.

'This one's more modern. Not far from here, overlooking the canal. It's got a balcony. It's pretty nice.'

Helen glances at the screen and whistles. 'I should think so, for that price,' she says.

Adam did say *around* seven hundred a week, didn't he? This flat is seven fifteen. If Adam is going to be paying the lion's share of the rent, she can't have him thinking she's taking advantage. She should stick to no more than seven hundred. Seven hundred is plenty.

She brings up the next tab. 'This one's cheaper. Not as close to the tube, but the rooms are bigger.'

'Yeah,' Helen says, but her voice is cold and Sara is starting to think she is bored of talking about flats, even though they have only just got started, and even though when Helen bought her flat last year it was all she talked about for months. What the colour scheme was going to be in each room, what bathroom suite she was going to have fitted, whether she should go with terracotta tiles for the kitchen or have the original floorboards repaired.

Perhaps something is wrong . . . They usually spend lunch breaks sitting together in what passes for the canteen at Decoded Media, or, if they're too busy, head outside for a cigarette break and a catch-up. But Helen has spent most of the day in the studio, recording the voice-over for the latest episode of *CTRL Shift* – her podcast about the impact of technology on people's lives. Maybe the recording didn't go well? Sara puts her phone face down on the table to show that she is paying attention.

'What's happened?' she says. 'Was Brian being a dick again?'

As Decoded's Head Producer, Brian has a hand in every podcast they release. If Helen is in a bad mood after a day in the studio, there's a good chance Brian has something to do with it.

'He was pissed off all day,' Helen says. 'Dylan didn't turn up for work again. Second day in a row. You heard from him?'

'No,' says Sara. 'Why would I?' Helen lifts an eyebrow. 'Hels, we went out, like, three times. And that was ages ago.'

Thinking back, it's hard to believe she ever dated Dylan. Not that he wasn't good-looking, or fun to hang around with. He was both of those things. Plus, he was smart, with a no-fucks-given attitude she'd found briefly exhilarating. But he could also be startlingly immature. Three dates were all it took to decide he was a long way off what she wanted – what she needed – in a relationship.

'I just thought he might have said something, that's all,' says Helen.

Sara shakes her head. Unlikely, she thinks. Dylan rarely bothers to stop for a chat these days, a far cry from when he used to spend half his day hovering around her desk, flirting. Plus, he isn't exactly known for keeping others informed of his whereabouts.

'Remember that time he went to Burning Man and forgot to tell anyone?' Helen adds.

'God, yeah,' says Sara. 'Never learns, does he?'

'Nope. He's in *so* much trouble this time.' Helen blows a pillar of smoke sideways. The wind catches it and carries it directly into the faces of a family of four sitting at the next table. Tourists, with matching anoraks and a map of London landmarks unfurling between them. Sara offers the dad an apologetic smile, even though they've chosen to sit outdoors on a chilly winter evening in Islington. Even though within an hour they'll be surrounded by goths, punks and City boys, all smoking and chucking as much booze down their necks as possible.

Sara picks up her phone, is about to show Helen the next tab – a two-bedroom maisonette in Muswell Hill – when Helen says, 'Don't you think it's a bit soon for you two?'

Here we go.

Helen's mood is nothing to do with Brian being a dick, or Dylan going AWOL. It's because she doesn't like Adam. She claims she does, but whenever Sara talks about him Helen's eyes begin to roll, and before long she disengages from the conversation or changes the subject. The two of them have only ever met once – an unplanned drink after they bumped into her on the South Bank – and Adam and Helen had both behaved weird, like wild animals circling each other at a wary distance. They'd disagreed on just about everything. Food, music, films, politics. When she asked Adam what he thought of Helen later that night, he'd half shrugged and said she *seemed* nice, which is exactly the sort of thing you might say about someone you don't like very much – a phrase that takes away as much as it gives.

'How long has it been now? Six months?' Helen says.

'Nine, actually,' says Sara.

'Not long, though, is it? Not really. I mean, you haven't even been to his place yet.'

His place. His soulless bachelor pad out in the middle of nowhere. Where did he say it was again? Farnham? Farnborough? One of those awful commuter belt towns, full of housing estates and business parks.

'Because it's miles away and there's nothing to do there. He doesn't even have a TV. It's a squalid little place he got in a hurry when he separated from his ex.'

Helen stubs what's left of her roll-up out in the ashtray then pulls her sleeves down over her fists to warm her hands. 'I still don't think nine months is a long time,' she says. 'How long was he with his wife? Ten years?'

Adam is not exactly in the habit of bringing up his ex-wife, but on the rare occasions he has, it's been with the kind of weariness that Sara expects comes from having spent too long in a relationship that should have ended years before it did. Could they have been together for ten years? A quarter of his life?

'Does it matter?' Sara says. 'They're divorced.'

Helen gives her a look, a smirk with one eyebrow raised.

'They're *divorced*,' repeats Sara. It's not like she's seen the paperwork with her own eyes, but she remembers the day Adam told her it had been finalised. It was their two-month anniversary and he'd taken her out for cocktails in Shoreditch to celebrate.

'You don't even know what he does for a living,' says Helen.

'He works for a start-up in Soho. He's Director of . . . something or other.' Her answer earns her another look from Helen. 'Hels, not everyone knows the ins and outs of their partner's job. I've known you for three years and there are parts of your job I haven't got a clue about.'

'But you're not moving in with me,' Helen shoots back. 'Besides, you know exactly what I do at work.'

This is only partly true. Sara knows Helen is the host of *CTRL Shift*. She knows Helen decides what topics the episodes are going to cover, that she commissions reporters, conducts interviews, and records the voice-overs that hold it all together. *How* she does all this and manages to make it sound so effortless, is a mystery. Like a kind of magic trick. One Sara hopes she'll have the skill to pull off herself someday.

But knowing, or not knowing, the details of someone's job doesn't mean anything.

'I know you don't like Adam,' Sara says.

Helen holds up her hands. 'That's not true—'

'Come on, Hels. I can tell. It's only because you don't know him,' she says. 'Once you spend more time with him, you'll see that he's really nice.'

Helen puts her hand on top of Sara's. 'That's just it,' she says. 'I'm not sure he is. Sometimes I think he's horrible to you. Leaving you in the lurch, cancelling plans at the last minute—'

'Because of his work—'

'Blowing hot and cold all the time. One minute he can't keep his hands off you, the next you don't hear from him for days.'

'It's not like that now,' Sara says. 'Yes, he could be a bit funny when we first got together, but he had some stuff to figure out, that's all.'

He was scared of being hurt. That's why he pushed her away. *I'm worried I'll fuck things up, that I'm not good enough for you*, he'd told her. All he needed was that bit of reassurance, to be told he was loved, that he deserved to be happy.

'Things are good between us,' Sara says. 'You're not there when it's just me and him. You only hear about the bad bits. It would be boring if I said, "Last night, Adam came round and we cuddled for hours and watched TV and had mind-blowing sex and it was all lovely." You only hear about the rows, or when I'm worried about something. But me and Adam are good now. And just because he's older than me—'

'A *lot* older than you—'

'—doesn't make it any less real. He's just asked me to move in with him, for God's sake.'

'And you trust him?' says Helen.

'Of course I do.'

Helen nods. 'I just worry about you, that's all. You know what some men are like.'

Sara does. The two of them have spent more hours than they can count, sat inside or outside pubs just like this one, talking about the men in their lives. Sometimes the good, but more often the bad. Like Helen's ex, who sent her threatening messages for over a year after they finished, even though he left her for someone else. Or Sara's former boss, who would look at her tits rather than her face whenever he spoke to her. Or the man who approached them outside this very pub last month, took a seat without asking and, when told they were having a private conversation, called them fucking lesbians and flicked his lit cigarette at them.

'Just because your last boyfriend turned out to be an arsehole, doesn't mean mine is,' Sara says. 'Adam's a good person. He's not like that.'

'None of them are . . .' Helen starts to say, then Sara's phone comes to life, vibrating hard against the table. Sara thinks about waiting for Helen to finish, but she'd rather the conversation end there. She picks up her phone, sees she has a new message. It's a cheesy selfie of Adam giving the thumbs up. In the background, the Eiffel Tower is lit up against the evening sky.

'Speak of the devil,' she says, showing the phone's screen to Helen.

It's good to hear from him, though she can't help feeling that a photo of Adam enjoying himself in Paris isn't quite what she needs from him right now. A moment later and the phone buzzes with a text: *Wish you were here x*, it says.

Me too, she thinks.

She wishes she were in Paris, or in the car with Adam, driving out of London to their week of walks and food and sex, instead of sitting outside a grotty pub in Islington, being made to feel bad by her best friend.

Helen slaps the table with both hands.

'I'm going to the loo. Same again?' She nods at their almost empty glasses.

'Please,' says Sara. Helen stands and disappears inside and Sara is relieved to have a moment to herself.

Yes, she and Adam have had their rough patches, but haven't most couples? And yes, there are things she doesn't know about him. She doesn't know the ins and outs of his boring job. She's never visited his middle-of-nowhere flat. And she knows next to nothing about his marriage. Though, on that last point, why would she?

She's going to move in with him, whether Helen likes it or not. She knows him, she loves him, and he loves her. What could be more important than that?

7

Catherine

There is only this thought, this feeling – this pain, this ache, this fear, this terror – and it fills me up and empties me out at the same time: *this cannot be real.*

It severs me from the world, leaves me hovering in the dark, a dream state somewhere between sleep and wakefulness . . . Until I'm wrenched back to reality by the sound of Charlie whimpering in his sleep. I get up and go to him, find him in the grip of a nightmare, tossing and turning, tangled in his sheets. His hair is damp with sweat and his face is flushed. I sit on the edge of his bed and try to soothe him, and my restless dream comes back to me in flashes.

Simon, trapped in our car, the smoke rising around him, tendrils dispersing into a silver cloud. It stings his eyes, forces its way inside him to scorch his lungs—

I stroke Charlie's forehead. 'Hush, now. Mummy's here.'

He moans, twists his head this way and that.

The inside of the car is glowing a frightful, flickering orange. Simon slams his forearm into the driver's side window, over and over – thunk-thunk-thunk – but it will – thunk– not – thunk – break.

Charlie awakens with a gasp, coughs and splutters, struggles for breath. When he catches it, he uses every last bit of it to let out an ear-piercing scream.

The car seats combust, jets of flame bursting from the headrests. The hood of Simon's coat catches fire. He tries to beat out the flames with his hands, sending smouldering embers floating through the car's interior. The sleeve of his jacket ignites—

I pull Charlie to me, but he fights me, screams unintelligible words through his tears, screws up his fists and hits me, thumps my chest.

'Charlie, it's Mummy,' I tell him. 'Shh . . . shh.' He looks *through* me, as if he doesn't recognise his own mother.

Fire ripples up Simon's arm and across his chest. He cries out, a drawn-out tea kettle scream that rises in volume and pitch—

'Shh, everything's OK.'

Nothing is OK.

Simon's blackened fists beat against the car window in a final desperate attempt to break free—

The bedroom light snaps on. Mum stands in the doorway in her nightie.

'Catherine? Oh, dear. Oh, love.' She hurries over. 'Let me take him.'

I don't want to let Charlie go. I need him and he needs me.

My husband is burning alive—

But I can't do this right now.

Mum lifts Charlie out of my arms and hoists him onto her hip. He wraps his arms around her neck and presses his face into her shoulder.

'There, there,' she soothes him. 'Shh.'

I cover my face with my hands. My head is full of pictures of Simon, trapped inside our car as it burns, a charcoal stick figure curling in on itself.

'What am I going to do, Mum?' I say.

She doesn't have an answer for me, but she comes to me and, with Charlie still on her hip, pulls my head onto her stomach and strokes my hair, and Charlie and I dissolve into tears.

Later on, Mum lies next to me with her head tipped back, snoring. Charlie is between us, sucking his thumb in his sleep.

I am on Simon's side of the bed. There's still a trace of him on his pillow. I bury my face in the smell of him. The scent of his aftershaves, both the one I buy him every year that reminds me of Christmas, and the sharp, citrusy Calvin Klein scent I know he secretly prefers and uses most mornings. I can smell his shampoo. Can smell his sweat. I breathe him in, over and over.

He will come home. He has to. Despite what the treacherous voice in the back of my mind keeps telling me.

Charlie mumbles, his face still blotchy and damp. I reach up and stroke his baby-soft hair and he quietens. He must sense something is wrong, but doesn't know what. I envy his not knowing. How I wish I could sleep, too. And in the morning, wake up with Simon lying here next to me.

But I can't drift off. My mind won't let me.

He's not missing. He's dead and he's never coming back.

No. I will not accept this. If it was him in that car, I would know. I would feel it, deep inside me.

My head is full of him.

The last time I saw him – not the last time we were together, arguing while he fastened his tie in the hall mirror – but the last time I really *saw* him. He was playing hide-and-seek with Charlie, and I came into the living room to tell him something and found him stomping around like a hungry giant, making crashing sounds with each footstep. He pushed his chin into his chest and put on a deep voice. 'I eat little boys for dinner, and I am *very* hungry! Where has that little boy gone?'

'He's not here!' Charlie shouted from behind the sofa.

Simon whirled around, plucked Charlie from his hiding spot and hoisted him in the air, then pretended to eat him, making nom-nom-nom noises and blowing raspberries on his tummy. Neither of them noticed me standing by the door, watching them. Loving them.

The last time he kissed me. On the cheek. On the lips. Other places.

The last time we made love – not the last time we had sex, which was over a month ago when Simon came home after a works do and his breath smelled of red wine and his fingers tasted of cigarettes. But the last time we made love, the last time we both really *meant* it. When everything flowed and we gave and took in equal measure.

The first time we made love.

The first time we met.

When I think of how we met, I don't recall the actual evening. Instead, I think about Simon telling the story at some dinner party or other, of how he saved me from being harassed by what he always calls a 'posh-looking fella, a rugger-bugger type'.

'Total creep, he was,' he'd say. 'Real nasty piece of work. He was getting quite abusive, wouldn't leave her alone. She asked me if I wouldn't mind walking her back to her dorm in case he tried anything, we got talking on the way and . . . that was that, really. The rest is history.'

The rest is history; our history. Fifteen years of being partners, fourteen of living together. Twelve of marriage, four of being Mum and Dad.

True, we are not the couple we once were, are not 'loved up' anymore. We argue, frequently. Sometimes we forget to be kind to each other. But that's normal, isn't it? For couples like us, who have been together forever, who are worn down with the responsibilities of work and childcare? It doesn't mean anything. We still love each other. Still know each other inside out. We are connected, even when we are apart.

I picture the telephone we made Charlie in the summer holidays using paper cups and a length of string. Simon on one side of the house, me and Charlie on the other, Charlie pressing the cup to my ear so I could feel the vibration of Simon's voice.

Vibrations. That's what we feel when we are close to someone. We know when they are happy or sad, or in pain. A bit of how they feel finds its way to us. So why didn't I wake up when Simon called me last night? If he was hurt – or if someone was hurting him – I would have known, wouldn't I? I would have *felt* it.

I reach inside myself, search for that bridge between us. It's still there. Which means he's still alive.

Simon? Can you hear me?

The silence is terrifying.

Even though I am lying next to Charlie and Mum, I have never felt so alone. The thought of going to sleep feels ridiculous, dangerous even. What if Simon is just the beginning? What if I wake up and Charlie and Mum are gone, too? Whatever will I do then?

I reach for my phone on the bedside table, dial Simon's number.

There's no answer – *of course there's no answer, he's gone, and he's never coming back* – but his voicemail kicks in, and hearing him speak brings me to tears, makes me feel closer to him and further away from him at the same time.

This is Simon. I'm not available right now but if you'd like to leave me a message, I'll come back to you as soon as I can.

21-11-2022

00.47 a.m.

'Before we do this, I want to know how you found me,' he says, then he stares at me, as if I'm going to give up the goods, just like that.

'How about this. You answer my questions first, then I'll tell you what you want to know.'

He shakes his head. 'That's not why we're here.'

That's exactly why we're here. He just doesn't know it yet.

'Do you have any idea how long I've been looking for you?' I say, because flattery goes a long way with people like him. 'The hours I've spent trying to figure out why you did what you did, how you managed to get away with it for so long? Come on, put me out of my misery. Talk to me, off the record.'

'Off the record?'

'Just you, me, and the truth. Then you'll never have to hear from me again.'

'It'll be over?' He gets this faraway look in his eyes, like he's picturing himself free of it all, like he can take back all the bad things he's done.

'Think about it,' I say. 'I mean, it's not as if anybody else has worked it out, right?'

'True,' he says, with a crooked smile, proud of himself. 'People only know what you want them to know. Only see what you want them to see.'

He wants to talk. Is desperate for someone to know just how damn smart he is.

'All right, I'll do it,' he says. 'Where do you want to start?'

'You tell me,' I say. 'It's your confession.'

8

Day Two

Sara

Sara arrives for work five minutes late, having stopped at the shop opposite Angel tube to pick up paracetamol, a bottle of water and some gum. Last night's booze is making her feel slow and heavy, like she's wading through a swamp. Her bones ache and her stomach churns. And it isn't only her hangover that's making the morning feel like far too much effort.

There was another selfie from Adam waiting for her when she woke up. This time he was outside a swanky-looking Parisian café, holding a cup of coffee up to the camera with a smug look on his face. And while it was nice to start the day with a message from him, she'd have rather he got back to her about the flats she's found. She sent him five links in all, in the hope he might say which he likes so she can arrange some viewings.

Maybe he doesn't want to move in with me after all? she thinks, then dismisses the idea. Of course he does. It was his suggestion. When he gets back she'll make sure he knows how him not replying makes her feel. Like he doesn't care. Like moving in together isn't important to him.

She types a code into the panel by the side of the office door, hears a low mechanical grind and pushes her way inside.

The offices of Decoded Media consist of two recording booths, six banks of desks, a small kitchen and a breakout area with two sofas and a range of oversized cushions. One side of the office – the cool side, as Sara thinks of it – is reserved for Editorial; all the hosts, reporters and journalists who work on the podcasts. There's Helen and the rest of the *CTRL Shift* team; Mike and Paul, the nerdy film obsessives from *Look Who's Talkin' to Me*; Lauren and Deepti, creators of the true-crime anthology series, *Unhinged*, and Dylan, who hosts true-crime podcast *The Push*. To Sara, even when half empty, the cool side of the office feels busy and alive in a way that the other side doesn't, especially the part where she sits – on a bank of desks with the other production assistant, Kate; Harriet, the HR lady; Steve who's Head of Accounts, and Brian.

She heads there now, hoping Brian is too engrossed in his work to notice her. He is wearing a giant pair of headphones and, on his screen, the waveform of an audio file scrolls to the left, plateauing and spiking like a heart monitor gone haywire. She moves behind him, but her reflection gives her away. He spins in his seat, takes off his headphones and gives her a look: *really?*

He can probably tell that she is late for no good reason, that she is hungover and tired because she drank too much and stayed out late. After the pub in Islington, she and Helen caught the tube to Camden, went to a club, danced until their feet hurt and then sat at the bar drinking shots of something. Tequila. She can still taste it at the back of her throat. If Brian was sitting any closer, he'd probably be able to get a whiff of alcohol under her perfume.

'Sorry, Brian,' she says. 'Won't happen again.'

He rolls his eyes. 'I seem to recall you saying something like that last time.'

Yes, she thinks, *that is what I said last time, but that was ages ago, and just because I'm the youngest here, doesn't mean you get to treat me like a child.*

She walks around to her desk with her head down, stewing over the unfairness of it all. The way he speaks to her sometimes . . . like he's a teacher and she's an unruly pupil who has forgotten her homework. If she isn't at her desk precisely on time, or if she is so much as one minute late back from lunch, she can count on him making a snarky comment. The next time he does it, she'll say something, she thinks. Stand up for herself. You can't do that to people these days – pick on them, single them out for special treatment. Just because you're the boss, doesn't mean you get to say whatever you like—

'Everything all right?' Brian says.

'Fine. I'm fine,' Sara says, hoping he can't read minds.

'Good,' says Brian. 'I've already had one staff member vanish off the face of the earth, I don't need another one disappearing.'

'Still no word from Dylan?' she asks, pointedly, because being five minutes late is in no way comparable to not turning up for work two days in a row. She looks over to Dylan's desk, eyes his empty chair. Make that three days.

Brian shakes his head. 'When he gets back . . .' He trails off, as if the trouble waiting for Dylan on his return is too big to put into words.

'He'll turn up,' Sara says. 'You know what he's like.'

Unreliable, she means. Not five-minutes-late-for-work unreliable, either. Dylan is one of those people – undeniably clever, but lacking in common sense. The sort of person who forgets the basics. Who goes to week-long festivals and forgets to tell anyone in the office. Who doesn't notice the battery has run out in his digital recorder halfway through an interview, then, when he goes back to do it a second time, forgets to turn the recorder on altogether. This, even after Brian has drummed into him, as he does all his staff, to never start an interview until you have hit record twice. Once on your main recorder, once on your backup.

For the rest of the morning, Sara focuses on getting through her work as quietly as possible. *Look Who's Talkin' to Me* is soaring up the podcast charts, despite the fact that, to Sara's ears, it sounds like two slightly drunk men talking over each other. It is Sara's job to give the episode a final polish, to place advertising triggers – pre-roll, mid-roll and post-roll – bleep out the worst of the swear words and clean up the audio, editing out the 'ums' and 'ahs' and 'erms', so that the tipsy-seeming hosts sound articulate and sober. By lunchtime she has the episode finished and uploads it to the server. She checks the production folder for her next job, sees that there is a file there waiting for her. A new episode of *The Push*.

Sara avoids working on Dylan's podcast if she can help it, and hasn't listened to an episode in months. Partly because she thinks that, despite its cult following, the podcast is going nowhere and should have been cancelled ages ago, but mostly because *The Push* was her idea.

She came up with it on a night out with Dylan. They were sitting outside a dingy pub on Tottenham Court Road and Dylan had been boring on about how he was going to take the podcast world by storm, once he found the right story.

'That's all it takes,' he'd said. '*Serial*, *S-Town*, *Up and Vanished* – with that kind of material, anybody could make a hit podcast. You get the right story, and the rest is easy.'

Sure, she'd thought. All you need is the right story. Plus, years of journalism experience, a brilliant ear for structure, good production values and incredibly thorough research . . .

She'd only been half listening. Her eye drawn to a man sprinting alongside a double-decker bus, slamming his hand against the window and screaming obscenities. The driver was either oblivious, or deliberately ignoring him. *That man could get run over if he's not careful*, thought Sara, and a connection sparked at the back of her brain.

'What about the London Bridge Jogger?' she said to Dylan.

'The what?'

Sara brought up YouTube on her phone and they watched the grainy footage of the jogger veering across the pavement, arms snapping out to shove the woman in the white coat.

'I remember this. What a psycho,' said Dylan.

'Right,' Sara said. 'And this footage was on the front page of every newspaper and all over social media. Everyone wanted to know who this arsehole was, find him before he hurt someone else. But then . . . nothing. The whole world has become obsessed with exposing film producers and comedians and musicians for being creeps and abusers, but this guy is still walking around a free man. And you know the worst part? Everything written about this case is all about *him*, the mystery psycho. The victim has never been given the chance to tell her story.'

Dylan slapped a hand down on the table. 'You could make a whole big thing of it. "The hunt for the London Bridge Jogger". Just think of the merch! Badges, T-shirts, hoodies.' He grinned.

'Maybe,' said Sara, though that wasn't quite what she had in mind.

A podcast devoted to hunting down the jogger was more than likely doomed. After all, the police had spent months trying to track him down. But there was still a story to be told here. About why some men think they own the pavement, the same way they think they own the world. And about the women they push out of their way.

They kicked the idea around some more, but it was clear they were on different pages. It wasn't this conversation in particular that led her to decide she and Dylan would be better off just friends. There were others like it, times when his boyish enthusiasm became tiresome, his no-fucks-given attitude plain irritating.

She broke the news over WhatsApp. *It's better that way*, Helen had warned. *Safer, even. Some men do not take rejection well.*

In the end, Dylan wasn't abusive, but he blanked her for weeks, ignored her in meetings, refused to talk to her. Occasionally, she would catch him glaring over his monitor at her, glassy-eyed, as if on the verge of tears.

'I feel bad,' she told Helen. 'He seems upset.'

'It'll do him good,' said Helen. 'He's a spoiled rich kid, used to getting his own way. You're probably the first person ever to say no to him.'

It was a full month before he broke his silence, skulking up to her while she was on a smoke break.

'You know that idea we had, about the London Bridge Jogger?' he said, and she almost laughed. First, at him jumping straight in like that, after a whole month of not speaking to her – no, *Hi, how are you?* or, *Hey, how's it going?* Second, because they both knew it wasn't *their* idea. It was hers.

'Would you mind if I pitched it to Brian?' he asked, when he might as well as have said, *Mind if I steal your idea and pass it off as my own?*

But when she replied, the oddest thing happened. She found herself saying she didn't mind, that he should totally do it, and that she thought he'd do a great job. Later on, she would think back on this moment and wonder why she did that. Rolled over, prioritised his feelings and ambition over her own. She didn't like what that said about her very much. Liked it even less three weeks later, when the first episode of *The Push* landed in the production folder.

When Sara listened to it, she got a sick feeling in her stomach. It was her idea, and she had just . . . given it away. All to make a man feel better about himself. Worse still, Dylan wasn't interested in the victim's story – or any woman's story, for that matter. *The Push* was a straightforward manhunt, only concerned with tracking down the jogger. And the most frustrating thing? It worked. Download numbers were among the best Decoded had ever seen.

Now, however, a year on, Dylan is struggling for new leads and audience numbers have halved. He spends most of his time in the office taking delivery of, and shipping out at the company's expense, merchandise he has made in support of the podcast. Pin badges, tote bags, keyrings. Black cotton T-shirts, with the silhouette of a jogger picked out in white and – Sara almost died the first time she saw it – Dylan's own face, hovering in the background, looking moody and mysterious. Every item of merchandise bears the same slogan: *I helped Dylan find the London Bridge Jogger.* Which would be fine, if the jogger had actually been found, but he's still out there and twenty-odd episodes of *The Push* have done absolutely nothing to change that.

Sara clicks play on the new episode and Dylan's voice fills her head.

Say what you like about Dylan. He might be unreliable, and arrogant with it, but he has perfected his podcast voice. It is calming and authoritative, somehow quiet and loud at the same time. It is also, Sara has to admit, albeit begrudgingly, quite sexy.

I'm investigative journalist Dylan Lesley. Welcome to this special update of . . . The Push. The podcast about the extraordinary case of the London Bridge Jogger.

Investigative journalist? As if. Twelve months after dropping out of his BA in Media and Communications and now he's an investigative journalist?

It goes without saying, but I'm going to say it anyway . . . if you haven't listened to the previous episodes, then stop, go back and listen from Episode One. I promise, everything will make a lot more sense if you do.

For our regular listeners, those who've stuck with us over the last twenty-five episodes, I want to say thank you. It's been a long journey, with plenty of challenges along the way, but I think you're going to be glad you came along for the ride. There's going to be a whole new episode next week, but I wanted to record this quick update to let you know that something big is coming. I'm pleased to say that all our hard work has finally paid off. After ten months of twists and turns, of false leads and dead ends . . . finally, listeners . . . we have a breakthrough.

Oh, and what a breakthrough it is . . .

Sara can *hear* Dylan grinning into the microphone.

As remarkable as it sounds, I believe we can now finally confirm the identity of the London Bridge Jogger.

She sits up in her seat.

I'll be taking this information to the police, but before I do, I plan to confront him and get his reaction on tape. After all these months of trying to track him down, I think I deserve this moment. And, dear listener, I think you do, too. So . . . Tune in to our next episode to find out how we got here, and to hear what the jogger has to say for himself. I cannot stress this enough . . . this is going to be big. So, tell your friends and family to subscribe, and in the meantime, don't forget to check out the merch page on our website. We've got T-shirts, keyrings, badges and a brand-new range of hoodies coming real soon.

I'm Dylan Lesley. Until next time . . .

Sara takes off her headphones.

Fuck. Maybe Dylan is going to take the podcast world by storm after all? So why isn't he here, bragging about having solved the case?

What if he went to confront the jogger, and the jogger didn't like what he had to say? Because one thing's for certain: whoever the mystery jogger is – the man who almost killed a woman just because she took up more space on the pavement than he liked – he's dangerous.

Sara calls over to Brian, waves a hand to attract his attention. He looks up, pulls off his headphones and cocks his head to one side.

'What is it now?' He sighs, as if the morning has been nothing but distractions.

'I think you need to listen to this,' says Sara. 'I think Dylan might be in trouble.'

9

Catherine

A family liaison officer visits. A small woman, dressed in jeans and a fleece, with a closed-mouthed smile that never seems to waver. She sits on the sofa for three hours, drinking endless cups of tea supplied by Mum.

'Rest assured we're looking into everything,' she explains.

Simon was last seen by a cleaner at his office building, catching the lift down from the tenth floor at 7.30 p.m. They know that much, but not much else. The CCTV cameras at the entrance to the garage at Jefferson Trading are on the fritz, apparently, so there is no footage of our car leaving the garage and therefore no indication of who was driving, or which direction the driver might have taken out of the City. They are trying to use number plate recognition to work out how and when the Mercedes got from central London to Epping Forest.

'We're speaking to his colleagues and his friends,' she tells me. 'And we're looking at phone records, any communication he's had with people over the last few weeks—'

'What about DNA?' I ask. Surely that's the best way to prove that the poor person they found in our burnt-out car isn't Simon.

'Absolutely. But these things take time, especially when there's fire involved.'

She lifts her mug of tea to her lips, takes a sip and swills it around her mouth, as if she has all the time in the world.

'Why are you here?' I ask. 'How do you expect to find him if you're sitting here drinking cups of tea? Why isn't it on the news, or in the papers? Why is everything so . . .' I can't think of the word.

There should be sirens and helicopters. People out there knocking on doors. It should be breaking news on every TV channel: *41-year-old father of one from South London, missing.*

Quiet. That's the word. Why is it so bloody quiet?

'I understand your frustration, Mrs Wells,' she says, 'but I assure you, the detectives are experts at what they do, and they've decided it's best not to release anything to the media until forensics have confirmed the identity of the remains found in the car. But I promise you, they aren't just sitting around. They're doing everything they can to find out what's happened to your husband.'

As she leaves, she turns at the front door and gives me a friendly pat on the shoulder that makes me want to knock her hand away.

'I'll make sure you're kept up to date, and you've got my number. If you need anything, or have any questions, just call me, OK?'

Why is everything taking so long? How is it that after two days, you know next to nothing about what has happened to my husband? How come, in a country with more CCTV than anywhere else in the world, you haven't a bloody clue where my husband went after he left work?

'And in the meantime, try and get some rest.'

'Thank you, I'll try,' I say, though even if I wanted to sleep, I couldn't. What if Simon tries to get in touch again and I miss his call?

She gives me a wave as she drives off and I am left looking out across the square we live in. The residents' gardens and the north side of the church that sits nestled back from the road. The old-fashioned red phone box on the corner. The bright-white Georgian houses, lined up like gleaming teeth. I have felt uneasy here before – during that spate of burglaries in the spring, or when we discovered some local students had been jumping the fence to smoke drugs in the residents' garden at night – but nothing like this. Now the square feels totally different. The house, too. It is all too exposed, too open to the dangers of the world. The houses still shine, but there is decay behind the scenes, cavities in unseen places.

I close the door and head inside. In the two minutes I've spent seeing the officer out Mum has armed herself with polish and a duster and is working her way round the sitting room. This is what she does now. If she's not helping with Charlie, she cleans. Flits from room to room like a chittering white-haired bird, darting in to swipe away a cup the second it's empty, or to steal crumbs off the coffee table.

The house has never been cleaner, and has never smelled less like our home. The faint odours that combine into our home's signature scent – fabric softener, Charlie's no-more-tears shampoo, Simon's aftershave – are all being washed away.

'They're useless,' I say to Mum. 'It's been two days now. How can they not know anything?' It feels like there's a stone lodged in my throat.

'Oh, love,' Mum says. 'I'm sure they're doing everything they can.'

Everyone knows the police are underfunded, that the government has slashed budgets and there are thousands fewer officers now than there were five years ago. Even if they are doing everything they can, that doesn't mean they are doing everything they *should*. And whatever they are doing, it's not enough.

Mum sets the polish and duster down and I follow her as she heads into the kitchen.

'They've interviewed his friends, been to his work, spoken to his colleagues. I bet they know something and aren't telling me. Why would they keep things from me?'

Mum licks her lips, as if she's about to give me a reason, but the words don't come. She turns away, switches the kettle on. If I drink one more cup of tea, I think I'll vomit.

I check my phone, just in case. Nothing from Simon, but there's a message from Lydia, sent half an hour ago: *Thinking of you today. No need to reply, but I'll check in later x*

She probably doesn't know what else to say. That's what it's like when terrible things happen. People don't want to risk saying the wrong thing, so end up saying nothing at all. At least Lydia is making the effort.

I go to Charlie in the sitting room. Wednesdays are one of the two days a week he doesn't go to nursery. Mum suggested she take him in anyway, but I thought it best if we keep to his normal routine. The truth is, I want him here. Having my beautiful baby boy with me, watching him play, makes me feel like normal life isn't so far away.

He is lying on his tummy on the rug, an array of plastic dinosaurs arranged in front of him. He picks up a two-inch-tall T-Rex, uses it to menace a triceratops twice its size.

For want of something better to say, I have told him Daddy is on one of his work trips. He's used to Simon not being here for stretches of three or four days at a time, and I'm not going to upset him by telling him anything different.

'Raar!' He shakes the T-Rex, mashes its jaws against the horns of the triceratops. I bend down. I want to hold him, feel his warmth against me.

'Come and give Mummy a cuddle,' I say.

He shakes his head, too engrossed in his play. I pick him up anyway and he squirms and twists away from me. 'Mummy, no!' He drops his T-Rex, reaches after it.

'Come on, Charlie . . .'

'I don't want to!' I walk him away from his dinosaurs, bounce him on my hip. 'I was playing. I was playing!' he cries.

'You can play in a minute. Mummy just wants a cuddle,' I say.

'Don't want to cuddle!' Tears come and he plants his fists on my chest.

'Stop that. Come on, little man,' I say, but he won't have it. He wriggles and fights me.

Mum is suddenly there, arms out. 'Oh, Charlie,' she says. 'Whatever's the matter?' To me she says, 'How about I take him to the park for some fresh air, hmm? It'll do him good. You can go and lie down, grab a few hours.'

Get some rest. Go and lie down.

What do they think? That I'll have sweet dreams and wake up refreshed and reinvigorated? My husband is missing, presumed dead. So, no. I don't think I will get some rest, thank you very much.

'He's fine here, Mum.'

Besides, what if something happens and she doesn't know what to do? What if he falls at the park and cuts himself, or if he picks something up off the floor? I have seen used needles in the park, used condoms.

'I can't leave him. He's upset,' I say.

'He's upset because you're upset,' says Mum.

'He's missing his daddy.'

Mum hitches in a breath to speak, holds it for a moment before she says, 'Of course he is, love. We're all going to miss him, very much.'

Going to miss him?

So she thinks he's gone, too.

How could she?

Simon adores Mum, often reminds me how lucky we are to have her around. And I always thought the feeling was mutual, that Mum adored him, too. She once joked there must be something wrong with him because he seemed too good to be true.

Now she's given up on him.

I turn my back to her and move into the kitchen, still trying to soothe Charlie, who has stopped fighting me but is unsettled, his body radiating heat, flopping this way and that.

Mum follows. 'Here,' she says, arms out.

'It's fine, Mum.' I rock Charlie, sing to him. '*London Bridge is falling down, falling down, falling down . . .*' He used to like that one when he was a baby, it used to send him straight to sleep. 'Shh now. *London Bridge is falling down, my fair lady . . .*'

When I turn back, Mum is holding out a cup of tea. She wants me to do an exchange: tea for Charlie.

'For God's sake, Mum,' I hiss. 'Can you *please* stop? I don't want any bloody tea. What help is tea? And for that matter, what help is scrubbing the place to within an inch of its life? It's like you're trying to wipe away any sign he was ever here.'

Mum sets the tea down on the counter and takes a step back. 'I'll do whatever you want me to do,' she says, in a small voice.

'Maybe you should just go.' The words are out of my mouth before I know they're coming and I watch the muscles in Mum's face harden as she swallows down the hurt.

'If that's what you want, love,' she says, but she doesn't move. She just stands there, no doubt expecting me to break down and tell her how sorry I am, that I didn't mean it and that of course I want her here. But I don't, because I do mean it. I don't want cups of tea. I don't want the house cleaning to within an inch of its life. I just want her to believe that Simon is still out there. What good is she to me if she's given up on him?

I take Charlie into the living room and get down on the floor with him. I hear Mum out in the hall gathering her things, then the sound of the front door closing.

I pick up Charlie's T-Rex and make it roar.

'Where's Grandma?' Charlie says.

'She had to go home, love,' I tell him. 'It's just you and me now.'

I'm used to it just being the two of us, sat at home waiting for Daddy, but this is different. Daddy isn't at work, or out for dinner with clients, or on one of his runs. He's missing. And the police are never going to find him, because they think he's dead, just like Mum does. That's why they haven't got any leads. That's why they come round and sit on my sofa drinking tea, when they should be out looking for him.

It's down to me, I realise.

I'm going to have to find Simon myself.

Something has happened to you and I'm going to find out what. And I will not sleep, I will not rest, I will not stop for a single second, until I bring you home.

10

Sara

Sara stays late at the office, keen to get back in Brian's good books, but also to avoid rush hour. Her hangover has got its second wind, and the thought of spending half an hour on a cramped Northern Line train to Elephant and Castle feels like it might just push her, and her stomach, over the edge. Plus, there's something nice about being in the office alone on a winter's evening, with only the electric hum of the vending machine for company. The stillness makes the day seem not so bad after all. Her hangover, Adam not replying about the flats, the Dylan thing . . . Which wasn't a thing at all, according to Brian.

It was a stunt, he told her. Dylan's attempt to drum up more subscribers.

'You tell me what's more likely,' he said. 'That I tell Dylan he needs to urgently address his drop in subscribers, and he just happens to find the jogger the very next day, or that he decides to put out a five-minute episode saying he *thinks* he's found the jogger, and listeners should tell all their friends?'

She thought about it for half a second.

'The second one,' she said. 'But then, why isn't he here?' Shouldn't he be in the office, working hard on his next episode – the one where he has to explain to his listeners that he hasn't found the jogger after all?

'I told him not to do anything stupid,' said Brian. 'Clearly he didn't listen, and now he's afraid to face the music. And so he should be.'

'I suppose,' said Sara, still not fully convinced. Dylan hadn't sounded like he was lying in the podcast, he'd sounded thrilled.

'Look,' said Brian, with an impatient sigh. 'If he really had found the jogger, do you think this would be the first we'd heard about it?'

He was right. Dylan would have shouted it from the rooftops, probably had a range of T-shirts printed touting his genius and handed one out to everyone in the office.

It was just like Dylan to try and bullshit his way out of trouble without considering anyone else's feelings. Never mind his listeners, what about the woman who was pushed? Has he given even a second's thought to how his little stunt might make her feel? Of course he hasn't.

It's seven thirty by the time she leaves the office, rides the tube down to Elephant and Castle and exits the underground onto New Kent Road. She considers taking the longer route home, past the fried chicken shops and the tanning salon, the Lebanese restaurant and the kiosk that fixes phones and sells e-cigarettes. But it's late, and she's tired. She wants to be curled up on the sofa, eating salty food and watching trashy television. She opts for the quicker route, winding her way through a warren of empty, amber-lit streets.

She has always hated London in winter. It's fine in Soho or Camden, or on Essex Road, where the streets are dotted with pubs and the pavements are alive with drinkers until the small hours. But away from the crowds, on a walk home alone in the dark, to a too-small flat that costs her half her wages in rent each month, the city feels bleak and hostile. She remembers her first winter here, how shocked she was to blow her nose and see crusted black snot in the tissue – the city's grime having made its way inside her. *That's* the real London, right there, she thought. That's what's hiding beneath the glitz and glamour.

An echo of footsteps behind her.

She glances back, sees a lone figure walking under the streetlights, thirty feet away. Probably nothing. Still, she quickens her pace. The road ahead is deserted and full of shadows, places for someone to hide in or jump out from. Maybe she should have taken the longer route after all? She turns a corner, sees her building up ahead. A black monolith against the charcoal sky, and one of the last brutalist-style tower blocks in this part of town.

She checks behind her again. The figure is still there. Close enough now for her to tell that it's a man, tall and well built, walking at speed.

It's nobody, she tells herself. *Someone on their way home from work, just like you.*

She crosses the road, looks back. A moment later, the man crosses, too.

Coincidence, she tells herself, though her heart quickens under her coat.

She walks a little further, then crosses back, checks again. The man follows.

Fuck. It's him. He's found you.

The shock of the idea dries her mouth.

She has been so careful. She makes a point of never sharing her address with anybody, unless absolutely necessary; has no contact with any of her extended family. How would he even know where she lives?

If he's followed you from work, he wouldn't need to know . . .

But then he'd need to know where she works, so he'd have to have heard her name credited in one of the podcasts she's produced, or seen her tagged in a social media post. And the chances of that happening are virtually nil. He probably doesn't even know what social media is, never mind a podcast.

But what if he does? And what if it's him?

She sprints the rest of the way to her apartment building with her heart in her throat, races across the car park, barrels into the lobby and slams a palm against the button to call the lift before she sees the 'Out of Order' notice taped to the door. Shit. She turns for the stairs, takes them two at a time, reaches the fifth floor with her legs on fire. She runs along the hallway to her apartment door, jams her key in the lock.

She stops, breathless. Listens for footsteps in the stairwell.

Has he got inside? Please don't tell me he's got inside.

She hears muffled voices, the sound of the TV in her neighbour's apartment, but no footsteps.

Once inside her flat she double-locks the door and puts the chain on. She should feel safer, but her panic has reached a crescendo. An invisible hand is wrapped around her throat.

In the living room, she backs up against the wall furthest from the door, stays there, waiting for a knock that doesn't come.

Nobody's coming. You're safe, you're OK.

But she doesn't feel OK. She feels like she is going to pass out.

She slides down the wall into a crouch, closes her eyes, focuses on deep breathing.

It wasn't him. It wasn't Dad.

Her dad is one of the bad men. Not bad in the wolf whistle, rub up against you on the tube, stare at your tits kind of way. He's worse than that. Much worse.

For the longest time she'd thought of Dad as two people. There was her real dad, who taught her how to ride a bike, laughed when she buried his feet in the sand on Morecombe beach, called her Daddy's girl and said that, even though Mum wasn't around anymore and it was just the two of them, they were still a family, a team. *What are we?* he'd say, and she'd answer, *A team!* He'd hold out his hand and she'd high-five him and he'd say, *Damn right we are.* And then there was Other Dad, who hugged her too tight and for too long, made comments about her figure or her clothes, and sometimes got this hungry look in his eyes when he was talking to her that made her skin itch.

It is Other Dad she remembers coming into her room at night, climbing into bed next to her, stroking her hair and breathing his booze breath on her cheek. Other Dad called her Daddy's girl, too. But he didn't mean it in the same way her real dad did.

By the time she reached her late teens her real dad was around less and less. It was Other Dad who was there when she got home from school. Other Dad who made her want to dress in big jumpers and long skirts. And it was Other Dad who, when he tried to climb into bed with her shortly after her seventeenth birthday and she pushed him away, fetched her a crack on the side of her head that made her ears ring for a full five minutes.

The moment he did it, he burst into tears and folded in on himself, lay on the edge of the bed sobbing. She sat, burning with hate for him, not knowing what to do, but in the end, she held him. After an hour or so he wiped his eyes and said, *What are we?* and she answered in a small voice, *A team.* When he held out his hand for a high five and she didn't move, he picked up her hand and pressed her palm against his and said, *Damn right we are.*

She knew then, though of course she'd always known, that he was not two people. He was just one broken person. She clung to this thought over the following months, until the day she passed her driving test. The next morning, she took his car keys and slipped out of his life without a word, driving his rust-bucket old Fiat south, to London, knowing he daren't report her to the police for fear of what she might tell them.

Now, whenever she thinks about her dad, she feels a hard ball of contempt rolling around in her belly. Black and solid. Polished smooth by the years of hate.

The idea of him appearing at her door is just . . . the worst. It is too much to bear.

But it wasn't him.

No, it was probably just your everyday random creep, intent on chatting her up, or doing something worse. And as ridiculous as that sounds, the thought makes her feel a little better.

She stays crouched down on the floor of her living room for a while, until the panic has subsided, and she begins to feel ridiculous, for thinking her dad had tracked her down to London when he probably doesn't give a shit; for allowing him to spark panic in her heart after all this time.

She moves to get to her feet, and it's then that she sees the phone, a black rectangle lying on its side, nestled up against the skirting board. It is well hidden beneath the chair, in a part of the room she has come to think of as Adam's corner. It's where he puts his things when he stays over – his bag on the chair, his jacket hanging from the back, so it doesn't get creased.

She reaches for the phone, catches the edge of it with her fingertips and pulls it out from under the chair. It doesn't look like Adam's phone. His is one of the latest models, expensive and with a great big screen, whereas this one is old and bears the marks of several years of use. Scratches on the screen and dents along the back and sides. But if it isn't Adam's, whose is it? Nobody has been in the flat but her since Adam left yesterday morning. It must be his work phone. He has complained plenty of times about having to carry around multiple phones. In the rush to get ready for his flight it must have slipped out of his jacket or fallen out of his bag. She wonders if he'll get in trouble for having lost it.

There's no point in texting him, adding to the unanswered messages she has already sent, but she takes her mobile out of her pocket and drops him an email to let him know she has found the phone. If he hasn't got back to her by the morning she'll go to his office and hand it in at the front desk. Someone there will know what hotel he's staying at in Paris and will be able to get in touch with him. When they tell him his girlfriend was the one to hand the phone in, maybe he'll feel so thankful – not to mention guilty for ignoring her – that he'll finally bother replying to her messages.

Thinking of him now, swanning around Paris having a great time while she's back in smelly old London being followed home by creeps, makes her feel that bit more alone. She wishes he were here. She might not feel so shaken up if he was.

She logs on to Twitter and Facebook. Adam doesn't really use either, but has, on the odd occasion, liked one of her posts when he's been away with work. She loves it when he does that. It's like he's waving at her from a distance. But there are no likes from Adam tonight. Not that it matters. He'll be back soon, and they can go and view the flats she's picked out. Within a month or so, they'll be living together. They'll come home to each other every night, eat dinner, take turns talking about that funny thing that happened at the office, or that stupid thing their colleague did.

Which reminds her . . .

She brings up Dylan's Twitter feed. Presumably he's told his thousands of followers he's found the London Bridge Jogger, too. It isn't right, misleading people like that. Maybe she should call him out? She could reply to one of his tweets. Something subtle, so he knows that not everybody is dumb enough to fall for his bullshit.

But when she checks Dylan's timeline, she sees no mention of the London Bridge Jogger. In fact, there have been no posts for the last three days. No obscure music or film recommendations, no funny gifs or memes. No tweets whatsoever. It's the same for his Instagram. Nothing since Monday. And for Dylan, who shares his every move with the world on social media, this is very strange indeed.

Back at the office, Brian seemed sure Dylan was in hiding because he knew he was going to be in trouble for lying about having found the jogger. But what if he's wrong? What if Dylan really is in danger?

21–11–2022

00.53 a.m.

'Would you say you had a normal childhood?'

'What is this, therapy?'

'No, it's just—'

'Then what's my childhood got to do with anything?'

Listeners always want to know about their childhood. To see if the signs were there. Bed-wetting, hurting animals, setting fires. Traits of sociopathy.

'I think it's interesting, to see where killers come from,' I tell him. 'Lots of people do.'

His eyes narrow. 'I didn't kill anyone.'

No, he didn't. But he tried to.

'So . . . a normal, happy childhood?'

He spreads his hands. 'Look, what do you want from me? I was a normal kid. Lived with my mum on a council estate. Went to school, studied hard, got good grades. I didn't get in any trouble. That's it, that's all there is to know.'

'Your dad wasn't around?'

He doesn't answer, but his eyes flick down to his wrist.

'I notice you looking at your watch there. Did he give you that?'

'Not exactly.' He pauses, licks his lips. 'My dad died in a house fire when I was six. The watch was one of the few things of his that survived.'

'I'm sorry. That must have been tough for you.'

'Can we change the subject?'

'I'm just interested, that's all—'

He turns on me. 'Are you fucking deaf?' he says, through clenched teeth.

'Calm down,' I say.

'Do *not* tell me to calm down.' I can hear his breath coming out in little snorts.

'OK . . . All right. We'll move on,' I say, soothingly.

We move on.

11

Day Three

Catherine

'Did you hear me?' a voice says, and the living room jumps back into focus.

I'm awake, I'm awake . . .

I wasn't asleep, not really. But I wasn't exactly present either.

I didn't even try to sleep last night. Instead, I sat at the kitchen table and made a list of everywhere Simon might have gone for drinks on the night he went missing. His favourite bars and restaurants in London, plus any that looked half decent – or that I thought Simon would think half decent – within walking distance of his office. Then I made a list of all his friends; at least, the ones I know about. The end result was full of holes and duplicates – *are Phil and Phillip the same person? Is Mark from five-a-side the same Mark whose stag do he went on?* and so on – but I felt better for having done it. Today I'll begin working down the list. Calling, emailing, messaging. Somebody must know something.

'Yes, I can hear you,' I say.

I have no idea what DI Carter has been saying. Something about watching television? I shake my head. I am dog-tired, and nauseous with it; eyes heavy and aching, hands shaky. The sort of tiredness I haven't felt since Charlie was a baby.

'Could I get a glass of water?' I ask, noting a slight slur in my voice. Chaudhari springs to his feet and heads to the kitchen, returns a moment later and hands over the water. I swallow it down, hoping it will make me more alert.

'Where were we?' I say, when I'm done.

'We just wanted to check something with you. About the night of the incident?' Carter says. *The incident*. So that's what they're calling it now.

Chaudhari takes a seat next to her on the sofa. He has his notebook with him and he flips open the leather cover, dabs the end of his index finger on his tongue and flicks back through the pages.

'Here we are.' He moves his pencil down the page as he reads. 'Monday afternoon: you picked Charlie up from nursery and arrived home around four. You put him to bed about six thirty, had a few glasses of wine and watched TV. Bed at elevenish?'

'Yes, that's right.'

He nods, looks over to Carter.

'We've been checking CCTV in the square,' she says.

'The square? You mean here?'

Of course she means here.

'We wanted to see if Simon came back home at any point during the day, perhaps while you were out,' Chaudhari explains, 'which, I'm afraid to say, he didn't. But it does look like you had a visitor that night, around 7 p.m.?'

My heart stops.

It's not like I outright lied. It's just that, at the point they asked me what I did on the night Simon went missing, I didn't believe Simon really *was* missing. I was still convinced he was crashed out on a friend's sofa, sleeping off his hangover. There was no need to explain in minute detail my every movement from the night before, especially as it had absolutely no bearing on things. I really did get home around four. I really did bath Charlie, put him to bed and read him a story. And I really did drink a few glasses of wine to unwind. I just wasn't alone for that last part.

'Oh yes, that's right.' I try to sound as if this piece of entirely inconsequential information has just occurred to me. 'A friend called round, after I put Charlie to bed. I think that might have been around sevenish, now you mention it.'

Mum enters the room bearing two cups of tea and places them down on the coffee table in front of the detectives. Yesterday's argument is still fresh enough to chill the air between us, but when she turned up on the doorstep this morning I decided the best thing would be to at least pretend to have forgiven her. I'll need someone to watch Charlie if I'm going to be out looking for Simon.

'Mrs Wells . . .' Chaudhari says.

'Yes. Sorry. What?'

Focus, Cat. Focus.

'So, you weren't alone that night?'

'Like I said, a friend came round. His name's Jonathan.' I hear my voice waver and hate myself for it. They're going to think this is something it isn't.

'And who exactly is he, this Jonathan?' Carter says.

Posh-looking fella. Rugger-bugger type.

'Jonathan Pearce. An old friend from med school. I've known him forever.' I glance over at Mum to see if she recognises the name. If she does, she doesn't show it.

'And how long was he here for?' DI Carter asks.

I know exactly how long Jonathan was here for. I texted him at seven to let him know the coast was clear, meaning that Charlie was asleep, and he arrived ten minutes later. We spent the best part of the next three hours sitting at the kitchen table, talking about this and that, working our way through a bottle of Sauvignon Blanc that he had been kind enough to bring, and once that was finished, another bottle I just happened to have in the fridge. He left at ten on the dot, said he needed to catch the ten twenty train and would need to make a dash for it.

'I don't know. An hour. Two, maybe?' How stupid am I being. If they have footage of him arriving, they'll have footage of him leaving, too. 'Perhaps a little longer? I wasn't really keeping track.'

Carter tips her head. 'Catherine, if you want us to find out what happened to Simon, you need to be truthful with us.'

'I *am* being truthful.' I feel my cheeks flush. 'I wasn't really keeping track of the time, that's all. I'm sorry.'

'We'll need to speak to him,' she says. 'If you can give us his details.'

'Is that really necessary?' I say. 'This has nothing to do with Simon going missing.'

'We'd just like to ask him a few questions,' says Chaudhari. 'Nothing to worry about.' But I am worried. There is a new coldness to the detectives. Not just Carter, who has her head tilted slightly and is studying me ever so closely, but Chaudhari, too. All the softness has disappeared, leaving him looking like an especially stern doorman. It's as if this one extra piece of information has given them cause to look at me anew.

As if to prove it, Carter says, 'Is there anything else you haven't told us? Anything you want us to know?'

'Of course not,' I say. 'I just forgot about Jonathan, that's all. I didn't think it was important. It *isn't* important.' I'm contradicting myself. I can't have forgotten about him *and* thought it wasn't important.

I'm making things worse with every word. They should be out there looking for Simon and now, because I lied, they will be looking in the wrong place and wasting valuable time.

When I come back into the living room after seeing the detectives out, for once Mum has not made me a cup of tea and is not cleaning. On her face is the look she used to give me when I was a teenager and she caught me smoking a cigarette behind the shed at the bottom of the garden, or leaving the house wearing too short a skirt.

'Jonathan Pearce? Catherine, really,' she says sharply.

12

Sara

The first thing Sara does the next morning is check her email, but there's nothing in her inbox from Adam, and only the usual spam in her junk folder. There is no reply to her email about the phone. None to her texts about the flats, either.

She types out another message – *Did you see the flats I sent you? Can you let me know what you think so I can book some viewings? x* – but pauses before pressing send. She looks at the unanswered texts she has sent over the last few days. Five little luminous bricks, stacked one on top of the other. Adding another to the pile isn't going to help.

And if you keep sending him messages, you're going to make yourself look desperate.

Desperate is not a good look.

Helen once told her that while they were sitting outside a pub and she was waiting for Adam to reply to a message, looking at her phone every two seconds. She always replies to his texts as soon as she sees them, but she knows that not everybody is the same. Some people like more space than others.

So, no more messages.

Over to plan B. She'll go to his office before work, hand his phone in at reception and let them handle it.

Over breakfast she googles: *Bitsaver office Soho*. There is no Bitsaver, but there's a Bitsave. She clicks through to the website, then on the Contact Us link and, when the page loads with the address and map, screenshots it.

It's a half-hour bus ride to Bitsave, time Sara doesn't begrudge. It is the perfect opportunity to catch up on *The Push*. Maybe Dylan is faking having tracked down the jogger, and maybe he isn't. If he is telling the truth, she'll be able to find out by listening to the last few episodes. Then she'll know if there is anything worth worrying about. She scrolls back four episodes, which should be enough to bring her up to speed, and hits play. Dylan's voice becomes the soundtrack to her passage through the city.

Welcome to Episode Twenty-One of The Push, the podcast dedicated to tracking down the London Bridge Jogger. I'm your host, Dylan Lesley, and today we're checking in with former Scotland Yard commander and friend of the podcast, Robert Pyne.

You may remember, we spoke to Robert right at the start of our journey to get his take on the jogger's potential motive, and again in Episodes Twelve and Thirteen, where we talked more about tracking down possible witnesses. I wanted to check in with Robert again, to see if there's anything we might have missed . . .

'It just seems . . . strange, doesn't it, Robert? All this time, and we're still no closer to identifying our man. But the footage has millions of hits on YouTube, his picture was everywhere – somebody must recognise him.'

'Oh, no doubt about that, Dylan, but unless they come forward, you're wasting your time. As I said when we first talked, I think the victim knew her attacker. That's why he's not been caught. She's protecting him.'

'And why would she do that?'

'Who knows? They could be boyfriend and girlfriend. Stranger things have happened.'

'And if she doesn't come forward, you don't think we'll ever find him?'

'The problem is, not only have you got an attacker who doesn't want to be found, but also a victim who wants to remain

anonymous. You can't find him, and you can't speak to her . . . so where do you go from here?'

'Exactly. Where do we go? What would you do next, if you were trying to find him?'

'All you can do is work with what you've got. And what's the one thing you definitely know about the jogger?'

'Nothing. I mean . . . that's the problem. We don't know anything about him—'

'Not true. Not true at all! You know that he jogs.'

'I suppose . . .'

'And he's in pretty good shape, so we can assume this isn't the first time he's strapped on a pair of running shoes. Start by asking what we can do with that piece of information. Nowadays, people who run like to track what they're doing. They wear smartwatches or fitness trackers, and they share that data online, post it on social media, that sort of thing . . .'

Behind the front desk of Adam's office, the company logo has been recreated in swirling pink neon. It backlights the receptionist's hair as she speaks on the phone, giving her a purple halo. She smiles at Sara, offers her a little be-with-you-in-a-minute wave. Sara takes a seat on a plush orange sofa.

The office is not quite what she expected.

A few months ago, she tried to surprise Adam at lunchtime, calling him when she got off at Oxford Street tube to say she just happened to be in the area and that they could grab something to eat, if he liked. Maybe have a picnic in Soho Square Gardens? No matter that she didn't 'just happen' to be in the area and had actually spent half the morning preparing picnic food she thought he might like. He didn't need to know that part.

'Ah, OK. Sure,' he'd said over the phone, sounding very unsure. 'I've got some things I need to finish up, but I'll be with you in about twenty minutes?'

When he arrived, a little over half an hour later, he refused to sit on the grass.

'I don't want to get my clothes muddy,' he said. He was in his usual work uniform of jeans, T-shirt and blazer, and Converse trainers. Smart, but it's not like he was wearing a suit or anything.

And when she took a series of Tupperware boxes out of her bag, containing smoked salmon sandwiches, a selection of expensive cheeses she had picked up from Whole Foods, a small bottle of Prosecco and two plastic glasses, he'd pulled a face.

'Really?' he said. 'I thought we could just go to Pret. Picnics are for kids, aren't they?'

So they sat side by side on a low wall and Adam ate his food in a hurry, checking his watch constantly. Twenty minutes later he said he had to get back to the office.

'Next time, don't just turn up out of the blue, OK? My job's not like yours. I can't just nip out for lunch when I feel like it,' he said, this disappointed look on his face, as if she'd done something wrong.

She watched him leave and wished she could go back in time and not bother with the picnic. Because when Adam said those things, it was as if he was talking about her, not the picnic. *She* was being unprofessional, *she* was behaving like a kid.

She apologised later that evening. When she thought about it, the surprise picnic hadn't really been for him, it had been for her. And just because she would have loved him to surprise her with a picnic lunch, didn't mean he would want the same.

Since that day she has had a picture in her head of his office as, while not big-bank formal, at least a very grown-up place to work. Instead, it is rather fun-looking, all bare brick and metal, exposed girders painted in bright colours, framed motivational slogans hanging from the walls. *The dictionary is the only place success comes before work!* says one. *Don't forget, the process is the goal!* says another. Through a glass wall, Sara can make out a breakout room with a row of fancy coffee machines, foosball and ping-pong tables, fridges full to bursting with food and booze. It is all so very different from her own office. Places like this make work look like fun. All the food, drink and entertainment you need are right here. In fact, why bother going home at all? No wonder Adam works such crazy hours.

'Sorry. Busy, busy,' the receptionist sings, when she hangs up the phone.

Sara approaches the desk. As she does, she feels around in her bag until her hand lands on the cold plastic of Adam's work phone. She puts it on the counter.

'I'm Adam Worthy's girlfriend,' she says. 'He left his work phone at mine, and I know he's away right now, but maybe someone could get in touch with him, or tell me what hotel he's staying at so I can let him know it's safe?'

The receptionist types at her keyboard, then shakes her head. 'I'm sorry, what was the name again?'

'Adam Worthy.'

'Adam Worthy?'

'That's right.'

She tries the computer again, then pulls a face. 'You're sure you have the right office?'

'Bitsave, right?' Sara widens her eyes and tips her head at the giant neon sign hanging behind the reception.

'That's us,' says the receptionist, 'but there are no Adams here. We have an Adrian? Adrian Robinson, the CEO?' She says it like it's a question, as if Sara might have got her boyfriend's name wrong, mixed him up with someone else.

'No,' Sara says. 'It's Adam. Adam Worthy.'

'Hmm. Nope, sorry,' the receptionist says with a little shrug.

Nope, sorry? What the hell does that mean?

She must be new, Sara thinks. That's what this is. She probably only started this week. She hasn't met Adam yet, what with him being away. Either that, or she doesn't know how to use the computer properly.

'Can you check again?' she says, but at that moment there is a ping and a set of lift doors open on Sara's left. A man emerges with elaborately spiked hair, wearing bootcut jeans and a grey T-shirt under a dark blue blazer. He has an iPad under one arm and is dressed so much like Adam usually dresses – like a middle-aged man trying just a little too hard to be trendy – that Sara feels the knot of tension across her shoulders slacken. She must be in the right place, after all.

'Here's Adrian,' the receptionist says, and she calls over to him. 'Adrian? Oh, Adrian? This woman is looking for someone called Adam Worthy. Says he works here?'

'Adam Worthy?' the man says as he approaches.

'Adam Worthy,' Sara repeats.

What is it with these people?

He shakes his head. 'Sorry, we don't have anybody here by that name.'

'But you are Bitsave?' Sara says.

'That's right. Fastest-growing fintech in London, but we run pretty lean. There's only twelve of us.' He smiles, like what's happening here is perfectly normal.

Sara takes out her own phone. Her screensaver is her favourite photo of her and Adam, taken last year on his birthday. Well, not exactly on his birthday, because he had to work that day, but the day after they had caught the train to Brighton, played on the slot machines in the arcades – ironically, of course – wandered down the Lanes, stayed in The Grand hotel opposite the squat skeleton of the burnt-out West Pier. In the photograph, they are arm in arm, grinning toothy grins against the wind.

She shows the man. 'This is Adam,' she says, pointing.

See? Recognise him now?

She expects him to smile or laugh. To say, *Oh, THAT Adam*, because perhaps Adam is known by a different name at work, a cool nickname he was given as a joke in his first week that just stuck. But the man's eyes narrow and he sticks out his bottom lip and shakes his head.

'Sorry. Never seen him before in my life.'

13

Catherine

For the rest of the afternoon the detective's questions hover around the house like trapped flies, and though Mum doesn't say another word about it, I can feel her judging me, even when we are in separate rooms.

She is waiting for me in the kitchen after I put Charlie to bed, small hands busy, drying the washing-up, opening and closing cupboard doors as she looks for the right home for things.

'You don't have to do that, Mum,' I tell her. 'Just leave them in the dishwasher, they'll dry themselves.'

'It's good to have everything put away,' she says. 'Everything in its right place.'

Is that meant to be a reference to Jonathan? Something to do with our past not being put away?

'What's that supposed to mean?'

Mum turns to me, eyes wide and enquiring. 'He's a friend,' I tell her. 'I didn't say anything to the detectives because it wasn't relevant. I've known him forever, and he just came round for a chat. You know, it's perfectly possible for a man and a woman to spend time in each other's company without anything untoward going on.'

She holds up her hands. 'I didn't say a word, love.'

'You don't have to. I can tell . . . And it was nothing.'

Yes, there was that moment when my head was swimming from too much wine, and I found my hand resting on his forearm, the warmth of his skin sending a tingle through my body. And there was that misplaced kiss at the end of the night, that strayed onto the corner of his mouth, that I had perhaps, if only for half a second, hoped would turn into something more. But that was just harmless flirting. It is what grown-ups do, especially after they have sunk the best part of two bottles of wine between them.

'He's just an old friend,' I say again.

A clatter of dishes, then Mum says, 'Old *boy*friend.' As if the fact Jonathan and I dated for four months has slipped my mind.

'That was a million years ago, Mum. Before I even met Simon.'

Not strictly true. There is an unfortunate overlap between my dating Jonathan and meeting Simon. A week or so, where I was yet to pluck up the courage to tell Jonathan it was over, and the reason I had been avoiding him wasn't because I needed to swot up for our end-of-year exams – a pointless lie; he knew I was always on top of my studies – but because I had started seeing somebody else.

But Mum doesn't know that.

'I didn't know you'd kept in touch, that's all,' she says.

'We didn't. I bumped into him at London Bridge, about six months ago. We went for a coffee, talked about old times, said we must do it again.' That part at least is true. 'And last week, he said he was free on Wednesday evening, and I said the easiest thing would be if he popped round to the house, after I put Charlie to bed.'

I am making it sound like I have only met up with him twice, once at London Bridge and once at the house last week. The truth is, I have seen him dozens of times over the last six months, in cafés and bars in South London. A quick coffee before picking Charlie up from nursery, a glass of wine on the few occasions Mum had Charlie for the afternoon. Stolen moments of time, moments of pleasure.

'He works at a surgery over in Crouch End,' I add. 'He's got two girls, a seven- and a nine-year-old. They've just bought a new house, wanted to be in the catchment area for one of the good schools up there.'

I don't mention that he is divorced; don't want to give her any more ammunition.

'So, you see?' I shrug my shoulders. 'It was nothing.'

As if I didn't put Charlie to bed half an hour early, so I had time to make myself look presentable before he arrived.

Did I want something to happen between us? Yes, and no. I mean, it's not like I planned to have sex with him on the kitchen table or anything. But I wanted to push the boundaries, to play in that electrifying space that exists between friendship and something more. And I wanted to be wanted, if only for an hour or two.

Mum sets her tea towel down, comes over and rubs my shoulders.

'You're tired, love,' she says. 'Why don't you try and get some sleep?'

I pull away. 'Can you please stop saying that? I don't want to sleep. I just don't want you thinking I was up to something behind Simon's back, when I wasn't.'

Mum drops her gaze to the floor and a rush of guilt dries my mouth. Even if she doesn't believe Simon is still alive, even if she is making me feel guilty about Jonathan, she is here. She is trying her best.

'I'm sorry,' I say. 'I don't mean to snap. It's just . . .'

'I know, love. You don't need to say.'

Something unlatches inside me. Relief, I suppose, at not having to explain myself. Mum knows what it's like to have someone you love taken away. When we lost Dad, she stopped being a person entirely for those first few weeks, was just a bundle of exposed nerves.

I give her a hug. 'You're right. I'm going to go and lie down.'

Not sleep, but lie down. Give my body a rest, if not my mind.

'You do that, love.' She goes back over to the kitchen counter, picks up the tea towel. 'I suppose things are different now, that's all,' she adds.

'Different?'

'Well, in my day we didn't have male friends. I didn't, at any rate. I just had your father. I didn't need anybody else.'

I take it all back. She is goading me, even at a time like this. Poking me and prodding me, saying things just to annoy me. I want to explode at her, but worry I might say something truly horrible.

Deep breath.

'It's no different,' I say, as I get up to leave the room. 'Jonathan's just a friend, like any other friend.' I tell her. 'I still need Simon, and he still needs me.'

Upstairs I close the bedroom door and collapse onto the bed.

I don't need this right now. And I don't deserve it, either.

I like Jonathan, I admit that. Not because he is a handsome and successful doctor, though he is those things, but because he likes me, and he listens. It can be lonely, being a mum. Nobody told me that before I had Charlie. Nobody said how much I would miss work, even the busy days, when I barely had time to use the loo between patients. Nobody said I would go out of my mind only having a four-year-old to talk to most of the time, or that the theme tune to *Peppa Pig* would play in my head until I thought I might go mad.

So, I like Jonathan, and he likes me, too. But it doesn't *mean* anything.

Why didn't I tell Simon I'd invited Jonathan over, or about the other times I'd met up with him? Because I didn't want him to think it was something it wasn't, or for the truth about the night we met to come tumbling out. Didn't want him to realise that the man he thought was harassing me that night in the bar wasn't harassing me at all, that he was actually my boyfriend, and I was the one who was being horrid to him. Jonathan was so bloody handsome and perfect, I'd got it into my head that it was only a matter of time before he dumped me, so made the spectacularly stupid decision to force his hand by getting off with a member of the rowing team.

That's why I didn't tell Simon.

Jonathan coming round; it really was nothing, and the police will find that out soon enough, but I wish I hadn't lied to them. I wish I hadn't lied to Simon, too.

And I wish I could sleep. Close my eyes and drift off so I don't have to feel anything, just for a little while. Tiredness is a too-warm blanket over my shoulders, loosening my limbs, trying to switch off my brain. But I mustn't sleep, not with Simon still missing.

I am wearing one of Simon's old . . . what-do-you-call-its . . . like a big towel with armholes. You wear them in hotel rooms, where they're white and soft and luxurious, but at home they tend to be more like Simon's: ratty and worn and missing the belt part. I'm wearing one of those, and I sit up in bed and reach into the pocket and take out my phone and my list of names.

I scroll through my contacts, trying to decide who to reach out to next. Old university friends? The couples we met at our antenatal classes? Simon became friendly with a few of the men for a while, bonding over 90s music and football. Or perhaps our old neighbours, from when we lived in Wanstead?

I stop scrolling, thumb hovering over Jonathan's name and number.

He'd come if I called, I know he would. Arrive at the doorstep to tell me everything is going to be OK – how I would love for someone to tell me it's all going to be OK. But I'm not going to call him. Of course I'm not. Because Jonathan and I are nothing. Just a silly flirtation, a distraction. And I can't afford distractions right now. I have a missing husband to find.

I need to get out there, I decide. Stop moping around in Simon's dressing gown and go and visit the places he might have gone on the night he went missing – the posh restaurants, and swanky bars. Show the staff his picture, find out if they saw him, and if they did, who he was with.

Somebody out there must know something. I just need to find out who that somebody is.

14

Sara

When she gets to the office, Sara only has to catch Helen's eye and it's enough for Helen to drop what's left of her bacon sandwich and usher Sara into one of the recording studios for some privacy.

'What's happened?' She closes the door, flicks a switch that turns on a red light attached to the wall outside that tells the rest of the office they should not be disturbed.

Outside, the sky was one giant cloud, and a biting wind gathered leaves in the gutters and made Sara's skin feel dry and tight, but now her T-shirt clings to her back with sweat and she can feel dampness spreading under her arms. She pulls at the neck, fans herself. Why is it so hot in here?

She wants to tell Helen what has happened, but can't speak, not right this second.

I'm sorry, Adam who?

Helen guides Sara by the arm, moves her over to the mixing desk and they sit next to each other. Sara puts her head in her hands.

'Tell me,' says Helen.

Sara pulls in a few deep breaths, thinks about what she wants to say, lays it out bit by bit in her head so she can get the words out. 'I went into Adam's work today' – *breathe* – 'and they said' – *breathe* – 'they've never heard of him.'

Helen screws up her face. 'What the fuck? What do you mean, they've never heard of him?'

'I don't know . . . I don't *know*,' says Sara.

Over the last hour her head has filled with worst-case scenarios. They crowd her thoughts, pile in, one after the other. He said that's where he works, and she remembers seeing it on his LinkedIn profile the first time she googled him, so how could they not have heard of him? If he doesn't work there, then where? Does he even work at all? He has a flash car and nice clothes. He must get his money from somewhere. Maybe he had a rich relative who died and left him everything, and now he doesn't have to work? But then, why bother faking it?

'Take a deep breath,' says Helen. 'Tell me from the beginning.'

Sara does. She tells Helen all about Adam's work phone – or *not* Adam's work phone – and as she talks she feels the cold hand of panic tighten around her throat.

'Definitely the right company?' Helen says, when she has finished.

She nods. There could well be another one with a similar name. But not another that would be listed on his LinkedIn profile.

'Maybe he got fired and didn't tell you? That happens sometimes. People get sacked and feel all embarrassed, pretend they're still working so they don't have to face up to it.'

Sara shakes her head. 'They'd never even heard of him, Hels. It's not that he doesn't work there now, he never has.'

'But he's on a business trip, isn't he?' says Helen.

Sara feels sick. Adam can't be away on business for a company he doesn't work for.

'Hey, hey. I'm sure it's nothing,' says Helen. 'When you speak to him, he'll probably clear everything up.'

She has tried calling him. The second she stepped out of the Bitsave offices, she tried, but she got his answerphone and hung up without leaving a message. Now, a part of her almost doesn't want to speak to him, because she's afraid of what he might say.

Sara wipes her eyes. Perhaps it is just a misunderstanding.

But what if it isn't?

She reaches into her bag, takes out Adam's phone and puts it on the desk between them.

'Can you get it open?'

Helen's eyes go wide. 'You want me to break into his phone?'

'Can you do it? Hack into it? You know about this sort of stuff, don't you?'

Plenty of episodes of *CTRL Shift* have been devoted to the darker side of technology. The dark web, hacking, bots that steal your identity. If Helen can't do it, she'll know someone who can.

Helen picks up the phone and presses the home button and the password lock screen appears. 'Maybe,' she says. 'Six-digit passcode. There are about a million combinations. Get it wrong a few times and it'll lock you out for ten minutes. Get it wrong enough times and it'll lock you out for good, or wipe itself. Even the FBI can't get into some phones. They have to get the manufacturer to do it for them. But . . .' she exhales slowly, 'it's an old model. Maybe I could get into it. It depends.' She puts the phone back on the table. 'He'll be back in a few days though, right?'

Two days, supposedly. He left on Tuesday morning for a four-day conference.

'Saturday. Sunday, maybe.'

'Well, there you go. He'll be back soon and you can speak to him, find out what's going on.'

Sara shakes her head. 'I need to know he isn't . . .'

She doesn't have to finish. She has shared so much with Helen over the last few years that there now exists between them a kind of telepathy, an unspoken bond that lets them convey the most important things without opening their mouths.

Helen picks up the phone again, weighs it in her hand. 'I'll try. No promises, but I'll try.'

'Thank you,' Sara says, feeling grateful and scared, but also determined.

A thought has been running through her mind for the last half-hour. She has tried to dismiss it, but it springs forward, as big and bright as the neon sign hanging in the reception at Bitsave: what if Adam is not who he says he is?

What if he is like her dad? Two people, instead of one?

21–11–2022

00.59 a.m.

Did she know, or didn't she? It's tempting to say she can't *not* have recognised her husband's blurry face on the front of all the papers. But the annals of true crime are full of oblivious wives who get a life-changing knock on the door one morning.

'You've been with Catherine for . . . how long?'

'Fourteen, fifteen years? Something like that. We met at university. Third year. I was studying economics, she was at Imperial, doing medicine. We were a good fit, back then. Made for each other. We were both driven. She was hard-working, principled – although not on the night we met.'

A sly smile, like a teenager, gleeful at having felt up one of his classmates behind the bike sheds.

'How do you mean?'

'She likes to tell this story about that night: her being harassed in a bar, me the white knight, stepping in to save her.'

'And that's not what happened?'

'Nothing like what happened. Truth is, she had a row with her boyfriend, this lanky rugger-bugger type. She stormed off, I caught up with her, offered to walk her home and she accepted.'

'You'd never met before then?'

'I'd seen her around, liked the look of her, but we'd never spoken. When I asked her who this fella who'd been giving her a hard time was, she looked me dead in the eye and said she had no idea. "Never seen him before in my life," she said. Even if I hadn't seen them together, I'd have known she was lying. She's a terrible liar.'

'She didn't want you to think she was taken.'

'Right. But even now, she tells the same story, when what actually happened is, she got drunk, had a row with her boyfriend, took a stranger home and slept with him within an hour of meeting him. After they had sex, she threw up and passed out on the bathroom floor. That's the truth. But it's not a very nice truth, is it? So she invented her own story. And that's the version she's sticking with.'

'She prefers the lie.'

'Exactly,' he says. 'People often do. Because sometimes, living with a lie is easier than living with the truth.'

15

Day Four

Catherine

When I park the car outside The Haymarket, the staff are already out front under the rain-slicked canopy, stacking chairs, sweeping up cigarette butts and swapping impatient glances as the few remaining customers drain their glasses.

'Looks like they're closing,' says Lydia. 'Come back tomorrow?'

Three hours of driving around the City, visiting bar after bar to show the doormen and bar staff pictures of Simon on my phone, and Lydia is ready to go home. I don't blame her. We have made no progress. Not one person has said they recognise Simon and now it's after midnight and the weather has turned against us. Lydia keeps rubbing at her left elbow – an old hockey injury that plays up sometimes – and checking the heater is on full blast. It is, but the cold still seeps into the car, the rain squalling against the windscreen. Any sane person would rather be home, where it is warm and dry, but being at home isn't going to help me find my husband.

'I want to keep going,' I tell her, fumbling for the . . . belt thing, whatever it's called. 'The more time passes, the less likely people are to . . . Why won't this bloody thing—'

Lydia reaches down, there's a click and my seatbelt snaps open.

'You don't want to waste any more time,' she says.

'Right. And this place looks . . .' *Simon*-ish, I want to say.

The Haymarket is a vast, multi-level bar, with a cocktail lounge and heated outdoor seating, and it's less than five minutes' walk from Simon's office. Of all the places we have visited tonight, this one looks the most promising. Not quite The Ivy, but fancy and full of itself, with tinted windows and a uniformed doorman stood to attention outside. No doubt it is ridiculously expensive.

Lydia leans forward in her seat, gets a good look at the front of the bar. 'I bet it's posh boy central in there,' she observes. 'Exactly the sort of place Simon might take clients. Want me to come with?'

'No,' I tell her, stifling a yawn. 'A coffee wouldn't go amiss, though, if you can find anywhere still open.'

'Consider it done.' She takes out her phone, rubs her eyes, starts to google.

Thank God for Lydia.

Sometimes, when we're talking, I'll think about something funny from the past, about someone we knew in senior school or university, and just as I'm about to remind her of it – *wasn't it funny when such-a-body did such-a-thing?* – I'll remember we didn't go to the same school, or university. We didn't even meet until we were in our thirties, at a life-drawing class in Waterloo. Despite my medical background, and Lydia's own interest in fashion and design, we were both rather hopeless at drawing the human body. One evening, as an octogenarian disrobed in front of us, Lydia leaned over and whispered that she'd really rather not spend the next two hours 'looking at his wrinkly arsehole', and proposed we go to the pub instead. Now, five years on, she knows everything about me. Some things I've told her; late-night secrets swapped after too many glasses of Pinot Grigio, but other things I have no memory of sharing. She just . . . knows. She intuits. Like we are identical twins. Like we share a part of each other's consciousness. Knowing she'll be here, waiting for me when I get back to the car, makes me feel a thousand times better.

I open the car door and step onto the pavement, rehearsing the lines I have already spoken dozens of times tonight: *Excuse me? Can you help? I'm looking for my husband. His name's Simon. He's gone missing . . .*

I'm not quite sure what happens next. One moment I am striding towards the orange lights of The Haymarket, and the next the ground is snatched from under me. I reach out to grab a nearby lamppost and my fingertips graze damp concrete, then there's a sound like a sopping wet towel hitting the floor and pain blooms along the right side of my body. I lie there, bewildered, looking up at the hazy night sky, rain wetting my cheeks and forehead.

I've had a fall, I think. Not fallen over, the way Charlie does, but 'had a fall', like an old person. The sort of tumble that breaks bones and leaves you bruised and shaken.

'Jesus. Are you OK?'

Lydia leans into view, and her twin is standing beside her. I turn my head, see the whole world in duplicate. Two buses passing by on the road, two doormen standing outside The Haymarket. The lights under the bar's canopy have merged into a quivering field of blinding light.

'Help,' I hear myself say, and I feel Lydia take my hand. She pulls me to my feet and immediately hugs me, tight enough to force all the air out of me. *Tighter*, I think. *Hold me tighter.*

'I've got you,' she says into my ear.

Don't let go . . . Don't let go . . .

But after a minute she releases me and takes a small step back. 'Better?'

'I don't know.' I have my eyes closed, can't bear to open them. How am I going to find Simon if I can't see?

'Look at me, Cat,' says Lydia. 'It's going to be OK.' I take a few deep breaths and open my eyes and – thank God – the two Lydias have merged back into one.I can see properly again. Relief floods through me.

'Sorry,' I say. 'Just . . . so tired.'

The tiredness. I can feel it, both inside of me and outside of me. Radiating from me, draining all the firmness from the world. There's too much *give* in everything. After three days without sleep, I am suffering from mild ataxia – loss of coordination, slurred speech, blurred vision.

'But I can't sleep,' I tell Lydia. 'Not with Simon . . .'

'Never mind that,' Lydia says. 'Let's get you sat down.'

She walks me to the car, opens the passenger door and lowers me into the seat. As she does, I catch a smell of myself: the pungent odour of sweat-through-sweat, like gym clothes that have been used too many times between washes. I've made sure Charlie is bathed every day, but I haven't had a proper shower since the morning I got the news.

'Ugh, God. I'm disgusting,' I say.

'Shut up. Don't you ever say that. You're beautiful. You're gorgeous,' Lydia says.

She does this when we're on a night out. Looks me up and down and gasps, says how beautiful I am, how she wishes her hair was as soft as mine, her skin as smooth and are those jeans new? *My God, they make your arse look fantastic.* She makes me feel beautiful, even when I'm not. Right now, I most definitely am not. My hair is a tangled, greasy mess, and the bags under my eyes are so swollen I can feel the weight of them resting on my cheeks.

'Let's get you home,' Lydia says, starting the engine.

I don't want to go. There are still people drifting around outside The Haymarket. There's still time. 'I feel better now,' I say. 'Really, I do. Let's just ask inside. It'll only take ten minutes, then we'll go.'

She shakes her head. 'Cat, you're exhausted. *I'm* exhausted. Andrew will start to think *I've* gone missing at this rate.' She catches herself. 'Sorry. My stupid mouth.' She grabs my hand. 'We'll come back another time, I promise.' She sounds like I do when I'm trying to coax Charlie out of the playground.

The drive through the City, across London Bridge and back to Cavendish Square, barely registers. I retreat somewhere – a Nothing Place, not asleep, but not quite awake – and only come back to myself when Lydia stops the engine.

'Here we are.' I look around, surprised to find myself outside my own home. 'Go and get some sleep. Dr Lydia's orders. I'll call you tomorrow and we'll decide what to do next.'

'Thanks,' I say, but I don't move. I don't want to go inside, don't want to be without her. 'Sorry. It all just feels so hopeless,' I moan, on the cusp of tears.

'If we don't have any luck with the bars, we can try something different,' Lydia says. 'Where was the last confirmed sighting of him?'

'At his office. One of the cleaners saw him.'

'There you go. Start there, retrace his steps. And try not to worry, we're going to find him, Cat. I know we are.'

I am so grateful for her that my chest hurts. I throw my arms around her, hold her close. 'What would I do without you?' I say. 'Thank you.'

For being there for me. For everything.

Even though tonight was a total failure, and I am being driven mad with tiredness, with Lydia by my side it feels like there is still hope. I am not alone.

I am going to find my husband.

16

Sara

After work, Sara waits for Helen on Islington Green, a small triangular park at the junction of Upper Street and Essex Road, which is well lit but offers some shelter from the wind. She takes a seat on a secluded bench and fires up Episode Twenty-Three of *The Push*, released just three weeks ago.

Dylan was absent again today. At lunch she sent him a WhatsApp: *Hey, you OK? Not seen you at work in a while?* There was no reply, no read receipt, either. She wondered if she should speak to Brian again, point out that Dylan's social media has gone dark. Suggest someone get in touch with Dylan's parents, make sure he's OK. But Brian was in another foul mood. He stalked around the office, muttering under his breath, and snapped at one of the interns. In the end, she decided to leave it.

Nothing in any of the episodes she has listened to so far suggests Dylan has been closing in on the identity of the jogger. Exactly the opposite, in fact. To Sara, *The Push* is the sound of a podcast not just running out of steam but, quite literally, crying out for help as it heads towards an inevitable and disappointing end.

> *As you know, we've spent the last week focusing on the one thing we actually do know about the London Bridge Jogger, which is . . . as you might have guessed . . . he jogs.*
>
> *Our hope was that his route across London Bridge might*

have been a regular one, and that he might have used an exercise-tracking app that shares his runs online. If we could find the male joggers who regularly took that route, at that time in the morning, we might be able to narrow down the suspect list, or at the very least, find new witnesses who were in the area that day.

By creating our own running profile on one of the most popular exercise-tracking apps – that, for legal reasons, we've been advised not to name – we were able to find dozens of runners who had logged their own times for a route that would take them over London Bridge, and a number of them would have been there around seven forty AM on the day in question.

The problem is data privacy. Getting someone's real identity from their online profile has proved to be impossible. We've been back and forth with these companies. None of them will share their user data unless a police warrant is issued.

Hate to say it, but it looks like we've hit another wall. That is, unless someone comes forward. That's why we're asking you, dear listeners, to help spread the word once more.

We want to hear from anybody who regularly ran that route across London Bridge early in the mornings in August 2018. It doesn't matter if they weren't there on that particular day, they still might be able to provide us with crucial information that could help us find our man. And if you're the person who helps us open up a new lead, we'll make sure you get some awesome The Push swag for your troubles. I'm talking hoodies, badges, posters, the lot . . .

Our mystery jogger is still out there, but with your help, I still believe we can—

A touch on Sara's shoulder. She starts, yanks out her headphones and whips her head around. It's Helen, standing behind the bench with a goofy grin on her face.

'Fuck! You scared the crap out of me.' Sara clamps a hand over her heart.

'Sorry, not sorry.' Helen, still smiling, looks over each shoulder in turn, as if she's in a spy movie and wants to make sure she hasn't been followed, then moves around to the front of the bench and takes a seat.

'I did it,' she says. 'I had to try a few methods, but in the end it was pretty straightforward. Obviously, I couldn't do a factory reset as you'd lose all the data, and any sort of Find My Device service was off the table. In the end I had to reboot it into recovery mode, then flash a password disable tool onto it from an SD card. Then I rebooted it again, and voila! No more password lock. Lucky for you it was a few years old – security is a *lot* tighter these days.'

Sara nods along, as if the process really does sound straightforward.

'You're a genius,' she says. 'So, what's on it?'

'Not a lot. Emails, messages. I didn't look too closely.'

Sara finds this hard to believe. Helen doesn't like Adam. Surely, having unlocked his phone, she'd be unable to resist taking a peek?

Helen's eyes exaggeratedly flick this way and that, then she retrieves the phone from her inside pocket and presses it into Sara's cupped hands.

'You know it's illegal, to break into someone's phone like that?' she says, with more than a hint of pride. Sara feels a swell of gratitude.

'I'm sorry,' she says. 'I didn't think.'

'Oh, it's fine,' Helen says. 'I quite enjoyed the challenge, to be honest. I like puzzles. Figuring stuff out.'

'So, why finish the puzzle and not look?'

'I thought it best if you were the one to do it,' Helen says, and she bites her lip. There's a hungry look about her, like she has just given Sara a present and can't wait to see it opened.

Sara considers it. She could press the phone's home button right now and have access to everything: call history, emails, texts. In a few seconds she would know where Adam really works, who he calls, the names of his colleagues, what he gets up to when he tells her he's working late.

It is the hungry look in Helen's eyes that stops her.

Helen would, Sara thinks, be almost happy if the phone revealed something awful. She probably wouldn't actually say the words *I told you so* – she's not a mean person – but Sara would hear it anyway, and from that day on it would become the background music to their friendship.

Sara weighs the phone in her hands. An innocuous-looking black rectangle that could, with the click of a button, turn her life upside down.

'Once I look, I can't take it back. I can't unlook at it, can I?'

'True,' says Helen, still unable to take her eyes off the phone.

'And he'll know I didn't trust him, that I didn't give him the chance to explain – and that might be exactly what he deserves . . .'

'Could be . . .'

'Or, maybe I've been thinking about Dad too much, you know? I don't want to be one of those fucked-up people who can't trust anybody because of something that happened to them when they were a kid. If me and Adam have a future, it has to start with trust, doesn't it?'

'Hmm . . .' says Helen.

'Besides, he's asked me to move in with him. We'll have to provide paperwork when we rent somewhere. Employee references, that sort of thing. The lie would have come out sooner or later, so . . . maybe he has a good reason for lying?'

Helen says nothing to this and they sit in silence, Sara squeezing the phone, wishing she had never found it, wishing she could break it in two.

'You know what? I'm not going to look,' she announces.

'Bullshit,' says Helen, with a small laugh. 'Come on, you made me unlock it. Just open it.'

'Hels! I'm serious.' Sara clutches the phone to her body, as if it were already open, the secrets inside already on show. 'I'll wait until he gets back,' she says. 'I'll talk to him. That's got to be the best thing to do, right? The grown-up thing?'

'It's one option,' says Helen.

'One more day, that's all. Two, maybe, depending on when his flight gets in.'

'You're really not going to look?' says Helen, disbelief in her voice.

'Really,' says Sara. 'I shouldn't have asked you to open it. I just got this idea in my head and . . .'

Helen puts up her hands in mock surrender. 'Fine. Although, after all that hard work, you owe me big time. First round's on you. And if you're not going to look, I don't want to hear another word about it. No more talking about men tonight. Deal?'

Sara holds up a hand, salutes with three fingers. 'Girl Scout's honour. We shall pass the Bechdel test tonight, promise.'

They walk down the Essex Road together, go into a pub that plays the kind of music they both like, songs they know all the words to by the Pixies, Nirvana, Foo Fighters. The music is loud and Sara pretends she has forgotten all about the phone. They take turns buying rounds of drinks. And all the while she is thinking, *Go. Just go, then I can look at the phone!* But Helen doesn't go, even when Sara says she is tired and they should call it a night. It is ten thirty before they leave and walk arm in arm back towards the busy part of Angel to wait at the bus stop.

'This is me,' Helen says as the 21 bus slows to a stop.

They hug and Helen makes a dash for the bus and Sara watches her tap her card and take a seat, and gives her a wave as the bus pulls away. As soon as she is out of sight, Sara sits down at the bus stop and retrieves Adam's phone from her bag.

A day is an awfully long time to wait, and the phone is right here in her hands, unlocked. If there really is a decent explanation, she could have it in a matter of seconds. And if there is something to worry about, if Adam really is like Dad, then isn't it better to know, then she can make her own choices?

She presses the home button and the screen comes to life.

There is no screensaver. No Facebook app, no WhatsApp or Twitter. There aren't even enough apps to warrant a second screen of icons. It's just the basics, as if nothing has been added since the day the phone was taken out of its box. Which makes sense. It's Adam's work phone, he probably only uses it for important calls and emails.

Sara presses the icon with a little picture of a telephone handset on it, taps the screen to view recent calls. She expects to see a long list of incoming and outgoing calls to various contacts, names for those stored in the phone book, numbers for those who aren't, but when the list appears it shows only five or six calls made over a four-week period. All are outgoing, to a number with no name next to it.

She taps the icon to show the entire list of contacts and there are none.

She presses the home button then hits the icon for messages. Five in all, most only giving a time and the name of a bar or club in an area of London – *Plumbers Arms, Victoria, at 9*, reads one. *Red Lion, Theobalds Rd, 8 p.m.*, another – but the most recent message is different. It was sent early in the evening on the night she last saw Adam, the night he woke her up in the early hours by taking a shower, then came into her room brandishing a cup of tea.

The Pit Bethnal Green 8.30 bring the money and don't fuck me around or you'll regret it.

What is this?

Why is Adam sending threatening messages to people?

She can't imagine Adam typing those words. It doesn't seem like something he would do. But, she reminds herself, Adam has lied to her. He is not Director of Something or Other at a trendy start-up in Soho. He doesn't work for Bitsave and he is almost certainly not away for a four-day work conference in Paris. He is not the person she thought he was.

So, who exactly is he?

17

Sara

The night bus barrels south, collecting and depositing passengers as it goes, a curious mix of young and old. Blurry-eyed business types, with loosened ties and briefcases balanced on their laps; young women in glittery tops and strappy shoes, on their way to dance through the night in Soho; drunks, swaying from side to side, arms spread like surfers trying to keep their balance.

Sara sits on the top deck, wishing there weren't so many people around her. She wants to disappear, to be alone where nobody can see her shame. As angry as she is with Adam, it's her own reflection in the window next to her she can't bear to look at. How stupid she is. Even her best friend told her something wasn't right about Adam. And every time, she made excuses for him.

She clutches the phone tighter in her hands. If only she could go back in time and not press the home button, unsee the messages it contains, then she wouldn't feel so shaken. Wouldn't feel like she is grieving for a version of Adam she left behind at that bus stop in Angel.

Is Adam a criminal? Her Adam? Who has always seemed so professional and wrapped up in his work? Adam, who has always seemed a little too grown-up for her?

Perhaps he does have a normal job, and whatever criminal activity he is involved in is just a sideline. Nothing too serious, nothing too sinister. But why pretend to work at one place if you have a perfectly legitimate job somewhere else?

Nothing is clear, other than the fact that she has been lied to. Not once, but hundreds, if not thousands, of times over the last nine months. Every time he stepped out to take a call or send an urgent email. Every time he told her he had to be at the office early for a meeting or stay late to finish a presentation.

They were supposed to be a team. They were planning a life together, had talked about having kids, for God's sake.

Sara feels sick. Feels sick and hates herself, and hates Adam, too.

What has he been up to? Sending threatening messages? And what about this oh-so-urgent trip to Paris? It can't have been for Bitsave, so what is it for? And why hasn't he responded to any of her texts for the last four days? He didn't even get back to her email about finding the phone—

Email. She forgot to check the phone for emails.

She wakes up the handset and opens the email app. There is nothing in the inbox, but three emails in the sent folder, the oldest dating from around a month ago. All have been sent from an anonymous email account, iknowwhatyoudid@mail.uk, and each is similar in tone to the threatening text message.

I know everything, says one. *We need to talk.*

Another says, *Don't ignore me. I promise you'll regret it.*

The final one is the worst: *If you don't answer me, I'm going to ruin everything for you. You'll lose it all. So, think on. Who would you rather hurt first?*

The text message was bad enough, but this? This is on a whole different level.

This is scary.

Sara reads through the emails again, sees that each one was sent to the same email address: simon.wells@jeffersontrading.com. Probably the same person the calls and texts were to.

Who is Simon Wells? And why has Adam been threatening him?

She opens Google, types in *Simon Wells Jefferson Trading*, then clicks search. The screen blinks and in the instant it takes to load she thinks about news reports, about police mugshots, Crimestoppers posters. When the screen refreshes, the first page of results throws up nothing unusual, nothing criminal-looking, at least. Just a list of online profiles.

The first result is for a LinkedIn profile. Sara clicks it. The page loads and in the top left is a small profile picture. She holds the phone up close, gets a good look.

Whoever Simon Wells is, his profile picture is a photo of Adam. The picture is tiny, cropped into a circle, but it really does look like Adam, even if it's a version of him she has never seen before. Adam in fancy dress, as a dull-as-dishwater business type, wearing glasses and a suit and a tie, with his hair oh-so-neatly parted on one side. He is smiling a small closed-mouthed smile and looking into the camera. *Trust me*, his expression seems to be saying. *I know exactly what I'm doing.*

Sara closes her eyes and takes deep breaths.

In for four, hold for one, out for seven . . . In for four, hold for one, out for seven.

When she opens her eyes none of this will be happening. The picture of Adam with someone else's name next to it isn't really a picture of Adam. It's just somebody who looks like him. An identical twin brother. Yes, that's what this is. Adam has a twin that, for some bizarre reason, he has never mentioned.

She opens her eyes and double-taps the picture. It enlarges, fills the phone's screen in high definition.

An identical twin brother, whose bottom two front teeth are slightly misaligned, just like Adam's. Who has the same tiny chickenpox scar at the side of his left eye. Who wears the same old-fashioned watch on his wrist.

Adam has not been messaging Simon Wells.

He *is* Simon Wells.

Sara slams the phone down on the empty seat beside her, grabs two fists full of her hair and pulls them tight against her skull. A sound like a scream fills her head, growing impossibly loud, and although she is on a busy night bus winding its way through the city, surrounded by businessmen with briefcases and young girls in strappy shoes and swaying drunks, she cannot help herself. She can't hold the scream in.

18

Catherine

Simon has gone away on business at least once a month these past few years, and has worked late more weekdays than not since he was promoted at Jefferson, so it's not as if Charlie isn't used to his daddy not being here, or me being the one to put him to bed. Usually, he takes it in his stride, but tonight he sits cross-legged on top of the sheets, a picture of defiance dressed in *Paw Patrol* pyjamas.

'Come on, get under the covers,' I tell him. 'It's past your bedtime.'

'But I'm not sleepy. Daddy lets me play *Angry Birds* when I'm not sleepy.'

'Good try,' I say, 'but I don't think he does. And I don't think Daddy would appreciate you telling lies to Mummy, either. Now, get under the covers.'

'He does!' he shouts, his face taking on an exaggerated version of the look Simon saves for when he is most offended. Face flushed with anger, eyes glaring beneath a comically big frown. 'I'm not lying,' he says. 'You shouldn't call people liars when they're telling the truth!'

Sounds like the sort of thing I might have said to him at some point, though I can't remember when. Perhaps he is telling the truth? I picture the two of them, huddled together at what should be story time, playing computer games, Simon whispering into his ear, *Shh, don't tell Mummy.*

'Fine,' I say. 'When Daddy's back you can play *Angry Birds*, but

Daddy's not here right now, and I'm asking you – no, I'm *telling* you – to get under the covers. It's time for sleep.'

He folds his arms. 'Don't want to.'

There is so much of Simon in him when he is like this. Not just his expression, but the way his cheeks colour and his breaths come out in bullish little snorts. Anger turns him into a miniature version of his father. Which is no surprise. Simon has always encouraged his combative side. Likes wrestling with him in the garden, watching him play with cars and toy dinosaurs and action figures. When Lydia bought Charlie a doll for his second birthday, Simon refused to give it to him.

'Little boys like playing with cars and trucks, not dolls,' he said. 'Can't we just let kids be kids without ramming gender politics down their throat?'

We argued about it – what would it matter if he played with it, so long as it was his choice, and so on – but in the end Charlie never did get his doll.

'So you're going to stay up all night, are you?' I say to him now, and he nods, as if the matter is settled.

The urge to leave him to it is strong, but instead I grab him by the arms and pull him up the bed, try to force him to get under the covers. He fights back, screams at the top of his lungs.

'Stop this. It's time for bed and you need to be a big boy,' I say.

He screams with such force and volume it feels like somebody has a drill pressed against my temple and is squeezing the trigger.

I put on my sternest voice. 'Daddy is going to be *very* cross with you when he gets back.'

That does it. He stops struggling. Looks up at me, lip quivering.

Simon has hit Charlie before. Only once, when Charlie was being especially naughty. A momentary loss of temper that left a bruise on Charlie's thigh. I remember inspecting it with my GP head on, worried someone might see the contusion and think the worst, but Simon told me not to be silly, said it happens to every parent at one time or another. He was probably right. Besides, I don't think it's the threat of a smacked bottom from Daddy that has made Charlie look so afraid tonight. It's me. It's because of my tone, and because – I am quite certain of this – he can feel the anger coming off me in waves.

What on earth am I doing? Shouting at him, making threats? He probably just misses his daddy.

I am the worst mother in the world.

'I'm sorry. Mummy didn't mean to shout.'

He scampers over to the far side of the bed, curls into a tight little ball.

'Charlie?'

Mum appears at the bedroom door, tips her head.

I don't want her to take over. I want to be the one to put him to bed. I need him to need me right now, but I don't have the energy to fight him anymore.

Mum moves to the other side of the bed and Charlie goes to her. She wipes the tears from his cheeks and strokes his forehead and I give up. I am beaten. I leave the room, go downstairs and try very hard not to hate myself.

It's the tiredness, that's what it is. Making me angry. Making me say things I don't mean.

Later on, I sit next to Mum on the sofa, while she pretends to read through a magazine, and go through every app I have ever used to contact Simon, then check all of his social media accounts, in case there have been any new posts.

There's a comment underneath a photo on his Facebook feed, a picture taken at Simon's work summer party a few months ago, of him sandwiched between Max and another colleague whose name I can't remember – Alex? Andrew? Something like that. The three of them are dressed in tuxedos, cheeks flushed, grins sloppy. Drunk, or getting there. They cheers the camera with glasses of champagne. Someone I've never heard of called Robert Collins has commented underneath:

Fantastic night, Si. Hope you can all make it over to Berlin for the—

The words blur on the screen. I screw up my eyes, blink a few times and try to bring them back into focus, but when I look again, they've become even less legible. They barely look like words at all. Floating lines and dots that refuse to organise themselves into recognisable shapes.

I need to stop.

I set the phone down and check the time. Half past eleven – where on earth have the last few hours disappeared to? Mum has fallen asleep beside me. The magazine has slipped off her lap and she is leaning to one side, head lolling, a glistening string of saliva hanging from the corner of her mouth.

I cough, loud and on purpose, and Mum jerks upright.

'If you're tired, go to bed,' I tell her.

She flaps a hand. 'Just resting my eyes.'

Go to bed, because falling asleep next to me like that . . . It's an insult. It makes me want to hate you.

'You were snoring.'

'Was I?' She rubs her eyes and – thank God – admits defeat.

'Promise you won't stay up all night?' she says.

'I won't,' I say. 'I might see if Lydia's still online, but I'll go to bed straight after.'

Lydia promised to call into The Haymarket over her lunch hour, and a number of the other remaining bars on my list, to ask about Simon. She had me text her a photo of him. *One of him in a suit*, she said. *They'll be more likely to recognise him in a suit.* I sent her the picture of the two of us from his colleague's wedding and wondered why I hadn't thought of that sooner.

Mum nods. 'If you need me—'

'I know.'

Just go.

When I hear the door to the spare room close, I move over to the bay window and part the curtains, peer out across the square.

Simon? Where the hell are you?

Despite what the police say, and the treacherous voice in the back of my mind, I know he's still out there. He has to be.

Movement outside. A shadow flits between the trees in the residents' garden. Probably a . . . a . . . what do you call them? Those things with matted fur the colour of mud that like to rummage through bins. Like dogs, but dogs that move like cats. Sometimes you hear them mating at night, an awful blood-curdling scream that sounds like someone is being murdered. Foxes. That's what they're called. Probably just a fox. I lean in, put a hand against the window to block out the room's reflections.

While the square itself is well illuminated, with streetlights casting orange cones of light at regular intervals, the gardens are in almost total darkness.

I could swear I saw something . . . there! A shadow, moving between the trees. Not low to the ground like a fox, but tall and upright. The wind, moving one of the taller bushes? I narrow my eyes, do my best to focus. Is it a person? Standing out there in the residents' garden?

Don't be stupid. You're overtired, you're seeing things.

But as I watch, the shadow shifts, steps to its left then slinks around the corner of the church.

Somebody is out there.

Simon?

I race to the front door, pull it open and run out into the street.

What Simon would be doing in the gardens at this time of night, I have no idea. But who else could it be? Perhaps there's some reason he can't come inside? He wants to – of course he *wants* to – but something, or somebody, is forcing him to stay away.

I move along the pavement, hoping to God that when I reach the corner of the square, I'll see him hiding behind the church. I'll run to him and he'll throw his arms around me and hold me, then he'll explain everything.

But when I reach the corner, the road that runs along the back of the church is deserted. Pools of orange lie in overlapping circles, the streetlights illuminating every inch of empty pavement. I call Simon's name, just in case, and my voice sounds terribly loud and afraid in the quiet of the square.

'Simon?' *Please be there.*

Nothing.

The emptiness of the square feels suddenly vast, as if I could get lost out here, even though I am in sight of my own front door. All at once I feel terribly aware of the cold surrounding me, the press of the pavement on the soles of my feet, the breeze snatching at my dressing gown.

How ridiculous I must look, standing out here in the middle of the night dressed like this, calling out for my missing husband like a madwoman.

The neighbours will think I've lost my mind.

I hurry back to the house, unable to shake the feeling that I'm being watched, even though I know it's just the tiredness playing tricks on me. How cruel of it. To make me think that the thing I want most in the world is right outside my front door.

21-11-2022

1.05 a.m.

'So, what was it? New witness? You dig up some CCTV from a new angle? Thought that might happen.'

He's trying to catch me out again.

'We're not there yet,' I tell him. 'I want to hear more about this double life of yours. How you made it work. It must have been difficult, not giving yourself away.'

He gets this smug look on his face, like it was the easiest thing in the world.

'If I was an idiot, it would have been difficult. But I'm not. As long as I stuck to my rules, I knew I'd be fine.'

'And you never slipped up?'

'Never.'

Not true, and he knows it.

'I notice you didn't make your social media accounts private,' I say. 'I could access all of them, see all your photos. Seems like a mistake to me—'

He shakes his head. 'If I'd wanted to make them private, I would have. It would have looked suspicious, drawn attention.'

'OK, take me through these rules of yours.'

He starts counting them off on his fingers. 'First you need a fake name, a fake backstory and a fake job. A dedicated email account and phone. A decent phone, too, not a cheap throwaway – you don't want to look like a drug dealer or some sort of hipster. Fake social media profiles. Fake LinkedIn, with a fake career history. Separate bank account. Cash payments, whenever possible. Empty pockets before going home. Throw away receipts from dinner, drinks, hotels or theatre tickets. Leave nothing behind, nothing to be discovered at a later date when the laundry is being done. Chew gum. Shower after sex. Be clean, but not too clean. Not suspiciously clean. Don't overdo the aftershave. Drink, but not too much. Keep your wits about you. Be sensible about where you meet. Busy places are best. You stand out in quiet places. Avoid parts of town you're likely to be recognised in. Keep public displays of affection to a minimum. Of course, all of this follows on from rule number one, the most important rule of all.'

'Which is?'

'Tell no one. No matter who you think you can trust, no matter how much you want to confide in someone, you keep your mouth shut. People are terrible at keeping secrets. And definitely don't even think about telling someone who is married. People tell their partners everything. Well, almost everything.'

19

Day Five

Sara

It is gone midnight when Sara arrives home. She tears around her tiny flat like a Catherine wheel, spitting out curses like sparks.

'Arsehole. Fucking arsehole! I can't believe this, I can *not* fucking believe this!'

She throws herself onto her bed, pushes her face into her pillow and lies there with her heart thumping in her temples.

Now she is back in her dingy flat, nothing feels real. Her boyfriend doesn't exist? Of course he exists. She is lying on the bed they had sex in less than a week ago, have had sex in hundreds of times. He exists, as sure as that is his scarf hanging from the coat hook in the hall, his toothbrush sitting alongside hers in the mug next to the bathroom sink, his photo as the screensaver on her phone.

He exists.

But she saw what she saw.

She gets up and goes to the living room, fires up her laptop and brings up the corporate website of Jefferson Trading.

On the About Us page, under a heading that says Our Team, there is another picture of Adam. In this one he is wearing a suit and tie, both navy blue, over a crisp white shirt. His hair is neatly parted and he has on expensive-looking glasses with thick black rims. Sara has never seen him wearing glasses before. They make him look old and serious. The suit doesn't help, either. He usually wears a jacket and jeans, T-shirts and Converse. When she first met him she thought he dressed a little young for his age, but she came to like it, thought it suited his energy. But on the website, he looks every inch the job title under his picture.

Simon Wells, Investment Advisor.

Simon has developed a wealth of cross-sector knowledge and experience, is RDR qualified and a member of the Chartered Institute of Securities and Investment . . .

She closes the website and types Simon Wells into the search bar. The screen blinks and fills with results. The first few entries – a film director, a doctor, a theatre designer – aren't the Simon Wells she is looking for, but halfway down there's a listing for a Facebook profile.

She clicks it open, and there it is, right at the top of the page. Adam's picture.

Simon's picture.

He is somewhere sunny, his face made of shadow, with a red V burnt into his skin above the neckline of his t-shirt, and he is grinning broadly, cheeks dimpled. If there was any doubt still left in Sara that Adam is really Simon, then this photo is the end of it. Those are *his* dimples, *his* smile. His teeth, too. He told her he wished he'd got braces when he was a kid, that one day, when he got around to it, he'd get them fixed. And she said, *Don't do that, I like you just the way you are*, but secretly she thought he probably should and wondered how much money he actually had, because everyone knows cosmetic dentistry is something only rich people can afford.

Sara steps away from her laptop, goes to the kitchen and searches for something to drink. She finds a bottle of gin and pours herself a double, reconsiders and makes it a triple. Gulps it down and wipes her chin on the sleeve of her jumper, then chain-smokes two cigarettes in a row.

Whatever horrible ride she is on, she wants to get off now.

She checks her phone. If there is a perfect moment for Adam to reach out to her to tell her there has been some dreadful mix-up and that this most definitely isn't what it looks like, then now – *right now, oh please, please, please, right now* – is it. But there are no missed calls or voicemails, no emails or texts. She extinguishes her cigarette, returns to the laptop.

Sara takes a deep breath and scrolls down Simon's Facebook feed to the most recent post. A photograph. Adam, dressed in a tuxedo, looking tipsy at some sort of formal dinner. He is sandwiched between two other men, also dressed in tuxedos and also a little drunk-looking. There is something about the three of them that screams privilege. Their haircuts, their ruddy complexions, the carefree look in their eyes as they 'cheers' the camera. Someone has commented underneath: *Fantastic night, Si. Hope you can all make it over to Berlin for the Expo. We'll show you English boys how it's really done.* The date on the post is from five weeks ago. Sara can't remember Adam saying anything about going to a fancy party last month.

Not that that means anything.

The next photo is of Adam in a posh-looking living room, large and bright, with a high ceiling. He is standing next to a big fireplace with a marble surround, a huge mirror hanging above it with an elaborate gold frame. He has his arm around a pretty, middle-aged woman, and the woman has a young child on her hip, a little boy of three or four, sucking the fingers of one hand and clutching a green plastic dinosaur in the other. There's no caption for the picture, but a dozen or so people have clicked Like.

Awww. Super cute, the only comment says.

Sara is not sure what makes her hover the mouse over the woman, something about the way the two of them are standing, a closeness that suggests they are more than friends.

A name flashes up beneath her cursor: Catherine Wells.

Her heart freezes.

A sister? Please tell me he has a sister he hasn't told me about. She is his sister; the little boy is his nephew.

She scrolls back up to the top of the page and clicks the About button, then clicks Family and Relationships, and reads: *Relationship: Catherine Wells – Married since October 12th 2006.*

Sara reads the words again, then the nausea rushes in. She clutches her mouth and races to the bathroom.

By three in the morning, Sara has taken all she can stomach. Adam was nothing online, a barely-there outline of a person, but with Simon it is different. With Simon, it is all here. A robust online life, all too easy to unpick and explore.

His real professional profile. A career history going back fifteen years, plotting his rise from assistant, to executive, to manager, to his current position as Trading Advisor. His social media: Facebook, Twitter, Instagram, all with posts in the last few weeks. Photographs. Lots and lots of photographs. In the vast majority of them is the little boy, or the woman. More often than not, both.

He's still married.

Adam – or Simon, whatever his fucking name is – is still married.

Adam is not Adam. Adam is Simon. And Simon has a wife.

Simon has a son.

Two years ago, they all went to Paris for a long weekend. They took lots of photos. One of them, a cheesy selfie of Simon in front of the Eiffel Tower at night, giving the thumbs up; another of him sitting outside a café, toasting the camera with a cup of coffee. Sara laughs when she sees them, compares the photos he sent her three days ago with the ones on his Instagram and actually laughs out loud. Then she curls up on her bed with her knees drawn up to her elbows, both of her fists bunched up against her mouth and the tip of one thumb held between her teeth.

She tries to figure out how she could possibly have been so stupid. To have fallen for this, she must be the stupidest woman on earth. The amount of lies he would have to tell, day in and day out, the sheer logistics of it . . . He must have slipped up, must have made mistakes a thousand times, and still, she had no idea.

Did he think she would never find out? That he could keep living two lives forever? Impossible. There is not enough time in the world for someone to maintain one family while they build another with someone else. Unless . . .

He never intended to make a life with you. You were never going to move in together, you were never going to have kids. Everything he told you, everything he promised, was a lie.

The bass-drum beat of her broken heart resonates through her body with such force it feels like it might shake her to pieces.

As the darkness fills her up, she wonders what she is supposed to do. How can she possibly be expected to get up and go to work and live her life, after this?

She doesn't know what to do next, though she knows what she *wants* to do. She wants to kill him. Adam – or Simon – whoever the fuck he is. For lying to her like this, for making her feel like the stupidest person to have ever walked the earth, she wants to kill him.

20

Catherine

The detectives call first thing, and DI Carter gives me another of those waste-of-time updates of theirs. Their enquiries are ongoing, they are still tracing Simon's movements on the night of 'the incident', still waiting for the DNA results that will prove it wasn't Simon in the car after all. Useless.

'I think someone was watching the house last night,' I tell her. 'They were standing out in the gardens.'

I can almost hear her sit up in her seat. 'You think?'

'Well, I was very tired, and when I went out to look there was nobody there. But they could have run away, couldn't they? It might have been Simon, trying to make contact.'

Is that a sigh on the other end of the line? 'And what time was this?'

'I'm not sure. Late. Midnight, maybe?'

The sound of typing in the background. 'OK, Catherine. We can have the CCTV in the square checked, but if it happens again, you must call us. Don't go out there yourself at night, OK?'

She doesn't believe me. Of course she doesn't.

As far as she's concerned, Simon's dead, so he's hardly likely to turn up in the communal gardens in the middle of the night. Or at any other time, for that matter.

Half an hour later, Mum has her bag over her arm and her coat on. She stalks from room to room, finding last-minute jobs to do that don't need doing. She doesn't want to leave me, but a part of her needs to get out from under the shadow of it all.

'I'll pick up some fresh clothes,' she says – never mind that she could wash her clothes here just fine – 'and I need to run a few errands, nip to the post office, the bank. Then I'll get us all something nice to eat. I'll be back for teatime. OK?'

She's started speaking to me like I'm a child again. I can't decide if it's being around Charlie that's done it, or if that's how she sees me now. Helpless, like a little kid.

She bends down with a groan and picks up Charlie. 'You take care of Mummy while I'm gone. Grandma will be back later, OK?'

'Bye-bye, Grandma.' Charlie hugs her back and sucks his fingers, wets the shoulder of her coat with saliva. She hands him over and goes to blot away the wet patch with kitchen towel.

I set Charlie down. 'We'll be fine, Mum. Really, we will.'

She looks as if she is on the verge of tears. I pull her into a hug and am awash with familiar smells; the leather of her gloves and her handbag, Lifebuoy soap and the Estée Lauder perfume she has been wearing all my life. It's tempting to stay there, my face pressed into the warmth of her coat's fur collar, surrounded by comforting Mum-smells, but there are things I need to do today.

'You're looking more like yourself,' she says into my ear.

I showered this morning, then took some time to stroke concealer under my eyes to hide the purple shadows, dab cream blusher on my cheeks and pull a brush through my hair. I don't want Mum to know how tired I am, how dreadful I feel. I want her out of the way.

'If you need anything, anything at all . . .'

'I'll call. I promise.'

Another hug for Charlie, then we wave Mum goodbye from the doorstep. The moment I shut the door I start getting Charlie ready.

Teatime. I think back to my childhood: getting back from school, homework in front of the television, food served around five thirty. Five hours away. Plenty of time for me to do what I need to and get back home before Mum knows I have been anywhere.

I sit Charlie down at the bottom of the stairs, button his coat and put on his shoes.

'Where are we going?' he asks.

'We're going on the . . . on the . . .' I can't think of the word. The train? Not quite. Why can't I remember . . . The tube, that's it. 'We're going on the tube, then we're going to visit a big tall building. You'll like it there.'

'Yay!' Charlie flings his arms into the air. He likes the tube, likes any sort of train.

I straighten up and the tiredness overwhelms me. My view of the hall lurches sideways and my legs unhinge. I grab the bannisters to steady myself.

Deep breath.

'Mummy?'

I close my eyes, try to focus on the feeling of the ground beneath my feet, the wood of the bannisters in my hands. These things are real, solid. Unmoving.

I open my eyes and, thank God, the world has stopped spinning.

'It's OK,' I tell Charlie. 'Mummy's OK.'

I'm too tired to be doing this. Last night I sat up waiting for Simon to call, obsessively checking his social media. Sleep crept up behind me when I wasn't looking, closed my eyes for me, bowed my head until my chin touched my chest. It took everything I had to fight it, to keep going.

I know what sleep deprivation can do. It is torture – literally, in some cases. Soviet Russia, Guantanamo Bay. Ten days without sleep, and vital functions in the body shut down; death soon follows. But long before that, lack of sleep can drive you mad. Patients used to come and see me – the grieving, the depressed, the sick – desperate for something to help them sleep. For lighter cases, sedating antihistamines might get them back on track. More severe cases required sedating hypnotics, or antidepressants. Zopiclone, Mirtazapine. Melatonin, to help re-establish circadian rhythms. One man who came to see me after losing his daughter had gone so long without rest that he was starting to hallucinate, seeing his dead little girl out of the corner of his eye. So I know what sleep deprivation can do, beyond the mood swings and lack of concentration, the headaches and paranoia. It can ruin you. Kill you, even.

But it won't come to that. Simon will be home soon and everything will be back to normal. Until then, until he comes home, I've got to keep it together.

His mother, my mother, the police; everyone else has let Simon down, but I won't.

'Are we going now, Mummy?'

You can do this. Simon needs you.

Max is there to meet us on the tenth floor of Simon's office building.

He is of a type, is Max. Though to be fair, he is of the same type as Simon. Tall and athletic, he wears middle age with moneyed ease. Nice suits, expensive shoes, a haircut that probably cost as much as mine.

'Catherine,' he says, his face a picture of sadness. 'I'm so—' His eyes flick down to Charlie and he stops himself. I accept a brief hug from him, then he steps back, unsure of what happens next.

'Do you want to come through?' he says. 'Or we could go out, if you prefer? Grab a coffee? Whatever works for you.'

'Actually,' I say, 'I was wondering if I could see Simon's office? Pick up any personal things he might have left behind. Photographs, that sort of thing.'

The last confirmed sighting of Simon was in this building. If I am going to retrace his steps, this is where I need to start.

'Of course,' Max says, glad to have something to do. He turns towards a set of glass doors, swipes a keycard and leads us out onto the office floor.

Jefferson Trading is a serious sort of place for serious business, and the offices have that expensive, minimalist feel to them. White walls, black carpeted floors. Glass meeting rooms with giant tables and big televisions mounted on the walls for video conferences with clients in New York, Hong Kong and Tokyo.

Eyes follow us as we pass through the office. People can't help but stare. Am I imagining the whispering?

That's Simon's wife. Did you hear what happened to him? Isn't it awful.

After what seems like an eternity we arrive at Simon's office. Max opens the door and, once Charlie and I are inside, closes it behind us. Thankfully, the blinds have already been lowered against the glass and we are no longer visible to Simon's colleagues.

'The police have . . .' He gestures, trailing off.

They have stripped the room almost bare, taken everything but the furniture, and that remarkable view of the city skyline.

'God knows what they were looking for,' Max says.

I pick up Charlie and carry him over to the window. You can see half of London from up here; a broad expanse of the Thames, riverboats like punctuation marks. In the distance, Westminster and the Houses of Parliament.

'Look, Charlie. There. Can you see the boats and the . . . and the . . .' I'm looking right at the thing, but can't for the life of me remember what they are called.

'Bridge, Mummy.' He gives me his silly-mummy look.

'That's right,' I say. 'And can you see the big clock?'

'That's Big Ben!' Charlie says, pleased with himself.

'Aren't you clever.' I lower him down and he presses his nose up against the window, pointing at one building after another – *Look Mummy, look!* – leaving tiny fingerprints dotted over the glass.

I dump my bag on the floor and search through it until I find paper and a grubby box of crayons.

'Can you draw a picture of the bridge and Big Ben while Mummy talks to Uncle Max?'

Charlie plants himself on the floor, legs folded beneath him. He tips his crayons out and selects a dark blue. Once he is suitably engrossed, I join Max over by the door.

'One minute you're helping them take their first steps, the next it's their first day at school. He'll be starting college before you know it,' Max says.

'Hmm,' I say.

'Simon said you got him into the school you wanted? That it was a real hassle.'

He is talking as if we've bumped into each other while out shopping at the weekend. I don't want to talk about schools, or how much Charlie has grown.

I don't reply and Max brings his head close to mine. 'We're all so terribly sorry. It's such a shock. Just . . . dreadful.'

'Simon's missing,' I whisper. 'He's not . . .' I can't say the word. 'He's just missing, Max.'

He blinks a few times. 'But . . . they said they found his watch?'

'Someone must have taken it. They found other things too, things that were *definitely* nothing to do with Simon. I would have known if those things were his.'

The rucksack, the hat, the flyer.

I want so desperately for Max to understand, for him to believe Simon is still out there. If anyone might feel that, surely it will be Simon's best friend?

'He's still alive,' I tell him. 'I know he is—'

'Catherine—'

My hand reaches for my heart. 'I can *feel* it.'

Can't you feel it too?

Max closes his eyes. He wants to believe me. Wants to, but doesn't.

'Look, Mummy!' Charlie calls from the other side of the office. He waves his half-finished drawing, a jumble of blue and orange swirls.

'Very good, Charlie! Keep going. Did you draw the boats? Don't forget the boats.'

Charlie looks over his shoulder, considers the scene for a moment then gets back to work.

Back to Max. 'When did you last speak to him?'

'As I was leaving the office that evening, just after seven.'

I experience a rush of jealousy, that Max saw Simon after I did.

'And how was he?' I ask. 'Did he seem . . . different at all?'

'He was just . . . Si. He was fine. Normal, I mean.'

'And you didn't see him after that? He told me there were work drinks.'

Max shakes his head. 'Must have got his dates mixed up. There were no work drinks that night. In fact, when I poked my head in to say goodnight, he told me he was going to pull a late one. Said you were out on a girls' night and that you had a babysitter, so he might as well make use of the time.'

So it isn't just me he lied to.

Max continues, 'That was the last time I saw him. And the police have asked everybody. Nobody here saw him after work.'

At least, nobody has *admitted* to seeing him. I picture him out with different women. His old PA who left abruptly – something to do with an inappropriate relationship with one of the senior managers. His opposite number at the Manchester office, with legs so long even I couldn't help but stare. She was flirting with him at the Christmas party, at least until Simon introduced me.

'Max, you don't think . . .'

A flicker of discomfort in Max's eyes, then he reaches over and takes my hand.

'Rubbish,' he says. 'Simon loved you, and you know how much he adored Charlie. That's not him. You know it isn't.'

I want to correct him – *loves* me, *adores* Charlie – but it is so good to hear him say those words that I don't.

'Thank you, Max,' I say, and he is suddenly overcome. A sob bursts out of him and now it's me comforting him, squeezing his hand. 'He's missing, that's all, Max,' I tell him. 'It's going to be OK. I know it is.'

He turns away and buries his face in the sleeve of his jacket, makes a motion with his hand that says, *give me a minute*, then opens the door and marches off across the office floor.

The door swings shut behind him and I cross over to the almost empty desk. The police have taken Simon's computer, his desk diary, lots of other things, probably. There are no files or papers, there is only a monitor, an Anglepoise lamp and a photograph in a dark wooden frame. The photograph was a Fathers' Day gift from Charlie I had framed a few months ago. It's a shot Simon took of the three of us on a Sunday-afternoon trip to the park. In it, we are sat on a picnic blanket, the camera looking down at us from the extent of Simon's reach. Simon and I are smiling up at the camera while Charlie is looking away, squealing with unrestrained glee at something or other.

What a happy time that was. One of those days that starts off entirely unremarkable but turns into something special without even having to try.

I pick up the photograph and spin round in the chair. 'Charlie, come and see—' But Charlie has gone. His drawing and crayons are there, but he has vanished. For a terrible moment I think that the big window must have somehow opened and that Charlie has, without a sound, tumbled through it and plummeted ten floors to the ground below.

'Charlie? *Charlie*?' I spring to my feet.

A small voice behind me: 'What, Mummy?'

He's OK. Thank God. Oh, my heart.

'Where are you?'

From under the desk: 'I'm *here*, Mummy.'

I roll back the chair and see that Charlie has made a cave out of the desk's underside. He has two plastic dinosaurs he must have smuggled with him in his pocket and is making them fight each other, dancing them around the rim of an empty wastepaper basket.

He's safe, thank goodness.

I move the chair back into position and take a seat.

'Be careful,' I tell him. 'Mind you don't bump your head.'

It's an odd feeling, to be sitting at Simon's desk, where he spent so much of his life. Five, sometimes six days a week, sitting right here, working away at his computer. Answering emails, taking calls, having meetings. All that time spent away from Charlie and me. All those hours, given away so easily. What a dreadful waste.

Stop it. Now you're the one talking as if he's gone. He's not dead. He's just . . . not where he's supposed to be.

Something must have happened on Monday. That morning he specifically told me he would be home late, that there would be work drinks.

What were you really doing that night, Simon? Where did you go? Who were you with? And why did you lie?

There are two desk drawers. I open the top one and find nothing but a mess of stationery. Post-it notes that have lost their stickiness, pens missing their tops, the worn-down nubs of pencils, dozens upon dozens of loose staples. The drawer beneath is deeper and contains a handful of manila files. I lift the top one out and thumb through it. Sheets of paper marked confidential. Tables filled with numbers, all meaningless to me.

Perhaps he found out something important about one of the

companies he works with that they don't want people knowing about? It sounds silly, but Simon has access to all sorts of information. Information that, if it got into the wrong hands, could do all sorts of damage . . .

There's a sound – *whump!* – and the desk jumps. I roll back the chair and Charlie is sat with his hands clasped on top of his head, his mouth hanging open in shock.

'Did you bump your head?' I ask, knowing the answer already. He emits a breathy high-pitched wail that I know is just the beginnings of a full-blown meltdown. 'Oh, dear me. I said to mind your head, didn't I? Come on. Come on out.' I grab an elbow and he scoots out from under the desk on his knees.

'I hit my head!' he wails.

'Let Mummy see.' I part his hair. 'Here?' He nods through his tears, pulls in hitching breaths between garbled streams of words. A snot bubble forms and bursts on his top lip.

There's no sign he has broken the skin. I pick him up and switch places with him, sit him in his dad's chair, kiss his forehead, wipe the tears from his cheeks and take a tissue from my pocket to clean his nose with. 'Poor you. Hold still . . . there we are.'

The office door opens. It's Max, looking a little red around the eyes but more together.

For a moment, I entertain the hope he has returned with some new piece of information that will make this trip worthwhile – a letter perhaps, that has arrived at the office and that, once opened, will explain everything, or a suit jacket that Simon left behind in one of the meeting rooms that has a clue hidden in one of the inside pockets – but he is empty-handed. As clueless as I am.

'Everything OK?' he says.

'Charlie bumped his head.'

'Oh dear.'

'He'll be OK.' I turn back to Charlie. 'Won't you, trouble?' In reply Charlie wipes his nose on the sleeve of his coat, then mutters something into his chest.

I lean in close. 'What's that, darling?'

'Want Daddy,' he says, sulkily.

'I know,' I tell him. 'But you'll see him soon.'

When I look up, Max is starting to tear up again, and something opens up inside me; a deep, dark well of hurt.

Why is this happening to me? What could I have possibly done to deserve this?

How stupid of me, to think I could come here and find some sort of clue to Simon's whereabouts. If there was anything to be found, the police would have already found it.

I pick up the photograph from Simon's desk and slip it into my bag.

'If there's anything you need,' Max says.

I nod. 'We'd better go,' I say, because I can feel myself starting to slow-blink, growing foggy-headed. The tiredness is coming on strong now. There is so much I wanted to do today, so much I'm going to have to do if I want to find Simon, but I don't know how I'm going to find the strength.

Max moves over to the window. 'Don't forget your picture, Charlie.'

Charlie has left his drawing and his crayons on the floor. Max collects the crayons and puts them back in their box then picks up the drawing and brings it over.

'Here you are.' He holds out the drawing, but Charlie jams his fingers into his mouth and hides behind my legs.

'Don't you want it?' He doesn't reply. The bump to his head has soured his trip to Daddy's office. 'Are you sure? Well, shall we let Uncle Max keep it safe for you, just for now?' You never know with a four-year-old. In an hour's time he might be crying his eyes out at having left it behind.

'Don't worry. I'll look after it.' Max turns it over, takes a good look at it. 'Wow! That's brilliant, Charlie. I never knew you were such a talented artist.'

Charlie *is* talented, I'm quite sure of that, but this drawing isn't one of his better efforts. The skyline has been reduced to a series of looping scribbles, London Bridge a tightrope-thin line over a churning purple Thames. Off to one side, two oversized stick figures stand holding hands beneath a turbulent sky of black and blue, like the biggest storm you have ever seen is moving in over the city.

* * *

At Bank station, the carriage doors open with a thump and a rattle and a handful of people step down onto the platform before a dozen more board to take their place.

'Are we getting off now?' Charlie is sitting next to me, legs sticking straight out, showing the dusty soles of his trainers to the passengers sitting opposite.

'Not yet, love,' I tell him. 'Three more stops.'

Normally I avoid the underground. It is too busy, noisy and smelly, and it can be stressful, even without a four-year-old in tow. But today the tube is a good place to be. The rhythmic rocking and shunting of the train soothes me. Life is simple down here. The tube moves from A to B, then back again. It stops and starts, people get off and others get on. It's a simple system, and deep down in the underground, surrounded by strangers, I can almost imagine that up there, on the surface, everything is normal. Simon is at work, in his office. Later on, we'll put Charlie to bed, take turns reading him a story, then eat dinner at the kitchen table, or on trays on our laps if there's anything good on television. Sleep next to each other, wake up with each other in the morning. If only I could stay down here forever, being carried from one station to the next, rocked from side to side, lulled to sleep . . .

An image swims into my consciousness. Waking up at the end of the line, an empty seat next to me where Charlie should be—

I come back to myself with a start.

Get it together, Cat. Wake up, wake up!

I look around the carriage, and although everyone appears to be minding their own business, with their eyes on their phones or newspapers, I have the distinct feeling they are only pretending not to look. That we are being watched.

The train barrels into the next station and comes to a squealing halt. I take Charlie's hand. 'Come on, we're getting off.'

He shouts his protest at the top his lungs. 'You said three stops! We only went two and you said three!'

'I know I said three, but I *meant* two.'

I pick him up and carry him out of the carriage, deposit him, kicking and screaming, onto the platform.

He pouts and sulks as we head up through the barriers at London Bridge and escape into the bright of the day. We push our way through groups of tourists until we are clear and continue our journey down Borough High Street. Still, that feeling that we are being watched, followed even, is with me. A prickle at the back of my neck. And Charlie is trailing behind, trainers scuffing the pavement.

'Keep up,' I tell him, but he continues to drag his feet. I look down to see that he isn't watching where he is going. Instead he has something in his hand, is sneaking surreptitious glances at it.

'What have you got there?'

He comes to a stop, thrusts his hands behind his back. 'Nothing,' he says.

'Show Mummy.' He shakes his head and I put on my stern voice. 'Charlie?'

He brings his left hand out from behind his back, opens his fist to reveal a small pin badge, black and shiny, with a slogan printed on it. *I helped Dylan find the London Bridge Jogger.*

'Who gave you this?'

'It's mine,' he says. 'I found it. It was under Daddy's desk.'

I don't recall seeing anything under Simon's desk except an empty wastepaper basket. Perhaps it was wedged in somehow, out of sight to anyone but a little boy playing with his toy dinosaurs.

I take it from Charlie, turn it over in my hand. What an odd little thing.

'Is it a button?' asks Charlie.

'Like a button. It's a badge. People pin them to their clothes.'

Something stirs at the edge of my thoughts, telling me that this badge is important.

'Can I have it back now?' Charlie whines. 'I found it, so it's mine.' He reaches up, grasps thin air with his splayed fingers.

'Just wait a moment—'

What is it? What could possibly be important about this little badge? My mind is a stone skipping over the surface of the water.

'Mummy, it's *mine*!' Charlie stamps his feet.

'Charlie . . .' I am about to tell him off for being naughty, and because he has to learn that real life isn't like the playground. Finders keepers doesn't apply in the real world. But then I think again. Perhaps he knows that this little badge belonged to his daddy. Maybe that's why he wants it so much.

'Stand very still,' I tell him, and I crouch down and fasten the pin badge to the front of Charlie's red duffel coat. It's probably nothing. Just a little piece of Simon left behind for Charlie to keep. In which case, maybe our visit to the office wasn't such a waste of time after all.

21

Catherine

The year before Charlie was born, Simon and I took a boat trip, a day-long tour of the Elaphiti Islands during a stay in Dubrovnik. It was supposed to be the highlight of the holiday, but I felt seasick the moment we were out on the open water. My stomach lurched along with the boat's rise and fall – or perhaps it didn't, and that was the problem. I spent most of the trip with my head in my hands praying for it to end. I have that same feeling now. Like my centre of gravity has been stolen from me.

I close my eyes, take deep breaths. Focus on just being still.

The visit to Simon's office has drained me of whatever energy was propelling me along earlier. But there's still so much more to do and so many unanswered questions, chief among them, where did Simon really go after work on the night he went missing? And why did he lie, not only to me, but to Max, too?

I lay my head on the arm of the sofa. The upbeat chatter of Charlie's cartoons, of *Peppa Pig* and *Bluey*, usually grates, but today it is a comforting white noise, easing me towards sleep. The urge to give in is so very strong.

Then sleep. What does it matter? Simon is gone, and you are so very tired, so sleep . . .

But it does matter.

I need to focus.

The badge. Perhaps it's of no significance whatsoever. It could just be a little trinket Simon found and hadn't got round to throwing away. Then again, the burnt rucksack the police showed me – the picture of the burnt rucksack – there were badges pinned to the shoulder straps, weren't there? Badges like this one? I wish I could remember what they looked like. I pretended I was taking a really good look, so the detectives would think I was doing a proper job, but in truth I was so relieved to be shown something that definitely wasn't Simon's that I all but dismissed it the moment I saw it. So it's possible the badge Charlie found is the same as one that was pinned to that rucksack. If it is, then the badge isn't nothing. It's a connection, a clue even.

I helped Dylan catch the London Bridge Jogger.

I remember the London Bridge Jogger, of course I do. Those grainy video stills were on the front of every newspaper in the country. I was as outraged as everybody else when I read about what happened. I remember talking to Lydia about it, sitting in her kitchen sharing a bottle of Pinot Grigio.

'That awful man,' I said. 'I mean, what sort of a person does something like that? He's clearly a psychopath. He wants locking up.'

'Absolutely,' she said. 'Bloody men.'

I also remember the London Bridge Jogger because Simon looked a little like the man in the video. The footage was so blurry and imperfect, you could pluck any middle-aged white man of medium build with short dark hair off the streets, put him in blue shorts and a grey T-shirt, and there'd be a pretty good resemblance. So, the jogger looked a little like Simon, and a little like Max. And if Jonathan weren't balding, he'd look a little like him, too.

I tried to joke about it with Simon.

'And where were you on the morning of August the third, Mr Wells?' I said, twirling an imaginary moustache, playing the part of detective.

'I was at bloody work, as you well know,' he said.

'And is there anyone who can corroborate that, Mr Wells?'

He looked almost angry with me. 'Rather poor taste, don't you think, Cat?' he said. 'A woman almost died.' Then he got all emotional, said it could have been me or Charlie who was pushed into the road, and that these days people can't even walk the streets without fearing for their lives, which I thought was a bit *Daily Mail* of him. But he had a point. It must have been very frightening for that poor woman. The randomness of it all. How could you ever feel safe again after something like that? You'd be forever looking over your shoulder, fearful that somebody might attack you out of the blue. The same man, even, seeing as the police never caught him. A fact that makes that slogan on the badge even stranger.

I helped Dylan find the London Bridge Jogger.

How on earth this Dylan person could claim such a thing is beyond me.

I boot up the laptop and google the phrase on the badge. The first link that loads is for a website about a podcast called *The Push.*

Join investigative journalist Dylan Lesley on his journey to crack the case that captivated a nation . . . and his mission to bring the London Bridge Jogger to justice.

The Dylan mentioned on the badge is the host of the podcast.

I click around the website, come across a sort of shop for fans with all sorts of things to buy. There are T-shirts and sweatshirts for men and women, there are tote bags and posters, and right at the bottom of the page, pin badges, like the one Charlie found under Simon's desk. A pack of three for £5.99. All the items have the same slogan on them, and some have the same image of the man's face I saw on the flyer. Presumably, the man pictured is not the jogger, seeing as he hasn't been caught – if he had, it would be on the front page of every newspaper in the country – so perhaps it is just a looming portrait, meant to look mysterious.

Simon is not a fan of true crime, and not a regular listener of podcasts. I would know if he was. People are evangelical about podcasts, like becoming a vegan, or watching *Stranger Things*. When they talk to you about them, they seem almost pained you don't share their enthusiasm.

This podcast is clearly quite a popular one. Aside from all the merchandise, there are special events. On the homepage is a list of live recordings that fans can attend. Meet the host, ask questions, enjoy a special DJ set by Dylan Lesley himself. There have been half a dozen or so of these events, spread out across the last two months, each one held in a pub or a bar across London. It is the most recent of these events, held last Monday evening, that catches my eye.

The Push: *Live – The Pit, Bethnal Green Road. 8.30 p.m. Q&A followed by DJ set by Dylan starting at 10 p.m.*

The Pit. That's the venue on the flyer the police asked me about. It wasn't a flyer for a band, it was for the podcast.

Did Simon go to the live recording of *The Push* the night he went missing? If he did, people must have seen him there. There'll be witnesses who might be able to say what time he arrived, what time he left, who he was talking to, all sorts of things.

I should tell the detectives, make sure they know that there is something linking Simon to the flyer after all. But they think I'm a liar, because I didn't tell them about Jonathan. And if they think I was trying to deceive them about that, what else might they think about me? That I'm involved in Simon's disappearance? His murder, even? I don't want them wasting more of their time, asking questions about me. I want them out there, trying to find Simon. Besides, why rely on them to make enquiries I can just as easily make myself?

I click on the website's Contact Us tab. A form pops up and I type out a short message for Dylan Lesley and hit submit.

21–11–2022

1.12 a.m.

He lights a cigarette, blows smoke out the window and fidgets with his lighter, snapping it open and closed, *flick-flick, flick-flick.*

'This podcast of yours,' he says. 'How many listeners has it got? A few hundred?'

Downloads are half what they once were, but that's all about to change. Soon *The Push* will be most downloaded podcast in the country, maybe even the world.

'More than that,' I say.

'Not much more, I'll bet.' He turns to me. 'The problem is, this whole thing – it's old news. Nobody cares anymore.'

He says it like he's sad for me, sorry that I've wasted all this time.

'Do you want to test that theory?' I say. 'I could still do it, if you like. Record a new episode, release it tomorrow. Tell them everything.'

'Everything?'

'The whole story.'

'Would you tell them you knew, but you chose to blackmail me for fifty grand instead of going to the police? How do you think that would play with your loyal listeners?'

He's talking like he's got some sort of leverage. As if my listeners – as if anybody – is going to believe a word he says once the truth comes out. I almost admire him for it. He's got nothing to work with, and he's still trying to shift the blame onto someone else.

'Any payment you make in exchange for me dropping the story

is fair compensation for the time I've spent working on it, don't you think?' I tell him. 'Unless, like I say, you'd rather do things differently? Because either way is fine with me.'

He looks like he's thinking it over, but I'd bet he's looking for a third option, a way he can come out of this with the money and his reputation.

'No . . .' he says. 'No, we stick to what we agreed.'

'You're sure?'

'I'm sure,' he says. 'People are brutal these days. You make one wrong comment on Twitter and they tear you apart. Last year, a bloke at work put his hand on a girl's back as he was passing her in the corridor – just being friendly, you know? Nothing meant by it. Next thing, she's complained to HR and he's clearing his desk. A twenty-year career, ruined, for what? Can you imagine what they'd do to me? They'd take away everything, starting with my job. I'd lose my home. Catherine, Sara. My *son*. That little boy . . . he's everything to me. The only truly good thing I have left. He's *mine*. Do you hear me? I'd rather burn it all down than lose my little boy. All because of some stupid podcast.'

As if the podcast is to blame. As if anyone's to blame but him.

He throws the rest of his cigarette out of the window.

'Let's get this over with,' he says.

22

Day Six

Sara

There is half a second of happy ignorance when Sara wakes, when the events of last night are so distant they might as well have happened to somebody else. Then all at once she remembers, and anger and sadness flood her system, picking up where they left off the night before.

She should have known.

The way he held so much of himself back, dipping in and out of her life when it suited, never inviting her to his home, or to meet his friends. She thought it was because he needed space, that he'd been hurt and wanted to take things slow. How stupid of her. It was never about that. It was because he has a wife and a child at home, a whole other life on the side.

Wait, that's not right. They're not the bit on the side. You are.

Right. They're the main event. She's just a distraction, the interval entertainment. No wonder he seemed to arrive late and leave early for everything, always changing their plans at the last minute.

Helen was right. He wasn't even that nice to her. Yes, he took her to fancy places, nice dinners and shows and swanky bars. But it was all on his terms. He was always the one in control.

Now that she thinks back, it seems as if all she can remember are little moments of control. Like the picnic, when he said she was being childish, or the times when he said she was being too needy. The clothes he said he preferred – which she made sure to wear when she saw him. The stud in her nose that she removed after he said she would look more professional at work without it. He was manipulating her, owning little pieces of her. Even the happy moments are spoiled now, because no matter how good they felt at the time, they weren't real. Not for him, at least.

God, how she hates him.

She reaches over to her bedside table, picks up her phone to dial his number and sees that she has a message from Brian: *You could at least have let me know if you weren't planning to turn up for work today.* Shit. What time is it? Nine thirty. She's already half an hour late. He probably thinks she's hungover again and can't face the commute. But there's no way she can go in today, not with her head in such a mess. She thinks about sending him some wild excuse – *Sorry, Brian. Hit by car, on life support* – but in the end opts for something more subtle that should keep him off her back for the rest of the day: *Sorry, Brian, gynaecological problems. Might be best if I stay home today.*

She hits send then calls Adam's number, hoping to catch him by surprise. She wants to explode at him, breathe fire on him. It rings twice, then goes through to voicemail: *The person you are trying to reach is not available—*

She hangs up, doesn't want to feel that she is shouting into a void.

For the rest of the morning she stalks around the flat, unable to sit, unable to stand, unable to do much of anything. She paces from room to room, propelled by her anger. She thinks about calling Helen, but isn't sure she can bring herself to explain what has happened, to hear the I-told-you-so in her bestfriend's voice.

I knew it! Didn't I say there was something off about him?

She isn't ready for that, couldn't bear to feel any more stupid than she already does. So she drinks coffee, smokes more cigarettes out of the kitchen window, and tries her hardest to resist breaking something. She searches for a distraction, anything to get Adam out of her head. She finds it in *The Push*, and in Dylan's soothing voice. Maybe this episode, released just two weeks ago, will be the one that explains how he tracked down the jogger?

Welcome, Push fans, to our latest episode. As always, I'm your host, Dylan Lesley. If this is the first time you're joining us, then we recommend you go back and . . . blah . . . blah . . . blah . . . You know the drill by now, right? Of course you do. So, sit back, relax, and enjoy a very special live episode of The Push, recorded in London just last month, where I sat down with a panel of experts to discuss the case.

Now, it's worth me saying that we had some technical difficulties at the start, so we're going to join the conversation at around the ten-minute mark. The voices you're about to hear alongside mine belong to body language expert Megan James, and the editor of the website, freethesheeple.com, Rik Johnson. And believe me when I say these two have very different takes on what really happened that day on London Bridge. I'll be back at the end with a brief update and a message from our sponsors. For now, enjoy . . .

'—sense of entitlement. You can see in the footage that his fists are clenched and his arms are at forty-five degree angles. He holds himself in a very determined manner, and this suggests to me someone who may well be a perfectionist. Perhaps someone very driven, in a high-powered, stressful career. His actions on the bridge could be seen as the equivalent of road rage . . . Pavement rage, if you will—'

'Rik, I see you're shaking your head there. You don't agree?'

'I see only two possibilities here, Dylan. You've got a man whose picture is all over the internet, and in all the papers, but nobody knows who he is? I don't buy it, not for one second. The question you have to ask yourself isn't why nobody recognises him – because without a doubt, plenty of people do. The question is: why is he being protected? And who is protecting him? To me, it's obvious. He knows things.

Classified things. I'm talking state secrets, UFOs, you name it. He's got collateral and they're frightened of what'll come out if he's put under the spotlight.'

'And the other possibility?'

'That this was nothing less than a state-sanctioned assassination attempt on sovereign soil. And in that case, it's less about who he is – likely CIA or FSB – and more about who she is.'

'But the police won't tell us. She's requested to remain anonymous.'

'And why might that be? What does she know? And why did they want her silenced—'

Sara turns off the podcast and rips out her headphones. What is she doing, listening to podcasts when her life is falling apart? Dylan's obviously fine. Find the London Bridge Jogger? He can barely record an episode of *The Push* without some sort of technical hitch, so the chances of him having got his act together enough to catch a wanted criminal are slim to none. This is all just a game to him, an opportunity to sell T-shirts and hoodies. There are, she concludes, much more important things to worry about.

She goes to her laptop, switches it on and brings up Simon's Facebook profile.

It's not as if she thinks a further look – sober, and in the cold light of day – will show her anything new, or might prove that Adam isn't really Simon after all. It is more that, right now, the scale of what has happened is too big to take in. It is planet-sized, so big it makes her feel like she must be going mad. Because it is madness, isn't it? Finding out that your boyfriend of nine months is secretly married with a child?

She clicks through one photo after another. There must be almost ten years' worth here. Plenty enough to build a picture in her mind of how Simon lives with his real family.

His wife's name is Catherine, their little boy's name is Charlie.

They have a big house on a Georgian terrace. Simon has photographs tagged with their location and most of them are in

South London, in or around Southwark or Borough, just fifteen minutes' walk from where Sara is sitting. The interior of their house is beautifully decorated and full of expensive furniture. The rooms have high ceilings and white walls, though the living room has one of those fancy-looking feature walls of richly coloured flock wallpaper, patterned royal blues and deep reds flecked with gold and silver. The kitchen has marble worktops and overhead spotlights, like something out of a cookery show. French doors open out on to a long garden with a luscious green lawn, perfect for a toddler to run around on.

Simon and Catherine are sociable types. They go to dinner parties with friends, have Sunday roasts in posh-looking pubs at the weekends with other mums and dads, buggies corralled around picnic benches in pub gardens. They went to the Proms last year. Holidayed in Florence two years ago; New York, the year before that. Croatia, the year before Charlie was born.

Charlie is four years old. He has his father's bright blue eyes. In all of the most recent photographs, he is clutching a plastic dinosaur and for his birthday, nine months ago, he was thrown a dinosaur-themed party and dressed up in a T-Rex onesie. There were dinosaur-shaped balloons and a dinosaur-shaped cake.

In most of the pictures of Charlie, he is with Catherine. She is often down at his level, on her knees or sprawled on carpet or on grass, surrounded by toys. And in all of the pictures, she is smiling, and not just for the camera. She smiles like she means it, like she can't help it. Her cheeks plump out, her lips part to expose a row of perfect top teeth, and her eyes turn into narrow slits. She looks happy. They all do.

Sara arrives at a fairly recent photograph. The Wells family at a picnic, tartan blanket spread out over the grass, a wicker hamper open by Catherine's knees.

He said he hated picnics. Said they were for kids.

Simon looks up into the lens and grins and Catherine does the same while Charlie dissolves into a fit of giggles between them.

Sara has a new sour taste at the back of her throat.

It is all so fucking unfair. They have everything and she has nothing.

If only his wife knew what he was really like. And what he has been up to these last nine months.

That would wipe the smiles off their faces.

23

Catherine

I text Jonathan the all-clear and ten minutes later he is standing outside the front door, a canvas doctor's bag hanging from his shoulder. His shirtsleeves are rolled up and his tie is skew-whiff, like he's just finished a hard day's work, though it is barely midday. Something stirs inside me, the memory of a feeling. To think I once had the energy to feel attracted to him, or to anybody, for that matter.

I usher him in off the doorstep.

The police think I lied to cover up something between us, which I did, but not in the way they think, and now they're watching. They'll see he's been here, on the . . . what do you call it? The things . . . the cameras. But I don't have a choice. I need to see him. At least Mum isn't here to make me feel bad. She has taken Charlie to the park to give me some time to myself.

'I was so sorry to hear about . . .' he says, the last few words obscured by the sound of the front door closing behind him. Still, I see a flash of Simon in the fire, the car filling with smoke and flames. The memory of a sound comes to me – that dreadful high-pitched scream from my dream – and my insides turn to ice.

'. . . came to see me.'

I shake the hallway back into focus.

'Sorry?'

'The police came to see me, at the surgery, told me what happened. They were asking all sorts of questions. Obviously, there wasn't much to tell, but I want you to know, I didn't say anything.' He widens his eyes. 'About us, I mean.'

A feeling like falling. I reach out a hand, steady myself against the wall.

'How are you coping?' he says, and I feel a flash of anger at him for asking such a stupid question – then catch myself. I mustn't let the tiredness do that to me; make me irritable and snappy. He's here now, that's all that matters.

'I've been better.' I move down the hall and into the living room. 'Mum's staying over, helping with Charlie. And Lydia has been brilliant, checking in every day. The police are . . . well, hopeless if you ask me, but they're around, if I need them. So . . .' I finish, standing by the fireplace on the opposite side of the room, arms folded.

'You've got support,' he says. 'That's good. And if there's anything I can do . . .'

'I need you to prescribe me something,' I say.

I could find what I need online. There are plenty of dodgy websites out there that sell prescription medication, without the prescription. But time is short, and I don't want to risk being ripped off, or being sent the wrong thing.

'I know I shouldn't ask, and if I was still registered it would be a different story, but I'm not, so will you give me something? Some . . .' What's it called? I had it before he arrived, knew precisely what I was going to ask for. 'Begins with an M . . .'

'Riiight,' he says, a long, drawn-out note of bewilderment. He looks down at the floor for a second, as if searching for something. 'So, that's why you asked me to come over?' he says, when he lifts his head.

I give him a look that says, *Why else?* As if I don't already know, as if our coffee shop chats and illicit text messages and kitchen table talks really were nothing, when some days, they were everything.

Sometimes, when Simon was away, or busy with clients every night of the week, meeting up with Jonathan was the only thing that kept me sane. And perhaps seeing me did the same for him. But none of that matters anymore. Whatever we were to each other was thrown into sharp perspective the moment the police told me my husband is missing, presumed dead.

'Sorry,' I say. That everything has changed. That we were something, but now we are nothing. That's just the way it has to be.

A weighty silence fills the space between us, full of potential – all the unsaid things that now must stay that way. Then Jonathan sets down his bag and comes to me, pulls me into a hug.

'It's OK,' he says. I lean into him, my face pressed against the warmth of his chest.

'I just need you to be my friend,' I say.

'Of course.'

I have never been more grateful for him. He is a good person, better than I deserve. He always has been.

We stay like that for a while. I let him hold me, calm me. I lose myself for a moment, then he pulls away, clears his throat. 'Now, what do you need?'

The prescription.

'I can't sleep,' I tell him.

'Ah.' His face softens and I know he's got the wrong idea. I don't blame him. He must hear those exact words spoken by a dozen patients every day.

'Sleep disturbance is extremely common for those who have suffered—' he begins.

'No,' I say. 'I don't mean that I need to sleep. I mean that I need to stay awake.'

He nods slowly, is in full-on doctor mode. 'And why is that, Cat? Why do you need to stay awake?'

'Because I have to find Simon. The police are useless, so I'm going to have to find him myself, but the tiredness . . . I can't focus, can't think straight. So will you give me something? Some . . .' Got it. 'Modafinil. Enough to keep me going for the next week or so, until I find him?'

Jonathan gives a small shake of the head. 'Have you talked to somebody about this?'

'Of course I have. I keep telling people there's been a mistake—'

'I didn't mean that. Cat, what you're experiencing here is perfectly normal. It's the mind's way of protecting you. The important thing to know is that help is available, there are people you can talk to. So, when you're ready, I can help you start that process.'

That's all I need. Another person who wants me to believe my husband is dead.

'Will you give me the drugs, or not?'

'Not,' he says. 'Drugs to keep you awake aren't the answer. What you need, for your mental and physical health, is sleep. Rest for your body, and for your mind. It's the best thing for you right now, and for Charlie, too.'

I had hoped for more from him. 'But what if Simon calls while I'm sleeping? What if he's in trouble and he calls again and I'm asleep and it's my last chance to speak to him . . .'

'Simon has *gone*, Cat. I know you don't want to hear that—'

'He's *missing*. My husband is missing, and nobody will listen to me when I tell them he's still out there and . . .' A wave of nausea comes out of nowhere, knocks me sideways. 'He's still . . . he's not . . .' I stagger backwards, sit down heavily on the sofa. A quivering, underwater version of Jonathan peers back at me, then rushes in.

'Catherine—'

'Don't—'

'Try and take deep breaths.'

'—touch me.'

'Just try and breathe.'

'He's not gone.'

'Nice and slow, Cat.'

'Simon . . . He's not gone. And *don't* call me that.'

'OK. OK.'

'Please . . . just go.'

'I want to help,' he says, a hand on my arm.

'Get off me!' He takes a step back, and the world steadies. Jonathan becomes himself again. Real. Solid. Here.

'You can't not sleep,' he says. 'You can already see what it's doing to you. There are no two ways about it: you don't sleep, and you'll . . .'

'I know full well what happens, Jonathan.'

'Do you? People who don't sleep fall to pieces, Cat. The neurons in their brain stop firing properly. They experience coordination problems, memory problems. Become irritable and paranoid. They hallucinate. Micro-sleep while driving and swerve into oncoming traffic, nod off while giving their toddler a bath and wake up to find them dead in three inches of water. And if you don't sleep for long enough . . .' He stops, a little breathless, takes off his glasses and pinches the bridge of his nose between thumb and forefinger. 'How many days now, since you last slept?'

I shrug. 'A few.'

Five. It is five days since I last slept.

He goes to his bag, opens it. 'I'm not going to prescribe you drugs to keep you awake. What I'm going to do is give you something to help you sleep. I know this is an awful time for you, but get some rest. I'm not saying everything will be better after a good night's sleep, but you may be better equipped to handle it.'

He takes out his prescription pad from his bag and a pen from his inside coat pocket, scrawls quickly over the paper and rips off the page.

'I'll leave it here, shall I?' He folds the prescription neatly in half and puts it on the mantelpiece. 'Look, if Simon is out there, I'm sure the police will find him. Right now, the best thing you can do is look after yourself, stay strong, for you and for Charlie. I'm sure that's what Simon would have wanted, too.'

The sound of Simon's name on his lips is an obscenity. Something explodes, black and red at the back of my mind.

'How dare you tell me what my husband would want.'

'I'm trying to help you—'

'Get out!' I shout.

He does. Closes his bag, picks it up and leaves, and I am left sitting alone in the living room, still dizzied, still burning bright with anger.

Jonathan is wrong, I know he is.

Do you? Because it's been five days now. Five days since Simon went missing . . .

Quiet. Hush. Jonathan is wrong. Sleep isn't going to help me find Simon.

I take out my phone, go through the usual checks. Nothing from Simon. And nothing back from the host of *The Push*, either. So I'll go and speak to him in person, and I'll do it tonight. Because I know exactly where he is going to be.

24

Sara

She knows from the Facebook posts that Simon and his wife live close by. There are too many pictures of cafés and pubs and parks in the area for them not to be living in Southwark or Borough. But that means they could be anywhere between Tower Bridge in the East and Waterloo in the West. She needs an address.

It's the burner phone she reaches for first. The battery has died, so she spends fifteen minutes searching the flat for a cable that fits. Eventually she finds one, plugs the phone in, waits a few minutes, then powers it up. She is reminded of how few apps it has on it. Just the basics, like it was fresh out of the box. No Uber, no Deliveroo, no Amazon, nothing she might be able to get his real address from. She opens the messages and thumbs through them.

Adam and Simon are the same person. Why would he use a burner phone to send threatening messages to himself? It doesn't make sense. Could he have been trying out the messages on himself, before sending them on to the intended recipient? That doesn't make sense, either. Unless . . . he was trying to make it *look* like he was being threatened. Has she stumbled across another scam of his? A way to make himself look like the victim, when he is actually the perpetrator? Because that's what he did to her, isn't it? Lots of times. She pictures him with his head down, eyes puppyish.

I don't deserve you, I'm not good enough for you . . .

People like him – City boys, banker types – are experts at

manipulation. They'll do anything to get what they want, even if it means trampling over other people. He's probably up to his neck in dodgy deals and insider trading. The sort of white-collar crime that should see him locked up for years. But people like him, white, middle-aged and middle-class, also have a habit of getting away with things. Even if she took the phone to the police – which she won't, because Helen said unlocking someone's phone without their permission was illegal – and they found out he'd been up to all sorts, he'd probably talk his way out of it. Walk away with a slap on the wrist.

No, the best way to get back at him is to hit him on the home front. Hopefully, once his wife finds out what he's been up to, she'll want a divorce. Take him for half of everything. Then maybe he really will end up living in a squalid little place in Farnham, or Farnborough, wherever the hell he said it was.

She double-checks the rest of the phone, just to make sure there's nothing else on it that might help her track down his address, and finds nothing new, apart from one solitary file in a folder called Backup. It's an audio file, a long one, too, judging from the size of it. It doesn't have a proper name, just a random-looking collection of numbers. She hits play, the screen dims, a media window appears, and the track begins to play.

Nothing. Just dead air. She pushes the timeline on with her thumb, just to be certain. Five minutes, ten, twenty. She lets go.

Music. A low-quality recording of some band or other, the vocalist doing a bad Bowie impersonation over jangling guitars and honking synths.

He sings: '*. . . falling to pieces without you. Whatever it was I did wrong, I'll take it all back if you want . . . Oh, baby don't leave me so blue . . .*'

The quality of the audio makes it sound like it was recorded off the radio. She has a brief recollection of Adam telling her he used to do that when he was kid, tape songs off the radio. She teased him about it.

'So you could listen to them on your Walkman?'

'Yes, actually,' he said. 'We didn't have iTunes or Spotify back then, and I couldn't afford to buy the latest singles. If I wanted to own a song, I'd have to record it using my tape player on Sunday afternoons, hold the microphone up to the speaker and press record at just the right moment.'

'Oh. My. God.'

'What?'

'You are *so* old.'

This is undoubtedly not one of those recordings, because who would bother to digitise old tapes of songs recorded off the radio a hundred years ago? But it is something like that, and it is the kind of music he likes. Old person music, from the 90s.

The singer launches into another verse: '*I'm a broken watch, last ticked when you walked away. A stopped clock, right twice, wrong a thousand times a day . . .*'

Sara presses stop. She doesn't want to listen to any of Adam's music anymore. Or Simon's music.

Forget the phone.

She turns to her computer and searches for how to find someone's address. In the end it is surprisingly easy. She arrives at 192.com, enters the name Simon Wells and the location London in the search bar. Forty people named Simon Wells are returned as living in the area. Each listing shows a possible age range, the start of a postcode and the first names of other people in the same household. Sara clicks to view the full record on the first entry and a registration form appears. The website tells her that for a small fee she can make up to twelve searches a month and access the full details of everyone on the electoral roll. All she needs to do now is look for a Simon Wells who lives in Borough, or Southwark, with a Catherine and a Charlie.

She goes and gets her credit card.

25

Catherine

'Are we going home now, Mummy?' Charlie asks. 'I'm cold.'

I crouch down in front of him. 'Let's make sure you're wrapped up nice and warm.' I put his hood up and make sure his coat – the one with the pin badge secured to its breast – is buttoned all the way to the top.

'Want to go home now,' he says. 'It's dark.'

It is just after 9 p.m., but it's not *dark* dark, given we are in busy central London, at the location of tonight's live recording of *The Push*. The streets are ablaze with neon signs that shimmer and blur when I try to focus on them, and the bars and clubs are all lit up and overflowing. And it's not as if Charlie is afraid of the dark – he doesn't even sleep with a night light on. But it is long past his bedtime. Ideally, I'd have left him with Mum, but she is at her prayer group tonight and won't be back until after ten. Besides, according to *The Push* website, tonight is the last of Dylan's live events. Tomorrow he could be anywhere.

'I know it's dark, love. But we'll go in a bit,' I tell him. 'Mummy needs to speak to a man first. It won't take long.'

'What man?'

'A man in there.' I point to the pub across the road.

According to the website, tonight's live recording of *The Push* was due to start at 8.30 p.m., followed by a DJ set from Dylan Lesley at 10 p.m. A little past nine and the windows of the pub are full of shifting shadows, and the music – a terrible heavy-metal racket – is so loud I can feel it thumping through the soles of my shoes. The live recording must have finished early and the DJ set has already started. Which means Dylan Lesley is inside the pub playing records, right now.

The Royal George is an awful place, the exterior walls covered in posters for bands, layer upon layer, as if the building were made of nothing but torn scraps of paper. Some of the customers have spilled out of the front door to fill a row of grey weathered picnic benches. Mostly young goth types. Lots of tattoos and piercings. Tall men with long hair, dressed head-to-toe in black leather, some of it covered in metal studs. Tough-looking girls in heavy eyeliner, clutching pint glasses and smoking. At the fringes of the crowd, two shifty-looking men in hoodies glance over their shoulders while they exchange wads of cash for little packets of God knows what.

Am I really going to take Charlie into a place like that? It doesn't even look like they could record a podcast in there. Perhaps that's why it finished early. Maybe it was too loud and they skipped the recording and have gone straight to the DJ set? Or perhaps I got the time wrong. It did say it started at 8.30 p.m., didn't it? Not 6.30 p.m?

Still, we're here now.

'Five minutes, that's all. I promise,' I tell Charlie. 'Once I've spoken to the man we can go home, OK?'

His chin dimples. 'I don't want to go in there,' he says.

That makes two of us.

I wish Lydia was here. She is stuck in Manchester, courtesy of British Rail – or whoever runs the bloody trains these days. *Sorry,* she texted back when I asked if she could come with me tonight. *God knows what time I'll be back in civilisation, will call if not too late. Thinking of you x*

'I know, love,' I tell Charlie. 'But I'll carry you, and you can keep your eyes closed the whole time—'

'But I don't *want* to—'

'Look! I brought Daddy's headphones for you to wear, see?'

I have an old pair of Simon's headphones with me that are ridiculously oversized on Charlie but that he loves to wear. We used to laugh when he put them on. Simon said it made him look like the cutest little fighter pilot in the world. I take them out of my bag, plug them into my phone and select a *Peppa Pig* compilation, songs about busy rabbits and silly Daddy Pigs. When I try to put the headphones on for him, he twists his head away.

'Charlie, please. For Mummy. Just for five minutes?'

'Don't want to!'

'And on the way home you can play games on Mummy's phone.'

He considers the offer, then nods, and this time he lets me put the headphones on for him.

'There's a good boy.' I make sure the volume isn't too high and press play, then pull up his hood and we are ready to go.

Across the road a bouncer stands guard, red forearms crossed over his barrel chest. I watch and wait, hoping he'll leave the door unattended at some point, but he stays exactly where he is, and after another five minutes I decide that we have waited long enough. It is dark and cold, and I am tired – so very tired. I can't let anything stop me from speaking to Dylan Lesley.

I scoop Charlie up and march across the road. I don't even look at the bouncer, I walk straight past him as if he weren't there, as if there were nothing amiss whatsoever in me, dressed in my winter coat and carrying a four-year-old, walking into that pub.

'She have a kid with her?' a voice behind me says. I don't stop to see who it belongs to. I step into the darkness and push my way into the crowd.

Inside, it is very dark but for the flash of neon lights, and the music is terribly loud. The floor is sticky underfoot, the air thick with the smell of body odour and alcohol. In spite of all this, the place is filled to capacity. People are wedged in shoulder to shoulder, three rows deep at the two bars either side of the long room, or gathered in little pockets, filling every available inch of floor space. We edge our way through the throng one small step at a time, squeeze our way through the crowd of broad backs covered in faded leather, until we arrive at a solid wall of human bodies, a traffic jam of people holding too many drinks in too few hands.

'Excuse me? Can you let me through?' I try. 'Hello? Can I get past, please?' But nobody acknowledges me and nobody moves. I might as well be invisible.

I stand on tiptoe, scan the room for the DJ. There, at the far side of the pub, in a little booth at the end of a packed dance floor. His lank hair hangs down over his face and he has one arm raised, fist pumping the air. In front of him, twenty or so people are dancing like maniacs, limbs flailing, bodies smashing together as if they're trying to hurt each other.

How on earth am I supposed to get through that?

Movement in front of us, thank God. An opening appears and I push on, use my free arm to carve a route through the crowd.

'Sorry, *sorry*. Can I get through? Please, let me through—'

I shove and elbow until we reach the edge of the dance floor. The music is louder here, pumping out of two giant speakers either side of the DJ booth. The bass thumps through my body. Feels like it is doing something unpleasant to my insides.

It will only be for a few minutes, I tell myself. Get across the dance floor, speak to the DJ. Find out if he saw Simon last week, ask if he'll put out an appeal to his listeners, and then we can go.

I hold Charlie that bit tighter, press his face into my collar, and step onto the dance floor.

The crowd heaves around me, smashes into me. Limbs thrash, lasers flicker. Stuttering lights burn my retinas, and all the while that dreadful thumping music deafens me, passes through me, shakes my bones. Leering shadows surround me. Hands claw at my clothes. Teeth and eyes flash in the darkness. Someone charges into me, clips my shoulder hard enough to make me almost lose my grip on Charlie.

This is madness.

It is, but I can't turn around now. The DJ is right there. He is only ten feet away from me . . . seven feet . . .

Charlie should be at home, in bed.

But we are so close. A few more steps and we'll be in front of the DJ and he'll be able to help us. For once, somebody will be able to help us.

You're going to hurt his ears; the lights are going to blind him.

He has his eyes closed and he has his daddy's headphones on

and . . . look . . . we're here now. We've made it and it's going to be OK. We have arrived at the booth and Dylan Lesley is right in front of me. He has his head down and his headphones on, eyes fixed on the turntables, hands darting about, fiddling with knobs and sliders.

'Excuse me,' I shout. When he doesn't look up, I try again. 'Ex-*cuse* me.' I wave my free hand to catch his attention. He lifts his head, parts the curtain of his black hair with one hand, looks at me, then at Charlie. The smile drops from his face.

'I need to speak to you,' I mouth.

He shakes his head, points to his headphones.

'*I need to speak to you*,' I holler.

Another shake of the head. This is pointless. I start to look for a way to access the booth. There must be a set of steps somewhere. I begin to move around the side, when a hand grips my shoulder.

The bouncer must have caught up with me.

I get ready to explain that I only need a minute, that I just need to ask the DJ a few questions, then I'll leave. But when I turn around, it isn't the bouncer with the bald head and the squashed nose standing behind me. It's Detective Carter.

26

Catherine

Charlie is asleep, curled up on the back seat beside me, the soles of his trainers pressed against my thigh. I, on the other hand, am wide awake. Alert in a way I haven't been in days. Right now the world is pin-sharp and full of detail.

Rain is a drum solo on the roof.

Outside, the lights of Soho. Hulking red buses. The blare of horns from black cab drivers. Theatres like ramshackle palaces. Starbursts of neon. The Strand. Waterloo Bridge.

Inside, the car smells of takeaways and leather.

The two detectives sit up front in sullen silence. I suppose they're annoyed, because I didn't tell them about the badge and Dylan Lesley. They must have worked it out somehow, why else would they have been there? But it is five days since Simon went missing – *five whole days* – and they have had so little to tell me about what has happened to him.

Did they think I wouldn't do whatever I could to find my missing husband? The father of my child?

I lean forward and my seatbelt pulls tight across my chest.

'What did he say? Was Simon there? Did he see him? What happens now?'

If Simon was there that night, then people must have seen him. They'll need to interview everybody. There'll be new CCTV footage to go through. They should be able to work out what time Simon left The Pit, if he was alone or with somebody. If he was followed, even.

My head buzzes and my heart leaps at the implications. This is how we're going to find Simon, I just know it is.

DI Carter turns in the passenger seat, her neat ponytail whipping behind her. She has a peculiar expression on her face, as if I've just spoken to her in a foreign language.

'Catherine, we talked about this already,' she says. 'We went through all this, back at the pub.'

We did?

There is a bright flash in the corner of my vision. A passing headlight. Or some electrical impulse, misfiring at the back of my brain.

We did talk about it. I remember now.

The scene comes back to me in pieces: Detective Carter escorting us through the crowd at the Royal George. The drinkers and smokers side-eyeing DC Chaudhari as he stood with us outside in the rain. I remember Charlie starting to cry and Chaudhari leading us to the patrol car, the three of us waiting inside while Carter made her enquiries. Fifteen agonising minutes passed before she came out. I heard a wolf whistle as she opened the passenger door, and a voice, presumably belonging to one of the smokers hanging outside the pub, said, 'All right, love?'

'Fuck off,' Carter said. There was a shower of laughter, then she was sliding in, closing the door and telling me the DJ wasn't Dylan Lesley, because he didn't turn up to host his own podcast event tonight. The man in the booth was a last-minute replacement.

You're sure it wasn't him?

The manager confirmed it, and his ID checked out.

Then where is he? Where's Dylan Lesley? Is he missing, too?

Catherine, calm down. I'm sure it's nothing to worry about. We'll talk to him. OK?

'Like I said,' Carter tells me now, 'we're already looking for him, and once we track him down, we'll see what he has to say for himself. If he knows anything about what happened to Simon, then *we* will find out. Leave the police work to us from now on, right?'

I sit back in my seat. 'Right. Yes, sorry.'

It is all there now. I can remember everything that happened after Carter found us at the edge of the dance floor, but until she reminded me, there was . . . nothing. A black hole.

It's the lack of sleep. My brain's ability to store and recall memories is declining, the connections between my short- and long-term memory no longer firing properly. I think back to the sleep-deprived patients I used to see at the surgery, how I would have to go over things again and again to make them stick. That's what's happening to me. Things are no longer sticking.

Are there other things I have forgotten? God, I hope not.

Five minutes later, DC Chaudhari turns the car into Cavendish Square. He parks up in front of the house, gets out and takes Charlie from the back seat, lifts him up onto his shoulder. I'm grateful for that much at least. I'm not sure I have the strength to carry Charlie right now. As Chaudhari heads for the front door, Carter unclips her seatbelt and turns in her seat.

'Catherine,' she says, 'listen to me.'

The dashboard is awash with amber light, but DI Carter is made of shadow.

'What you did tonight, taking Charlie to that place, it's not acceptable.'

A telling-off. I thought one might be coming.

'Yes, I know,' I say. 'And I'm sorry. I wouldn't dream of taking Charlie somewhere like that usually – it's just that . . . Well, you know.'

The badge, the podcast. Dylan Lesley. Someone had to do the detective work.

She blows out a stream of air, as if she is trying very hard to keep her temper in check.

'I've got a little boy myself, about Charlie's age,' she says.

'You have?' I'm surprised, didn't have her down as the mum type, with her perfect ponytail and pristine pencil skirt. 'My little boy's safety is my number one priority, always. And if I started to behave like it wasn't, then I'd hope someone would pull me aside and give me a bloody good talking-to. Do you understand? Because what happened tonight, it can't happen again.'

'Yes. Like I was saying, I wouldn't usually—'

She ignores me. 'I need to be sure that Charlie is safe with you.'

Of course Charlie is safe with me – of *course* he is.

'It was a silly thing to do,' I say. 'A one-off, I swear.'

'And what happened in the car back there? You're disorientated, forgetting things, making poor choices. You look like you aren't taking care of yourself, and I know this is a very difficult time for you, but if I think that you aren't taking care of your little boy, then I'm duty-bound to take it further. Do you hear me?'

My stomach drops.

She is talking about contacting social services, about taking away my baby.

'He is safe with me, I promise he is,' I cry. 'I'm his mum.'

The possibility that I could lose Charlie . . . It is unthinkable.

Carter's shadow doesn't move, and although it is too dark to see her features, I can feel the cold weight of her gaze pressing on me. I deserve it. How awful of me, taking Charlie to that horrible place. What was I thinking?

'I'm sorry,' I say. 'I'll never do anything like that ever again. I promise.'

A moment of quiet, then the shadow in the passenger seat shifts.

'Good,' Carter says.

I get out of the car and scurry to the front door.

DC Chaudhari must have handed Charlie over to Mum, because he is empty-handed as he passes me on the way back to the car. 'G'night, Mrs Wells,' I hear him say. I can't bear to look him in the eye.

I keep my head down and don't lift it until I am at the door. Mum is there waiting for me, stood in the hall with her arms folded, her lips a thin white line.

21–11–2022

1.17 a.m.

He tells me that he was at the launch party for *The Push*, and I make out like it was the most audacious move in history, like he's some sort of criminal genius.

'I can't believe it,' I say. 'Weren't you worried someone would recognise you?'

'It was a rush,' he says, which makes sense. It's not quite returning to the scene of the crime, but it's not far off. He continues, 'We had a little conversation, you and I, do you remember? I even wished you luck catching the bastard. And then you tried to flog me a T-shirt and I knew, in that exact moment, I was safe. You were more interested in selling merch than catching me.'

I want to ask him how that worked out for him, but he's on a roll now, so I let him keep talking.

'That was the night I met Sara,' he says. 'She told me she was a colleague of yours, asked what I did for a living. Of course, I had no intention of telling the truth, so I made something up. Told her I worked at a start-up. Didn't think it would matter. Pretty young women are rarely interested in what middle-aged men have to say for themselves. But for some reason, she kept talking to me and I could tell she liked me. It occurred to me it might be useful to have someone on the inside, someone close to this podcast business, who could help me keep tabs on you, just in case. That's when I came up with Adam.'

'A whole new identity, just to keep an eye on me?'

'That was part of it.'

'And the other part?'

'Adam was a chance to be someone different. And the more I pretended to be him, the more real he felt. I mean, he isn't me – but he is me at the same time. He was a chance to start again, I suppose. You ever think like that? Ever wish you could start over?'

'Can't say I do.'

He smiles. 'You're young. You haven't made any mistakes yet. Get to my age, look in the mirror, and all you see is the bad things you've done. They're like . . . scars only you can see. Every year there's more of them, and you get uglier and uglier, and you wish you could go back and do things differently, but you can't.' He takes a breath. 'I liked Sara. Young, attractive. I liked how she made me feel. But the chance to start over? That's what I really wanted.'

27

Day Seven

Catherine

The jacket, the badge, the rucksack, the podcast. Dylan Lesley going missing. It all means something, but what? I can't keep my thoughts straight. Moments of clarity come, but are brief. When they end, it isn't with a tailing off or a slipping away, but a sudden, jolting awareness that I've lost the thread, minutes, perhaps hours ago.

Start again, Cat. I tell myself. *Concentrate. Go back to the beginning.*

The jacket, the badge, the rucksack, the podcast . . .

I sit at the kitchen table for most of the night, watch Charlie doze on the baby monitor. Even if I wanted to sleep, I don't think I could. I'm not sure I know how to turn my brain off anymore, though it's not exactly switched on, either.

At some point I hear the soft clunk of the front door opening and closing. My heart jumps and I get up and go and stand in the hall, listen hard in the dark. Of course, it's nothing. There's nobody there. Simon has not come home—

Because he's never coming home—

Shut up.

It's the tiredness, making me imagine things. Forget things. Stealing words out of my mouth.

I am not myself.

I head upstairs. As I walk past Charlie's room, I hear him calling out in his sleep. Perhaps he is missing Simon in his dreams? I should go and comfort him, but the shame of what I did tonight is too much. Taking him to that place. Perhaps he'd be better off without me. For tonight, at least, I'll let Mum take care of it.

I go to the bedroom and get under the covers. Am reminded anew of the chill of a half-empty bed and the hollow in my chest.

God, I miss him.

His smile and his smell. Our rows and our make-up hugs. The sound of him moving around the house, of him coming home after a long day at work, putting his bag down in the hall and hanging his jacket up with a sigh. I miss knowing he is with me, even when we are apart.

Eventually the birds start calling across the square and dawn draws a hazy purple line between the curtains. The bedroom grows lighter, illuminating the happy mess of Simon's things. Clothes spilling out of the laundry basket, his work trousers draped over the back of a chair. A pair of dirty socks balled up in the corner. It's the only room of the house Mum hasn't cleaned, and I want to keep it that way.

Movement on the baby monitor.

Charlie stirs, balls up his fists to rub his eyes. He calls for me, and I am awash with relief. I drag myself up out of bed and go to him. Mum intercepts me in the hall, emerges from the spare room in her dressing gown. My vision isn't good this morning. My eyes prick and sting. Mum is blurry at the edges. Ghostly. I wipe the gunk out of my eyes, try to bring her into focus.

'Morning, darling. Did you get some sleep?' The residue of last night's anger gives her voice a wavering edge.

'A little.'

I'm not sure sleep is the right word for those moments I drifted away. Not asleep, but not awake, either.

'Oh, good for you.' She looks down the hall towards Charlie's room. 'Why don't you get a few more hours? I can see to him, if you like?' She isn't a good enough actress to pull it off, can't inject the right level of softness into her voice to make me think she is offering out of kindness, rather than looking for an opportunity to keep me away from my own son.

Tread carefully, Mum.

'It's OK. I can do it,' I say.

'You're sure?'

'I'm sure.' *Leave it, Mum.*

She doesn't retreat and, in the end, I have to step around her to get to Charlie's room. She follows and, as I say good morning to Charlie and get him up and dressed, I feel the weight of her gaze on my back. After what happened last night, she wants to make sure I'm capable of looking after him.

I go through his drawers, find underpants, trousers, T-shirt and jumper. Those things for his feet. What are they called again?

Socks, stupid. How are you supposed to look after him if you can't even remember what socks are?

He missed his bath last night, thanks to me, so I give him a quick wash at the bathroom sink and put on his underwear. He shoots his arms in the air so I can put on his T-shirt and jumper. I must do a good enough job because, once Charlie is dressed, Mum claps her hands and says, 'I'll make us some breakfast,' and I hear her soft footsteps on the stairs.

I lift Charlie down off the bed, set him on his feet.

'Ready for some breakfast?' I say. He nods earnestly, then beckons me to bend down close.

'What is it?' I ask him.

'I've got a secret,' he whispers. He likes secrets.

'You do? What sort?'

He presses a finger to his lips.

I am too tired to be playing games. 'Well, you can tell Mummy, because Mummy promises not to tell anybody else, so that makes it a double secret, doesn't it. Which is even more secret.'

Shaky logic, but good enough for a four-year-old.

'Daddy came to see me last night,' he says, 'but you can't tell anybody.'

'He did?' Poor Charlie. He is missing his daddy, even when he's dreaming. 'And what did Daddy say?'

'He said he was going to take me on holiday.'

'Aww, well isn't that nice? Come on,' I say, 'let's go and see what Grandma has made for breakfast.'

I hold Charlie's hand and we go down the stairs together, one slow step at a time. When we reach the bottom, he races off to the kitchen while I pause. Something is different in the hallway. Out of place. Simon's running shoes aren't by the door anymore. They've been cleared away, too.

Charlie asks me to take his favourite dinosaur colouring book down off the shelf, but when I go to get it for him it isn't there.

'It must be with your other things,' I tell him, but he shakes his head, near tears.

'Daddy put it on the shelf,' he insists.

'Why don't you play with your fossil instead?' I say, by which I mean the replica dinosaur tooth Simon bought him from the shop at the Natural History Museum. It's about an inch long, the colour of dark stone and surprisingly heavy. We keep it on a high shelf, not because it is valuable but because it is small and a little sharp along one edge. Charlie could easy lose it, or damage the furniture with it, though he usually just likes to hold it and look at it.

I take it down and it's then that I notice that the binder we keep our most important documents in is upside down. Mum must have reorganised the bookshelves. Just one more way she can feel like she is helping, without actually doing anything helpful.

'Mummy?' Charlie tugs at my sleeve.

'Remember to be careful. T-Rex fossils aren't easy to come by.' I hand him the plastic envelope with the replica tooth in it without looking, feel him take it from me.

'It's a Baryonyx tooth, Mummy,' he says as he walks away, as if I'm an idiot.

I flick through the binder's contents. Charlie's birth certificate, the deeds to the house, copies of our wills, our marriage certificate . . . Everything is here as it should be, everything but our passports. I set the binder on the table, go through it again to make sure they aren't hidden between other papers.

Simon's, mine, Charlie's. They're all gone.

Perhaps the police took them? They carried away so many things in such a short space of time. It's possible they would have taken Simon's passport, but I don't remember telling them where it was kept. Even if they did, what reason would they have for taking mine, or Charlie's?

I call out, 'Mum?'

'Yes, darling?' A moment, then the door opens and Mum appears, polish and duster in hand. She looks down at the open binder on the dining table. 'Have you lost something, love?'

She sounds innocent enough. But then, she would, wouldn't she?

'Mum, have you moved our passports?' She screws up her face, as if perplexed by the question. 'I always keep them in this binder, and they're not here.'

A bemused shake of the head. 'You must have moved them and forgotten about it.'

'No,' I say. 'I really don't think I have.'

I haven't, have I? Yesterday I lost fifteen minutes at the Royal George – but this is different. There is absolutely no reason I would move our passports. None.

Mum takes a breath. 'Nobody has moved your passports,' she says. 'I *certainly* haven't. How could I? I didn't even know where you kept them.'

True, she wouldn't know our passports are all kept together in the blue folder. But she could have found them, if she'd taken the time to look. Last night, when I heard a noise and stood in the hall, listening in the dark – what if that was Mum, going through our things?

'Why would you do that, Mum?' I say, trying to keep my voice calm for Charlie's sake.

She folds her arms over her chest. 'Catherine . . .'

'They were right here. *Somebody* has taken them.'

'I do not deserve this. Really, I don't.'

'It's not about who deserves what. It's a matter of facts. Somebody has moved our passports. It wasn't me, and it can't have been Charlie because he isn't tall enough to reach.'

'So it must have been me?' she says.

A moment of loaded silence.

Yes, it must have been you. It can't have been Simon because he is still missing, and nobody else has been here apart from the police, and I was in the room with them the whole time. So it must have been you.

'If you give me five minutes, I'll help you look for them,' she says, then she turns and heads back to the kitchen.

Did she take them because she thinks I'm going to take Charlie away, or because *she's* planning to take him away? That makes more sense. If she had my passport, I wouldn't be able to follow. Has she been speaking to the detectives? There was that five minutes yesterday, when DC Chaudhari brought Charlie inside and I was sitting in the car with Detective Carter . . .

Or perhaps Jonathan spoke to them? He seemed angry and upset when he left. Might he have decided to get back at me by speaking to the police and telling them he thought Charlie wasn't safe with me? It doesn't seem like him, but men can be so unpredictable when they don't get what they want.

I know I'm tired, but I'm not insane. Things really are going missing, people really are watching the house.

Somebody is out to get us – me and Charlie – I'm sure of it.

I move over to the window, part the curtains and look out across the square.

In the residents' garden, a couple are sat side by side on a bench, facing the house. They are dressed in the uniform of the well-to-do, him in a pair of bright red slacks, her in a flowery headscarf, like something the Queen might have worn. Matching Barbour jackets and wellingtons. They fit right in. Look exactly like the sort of people you might expect to find sitting on a bench in Cavendish Square, and I mean *exactly*. They're too perfect, like actors playing the part of people who might live here. I don't recall seeing either of them before, don't remember them from any of the residents' association meetings. I watch them talking to each other, see their lips moving, wonder if they are talking about me. Or if they are only pretending to talk. They look old, but are they too old to be undercover police officers?

You're being paranoid, Cat.

Am I? Because DI Carter turned up at the Royal George last night and not even Mum knew I was going there, which means they must have been watching me. Following me, even.

A thump and a clatter on the other side of the room, followed by a cry from Charlie.

'In a minute, love,' I say.

It makes sense. They don't trust me. They think Simon is dead and that I was going behind his back with Jonathan. I wouldn't be surprised if they have me down as a suspect in his disappearance.

From somewhere far away, I hear Charlie crying. He has probably dropped his fossil down the back of the sofa.

'Didn't I tell you to be careful?' I say.

They must be worried sick I'm going to make a run for it, take Charlie and jump on a plane and disappear into the sunset. How infuriating. They're wasting all this time watching me, instead of trying to find Simon.

Charlie tugs at my sleeve.

'Yes, I know, love. I'll get it in a minute—'

Simon's disappearance is something to do with the podcast, I'm sure of it. Something to do with Dylan Lesley, too. Last night, they were so calm about it all, but if he has gone missing—

There is a rush of air. Mum is suddenly beside me.

'Catherine! What are you doing? He's hurt. He's *hurt*!' she shouts.

I am shocked back into the room.

I look down.

Charlie isn't whimpering because he has lost his fossil. He is holding out his hand to show me where it hurts. Blood is pouring from his fingers, streaming down his arm. He emits an ear-piercing cry that cuts right to the heart of me.

I look around the room, see the fossil tossed aside on the floor. Charlie must have cut himself on it.

Mum scoops him up, hurries to the kitchen.

'Why weren't you watching him?' she says, as she carries Charlie over to the sink and sits him on the counter.

'I was,' I say. 'I *was*.' She doesn't even acknowledge the lie. She turns on the tap, lets the water run cold.

'Let me see,' she says to Charlie. 'I know it hurts, but let Grandma see.'

I try to tease Charlie's arms apart so we can get a look at his injured hand, but he squirms away from me, holds himself tighter.

'I think . . . you should give us some space,' Mum says.

Some space? He's my little boy.

'But I'm his mum,' I say.

She fixes me with a withering glare. 'Then for God's sake, start acting like it.' And she thrusts his bloody hand under the running water.

28

Sara

A couple dressed in matching quilted jackets and wellingtons are leaving Cavendish Square's residents' garden when Sara arrives. They walk arm in arm, offer her a polite smile that doesn't quite reach their eyes. Perhaps they're looking at her that way because they can tell – by her H&M padded parka and her lace tights and the stud through her nose – that she is not a resident of the square, and therefore not strictly allowed in the gardens. Or maybe it's something else. She can't help but feel exposed, as if everybody she passes on the street *knows*. How could they not? People must be able to tell just from the way she walks. They must be able to smell it on her like perfume. She's a fool. An easy mark. Always has been.

Once the couple have passed by, she catches the still-swinging wrought-iron gate leading to the gardens before it shuts. Inside, she sinks down behind the collar of her coat, walks the gravel track between the trees until she finds a wooden bench, not quite opposite, but with a good view of the house.

It looks like all of the other houses in the square. Beautiful. Pristine.

The brickwork of the ground floor is painted bright white. Grey stone steps lead up to a black front door with shining brass fittings. Two cars are parked out front. A BMW and a Range Rover. Posh people cars. Sara looks for signs of activity, but the day is bright and the windows of the house are full of reflections.

This is where Adam lives.

Simon.

With his wife, and his son.

Not some poky bachelor pad in the middle of nowhere, the fictional apartment he couldn't bear to have her visit, but here, in this beautiful square, with its rows of uniform houses and an old-fashioned red telephone box on the corner. A version of London straight out of a Richard Curtis film, where everybody is terribly uptight, stuttering their way through perfectly cosy middle-class lives.

Is she really going to tear it all apart? Because that's what's going to happen the moment she knocks on that door. Everything will change—

People are going to get hurt.

Why should you be the only one?

She wipes her eyes with the sleeve of her coat, looks away from the house and down at her feet. She runs a hand over the wood of the bench, finds a screw not quite flush, its edge cold and sharp, and presses the pad of her thumb against it until the metal bites.

Being here, seeing his real home, twists something inside her she thought couldn't be turned any tighter. Why would he decide to fuck up her life, when he has all this?

It is beyond cruel.

They were going to build a life together. Renting a flat would have been the first step. Then buy somewhere, once she was earning proper money, start thinking about raising a family. That's what Adam said.

She removes her thumb from the screw and looks at the red and white cross etched into her skin. She squeezes the wound against her index finger until a line of blood emerges and her thumb throbs.

How can she have been so stupid? She promised herself when she left home she would never let herself be mistreated like that ever again. And yet . . . here she is.

Shame thickens in her throat, threatens to overwhelm the anger that has brought her here. But she is not the one to blame. *Simon* is. He never loved her, was never going to move in with her. She was nothing but a B-side to him. He is the worst kind of person and she is going to be a thousand times better off without him. Everyone would be better off without Simon Wells in their life. And that's why she must tell his wife what kind of a person her husband really is. She deserves to know. And as for him? He deserves everything he gets.

She looks up at the house.

He's probably in there, right this second. Playing happy families and waiting for the right moment to sneak away so he can text her, tell her how sorry he is for not replying to her messages, certain that he can worm his way back into her good books, and back into her bed.

His wife deserves to know. And he deserves everything he gets.

She is going to do this. Walk right up to that front door, ring the bell and tell Simon's wife exactly what he has been up to. Because it is the right thing to do.

It is the only thing to.

29

Catherine

I have zoned out again, retreated to that nothing-place between sleep and wakefulness. Wait . . . that isn't quite right. I'm not *between* anything. I am in a place that exists in its own right, where the nothingness feels like a living thing. It surrounds me, forces its way down my throat. I breathe it in like smoke, thick and black. Like the smoke Simon breathed in when he was – *fire ripples up Simon's arm and across his chest and he cries out* – trapped in our car – *a drawn-out tea kettle scream that rises in volume and—*

Someone is shaking me.

I lift my head, surface through the smoke. The cool lines of the kitchen swim before me and the world pulls itself back together.

Panic brings me to my feet.

Charlie.

He was hurt. There was blood streaming down his arm. He needed me, was crying out for me, and I ignored him.

Mum is next to me. 'He's OK,' she says. 'It looked worse than it was, see? He's in his room, having some quiet time.'

The baby monitor is on the table. Mum picks it up and shows me the screen. Charlie is on his bed, playing with his dinosaurs. The thumb of his right hand is white, wrapped in something . . . What's it called? A bandage. His thumb has been bandaged.

'Oh, thank God.' I move to go to him but Mum touches my arm.

'Catherine,' she says. 'There's someone here to see you. She says it's important.'

Only then do I realise there is a stranger in my kitchen.

A young woman, in her early- to mid-twenties, is standing over by the door. She is wearing a black parka coat over a black dress. Lace mesh tights, nose stud, Dr. Martens boots. She'd look right at home with the customers of the Royal George, which means she's not police. She's too casually dressed to be a police officer.

I give Mum a look. What is she doing, letting people in the house like this?

'What is it?' I say to Mum. She stares back at me with blank insistence and I turn to the woman. 'What do you want?'

'It's about your husband,' the woman says, her voice barely above a whisper.

For the briefest of moments, I entertain the idea that she is here with good news. I picture Simon, groggy in a hospital bed, tubes down his throat, machines bleeping in the background. He's confused and disorientated, and he's asking for me. This woman is here to tell me that he is alive, but I must come right away. He's going to need a lot of help getting through this, but he's going to be OK. *We* are going to be OK.

The woman stands stock-still, staring straight ahead. Shoulders hunched, cheeks flushed pink. There's an air of tension around her, as if she might bolt for the door at any second.

'Well?' I say.

She blinks, stutters, 'I'm sorry.'

So she is police after all. The DNA tests have come back from the lab. The body in the car is Simon's. He was never missing.

I'm off my chair, moving on unsteady feet towards her.

'Tell me,' I say. 'Just say it.'

The woman's mouth opens and closes but no sound comes out.

She takes a step back, presses herself up against the doorframe. Mum's hands are on me, tugging at my clothes, trying to hold me back. I push her away, move forward until I am almost on top of the woman. I grab two fistfuls of her coat.

'For God's sake, just say it!'

I want to hear her say the words, because once she tells me Simon has gone, that will be the end of everything, and right now I need it to end. I want it to be over. I shake her and a sob bursts out of her. She twists her head so she doesn't have to look at me.

'Just say it!' I scream at her.

And then she does.

'I didn't know he was married,' she says.

What is she talking about? If she didn't know, then why on earth is she here?

'I promise,' she says.

I can't make sense of what she's trying to tell me.

I let go of her coat as a shout comes from behind me and Mum, moving with a speed I didn't know she was still capable of, inserts herself between us. She grabs the woman by the shoulders, turns her, pushes her out of the room, her voice a shrill cry.

'How dare you come here!'

The young woman is crying fully now, her words swamped with tears. 'I didn't know about you, I swear,' she says. 'I didn't even know his real name.'

I stand there, shaking my head while Mum rages.

She shoves hard enough to send the woman tumbling down the hall. Her legs tangle and she goes down, hands out in front of her, palms hitting the floorboards with a hard slap. Mum doesn't let up. She wraps her arms around the woman's middle, hoists her upright and half carries, half drags her, to the front door.

What is going on here? Nothing makes sense. What is Mum doing, pushing this woman around?

And then, all of a sudden, it hits me.

This woman was something to Simon.

Simon was something to her.

That's why she's here. Simon had some sort of one-night stand and she has come to tell me about it. Why would she do that? Surely she hasn't come here to tell a dead man's wife she fucked her husband?

Mum fumbles with the latch, wrenches the front door open. 'Get out!'

'You should know what kind of person your husband is,' the

woman shouts over Mum's shoulder. 'He lied about *everything*. I didn't know you existed. I didn't even know he had a son.'

'Just go!' Mum says.

'He's a fucking liar—'

'Get out! Get out!'

I get a final view of the girl's trembling mouth, then Mum gives her a two-handed shove and there is a clatter of feet and a crash outside on the pavement and the door slams shut.

Mum marches back into the kitchen. 'Stupid girl,' she says. She throws her arms around me, speaks into my ear. 'Don't you listen to her. Simon would never do something like that.'

I take a shaky step backwards, sit down before I fall down.

Mum's right. The idea that Simon has been running around, having flings with girls half his age? It's ridiculous. He's not a bloody teenager, who can't keep it in his pants. He's a middle-aged man, with a beautiful home and a beautiful family. He has no reason to look elsewhere, because he is quite happy with what he has right here, thank you very much.

He is happy with me, with us.

Isn't he?

30

Sara

There is enough force in the old woman's shove to send Sara down the stone steps, arms pinwheeling. She spills out onto the pavement, crashes against the bonnet of a Range Rover.

The physicality of the last few minutes has left her shaking and breathless.

Don't they understand that Simon's wife isn't the only one who has been wronged? So you just found out your partner has been having an affair? Imagine finding out he has a secret family, that he never loved you, that you never knew the real him.

She runs back to the front door and hammers on it with her fist. Crouches down and peers through the letterbox. She gets a widescreen view of the hallway leading through to the kitchen, can make out two figures hunched on the floor, entwined. The old woman with her arms wrapped around Simon's wife, stroking her hair.

Sara puts her mouth to the letterbox.

'He's the one you should be mad at, not me,' she shouts. 'He told me his name was Adam. He *told* me he was divorced.'

She straightens, gives the door a kick with one of her boots hard enough to rattle the letterbox, then lets out a scream through gritted teeth.

She wants to cause a scene. Wants the neighbours to come out and stand on the doorsteps of their fancy houses, so they can hear what kind of a man they have been living next door to.

And she wants someone else to suffer, for a change.

But the door to number 37 stays closed, as do the doors of the houses either side. Turning to face the square, Sara sees that it is empty of people. How is that even possible in central London, less than two minutes' walk from the tube?

A breeze bothers the trees in the communal gardens and small birds flit silently between the bushes and the roof of the church. The square is a picture of calm, while Sara's insides are on fire. She wishes she could burn the whole place down. The stupid gardens, the stupid church. The posh cars and the posh houses and all the posh people inside them.

She steps down onto the pavement, unsteady on her feet, a sick feeling in her stomach. Her legs carry her a short way down the road, some small part of her brain pointing her in the direction of the bus stop.

You shouldn't have come here.

She wanted to make sure his wife knew the truth, because it was the right thing to do. And she wanted to hurt him, to make him suffer.

And hurt her. You want to hurt his wife, as well.

She did. She wanted to hurt Simon's wife, because she has everything and Sara has nothing. But now it is done, it doesn't feel like she thought it would. She has no sense that she has done the right thing, or that she has set in motion his downfall. And now, Simon will get back from his trip and somehow, he'll smooth everything over. Claim it was just a stupid one-night stand, that it meant nothing. He'll promise to be better, swear he's never done anything like it before and never will again. They'll fight about it, but eventually he'll talk her round. And she'll forgive him.

He's going to get away with it.

Sara picks up her pace. She needs to get away from here. To be anywhere else but here as soon as possible. She'll call Helen, go round to her flat and tell her everything.

Footsteps behind her. A shrill voice calls out, 'You! Wait there!'

Looking back, Sara sees the front door of number 37 is wide open. The old woman has emerged from the house and is coming for her in a scuttling run, slippers slapping against the pavement, one accusing finger raised.

'You *stupid* girl,' she screeches.

At school, Sara never was the sort of kid who could take a telling-off. She would burst into tears if a teacher so much as raised their voice at her, and now some childhood instinct kicks in and she freezes where she stands.

'Stay away from my daughter, do you understand?' Catherine's mother says.

Sara struggles to find her voice, but there is enough anger in her to remind her that she is a grown woman and she is not the one who has done something wrong here.

'She deserved to know,' she says.

Catherine's mum's eyes go wide and she points back to the open door of the house. 'Have you no decency? My daughter is grieving. She has just lost her husband.' Her finger comes back round, is inches away from Sara's chest. 'Stay. Away. Do *not* come back here, ever.'

Sara finds herself nodding, even as she processes the old woman's words.

Grieving?

People talk about grieving after a divorce or a break-up. God knows, over these last few days, Sara has felt some of that grief. A longing to turn back time, a desperate need to shake the horrible feeling that everything is broken and that things will never be the same. Surely the old woman can't be talking about that? Catherine only found out her husband was a cheating arsehole ten minutes ago.

Catherine's mother turns away and starts walking back to the house. Sara is forced to run to catch up with her.

'Wait.' Sara tugs at her sleeve, and the woman spins around, still furious.

'Just go!' she demands.

'What do you mean, grieving?' Sara says.

The old woman's face darkens. She brings her hands up to her cheeks. 'Oh, God. What an awful mess.' She takes a few shuddering breaths. 'Simon . . . he's . . .' She doesn't say it, doesn't have to.

Sara can only stand there, open-mouthed.

She can understand them wanting her to go away and never come back, because then they'll be able to pretend she doesn't exist and therefore her relationship with Simon never existed, either. But telling her he is dead?

What utter bullshit.

'You're telling me Simon's dead?' she scoffs.

Catherine's mum raises her eyes to the sky. She looks genuinely upset. Even manages to add a tremble to her voice, as if she is trying very hard to hold it all together.

'Last week,' she says. 'There was some sort of . . . accident. They found his car in Epping Forest, it had been set on fire and he was . . . he was inside it. He . . .' Deep breath. 'He . . .' Her last word is little more than a squeak.

This is *literally* unbelievable.

'You can't be serious?' Sara says.

Catherine's mum wipes her eyes with the back of her hand. 'I think you should go now,' she says.

'He's not dead—'

'Speak to the police if you like. Detective Carter, at Southwark Police Station. I'm sure she'll be quite happy to tell you the whole story.'

The old woman reaches out with a shaking hand as if she is going to touch Sara on the arm, but she stops short. 'Please do the right thing and stay away,' she says, and with that she turns and walks back to the house.

Sara starts after her. 'Hang on . . .'

She follows, but before she has set foot on the grey stone steps in front of number 37, the sound of the front door slamming shut echoes around the square.

They're mental, the lot of them. Him, his wife, his mother-in-law. They've lost it. The best thing to do now is to get far away from them.

Sara heads towards the bus stop and takes out her phone, calls the number under Adam's name. There's no answer – of course there's no answer. He was probably upstairs at the house in Cavendish Square, hiding in one of the bedrooms while his wife and mother-in-law got rid of her.

The call goes through to his answerphone. She waits for the beep.

'Hi, *Simon*. Guess what? I just met your wife and mother-in-law, though you probably already know that, don't you? And you know what? They're both as fucked up in the head as you are. Don't call me. Don't email me. Don't contact me, ever again. I hate you.' She hangs up, scrolls through her contacts, selects his number and blocks it, then deletes it.

For all she cares, he might as well be dead.

31

Catherine

I sit in the living room, on Simon's chair, dimly registering the world moving around me. Mum standing by the window, staring out between a gap in the curtains, muttering under her breath, *How dare she. How bloody dare she.* Charlie, scooting around on his hands and knees, action figures and plastic dinosaurs spilling out of his toy box. He comes up to me, hands me something small and cold. A toy . . . something or other. What are they called again? Sharp points that dig into your feet if you stand on one. Doesn't matter.

Mum feeds Charlie, puts him to bed. Walks me upstairs to kiss him goodnight. I sit with him for a while, stroke his hair and think about how much he looks like Simon. I kiss him anyway and wander back downstairs, find Mum back on guard duty by the window.

She parts the curtains and peers out into the square. 'The nerve of the woman,' she says. 'I'm lost for words. Really, I am.' Though clearly she is not, given she's been muttering like this for the last four hours.

'I don't want to talk about it,' I tell her.

I don't want to talk about it because I don't want to think about the woman in the black coat and the black dress. Younger than me – a lot younger – prettier than me, too. Standing in our kitchen in her lace tights and heavy boots. Long brown hair. Petite, girlish frame. Slim legs. Slim all over, apart from her chest. I bet her body is firm and her skin is smooth. I have never been what you would call petite, but my body was firm once, and my skin, olive rather than pale, was smooth and free of wrinkles.

I hate her and I don't want to think about her.

Mum says, 'Probably all in her head. Just a silly girl with a crush. It happens. An older man like Simon? Handsome, successful.'

'Mum—'

'People can imagine all sorts of things, that they have a relationship with a person, even, when the reality is nothing of the sort.'

'Mum, stop. Please.'

I want her to be right. I can imagine a younger woman having a crush on Simon, being infatuated with him. He is handsome, he is successful, and he can be oh-so-charming when he wants to be. People get crushes on people. It happens all the time. I should know.

You wanted Jonathan in that way. You thought about sleeping with him, didn't you?

When I was alone in bed at night, waiting for Simon to come home. Yes, I thought about Jonathan that way, but when the moment came, when I felt we were close to crossing a line, I pulled back.

Wouldn't Simon have done the same?

Surely he would have.

But as much as the years have entwined us, they have pulled us apart, too. We live separate lives, overlapping only at the fringes. A hurried breakfast as we get Charlie ready for nursery, a late dinner in front of the television before bedtime. Huge parts of our days – our lives, even – aren't shared with each other. Then there's his constant work trips – away for days at a time. Oh, God, his work trips. Don't tell me he was with her when he said he was away with work?

Don't even think that, Cat.

What was it Max said? *Simon loved you . . . adored Charlie.*

He loves me, he loves us.

There's something else.

She said he told her his name was Adam. I've come across that name before. Not heard it, but seen it.

What was the play again? One of those shows you had to book tickets for months in advance. Simon said he'd get us tickets and when they arrived I recognised the theatre logo on the envelope.

I messaged him to let him know and he texted back, *Good seats?* So I opened the envelope and was delighted to see that they were very good seats indeed. Then I noticed there was someone else's name on the tickets, and on the front of the envelope, too. Our address, but someone else's name. Instead of Mr Simon Wells, it said Mr Adam Worthy.

How I am remembering this now, when I can barely remember how to dress myself, I don't know. But I can picture it, this seemingly insignificant detail, as clear as day. Can see Simon arriving home late, as always. Me, fussing around in the kitchen, finishing the washing up, desperate for an hour of adult conversation before bed.

'Look at this,' I told him that evening, showing him the tickets. 'They've put someone else's name on them. Isn't that weird? Will it matter?'

'Must be a computer fuck-up,' said Simon. 'I'll sort it.' And he spirited the tickets away, as quick as you like. A week or so later another pair arrived, with the correct name this time, although for a different date, and the seats were even better.

'They upgraded us . . . because of the mistake,' he told me.

'Oh, good,' I said. 'I was worried they'd say we couldn't go because we weren't *Worthy*.' I waited for him to laugh, proud of my little joke.

'Sorry, what?' said Simon, not even looking up from his phone.

'Never mind.'

An admin mistake. Happens all the time. I didn't think there was anything sinister about it. And maybe it *was* nothing and I'm being paranoid because I haven't slept in almost a week.

Or, maybe Simon took *her* to the theatre, too, and it wasn't their mistake after all. Maybe it was his mistake, his fuck-up.

Was he normal during the show? Did he seem like he'd seen it before? Laugh too much, or not enough? I can't remember. It was six months ago, more than that even. Surely whatever was going on with this woman can't have been going on since then, can it? It can't have been anything serious?

Don't tell me I had already lost him before he disappeared?

32

Sara

'Bit convenient, isn't it?' says Helen, when Sara tells her what has happened. 'You go to expose him for the lying, cheating bastard he is, and he just so happens to have died in a terrible accident? When did she say it happened?'

'A week ago,' says Sara.

'Did you tell them he's texted you since then? That he was still pretending to be in Paris five days ago? They're mad, the three of them. Stark raving. And *him* . . . Jesus Christ. I never liked him, but *this*?' She knocks the last of her double whisky back and slams the glass down onto the table, grimaces and sucks in air through her teeth.

'I just thought he was a bit of a twat,' she continues. 'An entitled wanker. I never thought . . .' She trails off, head shaking in disbelief. 'What an absolute *arsehole*,' she concludes.

'Yeah, total arsehole,' says Sara.

They are on Essex Road again, sitting on a bench outside the same pub they met at a week earlier, back when Sara told Helen she was going to move in with Adam. It is a familiar spot for Sara, and in this strange new world, where someone will look you in the eye and make up stories about a relative dying – dying *horrifically*, at that – she takes comfort in the familiar. The row of slightly run-down shops opposite – internet café, dry-cleaners, pet store that never seems to be open. The café-cum-juice bar one door down, people sitting out front on rickety folding tables, drinking coffee and smoking cigarettes. The empty takeaway container at her feet. The stale odour of the half-empty ashtray on the table between them. These things, big and small, make her feel almost normal, almost sane.

'Why didn't you tell me what was going on?' Helen says.

Sara sniffs, tears up again. 'I don't know,' she says, but she does. Because she was ashamed, and because she didn't want to hear her best friend say, *I told you so*. Now she wishes she had told her sooner. Helen has not once said *I told you so*. Not yet, at least.

Helen pulls her into a hug and squeezes her tight. 'It's going to be all right. I know everything feels mental right now, but it's going to be OK.'

Sara nods. It will be OK, eventually. She will get through this, somehow. Right now, it's Simon's wife she can't help thinking about. The way she looked when Sara was shown into the kitchen, sitting at the table in a stupor – not quite asleep, but not exactly with it, either. Hair all over the place, eyes like pits, so red and raw they hurt to look at.

'She seemed so well put together in all her photos,' she tells Helen. 'All prim and proper and posh. One of those yummy-mummy types. But when I saw her, she looked like a homeless person. Like she was strung out on something. On the edge, you know?'

'All part of the act,' says Helen. 'Like you said, they're trying to scare you off.'

'I suppose,' Sara says. 'The way she looked, though? I don't know if you could fake that.'

'Maybe she already knew? Maybe he came clean, and they've been fighting about it all week. That would explain why she looked like shit, wouldn't it?'

It's not a bad theory.

Sara thinks back to the last time she saw Adam. His behaviour was so strange, so unlike him. When they had sex that night, it had felt different. He said it was pre-flight nerves, but it must have been because he knew he was going to leave and never come back. And still his hands were all over her.

Self-hate churns inside her, makes her feel queasy.

Helen releases Sara from her hug just long enough to roll a cigarette, then puts her arm back around her and they huddle together, passing the roll-up back and forth.

'I fucking hope he is dead,' says Helen.

'Me too,' says Sara.

Does she? Even if Adam didn't really exist, she had loved him. Him leaving her is one thing, him being dead is another entirely. Her mind is suddenly full of what-ifs, alternative futures that no longer have the chance to play out. What if he loved her, too? What if he was planning to leave Catherine to be with her, and when he talked about them moving in together and starting a family, he really meant it?

So what? If he did it to her, he'd do it to you.

True. He's a liar. A cheat. An arsehole. But that doesn't mean she didn't love him.

What if he really is dead? If the strain of living two lives got too much for him – *That's not what this is* – and he took his own life because it was too much to bear and now a woman has lost her husband and a little boy has lost his daddy? If that is what has happened – *It isn't. It most definitely isn't* – then she played a part in that. Unwittingly, yes, but still. And now all the hate inside her will have nowhere to go, because you can't hate someone who has killed themselves, you just can't.

She buries her head in Helen's shoulder. 'I really loved him,' she says.

'I know you did. But he wasn't real.'

'I miss him.'

'You miss who you thought he was.'

'And now he might be dead . . . because of me, because of what we did.'

Helen pulls back. 'Look at me.' She pinches Sara's chin between her fingers and lifts her head until their eyes meet. 'He's not dead. Do you hear me?'

'But what if he is?'

'He isn't. They're crazy. You said it yourself, they're just doing this to frighten you.' Helen leans back and rummages in her bag for her phone. 'Look, I'll prove it.' She angles the phone so they can both see the screen.

'What are you doing?' says Sara.

'If he's dead then it'll be in the news, won't it?'

Sara watches as Helen begins typing in the search bar. 'What was his name, his real name? Simon . . .'

'Simon Wells.'

Helen types, then hits the News button at the top of the page. 'There. See?' she says. 'News. Simon Wells. Nothing. Nada. Zilch.'

She's right. Not that the search results are entirely empty. A list of articles pops up, but they look random. An article about H.G. Wells' great-grandson, two about the Bank of England, another about the Rolling Stones. Nothing about anybody dying in a fire.

'This is just stuff that mentions other people called Simon Wells, that's all,' Helen says. 'And the most recent is . . .' She checks. 'Six weeks ago. There's nothing about any burnt-out cars, or about anybody dying in a fire last week. Nothing. It's all bullshit.'

'Yeah,' Sara says.

Helen keeps going. 'What did that old bat say? They found his car in Epping Forest?' Sara nods.

Helen searches again, types in *Epping Forest Car Fire Body*.

'I'm telling you, he's not dead. They're a bunch of psychos, that's all. It's a load of old bollocks,' she says, and she hits search.

21–11–2022

1.21 a.m.

'How did it feel, to go viral?' I ask him, and he gives me a confused look. 'The CCTV footage,' I explain. 'It was all over the internet. News sites, social media. The video of the push was everywhere.'

'Newspaper,' he says. 'That's where I saw it. On the tube, on the way to work. The woman opposite was reading the *Metro*, and there I was, on the front page. *Hunt for London Bridge Jogger Who Pushed Woman in Front of Bus*, it said, or something like that. There was a blurry picture, too – not blurry enough, if you ask me. Half the people in the carriage must have been reading the same story, and I thought . . . that's it, I'm finished. Any second now someone's going to recognise me. But nobody did. I thought the police were going to come for me, because it was me, in that photo. Me on the front of the newspaper, me in the CCTV footage. But the police didn't come. Nobody came. For whatever reason, people couldn't see it.'

'What about the people who were close to you? Family, friends?'

'Didn't make any difference,' he says. 'Catherine even made a joke about it. "Where were you on the morning of August the third?" she said, like she was Poirot. So she *knew* it looked like me, and maybe on some level she knew it *was* me . . . But at the same time, she didn't. Because it didn't fit with who she thought I was. Didn't stop me panicking, mind. I told her some lie about being at work that shut her up. But in those few seconds, I felt this . . . rush of hate for her. I wanted to pick up my plate and launch it at her head. It was the stress. Every time I closed my eyes, I saw that front page, that CCTV footage of me, jogging. It was the same the next day, and the next. The day after that, things got easier.'

'Easier in what way?'

'That's when they arrested the American. I could see why. He looked like me. Handsome, similar age, similar build. Even after his lawyer proved he wasn't in the country at the time, people still thought it was him.'

'So why do *you* think nobody recognised you?' I ask him. 'Because I look at that footage, and you're right. It's you. It's so clearly you.'

'Because when people look at me, they don't see someone capable of doing something like that. Like I said, they only see what you want them to see. And they only see what *they* want to see, too.'

33

Day Eight

Catherine

Mum guides me to the car, folds me into the back seat, moving my limbs for me one by one.

'Seatbelt on, love,' she says. I don't move, don't have the energy. She does it for me, pulls the belt across my chest and clunks it into place, then shuts the door and hurries back inside to get Charlie.

Mum is in charge now. She tells me when to sit and when to stand, when to eat and when to drink. This morning she ordered me to take a shower, then stood on the other side of the curtain, calling out instructions to make sure I made a proper job of washing myself. Once done, she dried and brushed my hair, then pulled it back into a ponytail, the way she used to when I was little. While I fussed with the breakfast she made me, she wrestled two suitcases down from the top of the wardrobe in the spare room, packed one full of clothes, the other with an assortment of Charlie's toys.

Charlie lay on his front on the living room rug, his head buried under the sofa.

'I can't find Tony!' He has lost his favourite toy dinosaur. A two-inch tall plastic T-Rex.

'Well, where did you last see him?'

'He was under here. I know he was!'

'You can play with him when we get back.'

'But I *need* him!'

So now we are going to stay with Mum, and we are bringing one suitcase full of clothes and two suitcases containing half the contents of Charlie's toy boxes.

It's for the best. I am done. Worn through to nothing. I haven't looked in the mirror for days now, but if I did, I would be surprised if I even had a reflection.

I can't look after myself. And I can't look after Charlie, either.

I sit in the car and stare out of the window at the residents' garden and wait for Mum and think horrible thoughts. About Simon, coming into the house at night while I'm out of it. About the things that have gone missing from the house – Charlie's toys, our passports. And yes, about him being with the girl in the black dress. The two of them in bed, bodies pressed together, enjoying the kind of passionate love we haven't made in years.

'Mummy?'

Charlie is beside me. Mum must have opened the other rear door and strapped him into his . . . his seat thing, without me noticing. I look up and see her disappear back inside to get the last of the bags.

Charlie kicks his legs. 'Are we going to Grandma's?'

'Yes,' I say.

'Why?'

'Because.'

Because I can't do this anymore.

'I want to play on the iPad. Does Grandma have an iPad? Mummy? Mummy? Does Grandma have an iPad? I want to play *Angry Birds*.'

'I don't know. You'll have to ask her.'

A distant part of me registers the clunk of the boot opening and closing, then Mum opens the driver's side door, throws her own bag onto the passenger seat and gets behind the wheel.

'Right. Is everybody ready?' she says, with forced cheer, as if we are about to go on a family outing to the seaside. As if all is well with the world and her son-in-law isn't missing, presumed dead, and hasn't been seeing some other woman for God knows how long.

'Yay!' Charlie cheers. Mum reaches back with a groan, fumbles for her seatbelt and pulls it down. Keys jingle in the ignition. The engine starts and I let my head fall, close my eyes.

I have a terrible ache in my chest, like I have swallowed something too large and it is lodged right in the centre of me. I press my hand against it, feel my heart beating too fast. Tachycardia. My blood pressure is probably through the roof. Or perhaps I'm having a heart attack?

The car doesn't move.

'Oh, whatever now,' I hear Mum say.

With great effort I lift my head.

Mum is staring at the rear-view mirror. I turn to look over my shoulder, see a silver car with tinted windows has pulled in tight behind us. The car's front doors open simultaneously and out step Detectives Carter and Chaudhari.

Back inside, Mum is ushered upstairs with Charlie, while I am asked to take a seat. Because that is what they do when they have bad news to break. I've been here before. I sit in Simon's chair, bring my knees up to my chest and hold myself tight.

The room is still, for the time being, though the ache in my chest remains and my heart is racing. I blink a few times, bring the two detectives into focus. It hurts to blink, feels like there are grains of sand trapped under my eyelids.

'Catherine?' Carter's voice is soft and slow. 'Can you hear me?'

I must look like I am somewhere else.

'I can hear you,' I say, the words running into each other. *Icanhearyou.*

'There have been some developments.'

I already know what they're going to tell me, but I suppose they need to make it official: the DNA test results have come back from the lab. Simon is never coming home.

'We've had the forensic results back,' Carter confirms.

Something readies itself to be uncaged inside me. I can feel it, stalking back and forth, dark and dangerous, with long claws and sharp teeth. In a few seconds the cage doors will be flung wide, and this *thing* will be set loose. The torture of not knowing – of being convinced he is still out there one minute, sure he is dead the next – will end, and the torture of knowing will begin.

'—and we can now confirm that, while some of the DNA extracted from the vehicle does match your husband's, the remains that were found in the car are not his.'

I'm dreaming.

'I'm afraid there was an issue at the lab which caused some unforeseen delays—'

I have fallen into the deepest of sleeps.

'—the body in the car has been identified as belonging to another man—'

What other explanation could there be?

'—and furthermore, we can say with absolute confidence that your husband is still alive.'

I slump forward, fall out of the chair onto all fours, and a low moan of shock slips out of me that sets my body shaking.

DC Chaudhari is on his feet. He hooks an arm under my elbow to help me up, but I shake him off, push him away. I don't want his help. They've been watching me at night, spying on me, accusing me of all sorts of things, when they should have been out there looking for Simon.

I try to stand but my knees buckle and Chaudhari catches me before I go down a second time and eases me back into the chair.

'Where is he?' I manage. 'Take me to him. I want to see him.'

Do I want to see him? After what I found out yesterday?

Yes, you want to see him. You need to see him.

Whatever he has done, whatever happened with him and that girl, he is still my husband, we are still joined up in a thousand different ways. Besides, maybe Mum is right. The girl had a crush, she got the wrong idea. Nothing happened between them, nothing that matters, at any rate, or that compares to our fifteen years together.

'Mrs Wells?' says Detective Chaudhari. 'We need you to be absolutely truthful with us.'

What is he talking about? They have just told me that my husband is alive, after a week of insisting otherwise, and now they are asking me to be truthful with them?

Chaudhari says, 'If you know where he is, Catherine—'

Carter jumps in. 'We know you've spoken with him. Tell us, Catherine. It's very important that you tell us.'

Spoken with him?

'You told me he was dead,' I say. '*You* told me that. I've been trying to find him. I told you he was alive and you wouldn't listen, you wouldn't believe me.'

Wouldn't listen to me then, aren't listening now.

'We know he's been here,' Carter says.

The lack of sleep has tipped me over the edge. It's the only explanation for what is happening, for why two police officers, who should be apologising for putting me through hell, are questioning me as if I were somehow responsible for my husband's disappearance.

Carter looks over to Chaudhari, pulls in a big breath. 'Catherine, the body in the car has been identified as belonging to Dylan Lesley. That was the man you were trying to speak to at the Royal George, wasn't it?'

Dylan Lesley.

The host of the podcast.

'Dylan was last seen on the twenty-first of November at around midnight, leaving The Pit in Bethnal Green. We know your husband was there that night, and we know he left with Dylan. Some time in the early hours of the following morning, Dylan was attacked and killed. And his body was put in your car and the car was set on fire.' She pauses, the muscles in her jaw tightening. 'We know that Simon has been here, Catherine.'

This is madness.

'Of course he hasn't been here,' I cry. 'I've been trying to find him. You told me he was dead and I have been trying to find him!'

Carter and Chaudhari exchange looks. She nods and he reaches inside his coat and pulls out a manila folder. He opens it, slides out a picture and holds it up to show me. It's a grainy black-and-white still from CCTV footage, enlarged to A4 size, that shows a man walking towards the camera. He has the collar of his coat turned up and part of his face is obscured by a scarf, but his eyes are visible.

'Simon. Entering Waterloo Station at five twenty on Thursday morning. Less than forty-eight hours ago,' Carter says.

'Rubbish,' I say. 'That could be anybody.'

Chaudhari holds the picture a little closer.

Despite the coat and the scarf, it really does look like Simon. Same build, same tilt of the head. Same eyes. Even the swing of his arms looks somehow *Simon*-ish. But it can't be him. Waterloo Station is only ten minutes away. If he were at Waterloo, he would surely have come home.

'He used an Oyster card, triggered an alert on one of his bank accounts,' says Chaudhari.

'No,' I say. 'No, no, no. That isn't . . . It's not possible.'

Chaudhari takes the photo away and puts it back in the file, takes out another, holds it up. It shows the same figure illuminated by a streetlight, wearing the same coat and scarf, moving past a familiar row of houses.

'Two hours earlier,' he announces.

The person in the photograph is hardly any clearer, though I have no trouble recognising the residents' gardens in the background, and the old-fashioned red telephone box on the corner.

'No,' I say again. 'Just, no. It isn't him.'

I refuse to believe that Simon is the person in these photos, because he wouldn't do that. He wouldn't have me believe him dead, when he is alive and well. Wouldn't come to the square and stand outside our house and not come in to see his wife and son.

'He came to see you, didn't he?' Carter says. 'Tell us where he is, Catherine.'

'I don't *know* where he is because I haven't seen him!'

'If you're helping him, or if somebody you know is helping him, then you could be in a lot of trouble. Assisting an offender, hiding them, lying to the police – these are serious criminal offences.'

The pain across my chest blooms.

Can't they see what this is doing to me?

There is a moment of quiet, just the sound of my short, sharp breaths and the rustle of paper as Chaudhari returns the photo to its file.

Carter softens. 'All right, Mrs Wells. OK.' She turns to Chaudhari. 'Can you get Mrs Wells a glass of water, please?'

Chaudhari stands and hurries out of the room.

'What he's done . . .' Carter looks towards the bay window, as if Simon is out there right now, standing in front of the house like he was in the picture. 'We have to find him,' she says. 'For his safety and for yours. And for Charlie's. If he approaches you, if he tries to talk to you, asks you to meet with him, you mustn't. And you must let us know, immediately. Simon is currently considered a suspicious person in relation to a homicide, Catherine. We think he might be very dangerous. Do you understand?'

Dangerous? My Simon? The man I have a son with? The man who I have shared the last fifteen years of my life with? Simon is many things. He can be difficult, thoughtless, infuriating, but he has never raised a hand to me, or Charlie – apart from that one time, when Charlie was being very naughty and Simon was very stressed at work. Simon is not, and never has been, dangerous. And he is most certainly not a murderer, on the run from the police, sneaking around London and coming to the house without telling me.

But then I think about the figure I saw standing out in the gardens. The sound of the front door opening and closing at night. The missing passports. Charlie's dream.

The tiredness, playing tricks on me. Please God, tell me it was the tiredness. Because if it wasn't, if Simon has been watching me, if he has come into the house at night to take our passports and speak to our son in secret . . .

If he has done all these things, what else might he have done?

34

Sara

When Sara wakes the next morning, she is in Helen's room, in Helen's bed. She is woozy with tiredness, hungover, too. Dry-mouthed, with the acid burn of whisky at the back of her throat. Christ, what happened last night? They were outside the pub in Islington, talking about Adam and his crazy wife – and his even crazier mother-in-law. Then Helen found the article:

> Emergency services were called to a report of a black Mercedes GLE on fire in Epping Forest . . .

Then what?

She knows she drank more, and that she cried, on and off, for a long time. And she knows Helen stayed with her, comforted her, and come closing time, called an Uber to take them both back to hers. She has a vague memory of talking about Adam, about how him being dead has turned everything upside down, made her question her hate for him. Even twenty-four hours ago, she couldn't have imagined things would turn out like this. So final, yet so unresolved. Simon has gone, and therefore Adam has gone. And he has taken with him the answers to all of her questions.

Just when she thought he couldn't possibly be any more of an arsehole.

Helen comes into the room, dressed for work with her hair still wet from the shower. She places a glass of water and a packet of paracetamol on the bedside table, takes a seat beside Sara on the edge of the bed.

'How are you feeling?' she says.

Sara props herself up on her elbows, winces as the throb at the base of her skull comes alive and fills her head, pulses to the rhythm of her heart. She swallows the tablets and washes them down, finishes the rest of the water.

'Like death,' she says, once she's done.

Which is true, but that's only the half of it. The headache and the churning guts do feel pretty crappy, but there's something else, too. An overriding emptiness, deep down in her stomach.

'Not feeling too great myself, to be honest,' says Helen. She leans in for a hug. 'Want me to tell Brian you're still sick?'

Sara groans. Her head is in too much of a mess to think about work, but she has given Brian the same rather unconvincing excuse two days in a row now. A third will probably be enough to get her fired.

'No,' she says. 'I'll think of something. I'll text him.'

'Don't forget. He seemed pretty pissed off yesterday.' Helen pats Sara's leg through the duvet. 'Listen, why don't you stay here? At least until things have calmed down a bit.'

'I'll be OK,' Sara says. 'Really, I will.'

'Please? You'd be doing me a favour.'

'I would?'

'I'll worry about you if you're on your own. I won't sleep properly. Won't be able to focus at work. I'll start falling behind. Brian will call me into the office . . .' She puts on a grumpy face and a deep voice, '"Helen, I'm afraid this isn't working out", and the next thing I'm out. Can't afford to pay the mortgage. The bank will take back the flat. Before you know it, I'm on the streets, sleeping under a bridge.'

Sara smiles. 'All because I didn't stay over?'

'All because you didn't stay over. I'll have to sell my body to get by.'

'Your body?'

'My magnificent body. I mean . . . I'd probably make a fortune, but the world of podcasting might never recover from the loss.'

'Your fans will be bereft.'

'Exactly,' says Helen. 'So, if only for their sake, go home, pack a bag, and I'll see you here later on. And tonight, we'll do something fun, OK? Scary movie marathon?'

'Maybe,' Sara says, not sure if watching a bunch of back-to-back horror movies will make her feel better or worse.

'Or, we can eat crap and binge *Drag Race*?'

That sounds more like it.

It's a relief to know she won't have to spend the night alone in her cold, cramped flat. Plus, Adam never came to Helen's place. There are no ghosts here, no memories of him.

The moment Sara hears the door to the flat close, she shifts over to the edge of the bed. Her coat is slung over a chair, just within reach. She stretches out and snags a sleeve, pulls it over and retrieves her phone from the pocket. She wakes it up, opens the browser and types five words into the search bar, the same five words Helen used to find the article last night. Sara thinks she will never forget that sequence of words. It is seared into her brain like a line from a prayer.

Epping Forest Car Fire Body.

Six short paragraphs, less than half a page. You would be hard pressed to even call it an article. Still, it's enough to confirm the old woman wasn't lying. Police called to a burning car in Epping Forest, a man's remains found in the wreckage. Detective Carter, keen to speak to witnesses, anybody who might have been driving in the area, caught something on their dashcam. It's all here.

He's really gone. He's not on some business trip to Paris. He hasn't left her to go back to his wife. He's dead.

She reads the article through again.

His death is being treated as unexplained . . .

What does that mean? Suicide? Don't they usually say a death isn't suspicious if it's a suicide? Plus, while some people do kill themselves by setting themselves on fire, isn't that usually as an act of protest, like that Tibetan monk in Vietnam in the 60s? If you're going to end your life in a secluded forest, there are about a million other, less painful and much quicker ways to do it.

So, an accident then?

She pictures Adam, driving too fast down dark forest lanes – he always did like driving fast. Something darts out of the bushes, a shadow caught in the headlights, there for a second, then gone. A sharp intake of breath as Adam wrenches the wheel sideways, loses control. The car spins, over and over, comes to a crunching stop as it collides with a tree . . .

Cars explode into flames all the time in films, but do they in real life? And wouldn't the police have been able to tell if that's what had happened?

So it probably wasn't an accident, either.

Then she remembers the texts, the selfies in front of the Eiffel Tower and the Parisian café, both pictures taken from his social media. How could he have texted her on Tuesday night when she was with Helen, and again the following morning, if, according to the article, he was already dead? It isn't possible. Somebody else must have sent those photos. Somebody who had Adam's phone and wanted her to think he was still alive.

Why would someone do that? And why would they have his phone – unless they took it from him?

Already queasy from her hangover, Sara feels her stomach clench and flip.

Adam wasn't real. He was two people, rather than one. And he had a burner phone with threatening messages on it that don't make any sense. Messages demanding money of someone and telling them to meet him in Bethnal Green the night before his burnt-out car was discovered fifteen miles away, with his body inside it.

He was wrapped up in something. And whatever that something was, it might have got him killed.

35

Catherine

I tell Max about the pin badge Charlie found in Simon's office, about the podcast and the girl, the murder of Dylan Lesley and Simon being on the run. And about the police thinking I'm a part of it.

It takes a while, because I keep forgetting the words for things, losing my train of thought. Sometimes I have to stop and rewind, go back on myself to fill in the missing details.

Plus, Max is afraid of me.

He keeps glancing over my shoulder, shaking his head at somebody outside the room – his PA, probably – to let them know he's OK. No need to call security. Not yet, at least. I don't blame him. When I caught sight of my reflection in the lift, I winced. I'm a scarecrow of a person. I look like I shouldn't be allowed out on my own. And if it was up to Mum, or the police, I wouldn't be. But here I am.

'Max, pay attention,' I say.

'Sorry. Go on, you were saying . . . about the, ah . . . missing passports?'

When I'm finished, he gets up and goes over to the window, presses his hands against the glass and looks out over that expansive view of the city. His office is on the opposite corner of the building to Simon's and faces downriver, towards the skyscrapers of . . . I forget the name – where the newspapers are, and the building with the pyramid on top.

'And you believe them?' he says. 'You think Simon actually . . .' He turns back to face me but doesn't finish.

'I don't know why he'd want to hurt that man. But it was him, in the pictures,' I say. 'Our car they found. His . . . you know . . . from the tests, at the scene.'

'His DNA?'

I nod. 'And he hasn't come home, Max. If he didn't do it, why hasn't he come home?'

'Maybe he's had some sort of breakdown?' Max says. 'This place . . . it can get to you. The workload, the pressure. It can make you . . .' He abandons the idea.

I'm sure burnout is common at Jefferson, but burnout doesn't turn you into a murderer.

'Maybe it's a mistake?' he says. 'They got it wrong once, right? What's to say they haven't got it wrong again? This is our Si we're talking about. He's not some bloody psycho.' He shakes his head, can't take it all in.

'I don't know, Max,' I say. 'I just need to find him.'

He let me think him dead. He stood outside our house, while I fell to pieces, and watched. Worse, he came inside, moved things around, took things. Crept into our son's room, while I was down the hall, and told him he was going to take him on holiday. Even if he didn't want to be with me, even if he *couldn't* be with me, he could have let me know he was alive, so I didn't have to feel like I was losing my mind. But he didn't. And I want to know why.

Max pushes his hands through his hair. 'Look, if he has actually done what they say he's done – which I find very hard to believe – then you've got to let the police handle it. They'll find him, sort it all out.'

Will they? After this past week, I'm not so sure.

'Help me,' I say. 'He must be with this girl. It's the only thing that makes sense.'

His shakes his head. 'If he was with her, why would she come and see you? Surely that's the last thing she'd do?'

He's right. Before she came to the house, I had no idea she existed. Why would she expose herself like that? Unless it was to throw me off the scent?

'What if she planned it that way?' I suggest. 'What if it was meant to look like one thing, but it was actually something else?'

'Like what?'

I can't think. My brain can't make the right connections. Why would he send her to the house? To get something for him? The passports, maybe? Or were they gone before she arrived? I can't remember. Everything is muddled up in my head.

'Cat, listen to me,' Max says. 'You're not well . . .'

He's right again. My eyes sting, my body aches. My heartbeat is all wrong and I feel this . . . heaviness inside me, like I'm being dragged to my grave even as I stand here. I need rest, need to sleep. But before I do, I'm going to find Simon.

'You're his best friend, Max,' I say. 'He must have told you something.'

If this thing with the girl has been going on for so long, Max must have known about it. Simon would have let something slip after one too many glasses of . . . that wine he likes. And if I can find her, I can find him. They might be together right now. And if they aren't, I'll make her talk. I'll make her tell me where he is.

Max takes a deep breath, swallows hard and breaks eye contact. There's something there, something he is wrestling with.

'What is it?'

He squirms, as if the truth is wriggling around under his clothes, searching for a hole to crawl out of.

'He said it was just a silly fling,' he says. 'That it was nothing, over and done with. He swore.'

'Tell me everything.'

He saw them together.

'Last summer,' Max says. He keeps his head down as he talks, refuses to meet my eye. 'I was out with clients, over from New York. You know what it's like, they always want to make the most of it, see the nightlife. We went looking for somewhere to get a late drink and ended up at a hotel bar near Piccadilly, just wandered in off the street, and . . . there was Simon. He was with this woman—'

'What did she look like?'

'Short. Mid-twenties. Dark hair. Pierced nose. Dressed all in black, a bit like one of those . . . what-do-you-call-ems . . .'

'Goths,' I say, surprised at how easily the word comes to me.

Some words are there when I need them, while others are missing, faded like the ghosts of old shop signs you see on the sides of buildings.

'They were just sitting at the bar,' Max says. 'They weren't *doing* anything, but I could tell something was going on, you know?'

I know.

I picture them. Hands touching, heads close, eyeing each other's hungry mouths. After everything that has happened, it still hurts, still twists something inside my gut.

'I pretended I hadn't seen them. Didn't want to make things weird.' Max gives me a sheepish look. 'Like I say, I was with clients. But the next day I asked him what he thought he was playing at.'

I find this hard to believe. Men guard their friendships as fiercely as women do, if not more so. They keep each other's secrets, cover for each other.

'You confronted him?'

He looks up then, face soft with concern. 'Believe it or not, Cat, I do care. About him and about you, too. Things like that, they never end well.' He brushes an imaginary piece of lint off his trousers. 'Besides, that sort of thing's a distraction. It's bad for business.'

Bad for business. That's why he spoke to Simon. Never mind that Simon was being a total shit to his wife. There are deadlines to meet, board meetings to be on time for, and if you are having an affair, if you are fucking two women instead of one, your mind isn't going to be on your quarterly targets.

'He told me it was nothing. Said that, yes, something had happened between them, but it was a one-off, a stupid drunken mistake. He swore it was all done with. Promised me it was over.'

'What else? Tell me.'

Tell me, because while the horrid details of Simon's affair are the last thing I want to hear, he might have told you something that will help me find her, and if I can find her, I can find him.

'He said she was obsessed, that she wouldn't leave him alone. He was trying to let her down gently. Said he didn't want her doing anything stupid.'

Her doing anything stupid? It's almost enough to make me laugh.

'Did he tell you her name? Where she works, where she lives?'

He shakes his head. 'He didn't introduce us. All he said was that he met her at some podcast launch thing . . . something like that. Said she worked there. God knows what he was doing there, didn't think he was into that kind of thing, to be honest. That's all he told me, I promise.'

A podcast launch.

Simon, Dylan Lesley, the girl. They're all connected to podcasts. If I weren't so tired, and if the world would keep still for more than a second, I'd be able to work out how.

'I need to find her, Max.'

He grimaces. 'Leave it to the police, Cat. I'm sure they'll track her down.'

'They can't,' I say. 'I didn't tell them about her.'

'Ah.' Max opens his jaw wide, scratches at the stubble on his cheek. 'Well . . . you must. Tell them he met her at a podcast launch, too. There can't be that many places making podcasts in London, can there? They'll probably be able to track her down that way. Let them worry about it, Cat. You focus on you and Charlie, yes?'

I'm no longer listening.

I say my goodbyes, tell him of course he's right, that I'll tell the police everything, then I ride the lift down to the lobby. Outside, I take out my phone and bring up the website for *The Push*.

I find what I'm looking for at the very bottom of the website. A small notice says: Copyright Decoded Media Ltd, 2021; and beneath that, an address in Angel.

36

Sara

Sara makes a brief stop on her way to Elephant and Castle, calls into the office and asks Brian if she can have a quiet word in one of the meeting rooms.

'You certainly can,' he says, in a detached sort of way that makes her think he is planning to fire her, so a meeting is just what they need right now. He marches off across the office floor and she follows, catching Helen's eye on the way.

You OK? Helen mouths, lifting her head above her monitor.

Sara shrugs and gives a small tip of the head that she hopes will convey that she isn't, but there isn't time to explain, then she follows Brian into the meeting room. He closes the door behind them, leans against a table and crosses his arms.

'Well?' he says, a look on his face that says, *Come on, explain yourself. And this better be good.*

Oh, it's good, all right, thinks Sara.

Her plan is to tell Brian just the basics: that Adam has died and that she's going to need some time off. That way, at least she'll have a job to come back to once she has dealt with whatever comes next. Even Brian wouldn't fire someone who's boyfriend has just died.

But when she tells him the news, he is so nice – *God, I'm so sorry, sit down, take your time, don't worry about work* – that it has an unexpected effect on her. This version of Brian is not the stern, robotic boss she has grown used to working for these past twelve months, and his kindness, while not unwelcome, brings home the reality of what has happened. It makes the muscles in her neck tighten and tears prick the back of her throat.

'I think he was murdered,' she says, the words spilling out of her before she knows they are coming. 'I don't know what to do. I think I need to go to the police.'

She thinks back to that moment, when she was sitting on the bench outside Adam's real house, debating whether to walk away or to knock on that door. Today is the same. She has a choice. She can throw away the burner phone, and there's a good chance – given she was nothing but a B-side to him – that this whole thing will go away. Or she can face it head-on, do the right thing.

'Are you in some sort of trouble?' Brian says.

Is she? There's the thing with the burner phone – unlocking it without the owner's permission – but she hardy thinks the police will care about that now. Besides, how will they know it was locked in the first place?

'No, I don't think so,' she says.

'Good,' says Brian. 'And do you need someone to come with you? I could move things around?'

The prospect of walking into that police station makes her feel small and afraid. Equally, the idea of anybody – even Helen – being sat next to her while she explains, in detail, how she was duped into a relationship with a married man, who wasn't even that nice to her, makes her want to cringe.

'Thanks, but no,' she says. 'I need to go back to the flat and pick up some things. I'll go after that, I suppose.'

'Whatever you need,' says Brian. 'We're all here for you.'

She pulls in a breath, holds it.

It feels like the moment she exhales, she'll be on a new path, one that leads to Southwark Police Station, where she will ask for Detective Carter, hand over the burner phone and tell them everything. And from there? Who knows.

Then Brian says, 'Have you eaten?'

She breathes out.

* * *

He takes her to a local pub, a run-down place that still smells of cigarettes even though the smoking ban came in almost fifteen years ago, and they grab a seat at a high table by the window that has folded beer mats stuffed under three of its legs, but still wobbles when either of them leans on it. They take turns scanning the menu.

'What do you fancy?' Brian asks.

'Soup?' It feels like she could manage soup.

Brian shakes his head. 'You need something more substantial.' He takes the menu out of her hands and heads to the bar, orders for both of them and returns to the table carrying a pint of lager for himself and a Coke for Sara. When her food arrives ten minutes later, it is a thick wedge of cottage pie. Heaps of mashed potato and minced beef and gravy piled high on the plate. Sara eyes it with caution, worries it is too much and that trying to force it down is going to make her throw up.

'I'll do you a deal,' Brian says. 'Eat half, and we'll say no more about it.'

She scoops up a forkful, puts it into her mouth and swallows. To her surprise it goes down easy, and it tastes good, too. It warms her insides, and while she knows the feeling is temporary, it goes some way to countering the emptiness inside her. In the end she clears her plate.

'I'm sorry for lying,' she tells Brian. 'It's all been so . . .' Horrible, overwhelming. Unreal.

'That's OK,' Brian says. 'I'm not surprised work wasn't top of your agenda.'

'Still,' Sara says. 'Would have been better to let you know, wouldn't it.'

'It would,' Brian says, not unkindly.

One of the bar staff comes over and takes their empty plates and leaves behind the bill.

'I've got this.' Brian removes his card from his wallet and lays it on the table.

Sara wishes the place were busier. Only a handful of tables are occupied, and she can already see the man behind the bar heading back to their table with the card machine. Once the food is paid for, there'll be no good reason for them to stay. It'll get awkward and Brian will make his excuses and head back to work. She wishes they could sit for a while longer. Perhaps because Brian is grown up in a way that she is not, and in a way that Helen is not, and right now she needs to talk to a grown-up. Or perhaps it's because Brian is an older man, and him showing her kindness meets some deep and fundamental need within her.

The man behind the bar comes back and taps Brian's card, hands over the receipt and saunters away, and Sara fully expects Brian to reach for his coat, but he doesn't.

'I know it doesn't feel like it at the moment, but whatever happens, it's going to be OK,' he says.

Sara feels the scratch of tears at the back of her throat again. Brian leans over and takes a napkin off the neighbouring table, hands it over without a word.

'You think so?'

'I know so.' There's a flash of something in Brian's eyes and he seems to recede into himself for a second, then he's back, leaning forward, elbows on the table.

'I lost my wife. Three years ago,' he says. 'She was cycling to work, and a lorry cut across her. He just didn't see her. She was caught between the lorry and a barrier.'

'Oh, God,' Sara says.

She has seen him five days a week for the last eighteen months and had no idea he'd ever been married, never mind that he had lost his wife. Though, she supposes, she never bothered to ask.

'I'm so sorry.' *For your wife, for you. For never asking.*

'I spent a long time feeling very angry. At the driver, mostly, but I was angry at her, too. She could have got the bloody tube to work, like everybody else, right?' A small smile. 'When I was in the thick of it, I didn't think things would ever feel normal again. It was like this . . . this really loud noise in my head, all the time. But it got quieter, eventually. And I don't know everything you're going through right now, or will go through later today, but all these things that are filling your head . . .' He puts two fingers on the table and slides them backwards, miming turning the volume down on a mixing desk. 'One day, they'll be nothing but background noise. There, but not there, you know? So, you go and do what you need to do. Things will be hard and weird for a while, but you've come this far. You'll get through it.'

It is not quite the pep-talk she could do with, but she takes some comfort from Brian's words. Things are hard, and they are definitely weird, but he's right. She has come this far.

'Besides,' he adds, 'I need you back at your desk as soon as possible. You're the best we've got.'

It is the only feedback he has ever given her, and despite all that has happened, she can't help but feel a swell of pride.

'You really think I'm good?' she says.

He raises an eyebrow. 'Of course I do. That's why I get on at you. I want you to push yourself, do the best you can. You know what? I thought you'd have your own podcast by now. You were practically chomping at the bit when you came for your interview. What happened with that?'

'Ha,' she laughs. 'I did have an idea, but *somebody* got there first.'

Brian smiles. '*The Push*?'

'You knew about that?'

'I heard some rumours. You should have pitched it. You shouldn't have doubted yourself.' He leans in. 'And between you and me, I think you'd have done a better job than Dylan has.'

'You think so?'

He nods. 'Anyway, forget *The Push*. I'm sure you have other ideas. We'll put something in the diary for when you—' Brian's phone is ringing. He signals his apology, takes it out of his inside pocket and answers the call. 'One second . . . Hello? Yes. No, I'm just up the road. What's up?' There is a long pause while he listens to what the caller has to say, during which Sara thinks about how kind he has been, and how clever. For a moment there, she completely forgot about the horrible afternoon ahead of her, and with the promise of a meeting to discuss her podcast ideas, she now has something to look forward to beyond the nightmare of this week.

Brian ends the call then turns to grab his coat from the back of his chair.

'I'm going to have to get back,' he announces. 'The police are at the office.'

'The police?' Sara's now-full stomach clenches. Fuck. They must know about the phone. Maybe they were tracking it? When she switched it on to find out where Adam really lives – *lived* – they must have tracked it to her flat, and now they'll want to know why she didn't hand it over sooner, why she read those threatening emails and messages and did nothing.

'They want to speak to me,' Brian adds. 'It's about Dylan.'

They're not here for her. Thank God.

'What do they want with Dylan?' Sara hasn't thought about Dylan since she last listened to *The Push* and decided he was most definitely faking having tracked down the jogger. Surely, the police won't be bothered about him lying on a podcast?

'No idea.' Brian shrugs. 'Sounded serious though. My guess? He's been harassing witnesses again.' Which sounds exactly like the sort of irresponsible thing Dylan would do.

They walk back to the office together, say their goodbyes at the front door and Brian leans in for what must be the most awkward hug the world has ever seen.

'Tell Helen I'll see her later,' Sara says.

'I will. Take care of yourself. Make sure you eat, and if you need anything, let me know. Times like these, you need your friends around you.'

Are they friends? She supposes they must be and that makes her feel a little better, too.

She heads for the tube, walks between the market stalls of Camden Passage and onto the main road, then goes down into the underground. There is a short wait in the oppressive heat of the Northern Line platform, then the tube arrives and she boards, travels through the rattling dark, back to Elephant and Castle.

37

Catherine

'Cat, are you there?' Lydia's voice is small and far away, but I am warmed by the sound of it, can feel myself sinking back into my body—

'Cat?'

I open my eyes, am thrown forward into the light of the day, the city moving around me. I'm in a black cab, on the way to Angel. My hand lies limp in my lap, clutching my phone, a call in progress. I must have dropped off, micro-slept. I put the phone to my ear.

'I'm here,' I say.

I have told Lydia everything. At least, I think I have. I remember flagging down the cab, Lydia's name appearing on my phone's screen, her shock at hearing Simon was alive, that he is wanted by the police.

'Where are you? I'll come and find you,' she says.

'I'm going to Angel to find this girl. She must know where he is. I need to know why he did this to me. I want him to look me in the eye and tell me why.'

'Cat, wait. I know you're angry, but stop—'

'As soon as I've spoken to him, I'll call the police, tell them where he is.'

I want to watch the two of them – him and the girl – being led away in handcuffs. Him for murder, her for – what was it Detective Carter said? Assisting a something or other?

'Please don't do this,' Lydia says. 'Stop the cab, go and find somewhere to wait. I'll be there as quick as I can.' I hear her moving around breathlessly, getting ready to leave the house.

'No,' I tell her. 'I want to do this—'

'Listen to me. Tell the driver to pull over. Do it now.' She is almost shouting. 'Stay away from her. *Promise* me, Cat. I don't want you to get hurt.'

She sounds tearful with worry.

'Cat? Are you listening to me?'

I know she means well. If the situation were reversed, I'd be telling her to stay away too. But I need to do this. It feels like I'll never be able to sleep again until I have answers.

'I love you and I'm sorry,' I tell her. 'I'll call you.'

I hang up.

I arrive at the offices of the podcast company, up a dirty side street not far from Angel tube, ready to plead and persuade, do whatever it takes to get them to give me her address. I'll make something up. Tell them a family member is on their deathbed, that I have been sent to collect the girl and take her to the hospital before it is too late.

In the end, there's no need. She's right there, standing outside the front door. I recognise her immediately: cheap-looking black duffel coat, mesh tights, heavy Dr. Martens boots that make her feet look too big for her skinny legs. She is talking to a tall, middle-aged man with threads of grey in his scruffy beard who is wearing those things for your eyes that help you see. Glasses. He is wearing glasses, with thick black rims.

Boyfriend? Another married man she's got her hooks into?

Hate unfurls in my stomach.

Tell him everything. Rip her life apart. See how she likes it.

Then they hug, stiff and unpractised. Faces turned away from each other. They're not a couple. He's just a friend, or a colleague. I'm even more certain of this when she turns and walks away from him without a further word.

From across the road I watch her head onto Upper Street, and I follow.

She is a slow walker, which is good for me, because the wet

pavement shifts underfoot, the ground never quite as still as it should be. Each step feels like a gamble, an invitation to fall.

I keep pace with her as she cuts through Camden Passage, between the market stalls selling bric-a-brac and second-hand clothes. She stops to slump her shoulders at the window of an estate agents and I stop too, wait for her to move on.

I don't want to confront her here. I want her to lead me to Simon.

I follow her to the tube, through the barriers, down the escalator and onto the platform. Onto a Northern Line train, going south. I stand in the carriage next to hers, watch her through the window.

Three stops, four stops, five.

Off at Elephant and Castle. Through the tunnels, and up the escalator into the daylight. Down New Kent Road. Left turn, through the side streets, to an ugly old tower block. Ten storeys of dirty grey concrete. The sort of neglected high-rise they are tearing down all over London to make way for newer, prettier, more expensive homes.

I watch her go inside and run to catch the front door before it closes. I step into a filthy-looking lobby. Drifts of leaves in the corners, a lift with an out-of-order sign taped to it. A smell like Charlie's sheets when he has wet the bed.

I hear the echo of her heavy footfall in the stairwell, grasp the handrail and climb the stairs after her.

21–11–2022

1.25 a.m.

'Tell me about that day, about the push,' I say, and he gives a little half-smile.

'You've seen the CCTV,' he says. 'You know what happened.'

Don't go quiet on me now. This is the crucial moment, what the listeners will be tuning in for.

'How about I tell you what I see,' I say, 'and you can tell me if I'm on the right track?'

He yawns into the back of his hand. 'If you must.'

'When I watch that footage, I see a white, middle-aged man, likely well-to-do—'

'What's well-to-do about him? All I'm doing – all he's doing – is jogging.'

'True, but jogging is primarily a pursuit of relatively well-to-do people. And he's jogging, and he clearly thinks the pavement is his own. You have to be a certain kind of person to behave like that, to see someone who might get in your way, and take action to remove them. I look at this man, and I see the embodiment of white male privilege.'

He rolls his eyes. 'That word. People like you love throwing it around, don't they? Like to use it as a stick to beat people with. Anyone who's white and male and successful must have had it easy. Never mind how hard they've grafted, that they started at the bottom with nothing—'

'That's not what I'm saying—'

'You think people like me are the problem. That we're screwing over the man on the street and don't give a shit about anyone else. All this rubbish, about the jogger being a banker, that's where it comes from. The demonisation of the white, middle-class male. And if they work in finance, all the better. Lock 'em up and throw away the key, am I right?'

I wouldn't go quite that far. Then again, maybe I would.

'You know, the number of CEOs who display traits of psychopathy is said to be one in five, which is about the same as prison inmates,' I tell him. 'The corporate world values those traits. They like aggression. Someone who lacks empathy can be cut-throat in business, they can do well for themselves.'

'Must be true, if you say it is.'

'To me, the most striking thing about the footage isn't the push, it's the fact he didn't stop to help. He just kept jogging. Because in that moment, she isn't a person to him, she's an obstacle. Something to be removed. That's what makes it so shocking. We see a man try to casually murder someone, then he goes about his day as if nothing happened. This sort of thing usually happens away from the public eye, but here . . . well, it's all on camera.'

He laughs. 'What rubbish.'

'Why is it rubbish?'

'Of course she was a person,' he says. 'For a while, I thought she was the most important person in the world.'

38

Sara

It is threatening rain when Sara arrives home. The sky is headache grey and the clouds so low it looks as if they might, at any moment, start pressing down on the apartment building, sending bits of broken masonry crashing to the pavement below. Despite the turn in the weather, Sara can't help but feel a little brighter. Not that everything isn't still horrible – things are *definitely* still horrible – but after her talk with Brian, she has a sense that better things are possible. Not on the horizon yet, but one day they will be.

Plus, something has woken up inside her. A long-dormant muscle at the back of her brain has started working again, started thinking about podcast ideas, stories she might want to tell. If Dylan can do it – lazy, arrogant Dylan – then she most certainly can. And yes, it does occur to her that the events of the last eight days would make for quite the story. Secret identities, affairs, burner phones, bodies in cars. Plenty for listeners to get their teeth into. But she only considers it for a second.

Too soon, she tells herself. *Much too soon.*

The lift is still out of order so Sara takes the stairs, turns onto her corridor and reaches into her bag for her keys. As she stops at her door, balancing her bag on her knee as she feels around, she hears a shuffling footfall behind her and peers back along the dimly lit corridor. Somebody's there. A figure, silhouetted by the light coming in from the small window at the corridor's end. Nothing unusual about that. There are over eighty apartments in the block, people come and go at all times of day and night. But whoever this person is, they are moving in a way that doesn't look quite right, a way that makes Sara want to find her keys and get inside as soon as possible. They barely lift their feet as they shuffle-walk forward, shoulders hunched, head down, one arm braced against the wall for support.

Probably a junkie, or a homeless person, looking for shelter from the oncoming rain. There's even a notice downstairs: *Please ensure the communal door is fully closed to prevent non-residents gaining access to the building. Stay secure, stay safe!* Did she make sure the communal door was fully closed before walking up the stairs? She did not.

She searches a little faster.

Come on, come on. She can hear her keys jingling around. They must be in here somewhere.

Down the hall, the shambling silhouette lets out a low gurgling moan. Great, Sara thinks. That's all she needs right now. To be accosted by a junkie on her own doorstep.

'*You*,' a slurred voice calls.

What the fuck? It's like something out of a horror film. A real live zombie, right here in her apartment block.

Sara's fingers finally close around the tangle of metal and plastic that is her keyring. She yanks the keys out of her bag, fumbles to find the right one. There are only four keys on the ring, why can't she find – there! She's got it. She pushes the key home, turns it. The front door springs open. A broken column of light spills out of the apartment, painting the floor and the opposite wall a translucent white and, at the same time, the zombie rushes forward and Sara sees that it is not a zombie after all. It is worse than that. It's Simon's wife.

His batshit-crazy wife.

Sara steps inside the flat, tries to slam the door shut, but Catherine pushes from the other side, the sound of her thickened voice echoing through the corridors.

'Is he in there?' she shouts. 'I want to see him. Let me in. *Let me in*!'

'Go away!' Sara braces her shoulder against the door. It should be no contest, she thinks, because she is young and Simon's wife is sick – so sick that she looks like a zombie. But then Sara feels her feet start to slide, the rug that runs the short length of the hallway slipping beneath her feet.

White, bloodless fingertips appear around the door's edge.

'Let me . . . see him.' Catherine's words are punctuated by the groans of effort. 'I want to see . . . my husband.'

'Leave me alone!' Sara slams her body against the door. There's a cry of pain from the other side and Catherine snatches back her fingers. Then the rug slips out from beneath Sara's feet and she plummets to the floor. She shoots out a hand, catches herself, but the door swings wide, close enough for her to feel the kiss of the wood on the very tip of her nose.

Catherine stands in the doorway.

'Where is he?' she says.

'He's *dead*!' cries Sara. Catherine steps into the flat and Sara skitters backwards on all fours, desperate to put some space between them, but Catherine looms over her, jabbing at the air with her finger like she is telling off a naughty toddler.

'You're lying,' she says. 'Why are you lying for him?'

How can she be lying? She saw the article. Simon's dead. Burnt to death in his car. Besides, Simon's mother-in-law *told* her he was dead.

Sara gets to her feet. Catherine clearly isn't well, but that doesn't mean she can come bursting into other people's homes.

'You need to go,' she says. 'You can't be here, you can't just—'

Catherine looks around the hallway, peers through the open door of the living room.

'Simon?' she shouts, craning her neck.

'You have to go!' Sara says, but Catherine moves towards the living room.

Sara steps in front of her to block her way, stands firm. Without even looking at her, Simon's wife raises a hand to push her aside, and that is about as much as Sara can take.

She puts her hands on Catherine's shoulders.

'I said, you need to go!' And she pushes – not hard, not nearly as hard as she wants to, but with enough force to send Simon's wife staggering backwards. She almost regains her footing, but her heel snags on the hallway rug that is now heaped in its middle. Her feet skip in the air for a second, then there is a hollow thump as she hits the floor. She doesn't cry out. She exhales once, a quivering breath of shock that sounds like the opening note of a song, then she is still.

Sara freezes.

The flat is suddenly quiet – so quiet that, to Sara's ears, it sounds loud.

She stares at the middle-aged woman collapsed on her hallway floor, not knowing whether to go to her or to get away from her. In the end, she retreats to the kitchen, slams the door and braces her back against it. She makes sure she has a solid footing, boots firmly planted on the linoleum, and waits for the shouting to start up again, for the pounding on the door to begin.

'I'm calling the police,' she shouts. 'Do you hear? You'd better get out of here.' Phone. Where's her phone? Fuck. It's in her bag, and her bag is out there, in the hall. She must have dropped it without thinking.

She takes a cautious step away from the door, keeping one foot planted firmly in front of it in case Simon's wife is right on the other side. She opens it a crack, peers through the gap. In the hall, Catherine lies where she fell.

'Do you hear me? You'd better go,' Sara calls out, equal parts hoping and fearing a response. But there is no movement, no sign that Simon's wife is conscious.

She opens the door a little further, tries again. 'Hello?'

Nothing.

There's no blood as far as she can see, but people can die from a hard fall. You read about it in the papers. Some middle-aged father of three gets clobbered by a kid outside an off-licence, knocks his head on the pavement and never regains consciousness.

I've killed her. I've fucking killed her.

It was self-defence. Simon's wife attacked her. She must have tracked down where she lives and followed her here. They don't send you to jail if someone is killed in self-defence, do they?

Of course they do. It's called manslaughter, idiot.

But this is different. They'll understand.

Oh, they'll understand all right. When they find out you were sleeping with her husband. When they hear that you were thrown out of her house yesterday.

Yes, but she only went there because she wanted his wife to know the truth. She was doing it for *her*, because she deserved to know what sort of man her husband really was.

Bullshit. You wanted to hurt her. You wanted her to feel pain.

She did. But not like this.

Sara emerges from the kitchen, treads as softly as her heavy boots will allow and keeps her eyes locked on Catherine as she moves over to her bag. She stands it upright and reaches inside.

Catherine stirs, pulls in a ragged breath that sounds like tearing fabric. Her eyes open, flick sideways and lock onto Sara.

'Please, no please,' she murmurs.

She's alive. Thank God.

'It's OK. I'll get help.' Sara pulls her phone from her bag, starts to dial 999.

'Noplease-noplease!' Catherine cries again, frantic now.

She's delirious. Probably concussed.

Sara shuffles closer. 'Don't worry. It's going to be OK,' she says. 'I'm just going to call—'

Catherine clamps a bony hand around Sara's wrist and holds it fast.

'No . . . police,' she says.

'You need help. You fell.'

'No. Police,' Catherine says again, bloodshot eyes wide, a thin line of drool unspooling from her bottom lip. Sara lowers the phone and Simon's wife releases her and slumps back, her chin dropping to her chest.

Wait until she's calmed down, Sara thinks, *then* I'll phone for an ambulance. Maybe get her cleaned up a bit first, because she looks a proper mess, and when the ambulance arrives, they'll want to know how she got in this state.

They stay like that for a while. Sara, crouched down in the hall next to Simon's wife.

'Just lie still. Take your time.'

Catherine does. She lies there, taking long, slow breaths. Breaths that, to Sara's ears, sound almost like words. Almost as if she is whispering. 'No police . . . they'll take him . . . they'll take my baby.'

39

Catherine

The girl. I remember. Seeing her at the office, following her. The tube to Elephant and Castle. That dirty old tower block. I went inside, climbed the steps after her. Then what? And why does my head hurt so much?

I'm used to the constant headache the tiredness has brought with it, the way it persists behind the eyes. Heavy and alive, never quite settling. The way it fogs the world like a warm breath on a bathroom mirror. This is different. A new kind of pain. Pulsing and red hot at the back of my skull.

I open my eyes and the girl is right there, leaning over me.

'Try not to move,' she says. 'You fell.'

I want to tell her to get away from me but the pain is all-consuming. Dizzying in its intensity.

'I'm sorry,' says the girl. 'It was an accident.'

'An accident.' *Anaccshident.* My voice isn't my own. What has she done to me?

'And I'm so sorry about everything else,' she says. 'I didn't know, I swear I didn't.'

If that's true, why is she helping him?

He could be here now, somewhere in the flat. I can't let him see me like this. I lean forward, try to get my legs under me. Movement fills my head with stars, makes me want to vomit. I slump back against the wall.

'Careful,' the girl says. 'Take it easy.'

Simon's not here. He'd have come out of his hiding place when he heard my voice. He must be holed up somewhere else, getting everything in order so he can make his escape. Skip the country, go somewhere the police can't reach him.

'Where is he?' I say.

'He's . . . he's gone!' she says.

He's left the country already. Of course. Why wait? The moment he got his hands on his passport he'd have caught a flight to somewhere far away. But shouldn't some sort of alert have gone off? Doesn't that happen if someone tries to use the passport of a supposed dead person to leave the country?

'Where?'

The girl shakes her head. 'I don't know what you mean.'

She knows he's a killer, and still she's lying for him. I almost feel sorry for her. What did he promise her? That he'd send for her once it was safe?

'He's left you,' I tell her. 'You're not special. He left me, and now he's left you. Don't you see?'

'I . . . I—'

'He's dangerous. He killed someone, remember?'

Her face clouds over. 'Killed someone?'

'Dylan. The podcast. *The Push*. I know it was Dylan . . . in the car.'

She blinks a few times. 'What's Dylan got to do with anything? Simon didn't even know him. I mean . . . he knew *of* him, but he didn't *know* him.'

Maybe Simon didn't tell her everything, after all.

'This must be so hard for you,' she says. 'Is there someone you want me to call? Somebody who can come and get you?'

She isn't listening to me.

'He's a murderer,' I say. 'And you need to tell me where he is.'

Her face is a question mark.

'I don't know what you're talking about,' she says. 'Look!'

She picks up her phone and taps it a few times, shows me the screen. The contents swim into focus. Text messages, a dozen or so. Links to websites at the top. A few old selfies from Simon in return, from our holiday in . . . wherever it was. And at the bottom, more urgent sounding messages, laced with desperation: *Adam? Is everything OK? Adam, call me x. Adam can you please call me? I'm worried x*

'See?' she says. 'He wasn't replying to my messages. I even went to his work – where he told me he worked – and they said they'd never heard of him and he hasn't returned any of my calls and . . . I don't know what's happening here.'

She rocks back, gets to her feet and stands above me, grabs two fistfuls of hair. She looks like she wants to scream.

'This is mad,' she says. 'Totally mad.'

I'm not sure what it is that makes me believe her. Perhaps it's the messages. The sense of barely contained panic in them, the mounting desperation as each one goes unanswered. I know that feeling.

I got used to Simon not coming home at a reasonable hour – he trained me into it, I see that now – but in the early days I used to send texts like that, when I was sitting up late at night, waiting for him, worrying that something awful must have happened. Because he said he would be home at ten and now it is nearly midnight and there's no sign of him and he isn't picking up his phone and he hasn't replied to any of my messages . . . *Should I call him? Or will that make me look overbearing? Will it make me look like a nag, like I am trying to control him? He hates it when I do that . . .*

Or, perhaps it isn't the text messages that make me believe her. Perhaps it's the slow slide into shock that is making her shake and shiver.

I know that feeling, too.

40

Sara

Sara swallows down the panic that is threatening to overwhelm her. The things Simon's wife is saying . . . None of it makes any sense. All this stuff about Simon killing Dylan and skipping the country? Simon's the one who's dead, not Dylan. Dylan's fine, isn't he? If he was dead, Brian would have known. He would have said something over lunch. Simon's wife is confused – grief can do terrible things to people, send them over the edge. Add to that a bump on the head? She's probably concussed.

Sara clears a space on the sofa, scoops up an armful of old magazines, dirty clothes and unopened letters, and dumps them on the floor. Another time and she might be more self-conscious about the mess, but today? The state of her living room is hardly the priority right now.

Simon's wife takes a seat, moving slowly, like an old person. She sits with her feet flat, her hands on her knees and her back straight. She is shivering a little, swaying. She looks like she is trying very hard not to throw up.

'Can I get you anything?' Sara says. Catherine reaches up and touches the back of her head, winces and sucks in air through her teeth.

'Sorry,' says Sara.

Though to be fair, you were the one who pushed your way into my flat.

Still, she wishes there were something she could do to make

things better, because the sooner Catherine feels better, the sooner she'll leave.

'I'll get some ice.' Sara heads to the kitchen. Once there she closes the door behind her and leans against it, takes a few deep breaths.

Simon's crazy wife is in her flat. And while she seems calm enough right now, fifteen minutes ago she looked just about ready to kill somebody. And if Sara hadn't pushed her, and she hadn't fallen, who's to say she wouldn't have?

The best thing to do is to keep her calm, then get her out of the flat as soon as possible. Call her an Uber, maybe. Make sure she gets home OK.

There is no ice in the freezer, but there is a packet of frozen peas. Sara wraps them in a tea towel, takes a few deep breaths, then heads back into the living room.

'Try this.' She hands over the improvised ice pack and Catherine takes it and gently presses it to the back of her head.

'Oh,' she says, closing her eyes.

It's a shame, Sara thinks, recalling those pictures of Catherine on social media; how happy and together she looked. Now her skin's all grey and papery, her hair's a rats' nest and her eyes are puffy and bloodshot. When she speaks, her voice is slurred, the words mushed together. Sara thinks about Brian, and about that noise he mentioned. The sound of grief that filled his head but got quieter over time. What if it doesn't get quieter? Sara thinks. What if it only gets louder? So loud that it drives you mad?

She wishes there was a way she could make Catherine leave. And perhaps, she realises, there is.

'Wait here.' She goes to the bedroom and returns a moment later clutching Simon's burner phone. She holds it out to show Catherine.

'Evidence,' she says. 'He left it here by accident,' she says.

'His phone?' Catherine says.

Sara nods. 'Not his proper phone. It's a burner phone, like drug dealers have. Only not really, because they usually have a pay-as-you-go, but it's the same kind of thing. If you take it to the police, maybe it'll help them work out what happened? There are messages on it, see?' She shows Catherine the screen, scrolls through the messages. 'Times, places. Then this: threats. Talk about money. I was going to take it to the police.'

Catherine opens the phone, begins clicking through the contents.

'This . . .' she says. She is pointing to the final text, the one that says, *The Pit Bethnal Green 8.30 bring the money and don't fuck me around or you'll regret it.*

'He must have gone to meet him there, before . . .'

'Before?'

Catherine's face clouds over. She blinks, shakes her head, looks back to the phone as if she's seeing it for the first time. Whatever she was thinking, it's gone now.

'There's some threatening emails, too,' Sara explains. 'And an old song. See?' She leans over, presses the phone's touchscreen to open the Backup folder. She touches the filename of the song, that random mix of numbers and letters, and skips the file forward twenty minutes. Music begins to play out of the phone's tinny speakers. Perhaps it was a favourite song of Simon's, she thinks. Maybe hearing it now is just what Catherine needs.

The song starts part way through; guitar, synths and drums kicking in all at once, the singer throwing himself into his Bowie impersonation.

'. . . *falling to pieces without you. Oh . . . whatever it was I did wrong, I'd take it all back if you want . . . Oh, baby don't leave me so blue . . .*'

'Was it one of Simon's favourites?' Sara asks.

'Shush,' Catherine says.

'. . . *broken watch, last ticked when you walked away. A stopped clock, right twice, wrong a thousand times a day. Without you to run me down or wind me up . . .*'

A voice interrupts the music. *Can we turn that off, please?* somebody says.

A different voice replies: *My car, my music.*

'Stop!' Catherine cries. 'That's Simon. That's Simon's voice!'

Sara hits stop, drags the little icon on the timeline backwards, starts the file playing again and they listen as the song starts over: '. . . *broken watch, last ticked when you walked away* . . .' And the voices start up again.

Can we turn that off, please?

My car, my music. We're here now, anyway.

Simon's voice. And, Sara realises, Dylan's voice, too.

Why is there an audio recording of Simon and Dylan talking to each other on Simon's burner phone?

There's a click, one of them turns off the music and the conversation continues.

Before we do this, I want to know how you found me.

How about this: you answer my questions first, then I'll tell you what you want to know.

That's not why we're here.

Do you know how long I've been looking . . .

'I don't understand,' Catherine says. 'What are we listening to?'

'I don't know,' says Sara, but the longer she listens, the more she thinks she does.

The audio file is not an old song Simon recorded off the radio. The music was playing *on* a car radio before the start of their interview. Sara thinks back to the last episode of *The Push*, that five-minute tease that promised listeners he was about to confront the London Bridge Jogger. And although Dylan's interview with Simon has just got started, and although neither of them has so much as mentioned the jogger yet, her brain is rushing ahead, making connections.

Epping Forest Car Fire Body, she thinks.

What was it Simon just said? *My car, my music.*

None of this makes sense. Or rather it does, but Sara doesn't want to believe it.

This can't be what it sounds like, can it?

Dylan told his listeners he was going to confront the jogger and now here he is, interviewing Simon.

The recording is poor quality, much worse than it would be through a proper digital recorder. But Brian tells all of the podcasters at Decoded Media to hit record twice, because it is all too easy to press the wrong button, to run out of battery, to accidentally erase a file and discover that all that time you spent asking questions was for nothing. If you don't have a second recorder available, use your phone. However you do it, always have a backup.

41

Sara

They sit in Sara's tiny flat in Elephant and Castle and listen as the room grows dark around them.

Occasionally, Catherine asks Sara to rewind.

'Play that part again,' she says. Or, 'What did he say? Go back, go back.' Because the audio quality is bad, and the two voices are frequently obscured by a loud rustling Sara knows is the sound of the phone's microphone rubbing against the fabric inside Dylan's coat pocket.

At other times, Sara stops the recording herself, drags back the white dot on the red line, so she can play a section over again. Not because the voices are muffled, but because she can't quite believe what she is hearing.

Simon is the London Bridge Jogger.

All those times she watched footage of the push, and not once did she think the jogger looked like Adam – who was surely younger and in better shape than the jogger, and most importantly of all, not a total psycho.

But now it seems all too plausible.

He's the one the police were searching for. The man in the CCTV that was on the front page of every newspaper in the country. The person Helen was talking about when she said, 'Only a man would do something like that. Only a man would push someone into the road, just because they *might* get in his way. Fucking men.'

Fucking men.

21–11–2022

1.29 a.m.

'Usually, if I run hard enough, I can outrun my anger.' His voice sounds far away, like he's back there in his head; sweat on his brow, Nikes pounding the pavement. 'Whatever's making me mad just sort of . . . fades into the background, gets smaller and smaller, until eventually, I leave it behind. But that day was different. That day it felt like . . . it felt like somebody had doused my soul in petrol and set it alight.'

'Why were you so mad?'

'Because of what she did. She used me, humiliated me.'

He peers into the darkness of the forest.

'Why did you push her?'

'I didn't set out to. I just wanted to talk, that's all. The run was a good excuse to be out, plus I thought I'd get all the anger out of me before I saw her, then we could sit down and talk things through. But I reckon I could have run a hundred miles and it wouldn't have made any difference. By the time I turned onto the bridge I was just about ready to explode. And that's when I saw her.'

'The victim—'

His head snaps round. 'Are you joking? She's no victim.'

'You saw her, and you pushed her—'

'She looked so . . . normal. Like nothing had happened. That's what got to me. It was like she didn't care, like she felt nothing.'

'You wanted to hurt her?'

'I wanted to make her care. I wanted her to *feel* something.'

'So, you pushed her . . .'

'I pushed her, and I kept on running.'

'Why her, Simon? Who was she to you?'

I need him to say it. I need it on record.

42

Catherine

I ring the doorbell and we stand on the doorstep, the rain soaking us through, slicking our hair to our foreheads, seeping through my shirt and jumper. I'd feel the chill of it, if I could feel anything other than the hate that is keeping me on my feet.

Simon is the London Bridge Jogger.

The very idea was unthinkable just a few days ago. Ridiculous, even. My Simon wouldn't do something like that. He just isn't that kind of man.

Now I know better.

When I asked Simon about the jogger that time over dinner, and he looked at me like I was crazy, I think a small part of me knew. Knew, but didn't want to dig any deeper, didn't want to scrape away at the surface of our relationship, because I was afraid of what I might find. Or *who* I might find. I know now that Simon has always been pretending to be someone he is not. He *is* that kind of man, always has been. He just tricked me into thinking otherwise. But is the same true for Lydia? Is our friendship as much a lie as my marriage to Simon was?

I ring the bell again.

'You're sure about this?' the girl says.

I nod, then she nods, too. Doesn't try to talk me out of it. She has a stake in this. She was something to him, he was something to her. As was Dylan. That's why she offered to drive me here in her beat-up old car. She wants to see how this plays out. Wants to get to the truth as much as I do.

Lydia opens the door and throws up her hands.

'My God,' she says. 'I've been worried sick. I must have called you a hundred times.'

Usually, she is a calming influence, the person who makes me feel most like myself. Today, every muscle in my body tenses at the sight of her. She looks different somehow: her face older, features sharper. Was she this thin the last time I saw her, like a stick figure drawn by Charlie?

She pulls me into a hug, squeezes me tight. The sickly-sweet smell of her perfume fills my nostrils, makes me want to gag.

'Oh, thank God you're OK.' She rubs a hand up and down my arm as she points her chin at the girl. 'And who's this?' she asks, and I'm not sure how to reply. I don't know the girl's name. And I don't want to, either. Is Lydia wondering if she is *the* girl, the one I told her Simon had been sleeping with? Or is she just unnerved to find me standing on her doorstep with a stranger?

'A friend,' the girl says, her head shaking, as if she can't help but deny the words, even as they come out of her mouth.

Lydia raises an eyebrow. 'Right. Well, you'd both better come in, out of the rain.'

We follow her down the hall, dripping water onto the polished floor. Once in the kitchen, Lydia slips into autopilot and starts making drinks. Gin from the drinks cupboard, lemon and tonic from the fridge, crushed ice from the freezer. As if it were a normal afternoon and we were about to embark on an hour or so of mindless chit-chat.

'You mustn't do that to me,' she says. 'I didn't have a clue where you were, what was happening . . .'

The girl looks over. She's waiting for me to take the lead, for me to tell Lydia we know what happened on the bridge, that Simon was the pusher, and she was the pushed. But now I'm here, somebody has stolen my voice.

Lydia is still talking, '. . . I even went round to your place, to see if you were there . . .'

Another look from the girl: *Tell her. Go on, tell her.*

I try to speak, but nothing comes.

'Well, you're here now. That's all that matters. You're safe—'

The girl says: 'We know about what happened on the bridge.'

Lydia doesn't turn around. The only sound is the clinking of ice as she loads it into the glasses. She takes a small knife from a drawer, begins hacking at the lemon.

'We know Simon pushed you.'

Lydia drops the lemon slices into the drinks, scoops them up and arranges the glasses in a triangle, carries them over to the table.

'I'm sorry. Who are you, exactly?' she says to the girl, then she looks over at me, as if she has just noticed that a crazy person is standing next to us in her kitchen.

'Did he threaten you?' the girl says. 'Is that why you didn't come forward?'

'What are you talking about?' Lydia sips from her G&T, ice rattling in her glass.

'We know what he did. We know the truth,' says the girl.

But I'm not sure we do.

Why not turn him in? If not on the day it happened, then later on, when it all came out in the papers and the whole world was looking for the man who tried to kill her by pushing her into traffic on London Bridge?

There has to be a reason.

She turns to me. 'Cat, what is this?' She gives me that look again, as if the girl is deranged.

'Simon's confessed,' the girl says.

Lydia pales, swallows, then pulls in a deep breath through her nose and downs the rest of her gin and tonic in one go.

43

Sara

Lydia's mouth twists into a jagged line. 'I am so, *so* sorry,' she says.

Which is bloody typical, isn't it?

Lydia is the victim here. She's the one who almost lost her life at the hands of that psycho, yet she's the one standing here apologising. Because isn't that what women do? What women who have been manipulated and abused and made to think that they are in the wrong all the time do? Isn't that what she used to do all the time with Adam, when he turned on her, snapped at her, made her feel stupid or small? *I'm sorry*, she would say – *don't be angry. Don't be annoyed* – thinking that whatever he said, however unreasonable he was being, she must have earned it. Must have *deserved* it.

Simon must have known how disastrous it would have been for him to be identified as the jogger. He'd have been publicly shamed, lost his job. Probably lost Catherine, too. You couldn't stay married to someone once you found out something like that. You'd never look at them in the same way again.

God only knows what he said to Lydia to keep her quiet.

Sara thinks about him now. His physicality: broad shoulders, powerful arms. She used to like that about him. That he was tall and powerfully built. Found it a turn-on. When he wrapped his arms around her in bed, she felt safe and protected. Now, the idea scares her. The things he is capable of . . .

Lydia covers her face with her hands and her voice is a strangled cry. 'I'm sorry, I'm sorry,' she says, over and over.

'It's not your fault,' Sara says. 'This is what he does. He uses people, lies to them, makes them feel like it's their fault when it's *his*. You mustn't blame yourself. He did this, not you.'

Lydia doesn't even look at her. Her eyes are fixed on Catherine, who is sitting at the kitchen counter, stony-faced.

'You're my best friend. Why would he . . .' Her head nods for a second, then jerks upright. 'Why would he . . . do that to you?'

Sara knows she is missing something here. And she realises that Catherine and Lydia are like her and Helen. Not everything that is said between them is spoken out loud.

'I know, I *know*,' Lydia says. She is weeping now, and she comes to Catherine in small steps, feet scuffing across the marble floor, arms held out in front of her, pleading. 'I didn't want to hurt you. It was a mistake, the stupidest thing I've ever done. I wish I could take it back, every single day, I swear.'

And all at once Sara understands.

Simon isn't the reason Lydia didn't come forward. Catherine is.

44

Catherine

I fade in and out. Sometimes I'm here, in Lydia's kitchen, listening to her tell me what I have demanded to know – the details of her affair with my husband – and sometimes I am elsewhere. Because while I need to know what happened, and can't stand the idea of there being any more secrets, sometimes what she tells me is too much to bear.

So much makes sense now. The distance Simon and Lydia cultivated between them; that she never wanted to come round when Simon was home, always wanted to meet at her house, or somewhere in town; that every time I suggested we get together as couples, me and Simon, her and Andrew, she always had an excuse. I stopped asking after a while. Thought it was because I was special, that she didn't want to share me with anybody else. Stupid of me.

They'd had a fight, her and Andrew.

'I was a mess,' she says. 'I came to see you, but you weren't there.'

I have always been there for her. Always.

'Where was I?'

She looks away, doesn't want to say. Thinks it'll make things worse. As if things could possibly be any worse.

'Where was I?'

She sobs, her chest heaving up and down. 'You were in Leeds, with your parents.' Not at Mum's but, 'with my parents'. I had known

Lydia for about a year when Dad died, and can think of only one occasion I went to stay in Leeds without Simon during that time, which was when Dad was in the hospital and we knew he had only days left to live.

'Keep going,' I tell her. She shakes her head, but I have to hear it. I meet her eyes with mine until she caves.

'I didn't know where to turn,' she continues. 'I came to see you and you weren't there and Simon said I could come in and we talked and he . . . he listened. I just needed someone to talk to, that's all it was. To help calm me down. He listened, and we had a drink and . . . and . . .'

Don't say it. Don't give me clichés at a time like this.

'One thing led to another . . . I'm sorry, I'm so sorry.'

My head fills with pictures of them. My husband and my best friend, in our kitchen, our living room, our bed. No, it would have been downstairs. They wouldn't have wanted to wake Charlie. I see the two of them, sitting side by side on the sofa. Lydia's long, tanned legs curled beneath her. Simon, reaching out to put an arm around her . . .

She's still talking . . .

'—were so bad with Andrew, I thought things were over, I honestly did, and Simon *listened*. He seemed to understand me and . . .' Lydia stops, shakes her head. 'I don't know what we were thinking. It was a moment of total insanity. We just . . . we thought . . .'

Thought what, exactly? That they were going to run away together? Is that what she's trying to tell me? After all that has happened, even though I hate Simon more than I could possibly hate anyone, or anything, the thought of it still claws at my insides. We were married – we *are* married. Doesn't that mean anything to people anymore?

Lydia says, 'He said he had somewhere I could stay, where I could go and get my head straight. A house in a town where nobody knew us, and nobody would bother us. He drove me there in the morning and I stayed there for the rest of the week. He came and visited when he could.'

I spoke to Simon every day while I was in Leeds, Skyped to check on Charlie in the evenings, called to say goodnight before bed. Every time he offered to come and join me, and every time I told him not to. I thought it would be best if he stayed in London with Charlie, then I could devote all my time to helping Mum.

Lydia wipes her eyes again but a fresh swell of tears wets them immediately.

'I didn't want to hurt you. I know how that sounds, but it's the truth. I wanted it to stop,' she says. 'After a week, I realised how stupid I was being, how much I missed Andrew. We started talking again, agreed to give it another go. I wanted to be with him, I really did. So I called Simon, told him it had all been a terrible mistake and that it was over. I said I was coming back to London first thing in the morning to work things out with Andrew, and he told me he understood, that he felt the same way. We agreed to put it behind us, to never speak of it again.'

I can already tell what she is going to say, because she doesn't know Simon like I do, doesn't know that he is often calm in the heat of the moment, that the switch, from kind and caring to angry and spiteful, comes when you least expect it.

'The day after, I caught the early train, got off at London Bridge. I wanted to get my head straight, so I went to get a coffee at a little place over the river. I was crossing the bridge, and the next thing I knew, he was there in front of me, and I was so shocked to see him. He was running towards me. He looked right at me – and he put his arms out and . . . I thought he was pleased to see me . . . I thought he was going to hug me.'

But he didn't hug her.

'Why didn't you turn him in?' the girl asks.

Lydia looks down at the floor, though her words are directed at me.

'I wanted to,' she says, 'but if I had, then everything else would have come out, and then you'd know, and you'd hate me for it. I couldn't bear for you to hate me, so I told the police I didn't recognise him, said I just wanted to put it all behind me. Which I really did. I just wanted to make it up to you. I was trying to be a good friend. I was trying to protect you.'

Lies. She knew what Simon was capable of, and she let me stay with him. She knew, and said nothing.

What sort of a friend does that?

And the fact she has been so nice to me, that she has been there for me? It doesn't make it better. It makes it worse. It makes it all so much worse.

45

Sara

Catherine gives Sara an address in Holborn. Her mum's house, she says, then she rests her head against the passenger-side window.

Sara starts the engine. 'Which way is best?' she asks, but there's no reply, and when she looks, she can see that Simon's wife is slack-jawed, eyes vacant. It reminds Sara of how her dad used to get after he'd downed most of a bottle of whisky. Not like he was dead behind the eyes, more like he was dying, right there and then. Little pieces of him flickering out one by one, like lights in an office building at the end of the day.

'Catherine?' Sara waves a hand in front of Simon's wife's face.

Nothing. She's gone. And Sara can hardly blame her.

Your husband and your best friend? She thinks. *Wow. Just . . . wow.*

Everything that has happened – the affair, the push, the podcast, the murder – it all comes back to that one night four years ago, the argument Lydia had with her husband. How different things would have been if it had never happened. Nobody would have heard of the London Bridge Jogger. She would never have met Adam. Dylan would still be alive. And Catherine would still be the happy, smiling woman she was in her online photos, instead of the broken person she is now. Wouldn't she? Or would Simon eventually ruin her life some other way?

Sara plugs the address into her phone, checks the route, then sets off. It is not far to drive, but it means cutting through the busiest parts of central London. They crawl through the heavy traffic of Elephant and Castle and cross the Thames at Waterloo. Streams of commuters make their way to and from home. Even though it is pouring with rain, with the myriad lights of the city mirrored red, yellow and green in the oily puddles and the wet pavements, there are more than a few joggers out tonight. Sara thinks about how easy it would be for one of those joggers to push somebody into the road. Imagines a body slamming into the windscreen, the screeching of brakes and the shattering of glass.

Simon is the London Bridge Jogger.

He's the man Dylan was searching for. And he was right under their noses this whole time.

Unbelievable.

He actually turned up to the launch party for a podcast that was all about catching him. And he came away that night with her number, having decided that a fake relationship with her would be the best way to keep an eye on Dylan.

What sort of a person does that?

She thinks of all the things she told him, the parts of herself she shared with him, and feels sick. Nine months she dated him for, and she never had a clue, not the slightest suspicion. Why would she? Adam wasn't a psychopath. He was clever, good-looking, sensible. He was normal.

He was none of these things. You didn't know the first thing about him.

Nobody did.

She takes some comfort in that. It wasn't just her he fooled.

Sara parks as close as she can to the address she was given.

'Catherine? We're here.'

Simon's wife stirs, blinks herself back to life. 'Here?' she says.

'At your mum's. You gave me the address, remember?'

'I did? Oh . . . Right, yes.' She reaches down and fumbles with the seatbelt release, but can't seem to make it work. In the end Sara does it for her, then gets out, goes round to the passenger side and opens the door for her, too.

Catherine gets out of the car, stands with one hand on the door and looks around. Her eyes are blank and bloodshot. Does she even know where she is?

'What are you going to do now?' Sara says.

'Sleep,' Simon's wife says. 'I'm going to sleep.'

She points herself towards a three-storey town house with a blue door and sets off without a further word. Sara watches her walk, ever so slowly, over to the house and climb the stone steps up to the front door with her legs shaking as if she were an old woman of ninety.

Don't look away, Sara thinks. It feels like if she looks away too soon Catherine will fall, and if she goes down, she might never get back up.

Catherine reaches the door and Sara turns to go, but before she has even taken a step there is a great scream that has her sprinting towards the house Catherine has just disappeared into.

The blue front door is wide open.

There is blood in the hallway. A wet crimson palm print on the wall, a bright red smudge on the bannister.

The old woman who threw Sara out of Simon's house is sat on the hall floor, half propped up against the wall, her head lolling to one side at an unnatural angle. The side of her face that Sara can see has blood on it, too. *Oh, God, she's dead*, thinks Sara, then the old woman's eyes flutter open and show their whites.

Catherine is down on her knees, shaking her mum by the shoulders.

'Mum? *Mum*?' she shouts, frantic. The old woman coughs, splutters, tries to say something.

'Mum?' Catherine leans in close.

'He's taken Charlie,' her mum says.

21–11–2022

1.34 a.m.

Simon

'She was my wife's best friend,' Simon says. 'She still is.'

Images come to mind as he remembers how Lydia seduced him while his six-month-old son was sleeping upstairs. Her sagging breasts, swaying back and forth as she moved on top of him on the sofa. The soft ripples in her thighs and the way the light played over her body, turning the purple stretch marks across her stomach silver. He remembers the overpowering floral stink of her perfume, that he worried would cling to the furniture for days. And he remembers her laughter, when she called him to tell him it was over.

'It's not like we were actually going to be together, is it?' she said. 'I mean, can you imagine?' Then she laughed, fully, as if she found the idea hilarious.

When he thinks about Lydia, he remembers these things, and he gets a sour taste at the back of this throat. He hates her, can no longer understand how he once felt so different. She is one of those women: the sort who trick good men into doing bad things. If only people knew what she was really like, maybe they'd understand?

Maybe they'd think she deserved it, too.

He considers telling Dylan all of this, because it is the truth and it wants to be told. But despite what Dylan thinks, tonight isn't about truth. It's about survival.

'I've answered your questions,' Simon says. 'Now it's my turn. How did you find me?'

A small shake of the head from Dylan. 'That's not how it works. You've told me who, but you still haven't told me why. I want to know why you did it.'

Simon shakes his finger from side to side, the way he does when he is telling Charlie off for being naughty. 'You want to know more, you've got to tell me how you worked it out.'

He looks away, peers out of the car window into the darkness of the forest, lets the silence do the negotiating for him. Sure enough, Dylan caves.

'Fine,' he says. 'I'll tell you. But don't fuck me around, or I'll make sure you go viral all over again.'

Simon holds his hands up in surrender. 'Just you, me, and the truth. Right?'

'Right,' says Dylan. He adjusts his jacket, makes himself comfortable, then says, 'You were right about the launch. When I met you, it didn't cross my mind you could be the jogger. Even when you started dating Sara, and I'd see you, I didn't suspect. You didn't fit the profile. You weren't a successful banker, or a CEO type. You were recently divorced, worked at a start-up in Soho, lived out in the middle of nowhere. You were just . . . Adam. You seemed a bit of a loser, to be honest. The way you dressed – clothes twenty years too young for you. It was all a bit . . . try-hard, y'know? What she saw in you, I've no idea.'

There it is, thinks Simon. That hint of jealousy in Dylan's voice. 'You still like her, don't you? That's what this is about. She rejected you and this is your way of getting even.'

'Rubbish. Sara and I are friends.'

'She can't stand you.'

'That's not true—'

'She thinks you're a joke.'

'Sure. Whatever.' Dylan crosses his arms and looks out of the passenger-side window, turning away from a truth he doesn't want to hear.

Well, he's going to hear it, all right.

'She told me about you,' Simon says. 'Said you were full of yourself, kept saying you were going to be the next big thing in podcasting when you could barely remember to turn your recorder on half the time. You're a rich kid college drop-out, sponging off your dad. Even your podcast is a flop. You're only doing it so you can sell T-shirts with pictures of your—'

Dylan's head snaps round. 'You don't know the first thing about me, or my family.'

'Oh, really?' says Simon. 'Dylan Carver, bastard lovechild of Peter Lesley-Thorne, CEO of the biggest media company in the UK, net worth of about a billion? He was number eighty-seven on the Sunday Times *Rich List last year. You're not the only one capable of doing a bit of research, Dylan.'*

Simon enjoys the moment of quiet that follows. Is especially pleased by how deflated Dylan looks: head down, arms no longer crossed but wrapped around himself. Like he might burst into tears.

'Sad, isn't it, when you think about it?' Simon says, because why stop when your opponent is on their knees? 'Your dad owns the biggest media corporation in the country, but you end up working at some shitty little podcast company. Let me guess. Any obligation he had to pay your way came to an end once you dropped out of university, and now he doesn't want anything to do with you? He's cut you off, hasn't he? That's why you're demanding hush money off me. That's why you're willing to give up your big exclusive for fifty grand.'

The look of hurt on Dylan's face warms Simon's soul. He waits for a response, is ready for the fight – needs it, even – but there's an unnerving stillness about Dylan. When he responds, his voice is calm and his words measured.

'I thought it was him,' he says. 'When I saw the video of the jogger, I thought it was Dad for a minute. Didn't look like him, not really. It was just . . . the way he pushed the woman, then kept on jogging, y'know? It's just the sort of thing he'd do. You're either in his shadow, or you're in his way. That's how it's always been with Dad. You remind me of him. People like you . . . you think you're better than everybody else, that you're always right and they're always wrong. You think you're

untouchable, but you're not. See, I didn't find you because of Sara. I found you because of you. Because you made mistakes.'

'What mistakes?'

'Six weeks ago I got an anonymous email from a listener. Just a link to a Facebook page – that was all. I opened it, and it was for someone named Simon Wells. And lo and behold, Simon Wells looked an awful lot like you. Only he wasn't divorced, and he didn't live in the middle of nowhere and he didn't work for a struggling start-up. Once I started looking into who he was, it all fell into place. One person, two lives. You should have made your social media private, Simon.'

'Who was it? Who tipped you off?'

'I've no idea,' Dylan says. 'But if I had to guess, I'd say your wife's best friend had something to do with it. Besides, you were sloppy. You used one of Simon's old Facebook photos for Adam's LinkedIn profile. The few tweets on Adam's timeline came from the area where Simon lives. Adam goes away for a conference, Simon goes away on holiday with his wife . . . I could go on. It's all there when you look for it. And whereas Adam didn't fit the profile . . .'

'So what?' says Simon. 'So do a million other people. You didn't send them emails and text messages. Didn't send badges and T-shirts to their office with your fucking face on them.'

'I was testing you. I knew you were living two lives. Why not three? Adam, Simon, and the jogger.'

'But you didn't know, did you? Before tonight, you didn't know for a fact?'

'I knew the type. I grew up with one. Plus, you look like him. You're middle-aged, you like to keep fit. You live nearby. You're not a banker, but close enough. I should have worked it out when I met you at the launch. I remember now. You were so . . . interested, and men like you are only interested in themselves.'

'But you haven't got any proof, have you?' says Simon.

Dylan says nothing.

46

Catherine

Blood on the carpet. A trail, leading from the hall to the kitchen, then over to Simon's chair, where Mum is sitting with a striped tea towel pressed to the side of her head. A terrifying amount of blood. Dark red ribbons and spots and spatters.

'Try not to worry. Head wounds do that, they bleed a lot,' says one of the . . . what are they called . . . wear green uniforms. He eases me away from Mum, pushes me aside so they have room to work.

'It's going to be OK,' I call from the doorway. 'Mum? Can you hear me? It's going to be OK.' But I'm sobbing and the words don't come out right. Mum gives me a puzzled look as an oxygen mask is slipped over her nose and mouth. She looks so old, everything about her so brittle. When did she get so thin? Her wrists, her hair, her skin.

'Few deep breaths for me now, that's it.' The Green Uniform squeezes a rubber bulb and Mum's breathing rattles and hisses. Why is she breathing like that? What did Simon do to her?

Shock is keeping the panic at bay. Keeping me from screaming the house down.

Simon's attacked Mum and he's taken Charlie. He hasn't left the country yet, but now he will, and he is going to take our son with him.

He said he was going to take me on holiday . . .

I want to run out of the house, want to *do* something that isn't just standing here waiting for the police – the bloody useless police – to arrive, but I can't leave Mum like this.

Another Green Uniform removes the tea towel from Mum's head and examines the wound. 'Mmm. You've had a bit of a nasty knock,' he says. He swaps the tea towel for a white cotton pad that turns crimson with shocking speed. One of Mum's arms is limp, the hand lies palm up in her lap, curled fingers stained pink with her own blood.

It *is* her blood, isn't it?

Such a horrible thing to think, but please tell me it's hers. Whatever else he might be – a cheat, a liar, a killer – Simon has always loved Charlie. He can be strict, and yes he has a temper, but he wouldn't hurt his own son, would he?

I see flashes of Simon, in bed with the girl, pushing Lydia into traffic, watching our car burn with Dylan Lesley inside it. I see him hitting Mum, knocking her to the floor and leaving her for dead. Hitting Charlie, too. Leaving a red palm print on his thigh. It was only the once, wasn't it?

The girl is still here. She speaks softly into my ear, 'It's going to be OK.' She puts an arm around me and the urge to push her away comes over me, but I'll fall if she doesn't hold me up. And she was the one who phoned the ambulance and the police, who found the tea towel and held it against Mum's head to slow the bleeding. Maybe she is not all bad. I don't know anymore.

There's a sudden commotion as detectives Carter and Chaudhari arrive, come marching in through the open front door.

'Mrs Wells—' Carter begins.

I rush to her. 'What took you so long? Do you see what he's done? This is because you wouldn't listen. I told you he was alive, I *told* you.'

'Catherine, please—'

'He's taken Charlie. You've got to find him, you have to bring Charlie back. He must have forced his way in and he . . . he hit Mum, she said it was him, she said it was Simon—'

Chaudhari shows me his palms. 'OK, Mrs Wells. Slow down.'

'They could be miles away by now. He could have left the country, he's taken our . . . our . . .' The things he took from the bookcase . . . I can't think of the word. 'You have to *find* them! You were right about him. He's dangerous. He's the jogger, he's the London Bridge Jogger—'

Carter blinks. 'He's—?'

'The man who pushed the woman on London Bridge. It was Simon, it was Simon. He's . . . he's . . .'

I can't find my breath. There is too much to explain.

Chaudhari says, 'OK, Mrs Wells. One thing at a time. Right now, let's just focus on Charlie.'

He's right. It doesn't matter if Simon is the jogger. All that matters is finding him, and bringing Charlie home.

Movement behind me. A Green Uniform emerges from the living room, pulling a . . . one of those chairs with wheels. Mum has a heavy blue blanket tucked in tight around her and her head is almost entirely wrapped in bandages. Her eyes are closed. She isn't moving.

Oh, God, oh God—

'Mum! Mum?' I go to her, take her hand, and she stirs. Her grey lips part and she lets out a moan. All she has done is try to look after us, and I have been so horrible to her and now look what's happened. It is all my fault. I should have been here.

'I'm sorry, Mum.'

'Looks like she's got a broken wrist and she's taken quite the knock to the head,' Green Uniform Two says. 'We're going to need to take her down to St Thomas's. Do you want to jump in the ambulance with her?'

Something tugs at my sleeve. Detective Carter.

'I'm going to send someone with her.' She turns to Chaudhari, directs him to the ambulance with a flick of her eyes, then looks back to me. 'You can follow on in a bit, but right now we need to ask you some questions. We need you to help us find Charlie. And we *are* going to find him. We already have a description of Simon out there and we're going to get one of Charlie out there, too. Every airport, train station and bus station will be on high alert. Trust me, he's not going to get far.'

Simon has been missing for more than a week and the police haven't even come close to finding him. They have failed at every turn. They insisted he was dead, when he was walking around London, when he was outside my front door.

They are the last people on earth I trust to find Charlie.

The ambulance's siren screams into life and I watch them take Mum away. Carter ushers me back into the living room.

'Back in a few minutes,' she says. She disappears upstairs and I hear the soft thud of footsteps through the ceiling. They're in the little front bedroom, the one Charlie was sleeping in when Simon took him.

'What are they doing up there?' I say to the girl. She's standing in the corner, trying not to take up any space in the room. 'They're wasting time. Again.'

The girl looks down at her boots, says nothing.

When Carter comes back downstairs she asks for photographs of Charlie. I pick up my phone, unlock it and hand it over. I can't face looking through it, because while there are lots of photos of Charlie on there, there are lots of photos of Simon, too.

Carter thumbs through the gallery of pictures.

'Do you know what Charlie was wearing when he was taken?' she asks.

Taken. The word hurts my heart.

'I don't know,' I whisper. I am a terrible mother. I can't even remember how my own son was dressed today. I was so set on speaking to Max, on finding the girl, I barely said a word to Charlie this morning. Can't even remember the last thing he said to me.

'But we think he was in bed at the time, yes? So he could be wearing his pyjamas?'

Did Mum pack his pyjamas? I'm sure she would have. But Charlie has quite a few pairs, and right now I can't remember what any of them look like.

'Yes, probably. No. I don't know . . .'

'That's OK, Catherine. You're doing really well.'

Am I? It doesn't feel like I am. It feels like I am useless, that I don't know anything that is going to help the police bring Charlie home.

'You need to start looking for them,' I say.

'We are, Catherine,' she says. 'Now, let's just focus on anything that might help us to find them, OK? Is there anywhere you think Simon might be heading? Somewhere he has connections, maybe? Family or friends in other countries?'

Simon has no other family, apart from us, not since his mum died. No friends who live abroad, either. But he has travelled all over for work. Been to more cities in more countries than I can count. He is clever. Has stayed one step ahead of the police, not just for the last eight days, but for the last four years. Ever since he tried to kill Lydia.

'You can't let him leave the country,' I say. 'He'll disappear. We'll never see him again—'

'We won't let that happen. We're going to find him before that happens,' repeats Carter. 'But if you can think of anywhere he might be heading that could help us work out his next move . . .'

His next move? I haven't the faintest idea.

After the things he has done, there is nothing left of my husband anymore. He's gone, and left behind a total stranger in his place. A stranger who is wanted for murder, on the run, and who has taken my child.

47

Sara

Sara wishes she were back home, or at Helen's. Anywhere but here, standing in the corner of Catherine's mum's potpourri-drenched living room, watching Catherine unravel as the detective fires questions at her. But it'll look weird if she tries to leave. It'll draw attention to her, and then they'll ask her who she is and what she is doing here.

Funny story, now you mention it . . .

She can just imagine what they'll think of her, how they'll look at her. As if she is *that* kind of person. The kind that has affairs, that sleeps with other women's husbands and doesn't care what damage they cause. They'll think she is complicit in his lies. Might even think she's got something to do with what's happened to Dylan. After all, she is the common denominator here; she had the affair with Simon, she worked with Dylan. She even came up with the idea for *The Push*.

The cottage, the one Adam booked for them; that's where she wants to be all of a sudden. Some place nobody knows her, where nobody can ask her questions that are going to make her feel like a bad person. If only she could take off right now, jump in the car like she did when she left her dad, drive straight there and close the door on the world. They were meant to stay at the cottage for a whole week, so she would have two whole days before she'd have to come home. And maybe she could extend the booking, or find another cottage to stay in nearby, just keep moving.

As tempting as the idea is, Sara knows she isn't going anywhere. She has to stay here, has to answer the detective's questions, do whatever she can to help them find Charlie.

Besides, she can't go to the cottage. Simon cancelled the reservation. He told her as much the last time he saw her, said he'd phoned the place and they'd agreed to hold the deposit so they could go another time, after he returned from his imaginary work trip.

He cancelled the reservation. Didn't he?

Sara looks over to Catherine, who is still talking to the stern-looking police detective, still trying and failing to answer her questions. What Charlie was wearing, whether any of his toys are missing, where Simon might have taken him.

'I don't know, I don't know, I don't know!' Catherine cries, and puts her head in her hands.

Sara doesn't want to hurt her any more than she already has, doesn't want to give her another reason to hate her, but knows she has no choice. All that matters now is finding Simon.

Sara clears her throat, tries to find her voice. 'Sorry . . .' she begins. The police detective turns to her, tips her head at an angle, as if she is seeing her for the first time.

'I think I might have an idea,' Sara says. 'Somewhere I think he might have been hiding.'

There is no response from Simon's wife. She is weeping, with her head bowed and her shaking hands clasped in front of her.

'And who are you, exactly?' the detective says.

'It's . . .' It's complicated, she wants to say, but the detective raises an eyebrow and Sara knows she can't delay the moment she has been dreading any longer.

'I was Simon's . . .' Her throat dries in an instant. She swallows, takes a big breath to steady herself, swallows again. 'I was Simon's girlfriend. Only I didn't know him as Simon, and I didn't know he was married, or that he had a kid. He called himself Adam, and I can explain all of that, but what's important right now is . . . We were going to go away together, on holiday, to stay in a cottage, this week. The last time I saw him he told me he'd cancelled the reservation, only . . .'

'Only?' the detective says.

'He might have kept it?' She shrugs. 'And it isn't far. It's only an hour's drive.'

The more she thinks about it, the more it makes sense.

When Adam came to see her, he was already on the run. That's why he was acting so weird. He told her he'd cancelled the reservation because of his work trip, but there was no work trip. So why mention the cottage? Why make a point of telling her he'd cancelled, if he knew that would be the last time he saw her? Because he was already planning his next move, that's why. Go to the cottage on his own, use it as a base so he could get back to London, take the passports and wait for the ideal moment to snatch Charlie.

'Sounds like we should check this place out,' the detective says. 'You've got the address?'

Sara nods. 'I can find it, in my email. My phone's in the car.' She hovers for a moment, unsure if she is allowed to leave.

'Go,' the detective says. Sara hurries out of the room, out the front door and back to the car. She retrieves her phone from her bag on the back seat, stands outside in the moonlight scrolling through her inbox.

Where is it?

Here. She's got it, the reservation email Adam forwarded to her.

She runs back inside, hands over her phone with the email open and watches while the detective gets on her radio and reads out the address of the cottage, says that they need to get some men there right now and that she is on her way.

She hands Sara her phone. 'You and me are going to need to have a talk,' she says, and Sara nods. That look in the detective's eyes is exactly the look she feared. She is being judged, thought of as a bad person.

The detective turns back to Catherine. 'And I think you should go to the hospital, be with your mum. I'll get someone to drive you.'

Catherine struggles to her feet. 'No. I'm coming—' She sways, almost falls back down, just about stays on her feet. 'I'm coming . . . with you.'

The detective puts a hand on Catherine's shoulder. 'Hospital. No arguments.'

'I can drive her,' Sara says. She wants the detective to see she is trying to help, that she is a good person after all but she gets another one of those harsh looks in reply.

'That won't be necessary.'

'S'OK,' Catherine slurs. '. . . I want her to.'

The detective looks as surprised as Sara feels. Her eyes flick back and forth between them, a faintly bemused look on her face, but in the end she doesn't hang around. She is charged up, doesn't want to miss the opportunity to be there when they catch Simon.

'Fine. I'm going to let Detective Chaudhari know you're on your way. We'll be in touch the second we hear anything.' A moment later she is out the door.

Sara helps Catherine to the car, eases her into the passenger seat and goes round to the driver's side.

'Let's get you to St Thomas's,' she says, as she fastens her seatbelt.

The hospital is definitely the best place for Catherine right now. The way she is shivering and shaking, slurring her words and zoning out every five minutes. She needs to be somewhere she can be looked after. Once they are there, Sara will hand her over to the other detective. Maybe he'll tell her she isn't needed anymore, that she can go home. She'll drive straight to Helen's, she decides. She'll be able to breathe again once she is back at Helen's.

Catherine throws back her head and pulls in a breath.

'Stop,' she says.

'Stop?' They haven't gone anywhere yet.

'I don't want to go . . . to the hospital.' Her words are slurred and sleep-filled.

'It's OK,' says Sara. 'Your mum's there. And the other detective is waiting for us—'

'Want to go to this place. Cottage.'

Sara can't imagine anything worse than being trapped in a car with Simon's wife for the next hour. Being around her is hard. It is scary, and it is exhausting.

'Right, yes. But . . .' she begins, but Catherine turns to her and fixes her with a look from those swollen eyes that is beyond desperate, and Sara knows she is going to drive her to the cottage. Not because of Catherine, but because however hard it will be, there is a little boy in the middle of all this. She pictures him now, blowing out the candles on his dinosaur-shaped birthday cake.

Sara knows what it's like to have a father who manipulates people to get what he wants, who lies to make sure he comes out on top. Who is dangerous to be around. No kid deserves that.

'All right,' she says. 'Let's go to the cottage.' She starts the engine.

21–11–2022

1.38 a.m.

Simon

Simon forces Dylan's face up against the passenger-side window, feels the soft give of his bloody nose and lips against his palm, the wetness of his gums and the sharp press of his teeth. Dylan's panicked breaths sound like the squeak of a dog's toy being squeezed over and over in a fist, and while he is of similar build to Simon – younger than him, perhaps stronger, too – he isn't fighting back the way Simon thought he would. The suddenness of the assault seems to have shocked him into compliance.

There is no new video footage of the push.

There are no new witnesses.

'Don't move,' says Simon. He reaches inside Dylan's jacket, feels around, finds what he's looking for in an inside pocket. A small plastic device with a red light on the top that tells him every word they have exchanged over the past hour has been recorded.

'Off the record? You must think I'm stupid. Now, don't move. If you move, I'll kill you.'

Dylan nods. 'OK-OK-OK.' He looks on the verge of tears. Good, thinks Simon. Keep him on edge, keep him scared.

Simon opens the car door and steps outside, moves off the path and into the fringes of the forest. He would delete the recording if he knew how, but he doesn't know the right buttons to press, so he searches for something heavy and solid. He spies a rock as big as his fist, picks it up then sets the recorder on the ground, holds it between his fingers, then snatches them away just before he brings the rock down. The device's screen explodes, sending pieces of broken plastic spraying into the air. He brings the rock down again and again, keeps going until there's nothing left but a hundred useless fragments of plastic and broken bits of circuit board. He kicks at the remains of the recorder with his foot, mashes them into the dirt, scatters them.

There, he thinks. That should do it.

He came prepared to give Dylan the money, having withdrawn all of Charlie's university fund and everything from the account he uses when he is being Adam. Though judging by Dylan's response to the sight of his own blood, to the sheer panic that gripped him when Simon hit him, Dylan's silence isn't going to cost him a penny.

Then he turns back to the car and sees the passenger door has been flung wide.

Dylan has gone.

Fuck. Simon stands still, listens.

He can hear the faint rushing of traffic on the North Circular Road, but the acoustics are strange in the forest. It's hard to tell which direction sounds are coming from. He keeps still, listens to the click and chirrup of insects, small animals moving around in the undergrowth. Something else, too. Something bigger than a cricket or a mouse. Twigs straining underfoot, the squelch of mud. A tension in the air, a breath being held . . .

Dylan.

Simon moves in the direction of the breaking twigs and the held breath, taking quiet, careful steps, resisting the urge to run and give away his position.

There, up ahead. A shifting shape, black on black, nestled up against the trunk of a fallen tree. Somebody crouched down, waiting for the right moment to make a break for it? He moves towards the shape, then a branch gives out a brittle crack underfoot and the shape comes to life, bounds away into the forest on all fours.

Just a fox. A fucking fox.

Simon puts his hand to his chest, feels his heart beating too hard against his palm.

Dylan has got away, and now he's going to tell the whole world what Simon has done, and while he might not have the evidence to prove it, if he shouts loud enough, people will start asking questions, and that will be very bad indeed. The web of lies Simon has spun is a delicate one. It relies on nobody picking at a single thread, lest the whole thing loses its shape and comes falling down.

Fuck. He's going to have to run, he decides. Go home. Tell Catherine his work trip has been brought forward, tell Sara something's come up. Catch a flight early tomorrow morning. Hopefully, he'll be in another country by the time he goes viral.

He wades back through the trees, reaches the path, turns left then right. He has nearly reached the car when the screaming shadow comes racing towards him and knocks him off his feet.

48

Catherine

—back to myself with a sickening start.

I surface from the Nothing Place.

Where am I?

In the car, with the girl. Driving to the cottage. We are going to get Charlie.

The rumble of the road passes through my body, rattles my skull. Tall shadows shrink and collapse into nothing as we drive by. All the while, sleep bullies me, sets my head nodding, shuts my eyes for me and drags me down into the dark. There's still some fight left in me. Some small reserve of energy that pushes back and has me jerking upright with a cry of alarm every fifteen minutes. Each time it happens, reality floods in, hits me like a tidal wave.

Simon's taken Charlie.

If we don't find them soon, I might never see my baby again.

I want to reach out to Charlie. Want him to know that Daddy isn't Daddy anymore.

Remember when we talked about strangers, Charlie? Remember we said that if a strange man tries to talk to you, you should walk away? And if he follows, you should scream and run as fast as you can? Well, Daddy is a stranger now. Run away, Charlie. Run as fast as you can!

Simon's voice comes to me: *Nonsense. He's fine, Cat. He's with his dad. He's having the time of his life.*

Don't listen to him. Block it out. Focus on the road. On the lights and the lines speeding south, the rumble of the car's tyres and the rush of the night traffic, the way the car is buffeted from side to side whenever a lorry charges by. These things are real. This car is real. The girl is real. I am real.

Simon's voice is not.

I peer out of the window, into the darkness.

Where are you, Simon? Where are you taking our son?

I can't see properly. Can't focus on anything.

My eyes are full of sand. Deserts' worth of sand. I must have that condition . . . People who stare at screens or leave their contact lenses in for too long get it. Glands become blocked and the tear film stops doing its job. Left untreated it can lead to corneal ulcers, even blindness. Am I going to go blind? Jonathan didn't say I would go blind if I didn't sleep.

Up ahead, I make out the ghost of a figure, caught in the beam of our headlights. I see it at a distance, at the side of the road. We draw closer and . . . it can't possibly be what it looks like, can it? Because it looks like somebody has left a child by the side of the motorway. A little boy, sitting beneath the two uprights of a flickering road sign, his blond hair ablaze under the glare of our passing. We zoom by and I spin round in my seat, astonished at the recklessness of it all. Leaving a child by the side of the road? Could there be anything more negligent? I catch another glimpse of him as he recedes into the night, and see that he is wearing pyjamas.

Charlie.

'Stop the car,' I scream. 'For God's sake, stop the car. He's there. He's right there!'

A squeal of tyres as the car slips sideways. The girl grips the wheel, steadies us. 'Who? *Who's* there?'

'Charlie. He's back there!' I slap my hands against the passenger window and try to look behind us but am blinded by headlights. 'You have to stop the car!'

The girl checks over her shoulder. 'I'm trying!'

She brings the car to a stop, and I am out the door, shuffling back along the hard shoulder, weaving across the concrete. Charlie is back there, under that road sign. He is all alone in the cold and the dark, and he is in terrible danger.

Traffic streams by. A storm of light and noise. Headlights swallow me whole, spit me out, leave me dizzied and blinded. I lift an arm to shield my eyes, locate the grey rectangle of the road sign, thirty feet away at the top of a steep embankment. I run towards it, run as hard as my exhausted body will allow.

Twenty feet away and my lungs are bursting.

Ten feet, and my body is on fire.

I crawl up the embankment on hands and knees, fingers digging into the dirt.

I'm coming, Charlie. Mummy's coming . . .

I climb the final stretch . . . and am there. The sign towers above me. I stand between its giant supports and—

Charlie has vanished. There is nothing here but the grass and the dirt beneath my feet.

Impossible. He was right here just a moment ago.

I turn on the spot, call for him, scream his name. Maybe he got scared and ran away? I scan the scrubland at the side of the motorway, can make out the vague shapes of trees and bushes, ditches and gullies he could fall into and hurt himself.

I shout into the darkness, 'Charlie? It's me. It's Mummy.'

He was right here.

You're imagining things—

But I saw him.

You're going mad—

I am *not* going mad. It was Charlie. He was wearing his dinosaur pyjamas and he was sat under this sign and he was all alone. Simon must have abandoned him, left him by the side of the road.

—because you haven't slept for over a week—

No! He was here.

—and you're seeing things.

I will not accept that. This is just like back at the house. I said things were moving around, said people were watching me, and I was right. So, why can't I be right about this? Why can't I be right, and Charlie be here with me, where he is safe?

A noise. I turn, but it's only the girl. She climbs up the last of the embankment then doubles over, breathing hard, with her hands on her knees.

'He was here,' I tell her. 'He was . . .'

Right here.

The girl nods, says nothing.

'You didn't see him? He was sitting here, and he was wearing his dinosaur . . .' The word has gone.

I turn in a circle, call his name a few more times, but I know it's useless. There is only the empty field and the bushes and the scrubland, the lanes of traffic below and the cars rushing by.

I collapse, sit down hard beneath the road sign.

Ten days. That's how long you can go without sleep before your mind and body shut down for good. How many days is it now? Seven, eight? I don't remember. But I know I am getting close to the end. How can I not be, when I am imagining little boys by the side of the road?

The girl comes over and takes a seat on the grass beside me.

'I think I'm going mad,' I tell her.

'Don't say that,' she says. 'It's all this, it's everything that's happened. It's just . . . it's a lot for one person.' She takes my hand in hers and her warm fingers interlace with mine.

'We're going to find him, and we're going to get Charlie back.' She sounds determined, like she really means it. I'm grateful that she is here, though it doesn't change the fact that when I look at her something curdles in my stomach.

The girl stands, takes a moment to brush the dirt and the grass off her dress.

She offers me a hand. 'Name's Sara, by the way,' she says.

An image flashes into my mind. Simon in bed with the girl, his lips pressed up to her ear, saying her name over and over . . . I shake it off. It doesn't matter anymore – *he* doesn't matter anymore. Besides, I'm too tired not to take her hand. She pulls me to my feet, and we begin to walk back to the car, hazard lights blinking in the far distance.

'Careful,' she says. 'Slippy here.' She takes me by the arm, guides me down the embankment and walks me back to the car, and when we get there she opens the passenger door for me.

'I'm sorry,' I say, before I get in. 'Didn't mean to scare you.'

'It's OK,' she says. I fall into my seat and she closes the passenger door and moves around the front of the car.

It's not OK. We could have crashed. I could have killed us both. All because I'm so tired I have started seeing little boys by the side of the road.

What have you done to yourself?

A vibration in my pocket. I take out my phone, hoping to God it's the police calling with good news. They have found Simon, Charlie is safe, the nightmare is over. But it isn't the police. It's Lydia. Her name in big bright letters on my phone's screen, along with a small circular picture of her I cropped from a selfie of us. In it, she is grinning wildly, the lower half of her face distorted by a giant wine glass. It used to make me smile when I saw that picture. Used to remind me of good times. Now her distorted face looks ghastly, like she is disfigured.

'News?' the girl – Sara – says, as she shuts the driver's side door.

I show her the phone's screen.

Why would Lydia be calling me? How could she think, for one second, that I want to speak to her ever again after what she has done?

I swipe the screen to decline the call, then lay my head against the car window and wait for Sara to start the engine. But a moment later we still aren't moving, and when I look over, I see that she is staring straight ahead, lost in thought.

'What is it?' I say.

'Lydia,' she says. 'Where did he take her?'

I'd have thought it obvious. 'The cottage, of course,' I say. He took Lydia there, was planning to take Sara there, too. I wonder who else he has taken to his love nest? The thought makes me want to gag.

But Sara is shaking her head. 'I don't think so. She said he took her to a house, in a town where nobody knew them, not a cottage in the middle of nowhere. And she stayed there for a week before she came back to London, before everything happened on the bridge.'

I've no idea why she is bringing this up now, why she is asking me questions about the time my best friend and my husband had an affair. How is this going to help us bring Charlie home?

I shrug. 'Does it matter? Let's go.'

'It's just . . . he told me he had a place in . . . Farnham? Farnborough? Somewhere like that.'

Farnborough. That awful house.

'His mum lived in Farnborough,' I explain. 'We sold her house after she died. They didn't . . .' How to explain Simon's relationship with his mother? 'They didn't get on. They reconnected when she became ill; he used to visit her. She only lasted another year. When she died, he couldn't wait to get rid of the place. Anyway, that was before . . .' Before what happened on the bridge, before the thing with Lydia.

'You're sure?' She looks at me.

I am not so far gone that I don't remember when my mother-in-law died. It was the month before Charlie was born. I was heavily pregnant at the . . . the thing . . . the funeral. Too pregnant to stand when the small congregation got to their feet to sing hymns. I hated every second of it. Hated these strange people coming up to me at the wake, eager to put their hands on my belly. Hated their bittersweet smiles, as if my being pregnant was somehow connected to Simon's mum's passing. Or worse, as if a part of her might survive in him.

'I'm sure,' I tell her. 'He sold it, just after Charlie was born.'

There were meetings with solicitors. Days when he would take off in the car first thing in the morning, drive over to Farnborough to sort through her things, and not come home until after dark.

'Definitely?' she says.

'Well . . . he must have,' I say.

It's not like I saw the paperwork. Not like I saw the money land in our account, either, but Simon has always handled our finances. Has always been the one to keep track of our incomings and outgoings. Managing money is what he does, what he's best at.

'It's not some . . . some fling with a woman half his age. It's a house. You can't hide owning a house, it's just not possible.' I laugh. It isn't meant to be a dig at her, the part about the fling, but I've said it now. I can't take it back. And it's not as if it isn't true.

Sara looks at me, and I can tell what she is thinking: that this is Simon we're talking about here. He has kept countless secrets from both of us.

'We should make sure,' she says. 'The police are checking the cottage, we should check the house, just in case.'

'And what if it's nothing?' I say. 'What if it isn't where he took Lydia because he sold it, like he said he did?'

She reaches over and plucks my phone off my lap.

'We could ask her?' She hands it to me.

21–11–2022

1.43 a.m.

Simon

Simon must have landed on something hard, a rock or a branch. There's a sharp pain in his kidneys and a catch at the top of his breath that wasn't there before. He pulls himself up onto all fours and tries to orientate himself. Good God, Dylan came out of nowhere. Hit him like a fucking bus.

A bright light flares ahead of him in the darkness. Dylan's face, illuminated by his phone's screen. He doesn't look as if he is about to cry anymore.

'You should have done it my way,' he says.

Simon gets to his feet, breathing heavily. 'You were recording me. You were going to take the money and ruin me anyway.'

'I had this plan,' Dylan says. 'I'd get the episode ready, then give you twenty-four hours' notice before releasing it. Time for you to get away, go on the run. Season Two – the hunt for the jogger continues!' He runs a hand under his bloody nose. 'Now . . . I'm not sure I can be bothered. Watching you squirm is going to be so much more entertaining.'

'Wait,' Simon says. 'I can get more money. Lots more money.'

They track everything at work, every time a payment is made, or money transferred from one account to another. But he can find a way, he's sure of it. An accounting error; those things take an age to come to light.

He pats his pockets, searching for the envelope of cash he brought with him, but there is no envelope. No phone, either. Dylan must have taken both. And then Simon realises, it's his phone Dylan is holding.

'Let's see,' says Dylan. 'Who shall we tell first?' His thumb hovers over the screen. 'Sara? Or Catherine?'

Simon closes the space between them, hands out, palms up, as if Dylan is holding the detonator to a bomb. And for Simon, he might as well be. His job, his home, his marriage, Charlie; he is about to lose it all.

'Huh,' Dylan says. 'Can't find Sara's number. Makes sense. You and your rules. It'll have to be Catherine.' He jabs the screen with his thumb.

Simon lunges forward as he hears the sound of the dialling tone. Dylan turns away, holds the phone out of reach. They collide, spinning in the dark, feet scuffing over the forest floor. Then Simon's elbow connects with Dylan's jaw and the phone drops. It would be lost in the undergrowth, were it not for the fact that the screen is lit up with Cat's name. They drop down to their knees, scrabble for it. Dylan gets there first, hand closing around the phone, which is ringing . . . ringing.

Simon snatches at Dylan's collar, heaves himself forward, puts both hands on the back of Dylan's head and pushes his face down to the forest floor.

The phone falls from Dylan's grasp. Simon wants to reach for it, end the call before Catherine answers, but if he moves, Dylan will be able to speak, and he can't afford to let Dylan make a sound. So he straightens his arms, locks his elbows and presses down as hard as he can. Dylan lets out a muffled cry, his arms flap and his heels kick, but Simon keeps up the pressure, pushing down with everything he's got.

The sound of the ringing phone is loud in the quiet of the forest.

Dylan struggles beneath him, but Simon will not let him up, will not give him a second to catch his breath.

A click. Catherine's voice: 'Hello . . . I can't get to the phone right now . . .'

Voicemail.

'Don't say a word,' Simon hisses. 'Not a fucking word.' He adjusts his grip, a twist of Dylan's hair held tight in his fist, then pushes down harder.

'Please leave a message—'

'Not one word.'

'—after the beep.'

Dylan has stopped fighting.

Simon pitches forward, grabs the phone and presses the screen to end the call. He rolls onto his side, exhausted, breathless.

'I told you . . . you don't need . . . to do this. I can get you money. I've got . . . money.'

Dylan does not reply.

Simon gets to his feet, gives Dylan a prod with the toe of his shoe. When that fails to rouse him, he drops down on his haunches, pulls at Dylan's arm, turns him over onto his back. Dylan's eyes are closed, his lips caked with dirt. Wet mud glistens between his teeth. Simon picks up Dylan's hand and checks for a pulse.

He's alive. Unconscious, but alive.

Simon stands, hands braced behind his head.

Fucking Dylan. This is all his fault. And while he might be unconscious now, he'll soon wake up, and when he does, he's going to ruin everything.

Unless he doesn't get the chance. To tell Catherine and Sara. To finish his podcast. To get out of this forest alive.

It comes to Simon then: his next move.

It will be the hardest thing he has ever done, but it could work. Could get him free from it all. From Dylan, from Sara. From what happened with Lydia. He can start again, somewhere new. Take Charlie with him, maybe Catherine – if she'll go along with it. She adores him, after all, and she's weak. She's always let him take the lead, she needs him . . . Plus, it would be easier having her there for Charlie.

But if she won't play along?

He can cross that bridge when he comes to it.

49

Sara

Simon's mum's place is a squat red-brick semi-detached house, tucked away in a dark corner of a quiet cul-de-sac, in an area of Farnborough that has most definitely seen better days. Some of the houses have graffiti-covered metal shutters on their windows and doors, many have weather-beaten For Sale signs posted in their front gardens. And even though they are still in sight of the busy main road, where the traffic roars by and the glow from all-night off-licences and fried chicken takeaways illuminates the pavements, there is a middle-of-nowhere quality about the place.

What was it Simon used to say about his fictional bachelor pad? Soulless, he called it, which always made Sara think of a cookie-cutter new build, lacking in history or character. This house isn't like that. It is about as far away from that as you can imagine. It is old, and it most certainly has character, just not the sort of character you'd like to spend any time with. It is soulless in its own way. Creepy, too. Maybe because it is a secret place, Sara thinks, for doing secret things.

She parks the car at the entry to the cul-de-sac, because if Simon really is here, she doesn't want him to know they are coming, and she wants to make sure they can get away quickly.

'Can you walk?' she asks Catherine, hoping the answer is no. If she needs to run, she doesn't want anything slowing her down.

'I think so,' Catherine says. 'I feel a bit better now.'

If anything, she looks worse. Her eyes are red slashes surrounded by purple bruises, her skin waxy under the orange glow of the streetlights. There is also, Sara notes, an unwashed smell about her. A mixture of sweat and sour bad breath, like a teenage boy's bedroom.

'I can go on my own, if you like,' Sara says.

'I want to come.' Catherine reaches down to unbuckle her seatbelt, and this time manages it without Sara's help.

Sara gets out of the car and goes round to the other side, opens the door, takes Catherine's hand and helps her to her feet. Catherine sways back and forth, one hand on the open car door for support.

'I'm OK,' Catherine says, as if she's trying to convince herself. 'I can do it.' She pulls in a big breath, lets go of the car door and takes a faltering step forward, stays upright.

They move down the road together, eyeing the house at a distance.

There is no car parked on the driveway, no sign of life in any of the windows.

When they reach the path that leads up to the front door, they both stop.

'If we see anything that doesn't look right, we're calling the police, right away,' Sara says, keeping her voice low.

Catherine nods, her eyes fixed on the front of the house. 'He won't be here,' she says, with a small, disbelieving shake of the head. 'He sold it. I know he did.'

Don't you get it yet? Sara thinks. *It doesn't matter what he told you. He lied about everything.*

Besides, Lydia had confirmed it.

Back in the car, Sara had been the one to make the call on Catherine's phone. Catherine wouldn't speak, so it was left to her to ask Lydia where Simon had taken her during their week-long affair. Eventually, Lydia said he took her to a run-down little house off a big main road in Farnborough. No, he didn't tell her it was his mum's place, but it was definitely in Farnborough, a little two-up two-down on a scruffy council estate, and could she please just speak to Catherine for one minute, please? Could Sara tell her that she was so, so sorry for everything, that she never meant for this to happen. She even sent an anonymous email to some website to try and make sure Simon—

Catherine had cut her off then, just leaned over and pressed the button to hang up the call.

Sara walks down the path to the front door and Catherine follows.

The house looks well kept, with a small, recently mown lawn, and two tall ferns footed in terracotta pots either side of the path. The curtains are drawn behind the ground-floor window and the front door's frosted panes of glass reveal nothing of what might be on the other side.

There's a doorbell. Sara presses it with her thumb, hears a chime from inside the house, and takes a few steps back. She wants to see the windows upstairs as well as those on the ground floor.

She listens, watches. Waits.

No lights come on in the upstairs windows, no footsteps come thumping down the stairs. There is no sign at all that anybody is home. Sara feels the tension across her shoulders slacken.

It's a relief, him not being here, but a disappointment, too. She wants to help catch him, to be at least partly responsible for his downfall. She pictures him being marched from the house in handcuffs, peering out of the rear window of a police car as he is being driven away. How wonderful it would be for him to see her at that moment, to realise she isn't such a fool after all.

Sara tries the doorbell one more time, just to be sure. Even hammers a fist against the door, but nobody comes. She turns to Catherine, who has made a tunnel out of her hands and has her face pressed against the ground-floor window.

'There's nobody here,' Sara says. 'We should go.'

Get back on the road. Go to the cottage. With any luck the police will have found Simon by now and Charlie will be safe, and this will all soon be over.

'Wait,' Catherine's face is still pushed up against the glass. She lifts one hand as a signal to keep quiet. 'Wait . . .'

Perhaps she's recognised something of Simon's inside?

'I thought I saw . . .'

Sara steps onto the lawn and joins Catherine over by the window. 'What is it?' she whispers.

'It looked like him . . .'

'Simon?' Sara readies herself to run but Catherine shakes her head.

Not Simon. Charlie, then. She thought she saw Charlie. But she also thought she saw Charlie half an hour ago, sat under a road sign by the side of the motorway.

'Let me see.' Sara switches places with Catherine, cups a hand over her eyes and peers through the window.

There is only a narrow gap between the curtains, but it is possible to make out the vague shapes of furniture in the darkness of the living room. Sofa up against one wall, a low coffee table, a big flat-screen television, its standby light a pinprick of red in the darkness.

'By the door,' Catherine whispers. 'It looked like somebody was there.'

Sara looks over to the half-open living room door. There *is* something there, an irregular black shape, half in and half out of the room. A person? It is hard to tell in the dark. Sara screws up her eyes, realises what it is. Someone has left a coat or a jacket hanging from the door handle, that's all. It's not a person, and it most certainly isn't a little boy.

She turns back to Catherine to let her know that there is nobody inside the house. But Catherine isn't beside her anymore.

Sara takes a step away from the window.

'Catherine?' she hisses.

Where the hell did she go? Sara turns, walks a short way back up the path, stops sharp as she hears a thud from somewhere behind the house.

'Catherine?'

A moment later she hears the sound of breaking glass.

21–11–2022

3.04 a.m.

Simon

The first thing Simon does when he arrives at Sara's is get a plastic bag from the kitchen and take it to the bathroom. He locks the door and undresses, bags up his clothes – Dylan's clothes – and gets into the tub, turns on the shower and lets the water rain down over his head and shoulders. He scrubs himself all over, paying particular attention to his hands and fingernails.

He wonders how much time he has bought himself. A few days? A week, maybe? Perhaps he should have dumped Dylan's bag somewhere else, instead of kicking it under the car. And there'll be CCTV at the tube stations – Walthamstow, Green Park, Elephant and Castle. On the streets, too. Though at least he won't look like himself in the footage. How ridiculous, he thinks, that he'll have been caught on camera walking around London wearing a T-shirt with Dylan's face printed on it.

He watches the filthy water circling the drain, and can't help but think about Dylan's body, how unexpectedly heavy it was when he switched clothes with him, slipped his father's watch over his wrist, dragged his body the short distance to the car and heaved him behind the wheel. Dylan was unconscious the whole time, so Simon can't possibly have seen him move as the fire took hold. Can't have seen him slam a desperate hand against the driver's side window. He'd have to have been awake for that to happen, and he most definitely was not. It was a trick of the light. A shadow in the flames.

There's no point in dwelling on it, he supposes. Dylan's dead either way.

He is almost finished when he hears Sara calling for him. 'Adam, is that you?'

He gets out of the bath, leaves the shower running to wash away the dirt, then hurries to make himself presentable – gargling mouthwash, splashing on aftershave.

'Only me,' he says, as he peers into Sara's bedroom. She is sitting up in bed, her phone in her hand.

'You scared the shit out of me,' she says. 'I was about to call the police.'

The police. The word makes his heart leap. He looks at the phone in her hand, her thumb hovering over the screen, and thinks about rushing her, grabbing it off her. Then she drops the phone and picks up a pillow, launches it at him.

'Give me a second, I'm all wet,' he tells her. He shuts the door, goes back into the bathroom and opens the window. He forces the plastic bag containing Dylan's clothes out through the gap, hears it hit the ground five storeys below, then closes the window, turns off the shower.

He needs time to think.

He moves to the kitchen, fills the kettle and switches it on. For the time it takes to boil he finds himself wondering if he is going to kill Sara. An image comes to mind of her face down on the bed, his hands pressing down on the back of her head . . .

Stop, he tells himself. You don't need to kill her. She doesn't know anything.

Yes, she's suspicious of him turning up at this hour – he can tell that much by the sound of her voice – but he'll talk her round. He has always been able to talk her round. The smallest hint of what she wants most in the world – a future together, a family – and she gets this faraway look in her eyes, will believe anything he says.

His life with Sara is a secret thing, with so few connections to reality.

Just one more hour, he thinks, one more hour in that make-believe world, before he says goodbye to it forever.

50

Catherine

My little boy is trapped inside his dead grandmother's house. I know he is. I can *feel* it. I don't know if Simon is in there with him – that connection between us has gone now – but I have to get Charlie out. I've got to save him.

Mummy's coming, darling.

The fog in my head clears, clarity descends. Charlie needs me.

I leave Sara, take the narrow path that runs down the side of the house, follow it until I reach the garden. Back when Simon's mum was alive, the whole place was overgrown with weeds but now the bushes have been trimmed back and, from what I can see in the dark, the lawn is neat and tidy. Did Simon do this? Has he been coming to his dead mother's house in secret to tend the garden?

There's a large pane of frosted glass in the back door. I rap my knuckles against it. 'Charlie?' I whisper. 'Charlie?'

Nothing.

I try the door's handle, turn and push. Locked. I take out my phone, wake it up and point it at the ground. There is a withered plant in a small terracotta pot by my feet. I pick it up and weigh it in my hand, then bring the bottom of the pot down hard against the corner of the window. There's a loud *thunk!* and a crack appears in the glass. I hit it again and this time the pot breaks in my hand, explodes in a shower of dry soil, but the window breaks, too. A shard of glass folds inwards, drops into the house and shatters on the kitchen floor.

It leaves behind a hole big enough to fit my hand through. I reach through the gap, feel for what I hope somebody has left behind – for what I hope Simon has left behind.

Please be there, please be there . . .

It is, thank God. I turn the key, unlock the door and open it.

I shine the phone's light ahead of me, step over broken glass and into the kitchen. It is nothing like I remember it from the few times I came to visit. Run-down and dirty, smelling of grease and boiled vegetables, with a broken cooker and one working gas ring that we had to use to boil the kettle for making cups of tea. Now it smells of nothing, and looks clean and modern. Spotlights in the dropped ceiling, black laminate work surfaces holding appliances: microwave, juicer, espresso machine, all sleek and new-looking, covered in buttons and blinking LEDs.

At the far end of the room, the door leading to the hallway has been left ajar. That's where I saw Charlie, hiding in the shadows.

I move through the kitchen, into the darkness of the hallway. A door to my right leads to an open-plan living space, a dining table surrounded by chairs in one area, a coffee table, sofa and television in the other. A chair, like the one Simon has at home.

'Charlie?'

He might be hiding. He is good at hiding, likes playing that game – what's it called? The one where I cover my eyes with my hands and he tears off laughing as I count down from fifty in a loud voice, then stomp around the house pretending to be a hungry giant. His giggling always gives him away, but I am often surprised by the tiny spaces he can squeeze into.

'You don't have to be frightened,' I tell him. 'It's only Mummy.'

I shine the light under the table. There's nothing there, only a cage of shifting shadows made from the legs of dining chairs. The sofa, then. He could be hiding behind it. I step towards it, lean forward and shine the light at the space between the sofa and the wall. It's too narrow, even for Charlie.

'Catherine!' A voice hisses in the dark. I whirl round, but it's only Sara, her features washed blue by the light of the phone's screen.

'What are you doing?'

I'd have thought that perfectly obvious. I am trying to find my son. He is hiding somewhere inside this house and I am trying to find him, but Sara comes to me on tiptoe and grabs me by the elbow. 'Come on, we've got to go.'

'But I saw—'

She tugs at my arm. 'The neighbours are going to hear.'

'He's here, he's—'

She marches back into the hall, plucks something from the door handle. A piece of clothing. She holds it out to me. 'It's a hoodie,' she says. 'That's what you saw. He's not here, nobody's here.'

I suppose it could have just *looked* like someone was peering into the room from behind the door, but the hoodie doesn't explain the feeling I have in my gut, that rock-solid certainty that Charlie is nearby.

'He's been here,' I tell her. 'I know he has.'

She gives me an exasperated look. 'You don't *know* he has.'

I don't expect her to understand. How could she? She isn't a mum. Has never known that bond between mother and child, never felt that irrefutable connection, deep inside her bones.

'Come on,' she says. 'Let's go, before we get in trouble.'

But I can't leave, not while there's still a chance Charlie might be here.

'We have to check upstairs,' I insist. 'He might be hiding in one of the rooms. We like to play—'

'We are *not* going upstairs.' She takes hold of my arm again. 'We need to leave. Now.'

If she won't help me, I'll look for him myself. I pull free of her, move over to the stairs and set my foot on the bottom step. I grip the bannister with one hand.

But when I go to take a step forward the staircase pulses; it shifts and shivers and all of a sudden there are far too many steps for a house this size. Dozens and dozens of them, as if the upper floor is a hundred feet above us. The longer I look, the further the top step recedes into the distance, the staircase becoming a never-ending climb upwards, to that dark and forbidding Nothing Place.

'Charlie?' I shout as the world slips sideways.

I hear the girl call my name as my legs give way and I am falling, the air passing by me for far too long. Then I collide with something hard and a new pain explodes in my shoulder. I hear a loud knocking sound, both inside me and outside of me, which must be my head hitting the floor.

'Jesus,' I hear Sara say. 'Are you OK?'

I am not OK.

There is a rushing sound in my ears, like they are full of water.

I feel the hard press of the floor against my side and know I am still, but the world will not stop spinning.

Hands touch me in the dark.

My arms, my shoulders.

'Catherine? Hold on.' The phone's light flickers around the room, then everything turns white. She has turned the room's light on. She comes back into view, gets down in front of me.

'Catherine, look at me,' she says.

I can't lift my head. It is the heaviest thing in the world. Every part of me is so very heavy.

Simon speaks to me: *It's too late, Cat. I've gone, and I've taken Charlie with me. You might as well sleep. There's nothing you can do now.*

I mustn't close my eyes. Mustn't sleep.

'Let's get you sitting up,' Sara says.

She hooks an arm around my middle, wrestles me up until I am on the armchair.

'Catherine, can you hear me? We need to get you to a hospital.'

'We need . . . find Charlie—'

What if he is hiding upstairs and we leave and then Simon comes back from wherever he is and takes Charlie away?

'We need to check upstairs,' I tell her. '. . . Might be scared. He . . . be hiding.'

Sara looks at me as if I am speaking a foreign language. 'I can't . . . I don't understand what you're saying,' she says.

'Upstairs! We need to check upstairs before we go.'

She screws up her face, shakes her head. 'I don't know what you're trying to say.'

How can she not know what I am saying when I am being perfectly clear?

'Upstairs! *Upstairs, upstairs, upstairs*!' What is so hard to understand about that? But then I hear myself, hear the malformed words coming out of my mouth – *Uh-uuurs, uh-uuurs!* – like a toddler imitating their parents' speech.

I can't speak. My tongue and lips are no longer working together.

I focus, manage to lift my head high enough to meet her eyes, try again.

'Uh-airs.'

'Upstairs?' she says. 'You want me to check upstairs?'

I nod and she casts an eye up to the ceiling. 'There's nobody here,' she says. 'If there was, they'd have woken up by now. We need to go.'

'Uh-airs. Pl-ees. *Pl-ees*!'

'We need to get you some help.'

'Cha-lee. Uh-airs.'

Sara licks her lips, considers it.

'Fine,' she snaps, and she straightens. 'I'll look upstairs, but as soon as I'm done we're going, and I'm taking you to the nearest hospital.'

'Uh-airs.'

'There's nobody here,' she says, but she goes anyway, and I hear her heavy boots begin to move up the stairs as she begins to climb up that never-ending staircase, to the Nothing Place.

51

Sara

At the top of stairs is a narrow, carpeted landing, with plain white walls and no windows. Three doors, one to her immediate right, two others at right angles to each other at the opposite end of the landing. All of the doors are closed.

Sara stands still, listens. There is no noise coming from any of the rooms. She puts a hand to her chest, feels the heavy beating of her heart and takes a few deep breaths.

This is stupid. There's nobody here.

She should go back, tell Catherine she checked the rooms and that they were empty. They must be. If anybody was here, they'd have woken up when Catherine smashed the window, or when she shouted Charlie's name, or when she fell into the coffee table and nearly broke her neck. This whole thing is nothing more than a giant waste of time.

But what if it isn't? What if Charlie *is* here, hiding somewhere, scared out of his wits?

She can't take that chance.

Two minutes to check the rooms, then they'll go, drive to the nearest hospital.

She grasps the handle of the door closest to her and, with her eyes squeezed tight and the tips of her teeth touching in a grimace, turns it and pushes. The door swings inwards, comes to a stop with a soft thump against something solid. Sara braces herself, gets ready to run but there is no sound from inside the room, no movement. She risks dipping her head behind the door.

It's a bedroom, done in the same clean, modern style as the rest of the house. Spotlights embedded in the ceiling, dark wooden dresser against one wall, a wardrobe from the same set pressed against another. An alarm clock blinks at her from a bedside table. It is all so neat and tidy, hotel-like in its sparse simplicity. No dirty clothes on the beige carpeted floor, no trinkets on the bedside table. The bed is unmade, sheets thrown back, although that doesn't mean anything, because it could have been left that way this morning, or three weeks ago. What is important is that there is nobody here. No sign of Charlie, or Simon.

She backs out of the room and shuts the door, makes her way along the landing.

The next door she opens leads to a bathroom, spotlessly clean, with a single toothbrush in a mug by the sink and a white towel hanging from the rail. It smells faintly of bleach, but nothing more. If this place isn't Simon's, then whoever lives here is a total neat-freak.

Sara shuts the bathroom door. There is only one room left to check now and her heart is returning to its normal rhythm. Another thirty seconds and she'll be done and they can get out of here.

Unlike the others, the final door has a keyhole, though there is no key inside it. *Please be locked*, Sara thinks, as she grips the handle. It is not locked. The door swings inwards and she is hit by a blast of stale air; a foul body odour stink that makes her want to gag. She turns her head, tries not to breathe it in.

Both the bedroom and the bathroom were fitted with contemporary blinds that let in a grey sort of light, enough to see by at least, but this room is in total darkness. Sara reaches a hand into the room, feels for a light switch. She pictures a gnarled claw finding her in the dark and her body vibrates with the urge to snatch back her hand, then her finger connects with hard plastic. She pushes down and a domed lampshade in the centre of the ceiling buzzes into life, casting a thick yellow light over everything. There's a brief moment while Sara's eyes adjust, then she takes in the sight before her and a shiver scurries up and down her spine.

This room is not like the rest of the house. It is neither show-house neat and tidy, nor decorated in the same modern style. The walls aren't painted bright white but are covered in a peeling yellow wallpaper. The furniture isn't black and sleek and contemporary, but old and heavy and aged. The carpet is floral – dating back to the 1970s, at a guess – and worn through in patches. Heavy pink curtains hang from the windows, preventing any natural light from entering the room.

To Sara's left is a large wooden wardrobe, next to it an ancient-looking dresser that holds a half-dozen dusty bottles of perfume and a hairbrush cobwebbed with fine grey hairs. A large hospital-style bed has been pushed up against the opposite wall. Its hulking frame is flecked with rust, flakes of blue paint chipped away to reveal the dull metal beneath. A blanket on the bed has been thrown back and the sheets have come loose to expose the mattress beneath. Dark stains map out the shape of a person.

Even as Sara feels her bile rise, she can't help but look.

One hand covering her mouth, she takes a step forward, sees that at the side of the bed there is a small gas canister connected to an oxygen mask perched on the bedside table. The mask is surrounded by half a dozen pill bottles, tubes of ointment, tubs of lotion.

Simon's mother's room.

Catherine said she died after a long illness. This must be where she spent her final days. Perhaps on her own, or with nurses coming in to care for her. Maybe, Sara thinks, they took her away when it got too bad. An ambulance came and they took her to hospital so she could breathe her last in a safe, clean space, rather than in this horrid room.

Or maybe they didn't.

Maybe she breathed her last right here, in that big old rusty bed, and those dark stains on the mattress were what was left behind when they took away her body.

Now

Simon

Charlie will not sleep. He cries for his mummy, does that breathing-crying thing Simon hates, where the words come out as honks between hiccupping breaths, as if his whole world is coming to an end.

'Shh,' Simon tells him. 'You'll see Mummy soon.'

Charlie's reply comes in the form of a high-pitched scream. He takes his crying up a notch, too, his face covered with snot and tears.

What has got into him? It wasn't as if he saw what happened back at Cat's mum's place, Simon made sure of that. Plus, for most of the drive here he was excited, happy to see his daddy. He sat in the back seat, sharing facts about the Triceratops, who was as big as a bus and had long horns on his head for fighting other dinosaurs. And once they arrived, he played happily on the rug for half an hour until he started yawning. Something about going to bed, about being upstairs, has upset him.

'You have to sleep,' says Simon. 'We're going on an adventure tomorrow.'

'I . . . don't . . . wanna . . .' Charlie's words are punctuated by desperate gasps for air. 'Don't wanna . . . go . . .' venture.'

'Of course you do. It'll be like being on holiday. You like going on holiday, don't you? We can go to the beach every day. Do you remember how to make a sandcastle?'

Charlie shakes his head. 'I want Mumm-eee.'

'I told you, you'll see Mummy later on.'

'Want Mummy now! And Grandma!'

'Come on, Charlie. Be a good boy. There's no need for all this fuss.'

Simon leaves the room, tries to let Charlie cry it out, but the screaming is so loud and anguished he worries it will attract the attention of the neighbours.

'OK,' Simon says. 'Let's go and find Mummy.'

There is no child seat in the hire car. He makes a note to pick one up the next day – you can't be too careful when it comes to these things. For now, he straps Charlie into the back seat. It's an old trick: put him in the car, switch the radio to something classical and drive around in circles for half an hour. Whatever it is – the dark, the movement, the ambient noise of the tyres on the road – a night drive never fails to send Charlie to sleep. It is a long time since they've had to resort to such tactics, but tonight is not a normal night.

Fifteen minutes later, Charlie's crying has calmed to a whimper. Twenty minutes, and he is sound asleep, angelic in the rear-view mirror.

Simon turns the car around and heads back to the house. Best not to push his luck. Best not to stay out any longer than necessary. People will be looking for them by now. No reason they'll be looking around here – this is his secret place. But still . . .

He drives back along the main road, turns into the cul-de-sac, and immediately notices something is amiss. There is a light on in the downstairs window of the house, a light that was most definitely not on when they left half an hour ago.

52

Catherine

Part of me knows I am sitting on a solid chair on a hardwood floor, in a room with four brick walls . . . but nothing is quite as *here* as it should be. The room slips and slides, the floor undulates and my stomach lurches. I grasp the arms of the chair, focus on the blank white space of the wall closest to me. Its stillness offers a few moments of respite, before it grows soft, becomes not quite liquid.

If I touch it, my hand will sink right in.

Simon whispers in my ear.

Rest, love. Sleep.

He's right, I need to rest. Not sleep, just rest. Five minutes, ten at the most. Then the girl can drive us to the cottage and the police will have found Simon, and Charlie will be OK. Everything will be OK. I need to rest. I can't go on like this. Can't keep fighting it.

I close my eyes – just for a second.

The room rocks me, a gentle toing and froing that makes me think of Charlie in his rocker, back when he was little. That serene look he used to get on his face just before he dropped off. As if all the day's crying and screaming had been leading up to that single moment of calm. We would watch him, Simon and I, and breathe a sigh of relief as the muscles in his little face relaxed and a half-smile played on his lips, as if he'd just learned a new secret. We'd warm our hearts to the soft huff of his breathing. Our son. So small and precious and peaceful.

Rest. Sleep. Just for a little while . . .

Things were good back then, before everything went wrong. Before Simon went missing, before I found out about the girl. When it was just the three of us in our beautiful big house. We were so happy. We could find joy in the most ordinary of things. Giving Charlie a bath and feigning outrage as he splashed us with water. Reading him a bedtime story and watching him drift off in the evening. Him coming into our bedroom first thing in the morning for cuddles and tickles. I miss those squeals of delight, miss the feeling of his warm body pressing against mine.

I miss him. Miss him—

Charlie's missing.

What am I doing? I can't sleep while Charlie is missing.

I fight against it, claw my way out of the Nothing Place and, bit by bit, regain control, emerge into the light, my thoughts becoming clearer.

Must stay awake. Mustn't sleep until we find Charlie.

I open my eyes, lean forward and try to push myself up off the chair. I almost manage it. For a few seconds I stand, upright and unaided, then my legs spasm, begin to wobble like Charlie's did when he was taking his first steps, then the floor is pulled out from beneath me. I pitch sideways. Can't get my hands out in time to break my fall. I go down hard in a clatter of limbs, lie there with my cheek pressed against the carpet and my right side singing out with pain.

I'll get up in a second. Need a moment to catch my breath.

That's right. Rest. Close your eyes.

I try to roll onto my front, but something is wrong. My limbs won't respond. It's as if the connection between brain and body has been severed.

Am I dying?

Want to call for the girl. Sara. I scream her name at full volume, but no sound emerges. I can't move, can't speak. And now it is only a matter of time before the darkness closes in, before I sleep for good.

A shadow passes over me.

The girl! Thank God, it's the girl.

Help me. I can't move, I can't move!

A pair of mud-flecked running shoes pass into my field of vision, there for a second, then gone. Not the girl, in those boots of hers that make her feet look too big for her skinny legs. Somebody else is here. I can't move my head. Can't turn to see who it is. All I can see is the floor, rising and falling. And something else, under the chair. Something small and green. I strain to bring it into focus.

A plastic dinosaur.

53

Sara

Sara switches off the light in the old woman's room – the *dead* old woman's room – and stands at the door, pinching her nostrils and covering her mouth with one hand. She doesn't want to breathe in that lingering odour of sickness a moment longer.

Why would anybody want to keep a room like this?

She thinks of her dad. Can't imagine that, when he dies, she'll want to save even the smallest piece of him, never mind a whole room. And although she has seen films and TV programmes where grieving parents keep their missing or dead kid's bedrooms frozen in time, she feels sure this is not the same thing. There's no love here. This is not a way of holding onto somebody, of feeling closer to them after they are gone. It's the opposite of that. The hospital-style bed, with its stained mattress and filthy sheets, the oxygen mask and the endless pill bottles, the strands of brittle grey hair trapped in the hairbrush. It all speaks of a painful and drawn-out end. Whoever has kept the room this way has created a memorial, not to someone's life, but to someone's death.

Why would Adam do such a thing?

He barely ever mentioned his mum. Certainly, he never said anything that might suggest he'd turned her bedroom into a museum after she died.

Sara comes back to herself.

Maybe Adam – *Simon. Don't forget now. Don't you ever forget who he really is* – has been here in the last few days, and maybe he hasn't. Whichever it is, there's no sign of him now, and there's no sign of Charlie, either. She needs to get back to Catherine.

She closes the door to the room and moves back along the landing, heads downstairs.

'There's nobody here,' she says to Catherine as she reaches the bottom step and turns into the living room. 'We should go. Get to the—'

She freezes in the doorway.

Catherine is sprawled on her front on the livingroom floor, her swollen eyes wide and fearful. Her mouth opens and shuts like she is trying to talk, or perhaps scream, but all that emerges is a low, desperate keening sound.

Simon is standing above her. He lifts his head, looks at Sara and grins.

'You, too?' he says.

She thought he might look different after all the horrible things she has learned about him. Thought that, if she ever saw him again, he wouldn't look like her Adam anymore. But he looks just like he did the last time they slept together, the night he said they should move in with each other.

He is not two people, she reminds herself. He is just one broken person.

For a second neither of them moves, then Simon steps over his wife's motionless body, and even though Sara knows she is trapped, that there is nowhere to go, she turns and runs back up the stairs.

54

Day Nine

Catherine

An unfamiliar off-white ceiling hangs above me. Too low, it presses down, then all at once recedes, moves up and away, leaving behind the shape of what looks like two spotlights. I try to bring them into focus, and they merge together, become one.

Beneath me, I can feel the give of a too-soft mattress and the scratch of a woollen blanket. I am in bed, but I'm not at home. Not in Mum's spare room, either. And what am I wearing? Some sort of nightdress. An old-fashioned white cotton thing, with a lace trim. I try to prop myself up on my elbows and pain spikes through my body. It radiates from the base of my skull, squeezes me like a fist. It wants to crush me, reduce me to nothing. I cry out and a shape hurries into the room, looms up beside me and lays a hand on my shoulder.

Am I in hospital? I must have had some sort of accident and am in the hospital.

'Shh. Don't try and get up. Just rest,' a voice says.

Simon's voice.

I'm so used to hearing it in my head that when I look up and see him standing over me, I can only stare, expecting this vision of him to dissolve into nothing.

I'm seeing things. I must be.

He is wearing that terribly concerned look he gets when he is waiting for a train, or for his gate number to come up at the airport.

'It's OK, I'm here now,' he says. 'Everything's going to be OK. Shh.'

I reach up, expecting my hand to pass right through him, but instead I feel the warmth of his skin, the whisper of his breath, the scratch of his stubble against my palm.

'*You*,' I say, my voice barely there.

He nods.

I am shaking. Tears come, great big full-body sobs that rip through me.

'What happened to you? What happened to you . . . where were you . . . where were you?' I pull in hitching breaths. 'They said you were dead, they told me you burnt to death in our car theysaidyouweredead!'

'You don't remember?' he says.

'I . . . I . . .'

I remember waking up in a half-empty bed, feeling angry at Simon for not being there, then the police being at my door. I remember them telling me Simon had burnt to death in our car. And I knew they were wrong, knew he was still out there. I remember looking for him, looking everywhere. There's something else, too. Something that makes me want to shrink away from his touch, but when I try and think what it is, it vanishes. Like a handful of smoke, the harder I try to hold onto it, the quicker it slips away.

'It's OK,' Simon says. 'Don't worry about a thing. I'm here now.'

He picks up a glass of water from the bedside table and brings it to my lips.

'Take small sips.'

'Charlie.' I try to sit up. 'Where's Charlie?'

'He's with me. He's safe.'

Oh, thank God.

I wrap my hands around his and he angles the glass for me and even though I don't want to drink anything, I take a few small sips. My throat constricts and I splutter and cough. Simon takes the water away, puts both hands on my shoulders and leans in close.

'I'm right here.' He picks up my hand and presses it to his chest. 'I'm here, love. I'm fine.'

He's here. That's a good thing, isn't it? My husband is alive, and he is here. So why this feeling of dread in my guts? Why does a part of me want to get as far away from him as I can?

'It's you I'm worried about,' he says.

Me? He's the one who's been missing. He's the one they said was dead. Why on earth would he be worried about me?

'You're not well, Cat,' he says.

Now he has said it, I don't feel right. My thoughts are a jumbled mess, like the double vision of the spotlight. Multiple streams where there should be one. Something feels very wrong. I feel rotten, deep down inside.

'You haven't been well for some time,' he says.

'I haven't?'

Is that what it is? This feeling inside me?

'Am I going to be OK?' I ask, dreading him telling me that whatever is wrong with me, it is not the sort of thing you get better from.

'Of course you are.' He smiles. 'Now I'm here to look after you, everything's going to be just fine, I promise.'

Thank God.

'I've missed you,' I tell him through my tears.

'And I've missed you, too,' he says.

I have been in some sort of accident and right now I am not very well. But Simon is here. Whatever has happened, whatever is wrong with me, we will get through it. We will face it together.

55

Sara

Sara is sitting on the floor at the foot of the metal-framed bed. Her hands are fastened behind her with a dressing gown belt, and the belt has been looped around one of the bed's legs.

No light filters in through the room's heavy curtains, and it is hard for Sara to orientate herself. She has lost all sense of the space around her, though she knows she's in his mother's room. Can tell by the feel of the wiry carpet beneath her and the cloying hospital room smell of sickness, the ghost of all those ointments and lotions, and other less pleasant things she'd rather not think about.

After trying to lift the bed – first by standing as upright as the belt will allow and pulling upwards, then by jamming her shoulder beneath the frame and pushing with everything she's got – she has come to the conclusion that it is too heavy for her to move. It is unnaturally heavy, immovable in a way that doesn't make sense. Only when she reaches down to the point where the steel leg of the frame meets the floor does she realise it is bolted down. No wonder. She traces her fingers over the metal bolts. Four of them, fat and solid and fastened tight.

She lets out a scream of frustration. Not that screaming has done her any good over the last God knows how many hours she has been here. Nobody can hear her, not with the rag stuffed in her mouth and the gag tied on top.

He did it all without breaking a sweat. Came racing up the stairs after her, bundled her into his dead mother's bedroom, prised her phone out of her hands and tied her hands behind her. How awful, that this terrifying strength was within him this whole time. That he could flick Lydia into the path of a bus like it was nothing, and could overpower Sara with ease. How had she ever felt safe with him?

She pulls in a series of long breaths, fills her lungs to capacity in the hope that it will help her think more clearly.

You're going to get out of this.

Of course she's going to get out of this. This can't be how she dies. Tied up and gagged in a dead old lady's bedroom, in some creepy house on a fucking council estate in Farnborough?

She touches the bolts with her fingers, feels the shape of them. If she could get them undone, perhaps she could lift the corner of the bed enough to slip the belt underneath, then pass the dressing gown belt beneath her and get her hands free. If she could use her hands, she could surely find a way out of the room. Bite through the belt, smash a window. Jump down to safety, run to one of the nearby houses and raise the alarm.

She pinches one of the bolts between the pads of her thumb and forefinger, applies as much pressure as she can, and begins to twist.

56

Catherine

I am so tired. Keeping my eyes open feels like an impossibility, but I don't want to close them, don't want to take my eyes off Simon. It's like that game we sometimes play with Charlie – what's it called? Something to do with footsteps?– where you can only move when someone isn't looking. It feels like if I stop looking at Simon, he might do something I won't like. So I mustn't look away.

He leans in, kisses my lips, my forehead. Strokes my hair.

'Get some rest, love,' he tells me. 'Sleep.'

'I need to see Charlie.' I don't know much right now, but I know I ache to see my little boy. I want to hold him, hear his voice. Just having him here will make me feel a thousand times better.

'You'll see him soon,' Simon says. 'Right now you need to sleep. We don't want to scare him, do we?'

He's right. People look scary when they are sick. The sight of Dad in hospital when I went to visit him before he died is seared into my brain. His face all grizzled and grey. His skull, close to the surface in a way it never had been before. I remember thinking how terrible it is that our final memories of the people we love are often like that, of them turning into skeletons even before they have passed away.

But you're not dying.

No, I'm not dying. Simon says I'm going to get better. But seeing me in this dreadful state might frighten Charlie.

'You'll bring him to me, as soon as I'm awake?' I plead.

'The second you wake up,' says Simon.

I don't know if I want him to stay or to go. I don't want be on my own, but he has to look after Charlie. He releases my hand, walks out of the room and softly closes the door behind him.

He's right. I need to sleep. Every part of me is crying out for it. I'm exhausted. Have never felt so wrung out. Even the smallest of movements makes the pain at the back of my head flare and catch fire.

What has happened to me?

I try to think back, to locate this accident in my memory. A car out of control? A tumble down some stairs? A fall in the shower and a crack to the head? There's nothing there for me to hold onto. It doesn't matter. I suppose it will come to me, sooner or later. For now, I lie in this strange bed – where did Simon say we were? I don't remember. I'll have to ask him when I wake up – and I wait for sleep to finally swallow me whole.

I close my eyes. And I am sinking.

57

Sara

The door to the room opens and yellow light from the hall throws a tall shadow over the floral carpet. Sara stops working on the bolts, one of which she has been able to loosen enough so that she should have it out entirely in a few more turns.

Simon flicks the switch next to the door and the domed shade on the ceiling buzzes into life. He comes towards her and, when she thinks he is close enough, she lunges for him, kicks out, tries to connect with the heel of one of her boots. But the dressing gown belt only has a little give, and he has judged the distance too well.

'Sara, please,' he says.

That tone in his voice, like he is telling off an unruly child, is the same one he used to use whenever she did something he didn't like. Hearing it now enrages her. She screams into her gag, kicks out harder, but he remains out of reach. He waits for her to stop and after a minute or so she does, because it is hard to keep her balance with her hands fastened to the frame of the bed, and it is hard to keep screaming when she has no breath to scream with.

'Are we finished?' he says, once she is quiet.

She breathes hard into her gag.

Simon sits down on the floor in front of her, cross-legged, fixes his gaze on her and smiles. He looks oddly at peace, like they have just sat down for dinner and a waiter has poured their first drink of the evening and all of the day's tension is draining from his shoulders.

'This was my mother's room,' he announces. His face cycles through a series of quick expressions as he looks around at his mother's things: the ointments and lotions, the oxygen tank and mask, the twisted rope of filthy bedsheets. His eyes come to rest on the dresser, with its hairbrush and dusty bottles of perfume.

'Not that she was much of a mother,' he adds. 'She had some . . . issues, you might say.' A sigh, a small shake of the head. 'When I was naughty, she used to lock me in my room and threaten to set fire to the house. She didn't mean it, but I'd be so scared. She'd scream at me through the door, say she wished I'd never been born.'

In all the time she has known him, he has not once spoken of his mother this way. The few times he talked about her, it was with the everyday affection people have for parents who are no longer part of their lives, but who they bear no ill feeling towards. There was none of this sadness in his voice, none of this hurt. She feels a flutter of sympathy for him, for the little boy he once was.

'At some point, I stopped caring when she went out, who she was with, how much she drank. I stopped trying to make her love me. It was better that way. Everything became so much easier after I stopped caring, you know?'

She does. Cutting her dad out of her life was the hardest choice Sara has ever made, but once it was done, once she gave herself permission to stop worrying about him, everything really did get easier.

Perhaps this room, this twisted museum to his mother's suffering, makes some sort of sense after all. And just because he has never talked about these things before, doesn't mean they didn't happen.

'Here's the thing,' Simon says. 'When I heard Mum was sick, I came back to see her. I sat by her bed and thought to myself: I'm going to tell you what a terrible mother you were.'

Did she tell Adam that she has this fantasy? That she dreams about being able to say whatever she wants to her dad, without having to hear him make excuses, without having to see him break down in tears?

'I thought I hated her,' Simon says, 'but she took my hand in hers, and said she was sorry. For everything. She loved me, of course she did. She made mistakes, but she loved me, and I realised I loved her, too. People make mistakes, Sara. Sometimes they do terrible things, hurt the people they are closest to. But if you love them, if you truly love them . . .' He sniffs back his tears, wipes his nose on the back of his hand.

She did tell him, she's sure of it. On one of those nights when she froze during sex and couldn't explain why and he said it was OK, that it didn't matter, that she didn't have to tell him anything she didn't want to.

He is lying. Using her own story against her.

He knows she knows what it's like to have a parent who doesn't care for you the way they should, who drinks too much and loses control.

Now he casts his eyes up to the ceiling, as if he's gathering himself. The room is still, the only sounds Simon's snuffling and Sara's heavy breathing against the gag in her mouth.

'I know I've made mistakes, too,' he says. 'I suppose . . . my childhood messed me up. *She* messed me up. But I'm just a person, trying my best. Just like you.'

Not like me, Sara thinks. *Nothing like me.*

'I knew this couldn't last forever. Me and you, Catherine and Charlie. I knew the time would come when I'd have to make a choice.' He pauses for a moment, then says, 'I knew the day would come when I'd have to leave them.'

Another lie. She is sure of it. Still . . . hearing him say it speaks to a part of her she thought was long dead, tries to wake it up.

He wanted to be with you. He did love you, he really did.

'I would have chosen you, Sara,' he says. 'Of course I would have chosen you.'

58

Catherine

Please God, let me sleep. I was so close.

Simon is alive, Charlie is safe, and while I know I am not well right now, that I have been poorly for some time, I also know I am going to get better. Simon has promised me that. He is here – wherever here is – to look after me, so I'm going to get better, and everything is going to be OK.

So why won't my brain switch off?

Why won't it let me sleep?

I come close, feel myself drifting into the darkness, then some fragment of memory will light up my brain and drag me back to the surface. Faces I don't recognise, places I have never been, like I am looking through a stranger's . . . what are they called? Like books of memories. People used to make them, only nobody bothers anymore, except for weddings. It's like one of those. Each turn of the page brings some strange new picture for me to try and make sense of.

Let me go. I don't want to look at any more pictures . . .

No more images of fire and flashing blue lights, of Simon's office building, towering above me. Riding the lift up to the tenth floor with Charlie's hand in mine. No more pictures of the rowdy bar. Charlie and me, surrounded by dozens of people dancing in the darkness. Of me trying to talk to someone, desperate to be heard over the terribly loud music.

And no more pictures of Lydia.

I miss Lydia. When this is all over, and I'm feeling better, we'll see each other again. Go out and drink too much and share our secrets. And the next morning, we'll text each other to complain about our hangovers, and to find out when we are both free to do it all over again.

There is another picture. A young woman in heavy boots and a black dress. I don't know this woman. Don't recognise her. But she carries with her a memory of a feeling. Lots of feelings. Disgust, hurt, anger. Something else, too. Affection? No, it's not that. It is not that I like her. But I care about her. She needs looking after, whoever she is. She needs protecting.

I try to cling to her image, to stop it flitting away like all the others, because she is important to me, this woman. I know she is.

Her name comes to me.

Sara.

The girl. She was with me in a car. We were in her rusty old car, driving somewhere together, looking for something . . . for someone.

Charlie. We were looking for Charlie.

My eyes snap open. I sit upright and the pain from waking consumes me, fills me up.

I remember.

Sara. Lydia. Mum. The podcaster who burnt to death in our car.

Simon. I remember the terrible things he has done.

And I know where I am.

59

Sara

When Simon shuffles forward and puts his hand on Sara's knee, she can't help but let out a cry. His touch makes her feel like there are insects moving around under her clothes – poisonous insects, that will bite and sting if she moves. So she keeps very still, and she clenches her teeth tight around the rag that has been stuffed into her mouth.

'Does that surprise you?' Simon says. 'That I was going to leave them for you? It shouldn't, because I love you, Sara.'

Hearing those words come out of his mouth . . .

It is disgusting. Stomach-churning.

'Ever since the day we met I wanted to tell you the truth,' he says, 'but I knew as soon as I did, it would all be over. I couldn't do that to you – to *us*. I wanted so badly to be the person you wanted me to be. Tried so hard to be good enough for you.'

I'm not good enough for you, not worthy of your love . . .

These things he says, they are designed to make her come to him, and she has always given him the reassurance he craves. Even now, a part of her feels the pull of it, pictures herself holding him, telling him, *Of course you're good enough, of course you are.*

He is crying, tears streaming down his cheeks. He doesn't bother wiping them away, he holds his head up, so she can see.

'Oh, I know this sounds . . . crazy, I know, but maybe you could come with us, with me and Charlie? We're going to go far away.

Come with us. We can move on from this, be a family. Isn't that what you've always wanted?'

It is, for as long as she can remember.

'Mmm.' Sara nods.

'I know it is. Because I *know* you. I know you better than anybody.'

He leans forward, slips a finger between her cheek and the gag. 'You'll have to be quiet. Charlie's downstairs. He's sleeping.'

She nods and he tugs the gag down, pinches the rag in her mouth between his thumb and forefinger and pulls it out with thick strings of saliva.

'Forgive me,' Simon says. 'We can get past this, I know we can.'

She retches, coughs and splutters, tries to catch her breath.

'Forgive me, and I'll be the person you want me to be.' He is up close now, eyes pleading. 'Say yes. Say you'll come with us. I'll make it right, I promise I will.'

That he could even say such a thing. It is ridiculous. It is laughable.

She nods. 'Yes,' she says, her voice a broken whisper.

A smile spreads across his face. 'You'll come?'

'I'll come.'

He plants small wet kisses on her forehead, her cheek, her lips – 'Thank you, thank you, thank you.' She shudders at his touch, but he doesn't seem to notice.

'You must hate me,' he says.

She shakes her head. 'No . . . never . . .'

She forces herself to soften, to give him a weak smile, and in return his shoulders droop and his features slacken.

'I don't deserve you,' he says. He lowers himself down, folding his legs beneath him and laying his head on her breast. 'The things I've put you through . . . Please, don't hate me.' He reaches his arm around her, holds her tight.

'Shh.' She moistens her lips. 'I don't hate you. I love you. You're Adam. *My* Adam.'

You're Simon. And I hate you.

He inhales through his nose, breathes her in. She can feel the tension flowing from his body.

'I know I've made mistakes.' His voice is muffled against her dress. 'But if you love someone, you forgive them their mistakes, right?'

'We'll go away together, start again,' she says. 'You, me and Charlie.'

'Yes. I know somewhere. They'll never find us.'

'Then let's go.'

Untie me. Untie me, then I can get away from you.

'When it's dark,' he says. 'It'll be easier once it's dark.'

There's no natural light in the old woman's room. It's hard to say how long she has been here – it feels like forever. It could be hours before it gets dark.

'Why don't we go now?' she says. 'Let's not wait. Untie me, and we can go wherever you like.'

He squeezes her tight, then gazes up at her with those blue eyes of his that have won her forgiveness so many times before.

'There are other things you don't know,' he says. 'Bad things.'

She feels close to winning his favour, to having him unfasten the belt that is holding her to the bed. And once he has done that, she can look for an opportunity to escape.

She can't afford to lose him now.

'It's OK,' she says. 'I know everything. And I forgive you.'

'Everything?' A flicker of surprise in his voice.

'None of it matters,' she says, but she feels him stiffen. He clambers to his feet.

'What do you know?' he says.

Fuck. She has said too much.

She hesitates, wonders whether she should tell the truth, or pretend she doesn't know about Dylan, and that he is the jogger. She imagines sitting here, legs cramping while he tries to excuse himself for murder, and attempted murder, and in the end, decides it is better to let him think there are no more secrets left to tell. The sooner he thinks he's in the clear, the sooner he'll untie her.

She keeps her voice calm, speaks as if the horrible things he has done are no more serious than cancelling a date at short notice, or ruining a picnic lunch.

'I know about what happened on the bridge,' she says, 'and about what happened to Dylan. But it doesn't matter. You are not your mistakes.'

He takes a step backwards, and another.

'Adam, please. Don't go. Untie me and we can talk about it.'

But it's too late. She has lost him.

'What I did to Dylan?' His hands clench into fists. 'He was blackmailing me, did you know that? He was going to ruin me. I gave him everything he asked for and he was still going to do it.'

He paces a circle in front of her.

'You didn't even like him,' he says. 'You told me he was annoying, arrogant, immature.' As if it is a valid excuse, as if the way she felt about Dylan means anything. 'This is *his* fault, all of it. He did this to me. He did this to *us*.'

He believes it, she can tell by the look in his eyes. He truly believes that everything that has happened is somebody else's fault.

Dylan might have been annoying and arrogant, and perhaps he was trying to blackmail Simon, but he didn't deserve to die. Didn't deserve for his body to be found in a burnt-out car on the outskirts of London.

She drops her eyes to the floor, can't bear to look at him for a moment longer.

'Sara?' he says. 'Look at me.'

It is too hard to keep pretending.

'Sara?'

She hears his footfalls move towards her and she looks up.

'It was *you*.' She can't hold back. 'You did this. You did all of it. You're a fucking psycho, you're sick, you're—'

He comes for her, grabs a fist full of her hair and yanks back her head. He has the rag, from out of nowhere, and his big fingers stuff it back into her mouth. He pulls the gag back in place, reaches behind her head and pulls at the ends to make it even tighter.

'Be quiet,' he says. 'For God's sake, be quiet. You'll wake Charlie.'

He pushes his hands through his hair.

'I would have walked away from everything to be with you,' he says. He is burning with anger. 'And now you've ruined everything.'

She doesn't respond and the next thing she hears is the door opening. There is a moment of heavy stillness while he hovers in the doorway. She can feel him standing there, the air loaded with his dark presence. Then the lights go out.

60

Catherine

I recognise the sound of Simon's footsteps out in the hallway, just like I can recognise dozens of other sounds my husband makes. The rattle of keys and coins in his trouser pockets as he walks, the sound of him breathing when he is concentrating especially hard, or the way he huffs out air like a bull's snort when he is angry. He is doing that now. I picture him, clenching and unclenching his fists, the veins on his neck standing proud. Usually, when he is like this, I tell him to go for a run, blow off some steam, and he'll come back an hour or so later, drenched in sweat but a good deal calmer. Now, I keep quiet. I don't make a sound.

Please God, let him think I'm sleeping.

He thinks I can't remember all the bad things he's done, and that is a good thing. If he thinks I don't know, he has no reason to hurt me.

The door swings inwards and I shut my eyes – not too tight, not so tight that it looks like I'm pretending.

Please don't come in. Please don't come in . . .

But he does. I hear the door open, then the pad of his footsteps moving towards me, coming to a stop by the side of the bed. I feel cold air on my forearm, the rhythmic flutter of his breathing. He puts a warm, rough hand on top of mine.

Don't move.

He hurt Mum, he tried to kill Lydia. And he attacked the podcast host, burnt his body in our car. If he thinks I'm a threat, will he kill me, too?

Pretend to be asleep. Wait until he's gone, then take Charlie and run.

Simon lets go of my hand.

Is he leaving? I haven't heard his footsteps move towards the door, but maybe he is walking quietly, so he doesn't wake me? It feels like he has gone. I can't feel his breath on my arm anymore, and there is no sound in the room that doesn't come from my own body, nothing beyond the thump of my heart and the throb of my headache.

He's gone. He must have. I count down from one hundred, just to be sure, then open my eyes.

'You're awake,' Simon says, and the shock of seeing him forces a cry out of me.

'Hey, hey.' He strokes my shoulder. 'Shh, it's only me.' He smiles that crooked-toothed smile of his. 'I didn't mean to scare you.'

I am too afraid to say anything.

'Do you want some water?' he asks, and I shake my head. I don't want to speak, don't want my voice to give me away. I just want him to go. 'I'm sorry,' he says. 'I was just standing here, thinking about how much I've missed you.' He brushes his thumb across my knuckles, back and forth. 'I'll leave you to it. You need your rest. I need you well enough to travel.'

He wants to take his sick wife, who doesn't remember all the bad things he has done, with them. That's why he is still here. That's why he hasn't taken Charlie and gone already.

'Travel?' I whisper.

'That's right. We're going away, just the three of us. Me, you and Charlie. We're going to take a long holiday, go somewhere far away where nobody can bother us. I think it's just what you need. What we all need.'

'I'm not well, Simon. You said—'

'Don't worry about that. We'll get you all the help you need once we get there.'

I squeeze his hand to show him how grateful I am.

'I know things have been difficult' – he squeezes my hand back – 'that this last week has been hard for you. It's been tough for all of us—'

You hurt Mum.

'—and I'm sorry about that, really I am. I know you've been worried sick, but I'll explain everything, I promise. Get some more sleep, then tonight we'll go, and when we get there, you'll be able to rest all you like.'

And you hurt Lydia. Pushed her. Tried to kill her.

'Doesn't that sound good? Just the three of us, somewhere warm and sunny. Charlie can play on the beach and we can lie in the sun and just relax, forget all our worries. We haven't been away in ages, Cat. You deserve a break, we all do.'

And you set fire to someone.

'Thank you,' I say. 'It sounds . . . perfect.'

There is a tremble in my voice, I can't help it. I smile at him, to show him I'm on his side, to show him that I'm happy to see him, and that I know nothing.

He studies me, looks at me the way the detectives looked at me back at the house, when they were convinced I had something to hide. I have always been a terrible liar. Yes, I managed to hide what was happening with Jonathan, but that was different. It's easy to deceive someone about what you did with your day if they never bother to ask.

'You really don't remember what happened?' he says.

Can he see my heart beating too fast under the blankets? Can he tell I am lying, just by looking into my eyes? Feel it, the way I could feel he was alive when everybody told me he was dead?

I shake my head. 'Nothing,' I say. 'I mean . . . I remember them telling me you were missing, and I remember trying to find you and then . . . nothing. I haven't been sleeping. I've been so worried. I didn't know how I would cope without you.'

Please, believe me.

Simon stares at me, looks *into* me. I hear the soft click of saliva in his throat as he swallows.

He knows. He knows I'm pretending and any second now he's going to lash out. Hurt me, perhaps even kill me.

'Maybe it'll come back to you?' he says, rocking on his heels.

He must be wondering what will happen, if we are in the car, or on a plane flying to God knows where, and it all comes back to me and I remember the things he has done and who he really is.

I can't let him think like that.

'Whatever happened, we're together now,' I tell him. 'That's all I care about. You, me and Charlie, together again. Nothing else matters.'

Believe me.

'That's good,' he says.

That look on his face. I have seen it before. When we have argued and I make the first move to reconcile. When he has closed a big deal at work and got one over on his rivals. When he plays a game with Charlie and refuses to let his four-year-old son win. *He'll never learn if we just let him win all the time*, he'll say, as he makes his final move. That's where I've seen that look before; it's the look he has when he has won, and, more importantly, when somebody else has lost.

'Wait here.' He leaves the room, not bothering to close the door behind him. I hear his footsteps race down the stairs, a door open and close and then he is on his way back, moving slower now but still too quick for me to do anything. A moment later he is standing beside me with Charlie in his arms.

Oh, my boy. My sweet, sweet boy.

The sight of him breaks me. He is safe, he is here. He isn't a dream. He is right here, wearing his dinosaur pyjamas. He's OK. Thank God, he's OK.

Charlie reaches for me, little arms stuck straight out, fingers wriggling.

'Mummy!' he cries. Simon carries him over to the bed, sets him down on the blankets. Charlie crawls over to me and throws his arms around my neck. My boy, my baby. The weight and the warmth of him. How good it is to hold him, to have him by my side.

'Careful, Charlie,' Simon says. 'Mummy's poorly.'

Charlie pulls back, gasps. 'Are you poorly, Mummy?'

Bless him. Bless the worried look on his little face. I pull him into me, hold him tight. Kiss him. 'It's OK, darling. I'm OK.'

'She's going to be fine, but she's going to need lots and lots of rest,' Simon says.

'Missed you, Mummy,' Charlie says, and my heart breaks and

mends and breaks all over again, all in a matter of seconds. He snuggles into me, burrows into my shoulder. Tears come. A sob shakes me and Charlie looks up.

'Are you crying, Mummy?' he says.

'Because I'm happy to see you,' I tell him. 'Happy tears. Remember?'

His face lights up, and he lays his head down on my chest and for the first time in what feels like forever, I don't feel like I am rotting from the inside out.

'Charlie?' Simon says. 'Remember how I told you we were going to go on an adventure tonight? Do you think Mummy should come on our adventure, too?'

Charlie plants his hands on my belly, props himself up. He turns to me with his blue eyes shining. 'Are you coming, too, Mummy?'

Play along.

People lie and pretend all the time. To keep the things they love close, people lie through their teeth every day. Pretend they still love their partner, pretend they are happy and satisfied with life, when all they really want to do is run away and start all over again.

If it keeps Charlie safe, I can pretend, too.

But what about Sara? She was upstairs, checking the rooms for any sign of Simon or Charlie. What if she's hurt? I can't just leave her here.

'Of course she's coming,' Simon says. 'Aren't you, Mummy.' And he flashes me another one of his victory grins.

61

Sara

The most effective way to turn the bolts is to crouch with her weight on the balls of her feet and her back pressed against the bottom corner of the bed's cold metal frame. The position is unnatural, like something out of a yoga class. It is impossible for Sara to hold for long. The belt cuts into her wrists, the bed digs into her spine, the tops of her thighs burn, and her calves cramp and spasm. After a minute or two, her body starts to shake and her balance goes and she has no choice but to stop, to sit down and stretch out as best she can. Rest until the pain fades and the pins and needles come and go.

Five minutes, she tells herself each time she stops. *Four minutes to recover, one minute to feel sorry for yourself, then back to work.*

She counts down the seconds in her head. When she reaches zero she gets up, gets back into position and picks up where she left off.

Part way through loosening the third bolt, her fingers begin to bleed. The more blood there is, the harder the bolts are to turn. She blots her broken fingertips on the threadbare carpet and keeps going, keeps twisting and turning, until the third bolt is loose and her fingers are on fire. She casts the bolt aside and rests.

Five, four, three, two, one, zero. Come on. Get up, get up, get up!

She starts on the final bolt and an hour or two – perhaps even three – later, she has that one out, too, and her fingers are so numb they no longer feel like her own. She collapses, rolls onto her side and lets the bolt drop from her palm.

She's done it.

Maybe she isn't going to die in this awful place after all.

All she needs to do now is lift the corner of the bed, slip the belt underneath, and she'll be free. Not entirely, but free enough to get her hands in front of her, then she can break a window – whatever kind of windows there are behind the dusty curtains. Use something heavy and solid. She looks around the room for something that might do the job. The oxygen tank is the size and shape of a small fire extinguisher. It looks solid enough, but not so big that she should have trouble lifting it. Smash the window, then climb down and go and get help. She'll need to be careful. It will be quite a drop to the ground below. She could snap an ankle, break a leg, even. But at least then she'd be outside, and she could call for help. Somebody would surely come.

It is hard to tell how long it has been since Simon turned out the lights. He could come back at any moment and God only knows what he'll do if he finds out what she's been up to.

Sara gets back into position, back braced against the bed, knees bent, her weight on the balls of her feet. Behind her, she grips the bottom rung of the bed's frame in her right hand, and gets the belt ready in her left. She draws a breath, grits her teeth, then lifts with every ounce of strength she has. The muscles in her arms and sides pull tight, begin to scream.

You can do this, you can do this—

It's no good. It's too heavy. She is going to break before the bed moves—

Don't stop, don't stop—

There is a crack and a small squeal of protest and the corner of the bed lifts off the floor. Not by much, but by just enough to pass the belt underneath it. She feeds the belt under the foot of the bed then lets the bed drop. It thumps back down onto the carpet and she falls forward, rolls onto her side and lies there, every muscle in her body shrieking with pain.

She's done it. She's free. Now she can break the window and—

A noise from outside the room.

Simon must have heard the bed thump down onto the carpet.

Sara heaves herself up, scurries back into position by the bottom of the bed and tries to make it look as if nothing has changed. She hears the hurried rattle of the key in the lock, then the door swings inwards. Simon's broad silhouette fills the doorway. He casts a glance over his shoulder, back down the hall, then steps into the room, closes the door as he flicks the light switch.

After so many hours in the dark, the sudden influx of light hurts Sara's eyes. She looks away and down, and her eyes come to rest on two fat silver metal bolts. They are right in front of her on the carpet, must have rolled forward when she dropped them.

Shit. Why wasn't she more careful?

As soon as he gets close enough, he's going to see the bolts and it's going to take him no time at all to work out what she has been up to. He might tie her up again. If he does, there's no way she'll be able to get herself free. She is too tired and in too much pain to go through it all a second time.

Or he might not bother tying her up. If he is angry enough, he might decide it isn't worth the risk. He might decide that the best thing to do is to shut her up once and for all.

62

Catherine

The clock on the bedside table reads a little after seven. Morning? It must be. We got here . . . when? It was night-time. So it must be morning now. Unless I've slept. I haven't, have I? I don't think so, but as I lie here, the light in the room dims and takes on a pinkish-purple hue, the shadows growing fuzzy around the edges. The sun is going down. He said he wanted to go when it got dark, that he wanted me to rest so I'd be able to travel in the evening. And now the evening is here.

What am I going to do?

He's expecting me to go with them. For the three of us to run away to some far-off country and start our lives all over again. A part of me wants to, but it's the part of me that's exhausted, that is tired of hurting, that only wants the pain to stop. Wouldn't everything be so much easier if I just gave in? If I stopped fighting Simon and just let him take control? Would it really be so different? To keep pretending, to run away with him and rebuild our lives somewhere new? Simon can make that happen, I'm sure of it. He is clever, resourceful. He'll have it all planned out.

But even if I can keep lying to Simon – hide the truth in my voice every time I speak to him, remember not to flinch every time he puts his arm around me – it will mean lying to Charlie, too. I'll have to pretend his daddy is something he is not. That he is a good man, a good father.

A noise from downstairs. I hear a door open, then Simon's voice.

'You stay here,' he says. 'I'm going to go see if Mummy's feeling better.'

I hear Charlie's excited reply. 'Then are we going on an adventure?'

'That's right. Now, you watch your cartoon and be good. I'll be back in a bit.'

The door closes. Simon's footsteps thump on the stairs.

Oh, God, he's coming.

I brace myself as he reaches the top of the stairs, hold back a whimper as I hear him approach the door. I don't have a choice. I can't fight him, I'm too weak. So I'll have to pretend, for as long as it takes. Until I'm strong enough to take Charlie and run.

But the door doesn't open. Simon's footsteps keep going, down the hall. He opens a different door and closes it behind him. The bathroom, I guess, or his mother's room – at least it used to be his mother's room. I hold my breath and listen. Can't hear what he is up to. But I can hear something else, from downstairs. A high-pitched voice, singing a vaguely familiar tune. It's Charlie, singing the theme to one of his favourite cartoons. What's it called? The one with the little bear who drives a car and . . . it doesn't matter. All that matters is hearing him sing. At least that's something. At least he isn't unhappy or hurt. He wouldn't be singing if he was.

Then I realise, Simon has left Charlie downstairs.

I swing my legs over the side of the bed and set them down on the floor, feel the soft carpet under the soles of my feet. Where are my shoes? Simon must have put them somewhere when he undressed me and put me in this awful nightgown.

I push myself up off the bed, stand upright, and am amazed to find that my legs can support me. I take two teetering steps forward, put my hands out and brace myself against the bedroom wall.

You're OK, you're OK.

As long as I have something to lean on, something to help keep my balance, I'm OK. I step sideways, move hand over hand, until I reach the door, then stop and listen. There's no sound from out in the hall, no sign of Simon.

I have to hurry.

I grasp the door's handle and turn it, open the door. There is a rush of cool air and Charlie's singing gets louder. The stairs are right there, just three steps ahead of me. I cling to the doorframe, step out into the hall and move forward, grasp the bannister and look down.

The stairs look normal. Fourteen steps, leading down to the ground floor. Not a hundred, or a thousand. Just fourteen. What happened earlier; it wasn't real. It was sleep, playing tricks on me. I put my foot on the first step, then retreat. What if I am halfway down the stairs and they change and there aren't fourteen steps anymore, but hundreds? What if I lose my balance and fall? I couldn't bear the thought of Charlie hearing me scream as I tumble all the way down to the bottom, of him finding me all twisted and broken.

Stop it.

Deep breath. You can do this.

But as I set my foot down on the first step, there is a noise from along the hall. I look up as the door to Simon's mother's bedroom is wrenched open.

63

Sara

Simon has taken a seat, facing away from Sara, on the moth-eaten velvet-covered stool in front of the dresser. He has his mother's hairbrush and is moving it back and forth over his hand, letting the fine grey strands of hair trapped in its bristles trail over his fingers. Sara can hear his breathing; slow and ponderous, each exhalation a sigh.

It is the oddest thing, the way he came into the room and just . . . sat down. He has barely looked at her, and hasn't come close to spotting the two silver bolts on the carpet. She should be glad, she thinks. Glad he has nothing to say to her, that he hasn't come to hurt her. It's as if he has forgotten she exists.

That's a good thing, isn't it?

So why doesn't it feel like a good thing? Why does him ignoring her make her feel like she's in more danger now than she has been at any time since she arrived at this horrid place?

If she were sitting a little further to the right, she'd be able to see his reflection in the dresser's pock-marked mirror, read his expression and get a sense of his mood. But she doesn't want to risk moving in case the noise attracts his attention. She can hear him, though, in a voice that is soft and small and not at all like his own.

'I don't have a choice,' he says. 'I don't want to do this, I don't. But sometimes . . .' He picks up a bottle of his mother's perfume while he searches for the right words, twists off the cap and sprays the scent on his wrist, holds it up to his nose and sniffs. 'It's like you always said, sometimes you have to burn everything down so you can start over. That's what I have to do. I don't want to leave you, but I've got to go, and I can't ever come back.' He slumps down on the dresser with his head on his arms. 'Forgive me,' he says. 'Please, forgive me.'

Is he crying? It looks like he is. Sounds like it, too.

After everything he has done, forgiveness is an impossibility. But not everything is lost. There's still a chance for him to do the right thing. He can let her and Catherine and Charlie go, and turn himself in. That's got to count for something. Maybe there's still some good left in him, Sara thinks. Maybe she can convince him to do the right thing?

'Mmm-mm,' she moans behind her gag, tries to inject the right note of sympathy into her voice, but Simon doesn't respond.

She tries again, '*Mmm*-mm.' *Si-mon.*

He whirls around in his seat. Eyes red, face wet with tears.

He drags a wrist under his nose. 'I told you to be quiet.'

'*Mm*-mmm—' she starts, but he gets to his feet and storms over to her, stoops down and clamps his hand around her lower jaw. She squeezes her eyes shut, screams behind her gag as he shakes her.

'I said be quiet.' A fine spray of spittle hits her cheek. 'Not one more word out of you, do you hear me?'

'M-mm-mm.' *I hear you.*

He releases her, and when she next opens her eyes he is back at the dresser, has picked up another bottle of his mother's perfume.

Oh, my God, Sara thinks. She knew he was crazy, but not *this* crazy, not hearing-voices-in-his-head crazy. But he must be. He wasn't asking *her* for forgiveness. He was talking to somebody else, even though there is nobody else here.

Is he talking to himself?

I don't want to leave you . . .

No, that isn't it. Who then? Who else would he want to forgive him?

His mother. He is talking to his dead mother. That's who he wants to forgive him. He thinks his dead mother is still in this room, and now he's talking about burning things down and she wouldn't be surprised if he means it, if he *really* means it. Set fire to the house with her inside it. Burn her alive, like he did Dylan.

She needs to get out of here.

The door to the room is closed, but Sara doesn't remember him locking it when he came in, which means the key is either in one of his pockets, or is still in place, sticking out of the keyhole on the other side.

Sara pulls the belt tight against her backside, tugs it forward so she can feel the hard line of it underneath her dress. She shimmies her hips from side to side, small movements that allow her to move the belt forward bit by bit, and soon the belt has passed beneath her and is under her thighs rather than behind her back. She stops, checks on Simon. He is still sitting there, toying with his mother's things. He's in another world. She can only hope he stays there. She puts the heels of her boots together and lets the belt slacken into a loop that she can swing over the tips of her toes in one smooth, silent motion. On the second try she does it. Her hands are still fastened at the wrists, but at least now they're in front of her. She checks on Simon again, keeps one eye on him as she leans forward, places her palms on the faded carpet, tucks one leg beneath her and gets ready to run.

The mirror, she thinks, before she sprints for the door. *Just because he isn't looking at you, doesn't mean he can't see you. Now . . . Go!*

She covers the space in five paces, grabs the door handle, turns it and pulls the door open. Behind her she hears the scrape of the stool's wooden legs snagging on the carpet. Bottles of perfume rattle over the dresser's top. He's seen her, he's coming for her, but it doesn't matter, because the door is open and she is going to escape, she is going to escape—

There is a ghost standing at the top of the stairs. A grey-faced woman dressed all in white, who looks up at Sara with coal-black eyes and opens her mouth to scream.

His mother. It's his dead mother.

Sara's heart races, and although her brain tells her to keep going, that it is not a ghost, because there's no such thing, her body recoils. She loses momentum and Simon's arms encircle her waist. He lifts her up off the floor, spins her away from the door and kicks it closed with a flick of his heel.

Sara screams and thrashes. She beats his arms with her fists, tries kicking him with her boots, looks for an opportunity to bite him, to sink her teeth into him. She does everything she can to break free, but he holds her tight.

'Quiet. You'll upset Charlie,' he says as he carries her back to the bed.

If he fastens her to the bedframe again, she is done for.

She drops her chin down to her chest and flicks her head back, hard and fast, feels the dome of her skull connect with Simon's face. There is a meaty crunch and a satisfying sense of give. Pain explodes at the back of her head, but he loosens his hold. She drops to the floor, scurries to the other side of the bed and turns to face him. He has his hands up covering his face, blood leaking through his fingers.

'What have you done?' He takes his hands away, glares at his bloody palms.

Sara looks for something to defend herself with. The oxygen tank. She dives for it, wraps both hands around the cool metal and lifts it up. As he comes for her she swings it to her side, then launches it forward, puts as much power into the motion as she can. She imagines it hitting him square in the face, his head snapping sideways, his body collapsing to the floor. But Simon ducks down low, blocks her swing. The tank connects with his forearm then hits the floor with a loud metallic clang and rolls away.

Simon catches her wrist and holds it fast. He squeezes, and she feels the pressure on her bone, her skin burning. The pain fills her head with stars. Her legs give way and she drops to her knees, and still he doesn't let go, still he keeps on squeezing.

She sinks to the floor and Simon lowers himself down alongside her, then climbs on top of her, straddles her, sits back with all of his weight on her belly.

She sees his big hands reach down, feels his fingers fasten around her neck and his thumbs press into her throat. She tries to scream but has no breath. She is going to die in the old lady's bedroom after all, and she is going to do it without making a sound.

It isn't fair, she thinks. He is so much bigger than she is, so much stronger.

And now the pressure isn't just on her stomach and around her throat, it's behind her eyes, a dark and terrible swelling, as if something inside her head is going to burst. There is sound in her ears, like the loudest microphone feedback she has ever heard, and it is getting louder and louder and—

All of a sudden, the pressure is gone.

She feels nothing.

Is this it? Am I dead?

She opens her eyes as Simon slumps forward. He falls like a cut tree, his full weight landing on top of her, his head resting on her shoulder and his open mouth pressed against her neck.

She can breathe again.

Simon is a dead weight, impossibly heavy. She wrestles an arm out from under him, pushes his shoulder until she can wriggle from beneath him.

The ghost is standing over by the dresser. Catherine, in a long white nightdress, holding the oxygen tank in both hands.

64

Catherine

I've killed him. Oh God I've killed him.

I drop to my knees, reach out and touch Simon's shoulder. Shake him, say his name. I don't want him to wake up, but I don't want to have killed him. But he is oh-so-still and there is a lot of blood – *so* much blood. A glistening black shadow, seeping into the carpet.

How am I going to tell Charlie? How am I going to tell him that Mummy has killed Daddy? What if he thinks this is all my fault? What if he never forgives me?

Sara is on her knees beside me. She pulls a gag down off her mouth and a rag out from between her teeth and gasps for air, then retches, spits a mouthful of saliva out onto the carpet and puts her hands around her neck, holds them there. She pulls in big breaths through her tears, then clambers to her feet.

'I think I've killed him. I had to do something,' I say. 'He was . . . he was . . .'

He was strangling her. Sat on top of her with his hands around her throat, and her body was shaking, her heels drumming against the carpet. I had to stop him. But for Charlie's sake, I don't want to have killed him.

Sara pulls at my arm, bloody fingers digging into my skin. 'We've got to go.'

Simon stirs, emits a low groan that sounds like a question. His eyes flick open. He is woozy, blinking into the light. He props himself up on one elbow and touches the back of his head. His fingers come away wet.

'I'm sorry,' I tell him. He is going to be so mad at me.

He looks up. 'You . . .'

By the time he is on his feet Sara has pulled me out into the hall. She shuts the door. There's a key in the . . . in the thing . . . the hole the key goes into, and she turns it, takes it out and throws it into the bathroom, then helps me down the stairs, keeps a tight hold of me until we are on the ground floor.

We burst into the living room. Charlie is there, on the rug, an iPad in front of him showing cartoons. He looks up, then springs to his feet, runs to me and wraps his arms around my legs.

My baby, my baby. I've got you.

Simon's not taking him anywhere. He is locked upstairs in his mother's bedroom and he's not taking my son anywhere.

'Are you feeling better now, Mummy?' Charlie says.

'Yes,' I tell him. 'Mummy's feeling lots better. So much better, that we're going to go on our adventure, just like Daddy said. Can you find your . . . the things for your feet?'

'Shoes!' He points down at my own bare feet. '*You* haven't got any shoes on, Mummy.'

'Never mind that. Go and find yours. Hurry up. There's a good boy.'

Sara comes back from the kitchen with a knife. She uses it to saw through the thing holding her wrists together, sets the knife down on the coffee table.

'Phone,' she says, stalking around the living room.

She finds it by the side of the television, picks up the handset and dials. I hear her start speaking to the operator. 'Police, please . . . it's urgent,' she says breathlessly.

Charlie has found his shoes. He runs over and hands them to me, then jumps up onto the sofa, sits down with his legs sticking out.

His little socked feet. His little toes . . .

'Where's Daddy?' he says.

'He's upstairs, darling. Now, keep still.' I try to push the toe of Charlie's foot into his shoe, but it won't fit. Why won't it fit?

'You have to do the laces, Mummy,' Charlie says.

Of course. Silly Mummy. The laces need to be unfastened before I can put his shoes on. I look at them, a hopeless tangle of black string that is surely far too knotted for anyone to unravel.

'Address?' Sara shouts. 'What's the address?'

I can't remember. I had it before, managed to retrieve it from somewhere in the back of my mind, but it's gone now. I look over at her, shake my head. Maybe there is something lying around with the address on it? One of those things that come through the door. An envelope. A bill, a letter—

An explosion above our heads. Sara's eyes turn up to the ceiling.

Charlie says, 'What's that noise, Mummy?'

It's Daddy, throwing himself against the door of Grandma's bedroom, and once he breaks it down, he's going to come downstairs and he's going to—

'Nothing, darling,' I tell him. 'It's nothing.'

Another crash. Sara drops the phone.

'Go,' she says. '*Go*!'

She is beside me, hurrying me, helping me.

I pick up Charlie, lift him up onto my hip. He is so very heavy. He cries out, 'My shoes! My *shoes*!' But there's no time. Sara opens the front door and we spill out into the quiet cul-de-sac.

I feel the chill of the evening breeze on my bare arms and legs. Smooth concrete beneath the soles of my feet. Soft grass as we run across the lawn, out into the road.

Where the hell is everybody?

Charlie wails into my ear and I shush him. 'It's OK, darling. It's OK.'

Sara is running at a full sprint. Is she heading for the car? I have barely made it ten feet from the house and she is halfway there, but I can't keep up. My legs don't want to work, Charlie is too heavy, and nothing is as still as it should be.

Houses loom over us, lean in at impossible angles.

Windows full of leering shadows.

I call for Sara. 'Wait for us!'

She slows to a stop, turns to look back.

'I can't . . .' I tell her. I take my next step and my ankle twists, snaps sideways. There's a crunch and pain spikes up my leg. I stumble, fall against the bonnet of a car. I can't carry Charlie any further.

Sara. Where is she?

I hear her. 'Come on!' she shouts.

She's in front of me. I shake my head, try to hand her Charlie. 'Take him.'

'Get up. You can do this!'

But I am too tired to take another step.

'You have to take him. Please.'

Simon is coming. He is kicking down the door to his mother's bedroom and he is coming, and I am too tired to go any further. She has to take Charlie, has to get him somewhere safe.

She hooks an arm under my elbow, tries to pull me up.

'Daddy!' Charlie shouts into my ear, stretching his arms out over my shoulder and the girl lets go, turns her head and looks back towards the house.

'Fuck,' she says. 'He's coming.'

65

Sara

Sara looks back towards the busy road and the lights of the passing traffic. If she were on her own, she'd have got away by now. She can't help but picture it, see herself taking off, leaving Catherine and Charlie behind. It's not like she'd just keep on running, she'd get help. Flag down a passing car, or burst into one of the shops and scream for them to call the police. And the police are already on their way, aren't they? Even though she couldn't give them the address, they'll trace the call, won't they?

But it will be too late by the time they get here.

Simon has lost his mind. He's a murderer, and he'll do whatever it takes to get away and take Charlie with him, and he's coming for them.

Fuck. She should have kept hold of the knife.

Sara lifts Charlie out of Catherine's arms. The wrist that Simon squeezed until she saw stars feels heavy and huge and has its own heartbeat. As it takes Charlie's weight the pain blooms, sends her dizzy. She transfers him to her other arm, feels his tears wet her cheek. He fights her, his cries a siren in her ear, '*Dad-eeee! Dad-eeee! Dad-eeee!*'

'Get up,' Sara tells Catherine. 'Up, up, up!'

'I can't—' But Catherine pushes off the bonnet of the car, puts one foot in front of the other and moves forward, taking drunken steps that are as much falling as they are running.

'Don't look back,' Sara tells her.

Sara doesn't look back either, but she knows Simon is coming. She can hear the slap-slap of his trainers hitting the pavement, getting louder as he gets closer.

They aren't going to make it, she thinks. He's too fast, and they are too slow.

If you were on your own . . .

But she isn't on her own anymore.

'Move,' she says. '*Move*!'

'I can't!' But Catherine keeps going, keeps taking one wayward step after another, and now they are passing the rusty old Fiat. If only she knew where the keys were, they'd be able to get inside and lock the doors, but Simon must have taken her keys when he took her phone. Forget the car. Keep going, don't stop, don't look back. Get to the road.

For a moment, Sara thinks they might actually get away. They are here now, at the main road. Cars race by. She would lift her free arm and try to flag one down if it didn't hurt so much, but it doesn't matter, they are here. There will be people. Someone will see them, someone will help.

Behind her, Simon's footsteps quicken then collapse into each other.

She feels a sharp tug against her scalp. An arm reaches around her neck and she cries out and his hands are all over her. Digging, pulling, prising. She hears Catherine's screams mixed with Charlie's, then there's a sound like a snap and Catherine goes quiet.

Sara folds her body around Charlie, hunches over him, holds him tight.

Don't let go. Whatever he does to you, don't let go. Someone will come, someone will help.

Then Simon's hand closes around her fractured wrist and squeezes.

66

Catherine

I pull myself upright, body heavy, vision blurring. Taste of blood in my mouth. Hard press of concrete under my hands and knees.

I look up, see Simon and Sara, feet scuffling over the pavement as they spin and twirl, dark figures made of orange light and purple shadow. Sara has Charlie held tight to her body, is trying to keep her back to Simon. I hear her shouting into her chest, '*No, no, no, no* . . .' then Simon grabs her arm and squeezes, and she is . . . like when someone touches a live wire. Her head snaps sideways, her body twists. She lets out a howl. Simon wrenches Charlie out of her arms, lifts him up and away. Sara crumples, hits the pavement beside me.

'Daddy's got you, Daddy's got you,' Simon sings to Charlie, but he is a gruesome sight, his face and clothes stained with . . . something . . . the thing that's inside you. Charlie screams, turns his face away, arms reaching for me. Seeing him like that, it is the cruellest thing. All my pains rolled into one, times a thousand.

'Mum-eee, *mum-eee*!'

'Hush,' says Simon, 'Daddy's here.' He passes a hand over Charlie's face to wipe away the snot and tears.

The headlights of the passing cars. Like . . . when cameras do that thing.

Bright flashes of light.

I see Simon take a step backwards between two parked cars, see him look over his shoulder, searching for a gap in the traffic. Why isn't anybody stopping? Can't they see what is happening here? Can't they see we need help? As soon as the road is clear, he's going to go. He's going to take Charlie away from me.

'Stop . . .' I plead with him. 'Please . . .'

Don't go. Don't take my baby.

'I can't leave him with you, Cat,' he shouts. 'It isn't safe.'

'He *is* safe with me, he is!' I cry. 'Don't take him, *please*.'

He turns his back, still searching for that break in the never-ending traffic.

I push myself up off the ground, launch forward. Three steps. I snatch a handful of Simon's shirt, pull hard and he tips backwards, Charlie swinging precariously on his hip.

'Let go!' He lashes out over the front of the car with his free arm and the back of his fist connects with my cheek. I hear Charlie scream, 'No, Daddy, no!' And now Charlie is lashing out too, little fists screwed up tight, hitting Simon in the face, over and over. Simon jerks his head back – *Stop that, little man!* Charlie pushes against him and squirms out of his grasp, thumps down onto the bonnet of the car. I snatch the sleeve of Charlie's pyjamas and slide him over to me, scoop him up, put him over my shoulder.

'I've got you—'

His screams echo through the surrounding streets. No, wait . . . Sirens.

Help is coming.

Simon hesitates between the cars, listens, then takes a step towards us.

'Give him to me, Cat,' he says.

Behind me, Sara is shouting, 'Come on. Let's go, let's go!'

It would be a waste of time to try and run. Simon is faster than us, he'd only chase us down, take Charlie off me.

'Give him to me,' he says again, and he gives that familiar look of exasperation.

I shake my head, hold Charlie tighter.

'Catherine. If I don't take him now, I'll only come back for him later,' he says.

A warning. A promise. That look.

He clenches his fists. 'He's my son.'

'He's mine, too,' I cry. '*He is my son, too!*'

He comes for us.

I slam my free hand into the middle of his chest, but he leans in, pushes against me with all of his weight, arms reaching for Charlie. The soles of my bare feet scrape back over the pavement. Our eyes meet, and for a moment the world empties out and it's just the two of us, me and my husband, in our very own Nothing Place.

He is not the man I thought he was. Not a good husband, not a good father. Never has been. But we are still joined up in a thousand different ways. I know the real him now. He'll kill me to get what he wants. And he knows I can't hold him back. I don't have anything like the strength to. A grin spreads over his face. He reaches out and his hand closes around Charlie's ankle.

Then I hear a rumble like thunder.

The left side of Simon's body is washed white.

A stinging sensation as Sara's hands land on top of mine. She screams, we both do, then we do that thing . . .

I forget the word now.

It's the name of . . . the thing. The Dylan thing.

It's what you do when you are backed into a corner.

When someone you can't stand is too close and you can't breathe.

When you have taken as much as you can take and all you want is for them to get away get away get away.

We do that thing. And we do it together.

Statement of Sara Caldwell

2 December, 2022 – 3.30 a.m.

Interview conducted by Detective Inspector Hannah Carter & Detective Constable Ellis Chaudhari

DI Carter – *Tell us what happened when you reached the main road.*
SC – But we've been through this. Twice already.
DI Carter – *And I'd like you to take us through it a third time. This is important, Sara. We need to be absolutely clear about this, OK?*
SC – Like I told you, he was trying to get Charlie and we stopped him.
DC Chaudhari – *Stopped him how?*
SC – We blocked his way.
DI Carter –*You pushed him.*
SC – No, we stopped him. Then he said something to Catherine.
DC Chaudhari – *Do you remember what he said?*
SC – Something about him being better off without her, without either of us.
DI Carter – *Is that when it happened? He said that, then you saw the bus was coming and decided to push him?*
SC – I didn't push him.
DI Carter – *Catherine, then. Is that when she pushed him?*
SC – No. It was him. He knew he was going to get caught, so he turned and ran.

DC Chaudhari – *Neither you, nor Mrs Wells, had any physical contact with him immediately prior to that moment?*
SC – None. You must be able to see for yourself, there must have been cameras. Or the driver of the bus, he must have seen. We didn't push him. We didn't kill him.
DC Chaudhari – *He isn't dead, Sara.*
SC – [no response]
DI Carter – *His condition is very serious. Multiple broken bones, significant injuries to the head and face.*
SC – But he's going to live?
DC Chaudhari – *They're not sure. If he does, these are still life-changing injuries. So, you see, it's crucial you tell us the truth about what happened, Sara.*
SC – I'm telling the truth. It happened like I told you. Nobody pushed him. He did it to himself.

The Push – Episode Twenty-Six

I'm your guest host, Sara Caldwell, and welcome to this special episode of The Push, the podcast about the extraordinary case of the London Bridge Jogger. If this is the first time you're joining us, we recommend you go back and start at the beginning. Things are going to make a whole lot more sense if you do.

In our last episode, Dylan told you he had something remarkable to share: that he'd finally tracked down the jogger, and that he was going to confront him before giving his evidence over to the police. And then things went . . . sort of quiet.

Well, listeners, a lot has happened since the last episode. And I want to start by talking a little about Dylan, who you may already know is no longer here, to tell you how this story ends.

The thing about Dylan is . . . he could be a real idiot sometimes. He used to walk around the office wearing a T-shirt with his own face on it, and that used to make me so mad. And he didn't make a cup of tea for anybody else in the office for like, a whole year, which sounds like nothing, but those of you who sit at desks all day long will know that . . . it kind of isn't nothing.

I don't want to be unkind, but if I'm honest, sometimes I thought Dylan behaved in ways journalists aren't supposed to behave, especially when it came to talking about, and to, the victims of the crimes he was reporting on. And that stuff . . . that isn't nothing, either.

But in the end, Dylan got his man.

After twenty-five episodes of The Push, he found the London Bridge Jogger. He confronted him, and he was killed for it. Dylan died in the most horrible way you can imagine. Listeners, it makes me want to cry when I think about it. My sympathies, and the sympathies of everyone here at Decoded Media, are with Dylan's friends and family, at what we know must be a very difficult time.

The man who killed Dylan was the London Bridge Jogger.

He was the man pictured in the CCTV footage that the police released after the attack on the bridge. Right now, this man is in hospital following a serious traffic accident. If he recovers, he's going to prison for a very long time. For Dylan's murder, for the attempted murder of the woman he pushed, for other crimes, too . . .

For all you true-crime fans out there, this story has got a bit of everything. And we know you'd love to hear all about it, and a part of me wants to tell you about it. But – plot twist – I'm not going to do that.

I'm not going to talk about why this man did the things he did, or the messed-up childhood that made him into the person he became. We're not going to interview psychologists and retired police officers to get their take, and we're not going to talk to the victims of his crimes, either, because . . . Well, look . . . I get it. I used to get a weird kick out of listening to podcasts about horrible assaults and murders and the damaged men – and sometimes women – who commit them. I think it was something to do with facing my fears. Like, the more I listened to these things, the more prepared I'd be if something ever happened to me in real life. Well, I don't know if I believe that anymore.

What I do believe is that people like the London Bridge Jogger look in the mirror and see something different to the rest of us. They think they're better than us, that they're worth more, that they deserve more.

The truth is, they deserve less.

We aren't going to name this man, not because we want to protect him, but because he doesn't get to have his story told. This isn't just a podcast. It's real life. The people he hurt are going to need time and space to put their lives back together. And we're going to give them that. If they want to tell their truth, in their own time, then that's up to them. But we're not going to speak for them, and we're not going to give this man any more time or space in our heads or in our hearts.

So that's it. The end. This is the final episode of The Push. There will be no Season Two.

Annoying, isn't it? There's nothing more frustrating than a crime podcast that leaves you hungry for some kind of resolution. And this is worse than that, because all the horrid details are right there, within reach.

But we're going to hold firm on this one. I'm sure the story will come out one day, but I hope it doesn't. I hope you're all left hungry.

I'm Sara Caldwell, and this is the final episode of... The Push.

67

Day Thirty

Catherine

Eyes open, heart racing. Pillow damp with sweat, cold against my cheek. Another bad dream. The third tonight. I reach out into the dark space on Simon's side of the bed to check he isn't there, to make sure my nightmare was just that, and I tell myself over and over, *Just a dream, just a dream . . .*

Simon isn't here. He's still in the hospital, with tubes up what's left of his nose, and machines to keep his heart beating and his lungs breathing.

If he does get better – and that's a big if according to the doctors – they'll look at trying to fix his face. A surgeon offered to explain it to me, launched straight into talking about bone grafts and screws and plates and taking skin from here and there, and I told him I didn't want to hear it. But now, there are hours when I think of nothing else. It is the obsession of my dreams; what Simon will look like once they're finished.

When I see him in my dreams, he rarely looks like himself. Sometimes he looks like a stranger, like any man off the street, and sometimes he looks like Max, or like Jonathan. And sometimes his face is a blur of pixels, like fuzzy CCTV footage.

They can do remarkable things these days, but even after the best surgeons in the land have finished with him, he won't look the same. He's going to hate that. He always thought himself so handsome.

It's no good. I am too restless to sleep.

I get out of bed and go to Charlie's room, stand in the doorway and listen to him breathe. Poor Charlie. He has a night light on now when he goes to sleep, because he has bad dreams too. Wakes up crying and won't settle until I bring him into our bed – *my* bed. Tonight, there's not a peep from him, though. He's sleeping through.

I wish I could do the same, but now my nights are broken. Nightmares and worries keep me awake. What will happen if Simon does get better? What will happen if we have to go to court? What will happen when we run out of money? Though to be fair, things aren't so bad on that front. Turns out Jefferson Trading have a rather generous Accident Cover policy and they've paid out a year of Simon's salary in advance, tax-free, straight into our joint account, rather than his. I shouldn't have been surprised to find out that Simon's salary was almost twice the amount he told me, but I was.

I worry about Mum, who refuses to take it easy, despite doctor's orders. And I worry about Sara, too. Isn't that the strangest thing? She slept with my husband – or at least a version of him – and now I lie awake worrying about her.

She came round this evening, comes round every few days now. Says she wants to make sure we're OK. Charlie adores her. They spend hours lying on the rug in the living room, playing with plastic dinosaurs and toy cars, and after I put him to bed, she sits with me in the kitchen and we have a few glasses of wine. Sometimes she smokes roll-your-own cigarettes out the back door and tells me about her work, about a podcast idea she's working on, a true-crime thing that focuses on the victims of crime, rather than the perpetrators. I told her it sounded like a good idea, so long as she leaves me out of it.

We don't talk about what happened that night, at least not out loud; though today I caught a look in her eye and could tell she was thinking about it.

'You mustn't worry,' I told her.

The fact that Detectives Carter and Chaudhari have stopped asking questions about that night only goes to prove they have nothing but our word to go on. The driver of the bus wasn't sure, apparently, if we pushed Simon, or if he fell. And while there was CCTV, the angle wasn't good enough to make out exactly what happened.

Fancy that.

'I'll try,' Sara said, rubbing the palms of her hands on her dress, as if trying to wipe dirt off her skin.

'Right, I'd better go and catch the bus,' she said, though she didn't move.

'Are you busy on Sunday?' I asked. 'I was thinking of making a roast, if you fancy it? My friend Jonathan's coming over, and you're welcome to bring Helen, too.'

We are friends, Jonathan and I. For now.

'Sure, if you like,' she said, as if she didn't care either way, though a smile spread across her face.

'I do like,' I told her. She needs people around her, needs a family, and I need a new friend. I haven't spoken to Lydia. Sometimes I pick up my phone and write out a text to her, out of habit, then catch myself. Perhaps one day I'll press send. But not yet.

I head back to bed, get under the covers, run the flat of my hand over the cool linen.

I used to hate being on my own in bed. I suppose I was afraid of what it told me about my marriage, what it told me about Simon. I'd lie awake into the early hours, waiting for him to come home, making up excuses for him. He's missed the last tube, or he's in the office working late on a big presentation and forgot to tell me, or his phone's out of battery and he's going to walk through the door any second now . . .

I don't hate my half-empty bed anymore.

It is a blessing. It is all mine.

The DNA in the car, the audio recording on Dylan's phone; Detective Carter told me it is enough. If Simon recovers, he'll go to prison for a long time. Whatever happens now, he is never coming home. It's just me and Charlie now. And Mum. And Sara, too, I suppose.

I rearrange the pillows, shift my body into the middle of the bed. Such a stupid habit, lying on one side when there's no need. It isn't a half-empty bed when you're the only person in it. It's just your bed, with room to breathe.

Room to breathe. I like the sound of that.

I don't feel restless anymore. I close my eyes and let sleep take me.

Acknowledgements

This book would not have been possible without the help and support of many people, but in particular I would like to thank:

Jane Snelgrove and the brilliant team at Embla Books, for their hard work at making this book a reality, and my fantastic agent, Stephanie Glencross, and Jane Gregory, at David Higham Associates, for taking a chance on me.

The tutors at City University, in particular Claire McGowan and Laura Wilson, whose early guidance helped shape the story. Special thanks to the brilliant Alexandra (A.K.) Benedict, the best teacher I know, without whom I would not have got to the finishing line.

Thank you also to S.J. Watson, who offered many words of wisdom, took the time to talk through my initial ideas and taught me how to keep putting the words down when it gets tough.

For help with medical questions on sleep, and lack thereof, Caroline Moss, and for help with questions on police forensics and identification of burnt remains, Kevin N. Robinson at Crime Writing Solutions.

My writer friends: Tom Newman, Jake Webb, Josh Winning, Lydia Gittins and Andrea Robinson, for the many hours we have spent talking about our craft and working through tricky plot problems.

Thank you to my mum and dad, for their continuing support – I hope you love the book – and thank you to the best dog in the world, Rufus.

Finally, thank you to my wife, Bailey, for sticking with me and believing in me. It means the world.

Author P S Cunliffe

P S Cunliffe was born and grew up in Newton-le-Willows, Merseyside. A musician, artist and writer, he holds degrees in Fine Art and Creative Writing. He has spent the last twenty years working in digital marketing for some of the world's biggest websites, and now lives in North London. For information please see his website at paulcunliffe.com.

About Embla Books

Embla Books is a digital-first publisher of standout commercial adult fiction. Passionate about storytelling, the team at Embla publish books that will make you 'laugh, love, look over your shoulder and lose sleep'. Launched by Bonnier Books UK in 2021, the imprint is named after the first woman from the creation myth in Norse mythology, who was carved by the gods from a tree trunk found on the seashore – an image of the kind of creative work and crafting that writers do, and a symbol of how stories shape our lives.

Find out about some of our other books and stay in touch:

Twitter, Facebook, Instagram: @emblabooks
Newsletter: https://bit.ly/emblanewsletter